GIVE NO QUARTER

JAMIE McFARLANE

Cover Artwork: Elias T. Stern

ACKNOWLEDGMENTS

To Diane Greenwood Muir for excellence in editing and fine word-smithery. My wife, Janet, for carefully and kindly pointing out my poor grammatical habits. I cannot imagine working through these projects without you both.

To my beta readers: Carol Greenwood, Matt Strbjak, Linda Baker, Kelli Whyte, Robert Long, Nancy Higgins Quist and Dave Muir and for wonderful and thoughtful suggestions. It is a joy to work with this intelligent and considerate group of people.

CONTENTS

FORWARD

One of the great joys I have as an author is the privilege of meeting and talking with members of our armed services. One in particular, Coast Guard Boatswain's Mate Class 2, Matthew Strjbak has respectfully stepped forward and requested, in the kindest way possible, that I clean up my ship class designations.

Upon review, I discovered that indeed I'd broken well-established conventions and as a result, made it difficult for those who are knowledgeable about such things to make reasonable assumptions based on these classifications.

To that end, I've made the following modifications going forward:

Class	Tonnes	LOA - Meters	Examples
Dart		< 10	
Cutter	180	30	*Sterra's Gift*
Tug	350	40	*Adela Chen*
Sloop	450	40	*Hotspur*
Light Frigate	1,200-1,800	50	*Banny Hill, Cape of Good Hope, Strumpet, Dulcinea del Toboso*
Frigate	4,500	120	*Justice Bringer, Peace Bringer, Intrepid*
Justice Class Frigate	5,500	80	*Fist of Justice, Hammer of Justice, Stark Justice*
Destroyer	8,500	140	
Light Cruiser	10,000	160	*Hipparchus*
Cruiser	12,000	180	*Walter Sydney Adams, Theodore Dunham*
Battle Cruiser	16,000	220	*George Ellery Hale, Messier*
Battleship	18,500	250	

PREPARATION MEET OPPORTUNITY

"We've got trouble, Cap." Ada's face appeared on *Hotspur's* forward holo display. A beautiful, ebony skinned woman, Ada, had sailed with us since darn near the beginning of our adventures. Originally a tug-pilot, she was one of the finest heavy-ship pilots I'd met and currently sailing five hundred meters off the starboard side in our recently captured Belirand light frigate, *Strumpet*.

We'd split the crew between the two ships – Silver, Ada, Jonathan, Nick and Marny on the light frigate with Tabby, Moonie and me on *Hotspur*. We were at least ten short from having comfortable crew complements for the two ships, but trusted crew was hard to come by.

"I see it," I responded.

We'd just emerged from fold-space five hundred kilometers from a Belirand supply cache. According to our newest crew member, engineer Moon Rastof, Belirand had unmanned and largely undefended supply caches sprinkled throughout all four of the settled star systems. According to Moonie, the locations were highly guarded corporate secrets and each cache was only used for a few stans. As a former engineer aboard Belirand's *Cape of Good Hope*, he'd recorded the locations of those his ship had visited. An action quite against corporate policy.

The trouble Ada was referring to was the frigate *Peace Bringer*, currently docked at the supply cache. Frigates were a particular brand of trouble for us - heavier weaponry by a factor of five than the light frigate *Strumpet*, and every bit as fast as *Hotspur* on a dead run. At a hundred twenty meters LOA (length overall) and a narrow beam, frigates were blisteringly fast and deadly to most ships smaller than themselves. The only advantage *Hotspur* had in combat against *Peace Bringer* was in maneuverability. We'd gambled on the cache being deserted and we'd lost in the most spectacular way possible. On a list of our mistakes, this might just be our biggest one - ever.

"We're being hailed," Ada said.

The one sensible precaution we'd taken was to approach with *Hotspur* in nearly full blackout mode. Its light absorptive armor made us nearly invisible to most ships unless they were actively scanning.

"Patching them through." That was Nick, my quick-talking business partner and childhood friend.

Our plan, in case we had any unexpected interactions with Belirand, was to switch on *Strumpet*'s original transponder. She'd show up as *Cape of Good Hope* and might get us past automated systems. In the event of actual human contact, well... I guess we were hoping word hadn't gotten around yet about the loss of the ship. No question about it, we might have done some hand-waving in that part of the plan as there was no possibility of someone in the Belirand fleet not having heard about the loss of *Cape*.

"Jonathan, I need you to back me up on this."

"We will," he replied simply. Jonathan, also aboard *Strumpet*, was an artificial life-form living in a manufactured human body. To be more specific, Jonathan was one of fourteen hundred thirty-eight individual sentient beings taking up residence in that body. It was Jonathan who had been nominated to interface with its human counterparts. The rest of the sentients preferred not to interact with the slow-moving world of humanity.

"This is *Cape of Good Hope*, Grossman speaking." I answered the outstanding hail *Cape* had received. Grossman was the name of the first officer of *Cape*, information I knew anyone from Belirand would have access to. "I wasn't expecting competition today." I hoped Jonathan could manufacture a response to what I knew would be an automated identification verification from Belirand. It was a lot to ask in such a short space of time.

A delay of several seconds followed, but he finally answered.

"Where the hell have you been, Grossman? The whole damn corporation's been out looking for you. Where's your captain?"

The forward holo projector popped to life showing a grey-bearded man in a poorly maintained vac-suit. The identification showed him as Kaeth Brunkow, a maintenance technician with Belirand. The vid panel in front of me started streaming Brunkow's private Belirand personnel files. I blanched, partially at how easily Jonathan had discovered the details, but also at the maintenance worker's rocky history.

"Captain LeGrande is dead, as is more than half my crew. I'm declaring an emergency, Brunkow. I need all available personnel to help when we dock up. You need to get that ship out of our way," I said.

"No can do. Nobody here with the certification to sail this thing," he said. "I ain't losing my job over this."

"I'll have your job if you don't," I barked. "I've twenty-five people on the verge of dying here and if any of them do because of your negligence, I'll see you hanged!"

Tabby, my fiancé and co-pilot muted the conversation and looked at me with raised eye-brows. "Laying it on a little thick, don't you think? Hanged?"

I shrugged. Brunkow's admission of no nearby crew was the best news we'd heard so far.

"That's bullshit," he pushed back. "You're not in my chain of command and I have specific orders that under no circumstance am I to move this ship. You're not shoving this crap on me."

I unmuted and sighed audibly, mostly for show. "You're right, Kaeth. I can't order you to do anything. It's just, things over here are pretty dire. How many people do you have who can help?"

He looked into the display thoughtfully and finally responded. "I've called in your emergency. It's just me and the kid, Rowser. Just set in close to *Peace Bringer*. We can ferry your people over through the starboard cargo bay. You're better off docking with *Peace Bringer* than this piss-ant station anyway."

"Copy that. Grossman out," I said.

"What are you doing?" Moon Rastof asked once I'd cut the

comm.

I ignored him. "You get that, Marny?" Marny, a heavily muscled former Marine from Earth, was our security officer and Nick's girlfriend.

"Aye, Cap. Jonathan and I are headed to the armory as we speak. Bring Moonie just in case we have system problems," she said.

"No frakking way are you doing an incursion without me." Tabby jumped ahead of me onto the short flight of stairs that led from *Hotspur*'s cockpit to the deck of the bridge.

I shook my head. I might be in charge of the expedition, but "Captain" felt like more of an honorary title some days. That said, she was right. Tabby and Marny were both physically superior to any of our crew by a considerable margin. Where Tabby was lean, brutal, and fast as a whip, Marny was powerful and extraordinarily strategic in her thinking. But with most of her limbs and spine replaced after receiving horrific injuries, Tabby had a significant advantage when it came to strength, endurance and speed. She'd been training with Marny and had recently become the dominant fighter. To Marny's credit, she accepted the change, recognizing the value to the team more than the loss of status.

Nick, always one step ahead of the team, anticipated Tabby's response and the fact that *Hotspur* would be empty if the three of us joined the quickly forming incursion force. "Liam, Silver will take command of *Hotspur*. She'll EVA as soon as both ships are zero delta-v with *Peace Bringer*."

We were taking some risk communicating while sailing so close to the much bigger frigate. If *Peace Bringer* had full-strength sensors running, they might pick up our line-of-sight communications. While a narrow laser beam focused on a single receiver was hard to detect, it wasn't impossible. When *Hotspur* went completely dark, we didn't even allow for vid-screens in the cockpit, much less tiny flashes of laser light.

"Suit up, Rastof," I said as we brought *Hotspur* to zero delta-v with *Strumpet*.

It didn't take a moment for him to complain. "I'm not tactically trained." Moon Rastof was a good ship's engineer and had a quick wit, but he lacked anything resembling a spine.

"We either take the ship or Brunkow figures out we're not on the same side and uses that frigate to blow us up," I said.

"There are only two of them. How would they mount an assault?" Moonie argued.

"Automated systems would most likely do it. The blasters on that frigate would shred *Hotspur* in forty seconds. And you're making my point for me. I doubt Brunkow will even be armed while you'll be in an armored vac-suit," I said.

"You shouldn't get greedy," he said. "We should just get out of here."

"Or what? They'll hunt us down and threaten our families?" I asked.

"Yes!"

"What do you think they're doing now?" I walked down the flight of stairs and placed my hand on his back, helping him stand up from the engineering station he'd become glued to.

"It'll get worse," he said, reluctantly coming to his feet before moving toward the lift that would take us to the berth deck where the armory and entry hatch were located.

"Not for me, pal. They murdered my father and attempted to murder my mother. Perhaps you don't get it, but Belirand has gone unchecked so long they believe their shite has lost its stink. Remember, not so long ago they abandoned you and your crew in the deep dark to starve to death."

"I still think this is a bad idea," he grumbled.

"Good thing it's not a democracy. If you want off after this mission, I'm sure the good people of Ophir will take you in. No doubt your skills would be in high demand. Today, however, you need to follow orders. The lives of my friends depend on us working together as a team. Once we step through that airlock, we're done arguing. Savvy?" I wasn't pleased I had to lay it on so thick.

He sighed heavily into the comms and accepted the armored

vac-suit I handed him. My peripheral vision caught sight of Mom's thin frame entering the deck through the aft-airlock. My HUD (heads up display) had alerted me that she'd boarded.

Transfer helm to Silver Hoffen, I instructed the ship's A.I.

As Mom brushed past us in the narrow hallway, she patted me on the shoulder and we exchanged a look. She'd no doubt heard my argument with Moonie and was concerned I was taking a reluctant, relatively unknown crewmember into a hostile situation. We both knew it was necessary, but I saw the concern in her face.

"Godspeed, Liam," she said before disappearing into the ceiling on the lift to the bridge.

"On my six, Moonie. Let's go." I handed him AGBs (arc-jet boots and gloves) that would give him maneuverability in zero-g outside the ship.

"Aren't you wearing an armored suit?"

"These are armored," I said, gesturing at the experimental grav-suits my original crew had received from the now-deceased Thomas Phillipe Anino. The suits were slightly thicker than ordinary vac-suits but had the armor characteristics of the much bulkier armored vac-suit Moonie wore. Even more impressively, our grav-suits had their own propulsion that utilized magnetic and gravitational fields instead of AGBs. To be honest, I didn't understand the physics, but I did know the suits were a serious upgrade.

I jumped through the exterior hatch into space. We'd come alongside *Strumpet*, keeping it between us and *Peace Bringer* with *Hotspur's* hatch on the space-side. For many, having nothing between you and the emptiness of the universe was overwhelming and caused feelings of panic. I monitored Moonie as he exited to make sure he'd be okay, then winced as he fired his arc-jets way too hard for the easy turn toward *Strumpet* where we'd join the no-doubt already formed incursion party.

"Take it easy, Moonie. Lighter on the arc-jets," I said as soothingly as I could.

"I've got it," he replied, the calm in his voice at odds with his jerky space flight.

"Liam, I'm getting a hail from Brunkow again," she said. "I think he's picking up on your EVA."

"Shit. Kill your suit, Moonie." I watched helplessly as he continued to flail.

Override Moon Rastof's suit, turn off arc-jets. As tactical leader, I was able to override many of my team's suit functions. I'd never had to exercise that control for a conscious member, however.

"Grossman, here," I replied to Brunkow's hail as I grabbed Moonie from behind to level out his flight.

"We're picking up on an EVA on the starboard side of your ship. Are you reading that?" he asked.

"Copy that," I said. "I sent a tech out to look at our starboard engine. We nearly lost it on the way in."

"I'm also picking up extra mass," he said. "I'm firing up the sensor package. Something isn't right."

"Frak! My sensors just picked up another ship. We have company, Brunkow. Open that hold door, I'm sending a fire team over. We're sitting ducks out here," I said.

"I don't know," he stalled.

I didn't blame him. We were pushing the limits of credibility.

My HUD showed *Hotspur* drop out of silent running and fire up her main engines. The blue glow of the engines intensified as Silver raked the side of *Peace Bringer* with a light salvo of blaster fire.

"Damn it, man. We're in the open. Get that hold open! It's coming around again and we're defenseless out here," I screamed.

Hotspur snapped around and rolled on her side, opening up with all three blasters, stitching a line of fire along *Peace Bringer's* hull.

"Hold is open. Go, go, go!" Brunkow screamed into the comm. "I'm warming up the defensive systems, they're almost online."

Moonie's extra mass slowed me enough that I was the last to land in the bay of *Peace Bringer*. I let him slide along the deck to arrest his own momentum. Marny, Tabby, and Jonathan were already waiting, stacked up against the forward bulkhead. It was my job to take point, with Marny as number two and Tabby bringing up the tail. Our cargo, Jonathan, and Moonie were supposed to be between Marny and Tabby. I wasn't sure if Moonie was going to make it and could hardly blame him. He'd never drilled with us.

"Brunkow, come get us. We need access to the bridge so we can run this bastard off," I said, taking my position. "He's really laying into us. I hope you have a suit on - we could breach."

The cargo bay's doors had already started closing and I watched as blaster fire neatly pinged off the heavy armor around the bay. Mom had reduced the intensity of the blaster rounds and I'd have been surprised if she was even making a dent in the warship's skin.

Atmosphere flooded the bay and a moment later the harried Kaeth Brunkow and a younger man met us at the door, holding heavy blast rifles. "We're on your six. Move out, Brunkow." I barked my orders using the voice I'd heard my late father use so many times before when he was looking to spur someone to action.

Whether I was actually channeling Big Pete, or Brunkow was just that freaked out, I didn't care. He took off at a dead run, something he was in ill shape to do.

"Bridge is here," he said, pulling up no more than twenty meters in.

My HUD showed that we were in the middle of the ship.

"I need bridge control," I yelled. "Jonathan, give him my ident."

"This doesn't look right," Brunkow said. His instincts weren't bad, but we weren't going to give him time to figure it out.

Tabby spun around, pulling a pistol from her thigh holster. "I'm not dying today, Brunkow! Frakking do it before we're torn to pieces. That sonnavabitch is gonna drop rockets up our ass if you don't move!"

"Lieutenant, stand down," I yelled. "He's just doing his job. Maintain discipline!"

Tabby darted glances back and forth between the panicking maintenance worker and me. "He's going to get us killed!"

"Stand down, Lieutenant!"

Tabby lowered her gun and the younger man, Rowser, chose that moment to point his heavy blaster at her chest.

"What's it going to be, Kaeth? The Lieutenant is probably right. If that bird has rocks, it'll open this tub right up," I said.

"This is ten ways to frakked up," he replied. *Peace Bringer, authorize LN-2016221895, full control.*

"Jonathan, check it," I said.

"You've got control, sir," he said. "We're running a diagnostic."

Tabby wasted no time and punched poor Chester Rowser square in the nose. The sound of breaking cartilage shortly preceded his fall to the ground. Before Brunkow responded, she'd spun and brought her heel into contact with his jaw, knocking him unconscious.

"Jonathan, can you use the access we have to lock out Belirand?" I asked.

"Belay that, Liam," Nick said over the comm. "You'd end up locking down the supply cache."

"Roger that, Nick. What's the plan?" I asked.

"You, Marny, and Moonie take the prisoners to the cache," he said.

"What do you have for me, pint-size?" Tabby asked. She'd picked up the new nickname on Ophir and was trying it out on Nick. He'd always been the smallest kid in our class at school and Tabby was the only person allowed to pick on him. Oddly enough, it was generally Tabby who enforced the rule.

"Really? Pint-sized?" Nick rarely complained, but this one he apparently didn't care for.

"Aww, don't listen to her, little man," Marny said.

It was unusual for us to talk quite so much while on a mission and I felt like we were losing focus. "Cut the chatter guys, we need to save it until we're in deep space."

My HUD lit up with green dots next to everyone's avatars - that is, except Moonie's. It was something we referred to as a ready-check and it communicated agreement. I didn't feel bad about Moonie not replying, as he had no way to know what we were doing. I realized that I'd placed us all in danger by bringing an untrained crewman along. Worse yet, he'd even warned me of just how uncomfortable he'd been and I'd ignored him.

"Tabby, undock Peace Keeper so Silver can bring *Hotspur* in. We'll transfer to the cache first, then load supplies onto *Hotspur*," Nick said.

It was a good plan. Not only did *Hotspur* have a generous five hundred cubic meter hold, but it had a single aft loading ramp that gave quick access.

"Copy that," Silver acknowledged.

"Just give me the word," Tabby answered.

"Marny, grab Brunkow. I've got the kid. We'll dump 'em on the station," I said. "We're on the move. Moonie, where'd you disappear to?"

"I'm headed to the cargo bay now," Moonie replied. I shook my head. Working for a corporation had ruined him. Wandering off in enemy territory was a good way to get killed.

Reduce gravity to 0.3g. I leaned over and zip-tied the kid's wrists and ankles and slung him over my shoulder. Marny was a step ahead of me and I jogged down the hallway after her. As I did, I took in the general décor of the ship. It wasn't quite the same fit and finish as the luxurious *Strumpet*, but I suspected that was because this was a working ship and not made for high profile passengers.

When we returned to the cargo bay, Moonie waited by the open airlock. I nodded as we passed him on our way to the station's large bay. The first thing that struck me about the cache was just how simple it really was. The entire thing was just a big steel box, large enough to hold supplies for a multitude of ships. "I didn't think Belirand kept these caches manned," I mentioned to Moonie.

"Normally they don't, but Belirand has more ships than they do crews. They must have needed *Peace Bringer*'s crew to have left her behind," he said. "You need to leave it here. I'm telling you, stealing fuel and consumables is one thing, stealing a ship... you can't come back from this."

11

"We're not having this conversation, Moonie. Get those stevedore bots fired up and online so we can start loading as soon as Mom lands," I said. "And lose the atmo in here."

Marny and I continued through the huge cargo bay, still loaded with our prisoners. We'd spied living quarters at the back and dropped our prisoners off in the conditioned space.

Thirty minutes later, Nick contacted me. "Liam, we're out of time. You need to get out of there."

"Roger that," I said and directed the stevedore bots to set down in *Hotspur's* cargo hold. "We're out of here, Marny." I clapped my hand on her back as we stepped inside and closed the hold. *Hotspur* broke free from the station and started sailing as we made our way up to the bridge.

"Jonathan, you made mention of asymmetric warfare. Is this what you had in mind?" I asked over the tactical channel joining our crew.

"A near perfect definition, Captain Hoffen," Jonathan replied.

"I can't believe your luck," Moonie interjected. "That could have failed for so many reasons."

The young engineer had already annoyed me and he didn't seem to know when to keep things to himself. We'd just about never had luck turn our way. Much to the contrary, I'd always felt like there was an invisible hand that seemed to make us pay dearly for any success we experienced.

"You know what luck is, Moonie?" Ada asked.

"What's that, Chen?" Even the way he said her name made me grind my teeth.

"Luck is when preparation meets opportunity. What do you think would have happened if Brunkow had smelled a rat? I'll tell you what - that frigate would have shredded us. Turns out the luck, as you call it, was all Belirand's. Today they had the opportunity to bury us and they failed. Why is that?"

"Because Brunkow was an idiot?" Moonie's voice was subdued. Pissing off Ada was hard to do and he was wisely hunkering down to weather the storm.

"No. Because a brilliant crew recognized and seized an

opportunity. If you want to keep sailing with us, you're going to need to find your A-Game and bring it. You nearly got my crew killed today with your frakking antics and you're completely oblivious to that fact. If it were up to me, you'd be back on that cache with Brunkow, waiting for Belirand."

"I hate to step in front of this, Ada, but bringing Moonie was my call. I shouldn't have put him in that situation," I said. "I nearly killed our crew today by bringing along a civilian."

"That's crap. We were all civil..." Ada's comm cut out and I looked at Mom whose eyebrows were raised in surprise at Ada's meltdown.

"Damn, Hoffen. That the way you see it?" Moonie asked, sheepishly.

"How's that?" I asked, looking back at him at the engineering station.

"That you shouldn't have brought me along. That I almost got us all killed?" The pain in his voice was evident.

"I put you in a bad spot, Moon. I didn't know your capabilities and threw you in the fire. Everything after that was on me."

"So you think Chen was out of line?"

"Don't push it."

BELIRAND MENACE

"Silver, this is Jonathan. Do you copy?"

"Go ahead, Jonathan," Mom answered. It was mind boggling just how easily Jonathan had adjusted to our speech patterns. I felt it was to my credit that I'd adjusted to thinking of Jonathan in the plural, although it seemed a small accomplishment.

"We've a docking harness on the keel of *Peace Bringer*. Are you familiar with this configuration?"

"Roger that, Jonathan. If you'll transmit the mating sequence, I'll bring her in," Mom answered, closing the comm.

"Docking harness?" I asked, looking at mom.

"Not uncommon on larger ships," she said. "Take the helm, I'll walk you through it."

"Aren't we too big?" I asked.

"She'll look pregnant," Mom quipped. "But it's efficient. *Peace Bringer*'s engines are powerful enough to handle the extra load."

"Do you have anything to report?" I asked, starting our time-honored sequence for handing over the helm.

"All systems are nominal," she answered.

"I relieve you."

"I stand relieved," she said.

"Is that really necessary with just the three of us on board?" Moonie asked.

"Discipline, Moon," I answered. "Mom, what am I supposed to do with this sequence?" My vid-screen was blinking with a data upload from Jonathan. It was little more than a few vectors and tolerance. "I don't get how we're going to lock in hard enough to survive transition to fold-space."

"You've forgotten your girl's history. Her name wasn't always *Hotspur*," Mom said. "She used to have an HMS in front of her name and with that comes with mating hard-points. All you need do is line her up on that vector and keep her under fifteen meters per second delta-v. The ship's harness will pull you in once you're within five meters."

"Moonie. Just for my peace of mind, would you validate we haven't covered up those hard-points with all the repairs we've made?"

"Can do," he said. "Just a minute."

I closed the distance between *Hotspur* and *Peace Bringer*, rolling over so we were belly-to-belly, the forward holo display showing our approach.

"Gonna need that verification soon, Moonie," I said.

"We're good to go," he said. "Sorry, her repair history is long and distinguished. It took me a while to wade through it. Would you believe you're not the worst thing to happen to her?"

I laughed. Moonie's wit was irrepressible.

"Jonathan, we're in position."

Cables fired from *Peace Bringer*'s belly, attachment pins embedding themselves into receptacles on *Hotspur*. I'd missed my spot by a few centimeters and the ship shuddered as the cables tightened, centering us.

"You've become quite adept with this ship," Mom said with approval. "I'd have been pleased to have lined her up as well." Coming from anyone else, it would have sounded like criticism. Mom, however, had flown hundreds of combat missions for the Marines and her praise was very welcome.

"I'll take that." I pulled her to me in a side-armed hug as we competed to descend the stairs to the bridge deck.

"Don't get cocky." She winked at me, quoting an old vid we'd shared when I was a kid.

"How hard is this frigate going to be to handle?" I asked.

"While I don't have many hours on full-sized warships, every hour I have is on a frig. They're pretty much one-trick ponies," she replied.

Moonie fell in line behind us as we loaded onto the lift and rode down to the berth deck.

"One trick?" Moonie asked.

"They're made to run," Mom said. "Any ship small enough to run her down won't survive her guns. Anything she can't outgun, she can outrun. Good for scouting, not as much for battles. Although there was a commander who made a name for himself by running a whole flock of these birds. Can't remember his name."

"Ivanov Kuznetsov," I answered. "Which was the name of Commander Sterra's ship when she visited Colony-40."

"Right. I should have remembered that."

"Be careful out here, Moonie. If you lose contact with the ship, we'll have a hard time finding you," I said as I opened the air-lock. *Peace Bringer* was still accelerating and if any of us got outside the range of the gravity generators, the ship would accelerate out from under us. Not a huge problem, unless you hit some part of the ship on the way past.

"Not likely. The gravity field extends several meters," he said.

He was right, but I also knew we were at the edge of the gravity generator's range. I looked forward, down the length of *Peace Bringer*. Even from the underside, it was quite a sight. She was as narrow as *Hotspur* at her waist and bumped out as she went forward. The bow of *Hotspur* was resting at about midline and she just seemed to keep going from there. To the aft, the oversized engines flared out, each of them capable of producing the same amount of thrust as *Hotspur*. Well, technically, it wasn't thrust, but according to my physics classes it had the same affect.

"You coming, Liam?" Mom asked as she slid down the safety line running into an airlock.

"Just enjoying the view." I grabbed the line and slid down next to her, braking with my hands in the light gravity. A familiar symbol in the long air-lock indicated a gravity shift that would orient us with ship normal if we continued. I palmed the lock's panel, closing the outer door.

Mom and Moonie grabbed handles that ran along the length of the airlock, allowing their bodies to transition with the shifting gravity that would spin them 180 degrees. The grav-suit I'd received from Anino allowed me to easily adjust to the change and I squirted past them through the open hatch above, landing easily on the deck.

Show ship's layout. My AI displayed a map. I was on a short deck that offered access to the lower engines. Five meters forward, the passageway elevated to join with the main deck above. I recalled stepping aboard the *Kuznetsov* and having it explained to us that the sloping passageways allowed for easy navigation when the ship lost gravity control. Often Commanders would reduce the gravity in combat to take advantage of considerably faster transit time for the crew.

Unlike every ship I'd sailed previously, *Peace Bringer*'s bridge was located amidships. Not quite dead center, but close enough. While not as romantic as being able to stare out, unaided, into the depths of space, it was a whole lot more practical. Both more armored and central, the location was chosen with little thought to the aesthetic.

I palmed the security panel on the aft bulkhead of the bridge. "Permission to enter the bridge."

"Permission granted," Tabby replied and the door slid sideways, disappearing into the bulkhead. Tabby snaked her hand around my waist before I realized she was standing on the threshold. Brusquely, she pulled me in, her hand slipping south. She accentuated her surprise kiss with a rough squeeze. Suddenly, her head pulled back and she let me go, her cheeks turning a light shade of crimson. "Oh, frak! Sorry Silver. Forgot you were with him." As far as I knew, Mom was the only person in existence that caused Tabby to feel embarrassment.

"Don't apologize to me. I've always thought he was particularly kissable," Mom said as she stepped through the doorway, placing her hands on each side of my head and kissing me on the forehead. I closed my eyes as my own cheeks now burned.

"What do you think?" I asked, grabbing Tabby's hand as we looked around the bridge. There was no winning when faced with Mom and Tabby, so it was better to redirect them.

"Not an ounce of fat on her," Tabby replied.

Overall, the bridge was much like the rest of the ship - Spartan. No wood inlaid panels on the chairs or fancy polished slate floors. What it gave up in opulence, it gained in functionality. There were a total of six workstations, the largest of which was actually the gunnery officer's station. It sat between the fire control room and bridge with a much larger series of vid-screens. Marny would be able to enter either via the bridge or fire-control room and communicate effectively with both teams. The next largest area sat dead center against the aft bulkhead and belonged to the captain. Two officer's workstations were on either side, one forward and the remaining two occupied the port side. Finally, a conference room was accessible through the forward bulkhead of the bridge.

"Do you mind?" I asked, gesturing to the captain's chair.

"All systems are nominal, Captain Hoffen," Tabby reported snappily.

I nodded with a grin. We continued the shift change procedure, where I learned that Brunkow had been overseeing a maintenance problem with the waste processor. I considered myself fortunate that it wasn't a problem with the actual septic system.

Stepping up into the captain's chair, I directed my AI to configure the available displays, then scanned the ship's statuses and found nothing Tabby hadn't reported. The displays were of higher resolution than I was used to and everything was extremely crisp; the colors vivid.

"Look at the forward bulkhead," Tabby said. "You won't want to miss this." She'd been standing in front of my chair, watching as I acclimated. Her eyes followed mine forward as she threw something from her HUD. In perfect timing with her throw, the entire forward bulkhead as well as the overhead displayed the exterior star field in startling clarity.

"That's amazing." My eyes searched for failure in the fabric of the vid screens and found none.

"Thought you'd like it." Tabby said, grinning. She knew me well enough to know I'd been fretting about the bridge's poor view of space.

"Jonathan, you've been quiet. Were you able to remove

Belirand's access from the ship's systems?" I asked.

"Mostly," he replied. "One hundred three of us transferred to *Peace Bringer*'s neural fabrics and we await the return of the remaining twenty-one. Belirand is quite advanced with their security technologies and we've had to engage directly."

"You've been at it for less than twenty minutes. My guess is you are seeing some of the best technology mankind has, as far as security goes," I said.

"Oh. Very much. But let's be clear. Mankind didn't craft the neural mesh in *Peace Bringer*," he said, matter-of-factly.

"Nick, are you listening to this?"

"I am, Liam. We've linked bridge comms," he said. His voice carried the slight lilt I'd come to associate with the fact that he already knew what I was learning.

"Where did they get it?" I asked.

"Norigans are what Belirand refers to them as, internally," Jonathan replied. "As we have had no reason to assign this species a human name, it seems reasonable."

"Are they dangerous?" I asked. Jonathan had the attention of everyone on the bridge.

"Not in the sense that you ask the question. Norigans are social bipeds, not dissimilar to humans." He gestured, lobbing the image of a short, bright-green, big-mouthed, frog-skinned, tri-fingered humanoid. The display showed the Norigan was not quite a meter tall and had an average mass of around thirty kilograms.

"You think we look like that?" Moonie asked, scandalized.

"Within the scope of sentient beings we've come in contact with, humans and Norigans are quite compatible. Your reproductive systems are similar, although we have no reason to believe compatible. You'd find their ordinary habitat to be oxygen poor, but survivable, and they communicate sonically using analogous language constructs," Jonathan continued.

"Ewww," Moonie said. Somehow it was funny when he said it. I wasn't sure why.

"What do you mean, 'not dangerous in the way I mean it?'" I asked.

"They are intelligent and technologically advanced, compared to humans. They have little guile and are easily manipulated."

"And a corporation like Belirand has no qualms about using them to gain technological advances. Those ass hats." I spat.

"Ass hat?" Jonathan asked. "We assume you are denigrating Belirand for amoral behavior. Would you please explain? Some of us believe you feel that Belirand is gaining a tactical advantage and you are opposed to this, while others believe there is some other reason for your indignation."

"I'm not completely sure what pisses me off so badly, but I guess I just don't like that they're a peaceful race and our first interaction with them is to put them to work. It feels that we should do something else, like show them paintings or music or dancing or something," I said.

"Nice," Tabby said, shaking her head at my inability to express myself. "I think what you're saying is Belirand hardly represents the human race well and you're concerned they're taking advantage of the Norigans."

"Right," Nick said. "Belirand doesn't want to keep humanity from the stars in order to protect us. They just don't want any competition. What I don't understand is what keeps other species from preying on the Norigans?"

"Humankind is the first species we've encountered that has developed cost effective interstellar travel. For others, the time and material cost is too great," Jonathan explained.

"If we share TransLoc with everyone, it wouldn't be that long before other species would learn of it. Humans really aren't capable of not sharing information," I said.

"A truth we often discussed with Thomas Anino," Jonathan replied. "The problem is not as simple as you describe, however, as with increased communication and contact, species like Norigans would learn to defend themselves."

"Or become enslaved if they didn't," Tabby added glumly.

I didn't want to think about all of the implications. What I had to deal with in front of me was enough for right now. "Ugh. Well, it won't matter at all if we sit here all day. I'm guessing Belirand is fixing to jump a fleet in our general direction and we'd better not be here. Even with all their resources, they won't like us swiping a fifty million credit ship."

"I think the actual number is closer to six hundred million," Nick said.

I whistled.

"Right. Belirand is so not letting this go anytime soon," Ada added.

While we weren't exactly sitting ducks while underway, sailing around in New Pradesh wasn't the safest thing we could be doing. No doubt Belirand would mount a response to our brazen raid. With *Peace Bringer* in our stable, however, I doubted they had enough firepower within several days of hard burn to push us out. That said, I didn't like sitting around.

I scanned my queue. We'd been in-system long enough for messages to have been relayed and picked up. My eyes lit on one I was looking for from Jake Berandor. I hoped he had good news. We'd made a deal to pack up the three stationary cannons taken from the Red Houzi compound. Unknown to me, these cannons had a manufacturer's kill switch that Belirand had taken advantage of when they attacked the Descartes Mining Co-Op. Berandor's message was simple: packages delivered, Nuage isn't safe.

I could have guessed the latter. Belirand had strong-armed the small Nuage nation to detain us when we were there last and we'd been forced to make a messy exit. Jonathan assured me he had a legal team working on clearing our names, but these things took time and held no guarantees. It was sad. I loved the Nuage people and the very nation itself. Big Pete had always told me, however, that sacrifice was giving up something of value for something you believed in. My crew had saved over eight hundred colonists on Ophir and forty-five crew members on *Cape of Good Hope*. We'd traded our ability to live amongst the civilized nations of humanity and if we had it to do all over again, we certainly would.

Using all available storage in Loose Nuts fleet, do we have sufficient room for Co-op cannons that were packed by Jake Berandor? It was a fairly complex problem I was throwing at my AI, but I knew it was up to the task.

"Sufficient storage is not available," the AI responded to my narrow question.

Are there alternatives? It was a first question you learned to ask an AI. They were very good at answering direct questions, but were even better at problem solving.

"If strapping were manufactured, the long barrels of the cannons could be strapped to cargo hooks along the keel of Strumpet."

I didn't need to ask if we had the capacity to manufacture the strapping as the AI would have stipulated that difficulty.

If we jump directly to Descartes location, how much time in hard-burn is required once we exit fold-space?

"Four hours nineteen minutes."

"That should work," Nick said over the comm. He'd obviously been listening in. "I'll start manufacturing those straps."

"Copy that. Ada, would you create a nav-plan? I'm sending the coordinates now." My AI presented a small, virtual package on my HUD which I flicked in her general direction.

"Can do, Liam. What are we going to do with those guns?" she asked.

"Feels like we've endangered the good people of Ophir and I'd like to give Captain LeGrande some real punch if Tullas shows up," I said. I was of course referring to Katherine LeGrande, the previous captain of *Cape of Good Hope* who, with her crew, had been left in the deep dark to die by Lorraine Tullas, an Admiral in Belirand's Central Security division.

"Transit time thirty-two hours," Ada replied. A notification appeared on my screen, requesting my approval for a fleet directive. My AI reviewed the contents and acknowledged its agreement to the effectiveness of Ada's plan.

"On your mark, Captain Chen," I said and lobbed the honors back to her.

The holographic display of *Peace Bringer* and *Strumpet* appeared to my right, showing the ships turning in unison, accompanied by the now familiar sound of TransLoc engines spooling up. I wasn't excited about the next part, which was a gut-wrenching moment when the universe felt like it was sliding backwards. Every color in the immediate vicinity smeared like a wet impressionist painting being wiped by a giant invisible hand. It was always the same experience as we entered fold-space, which fortunately dissipated quickly.

"I never thought I'd be grateful for a completely armored bridge with no view of space," Tabby said. She'd changed her workstation's translucent wraparound screens to show the stars as they would look near our old home, Colony-40. If we had armor-glass, the stars would have been jittering around us as we wound our way through fold-space. That was an unnerving view I wouldn't miss.

"We have thirty-two hours before we drop out of fold-space," I said, raising my voice slightly so everyone knew I was addressing the room. "There are five of us and I want two people on duty at all times. Tabby and I will take first shift and I'll send assignments out after that. Feel free to find a bunk and make yourself at home, generally."

"Sweet! Dibs on the captain's quarters," Moonie said, springing to his feet and dashing out the bridge door.

A PIRATE'S LIFE

A familiar whistle sounded. I turned my chair and looked up from my studies. Tabby and I had spent the better part of our six-hour shift taking overview coursework on the General Astral Frigate Mark VI. As warships went, we were small; one hundred twenty meters LOA and four point five kilo tonnes. While we were able to sail her with just two people, the ship was capable of hosting as many as eighty souls. A more reasonable minimum crew would be closer to twelve. Fewer crew put us in danger of not being able to man the guns or tend to any number of other emergencies in a true combat situation, not to mention the simple grind of bridge watches. Where we would come up with an additional seven people we could trust, I had no idea. It was enough to make my head hurt, but we could only truly respond to one issue at a time.

The whistle sounded. I'd become distracted. Once again, I turned my attention to the door. An incredibly high-resolution vid-screen on the bridge door showed Jonathan standing patiently outside; fifteen minutes early for his shift.

"Permission to enter bridge," he asked, once I acknowledged his presence.

"Permission granted." The AI opened the door upon hearing my reply.

"Greetings, Tabitha and Liam. I trust your watch was satisfactorily quiet."

"Roger that, Jonny Boy," Tabby said. Her response told me she was getting antsy. Six hours of sitting was about as much as she could take. Fortunately, the ship appeared to have a first-class exercise facility in the bow and we'd burn off some of her angst in a few minutes.

"How hard is it to change the ship's transponder signal? We'd

24

like to rename her." My query caused Jonathan to turn before he sat at one of the available workstations.

"Transponders are simple mechanisms and easily reprogrammed. It won't help with your registration at any reputable port in human space as *Peace Bringer* will have been reported stolen," he said.

I knew what he was saying to be true. If our registration wasn't recognized, the station authority would attempt to seize our ship, at least until we could clear up provenance, something we had no real hope of accomplishing.

His comment, however, got me to thinking. "How many non-reputable ports are you aware of?"

"The list is ever-changing, as are their locations, but currently we're aware of twenty-three stations that do not recognize the Ordwall Conventions," he answered.

"Where?" That there were twenty-three of these stations, I found remarkable. I'd previously only heard rumors about them.

"Scattered around the four settled solar systems. There are fewer in Sol than in Bethe Peierls, New Pradesh and Tipperary." His tone grew grave. "I feel I must warn you, Liam. These stations are to be avoided. Most are run by locally powerful entities who manufacture their own laws."

"Thugs, pirates, outlaws and miscreants?" Tabby asked. "I'm already starting to feel all warm and tingly. You know, we're outlaws now. Thugs even." She loved needling Jonathan with half-truths and innuendo. For their part, they seemed to enjoy the puzzle of decoding what she said.

"We feel that yours is possibly too strong of a characterization to be spread so liberally across such a large number of groups, but there are those of us who agree with your general analysis." Jonathan's speech became more formal when replying to Tabby.

"Jonathan, how difficult would you find it to change the transponder's signal to a new ship's designation?" I asked.

"There are a number of issues in showing up as an unregistered ship in most ports. Given the origins of this particular ship, we believe this to be a reasonable alternative. Instead of modifying the current transponder, we have already taken the liberty of manufacturing a new transponder. It awaits a final name to be burned into the permanent circuitry. To do otherwise is detectable," he replied.

"*Intrepid*," I replied.

"A brilliant choice," he said.

"Oh?" I hadn't expected him to have much of an opinion on the subject.

"We had a lottery and *Intrepid* was my individual choice," he said. "*Intrepid* was only chosen by six percent of us. Most thought you would choose *Atropos*; a logical choice if you were familiar with the fictional representation of Horatio Hornblower; his first ship being HMS *Hotspur* and second being *Atropos*. My voting bloc's choice was for a more contextual name; a description of purpose, that is, to be fearless or adventurous."

It was one of the risks of talking with Jonathan; ask a relatively simple question and receive a lengthy answer. Most of the time, I was up for it, especially on long trips. "You do lotteries?" I'd extracted the one point he'd made that I found interesting.

"Constantly. It is a game mechanic Thomas Anino taught us. We've found that betting on human behaviors provides considerable entertainment."

"What do you win?"

"Your closest analog is esteem," he said.

"Let me guess. Tabby is the source of a lot of lotteries."

"It would seem an answer to that question would put us at a disadvantage. We are willing to admit we find your young life-mate to be fascinating."

"Damn skippy you do," Tabby said.

A second whistle alerted us to another request for bridge access. It was Mom carrying a tray with three cups of coffee. I recognized the cups as the ones we'd discovered on *Mastodon*. They had mini grav-generators built into the base and, as a result, were virtually spill proof. It wasn't like Tabby or me to go six hours without a stim-drink like coffee, but we'd both been so absorbed in the new ship literature that our shift had passed quickly.

"Thank you!" I said, meeting Mom at the bridge door.

"There are two galleys," she said. "Ward room and general. Neither have anything fresh and I'm sorry about the crappy coffee."

I took a sip. It was bitter, as synth-coffee always was, but having gone so long with nothing made up for the bad flavor. "Works for me. Tabby and I are going to explore. Have you seen Moonie?"

"He's holed up in the captain's quarters," Mom said, smiling.

"Seriously?" Tabby asked.

"The officer bunks are very comfortable." Mom replied, looking to minimize drama. "You have to hand it to Belirand; they know how to fit a ship."

"I'm gonna fit it with something," Tabby said, still focused on the problem named Moonie.

We handed the watch over to Mom and Jonathan, exited the bridge and found ourselves in a starboard passage that ran the length of the ship. For as long as we'd been onboard, we'd only been in the hold, this passageway and the bridge.

"Where to first?" I asked.

"I want to oust Moonie from the captain's quarters," she said, bouncing on the balls of her feet.

"No. That'll work itself out. I want to see the ship. Let's go forward." I pulled her along behind me. She could have stopped me, but she let me lead. I stopped at the first door on the port side of the hallway. 'Fire-Control' was the label above the security panel. I palmed the door open and stepped through the hatch. From the bridge-side door, we'd been able to see into the room, but I wanted a closer look at the four smaller weapons control stations as well as the pass-through station where the gunnery officer could communicate with the bridge as well as the gunners.

"Makes me feel like we're short-handed," Tabby acknowledged as we stepped out.

"I've got some ideas about staffing, but I'd like to talk with everyone about it," I said. "We started out as a company, but I just don't feel like that's what we are now." We headed forward again, my HUD displaying each room's function as we passed by. I couldn't help but stick my head into each for a quick look.

"How aren't we a company anymore?" Tabby asked.

"Loose Nuts is still a thing, but what's a company if it doesn't have a profit motive?"

"Hard to say. Stealing a hundred fifty thousand credits in supplies, not to mention a ship worth six hundred million, is quite a profit," she retorted. "We crossed a line back there. Every major government will consider us pirates from this point forward. No one will care about our motives."

"Trying to cheer me up?"

"Turn here," she said. The passageway had come to a fork. If we stayed on the starboard side of the hull, we'd be forced down to Deck-3. Tabby herded me to the left and then right and we were once again headed forward. "I get it and I'm in - for whatever. What's next though? Turn here."

I misunderstood which direction she was indicating and attempted to turn back to the starboard where a passageway ended in an air-lock. We'd made it to the ship's main air-lock. "I don't want to go outside," I laughed. Tabby, however, had already palmed open the hatch opposite, grabbed my shoulder and was pulling me backwards into what I knew to be the crew's mess. "Where are you dragging me?" I had no choice but to follow as she worked her way around the long, polished mess tables and through another hatch.

"Here!" she exclaimed. We'd entered a long, curved room dedicated to exercise. There were numerous stationary running tracks, a half-court pod-ball arena, weight lifting equipment and a boxing ring. It didn't take a genius to guess what she had in mind, as she tossed me a protective sparring mask and gloves.

Thirty minutes later, exhausted and battered, I refused to stand up one more time. For a few minutes, I'd felt like I was keeping up, but she just kept relentlessly hammering me. I'd backed her down a couple of times and had my share of lucky hits, but I was no match for her. At least she didn't feel compelled to point it out.

She held a glove out to me in a friendly gesture meant to help me up and I grabbed it. I've always had a penchant for doing the wrong thing at the right time - and this proved to be another one of those times. As I grabbed her gloved hand in my own, I rolled back, pulling her with me, using my leg to throw her. With just about anyone else, it would have been a brilliant maneuver. With Tabby, it was suicide. She lithely used her momentum and spun around, lifting my body from the mat just enough to snake her leg around my arm and neck. When she levered her foot beneath her knee, I found myself on the wrong side of a choke hold. For a moment, I didn't have enough wits about me to tap the mat with my free arm and her legs tightened, cutting off the flow of air to my beleaguered lungs. Fortunately, Tabby was waiting and loosened immediately once I signaled.

"I think you just wanted to get between my legs," she said, lying next to me on the mat. I smiled. She had a filthy mind and I liked it. I twisted around and slid up on top of her, my arms trembling from our workout. From the look on her face, she thought my shaking was something else.

"Carry me," I said and collapsed. I kissed her neck and made my way to her earlobe, nibbling gently. Not one for being on the bottom, Tabby rolled us over. She was considerably friskier than I could manage at the moment; kissing and groping me. I did my best to keep up with her until she abruptly popped upright and pulled me to my feet.

"I bet the head is amazing." She sprinted to an open hatch, throwing gloves and protective gear to the deck as she did. I scooped up her vac-suit and suit-liner as I followed the trail of clothing to a brightly lit public shower room. I counted fifteen individual streams of water shooting from the walls as she ran naked through them splashing and whooping it up. A more beautiful sight I couldn't imagine. I cursed my body's failing muscles and removed my own vac-suit. Once naked, I fended her off just long enough to feed the clothing into the oversized suit fresheners.

Once we finished showering and were dressed, I still didn't

want to move. "I'm exhausted," I said. We'd burned two of my six-hours of rest and were standing in the galley of the general mess-hall wolfing down meal bars and electrolyte juice.

"We should check out the Forward Observation Lounge." Tabby stuffed a thousand kilo-calories of bars into her suit.

My HUD informed me that we were only a single hatch away, so I led her forward. For a moment, I'd forgotten we were in fold-space. I looked out, expecting the ordinarily serene view of space I was used to on long trips. The jumping view in front of me was less disturbing than it had once been, but it still wasn't my favorite.

The lounge was set up with reclining seats embedded into the sloping deck, giving its occupants a place to comfortably sit or lie while staring out at the stars. I pulled Tabby down as I slumped into a padded chair.

Set alarm, fifteen minutes before my next shift.

She lay next to me and rested her head on my shoulder, hand across my midsection. Her earlier words haunted me. I had just made us all into pirates. Tabby was right; it wouldn't just be Belirand who had it in for us now.

"Yar," I murmured as I slipped off to sleep.

DESCARTES CO-OP

I was always grateful to drop out of fold-space. For whatever reason, the thought of slicing through the fabric of space still freaked me out. It wasn't as if we didn't have the capability to recover from such a drop, but the idea of where we might end up bugged me.

"Jonathan, are we picking up any nearby ships other than *Strumpet*?"

"No, Captain. The sensors on *Intrepid* are extraordinarily sensitive and there are no ships in near space," he answered.

Establish bridge-to-bridge link with Strumpet. A pleasant chime acknowledged the command's success.

"What's your sit-rep, *Strumpet*?"

"We're tired, but status is green." Ada's reply wasn't surprising. With just her, Nick and Marny, they were sailing ridiculously short-handed.

As promised, Jake Berandor had packed and moved the three defensive cannons to this arbitrary location in space. We were relatively close to Descartes, but far enough away that no one would just happen by the location.

"Let's raft up while the bots load the crates and we can have a confab. That work for you all?"

"What kind of food you have on that tub, Cap?" Marny asked.

"Meal bars and protein powder." I wasn't complaining. While I'd learned to enjoy the food Marny cooked, I'd grown up on meal bars and could go either way.

"I just pulled out chocolate cupcakes," Marny said. "And a fresh pot of coffee." She really knew how to hit below the belt.

"We'll be over just as soon as we establish zero-delta," Tabby answered for me. Mom and Tabby had joined Jonathan and me for the final hour of our approach into local-space.

"How about you bring a cupcake back for me," Mom said. "I'll man the bridge here. I feel squeamish leaving the bridge empty."

As soon as she said it, I recognized the wisdom in her words. "You're right and I'll get Moonie to oversee the loading process."

It took twenty minutes to arrive at the exact location Jake Berandor and I had agreed on. I transmitted a low power encoded burst and the packages, previously dark, illuminated on our sensors. With Mom on the bridge and Moonie in the hold, Tabby, Jonathan and I walked across the catwalk that joined *Intrepid* to *Strumpet*.

Ada and Marny met us on the other side and we exchanged hugs before heading to *Strumpet's* well-appointed bridge. We might be pirates now, but this was my family. We joined Nick at the highly polished conference room table next to the bridge where Marny had thoughtfully placed cupcakes and mugs of coffee in anticipation of our arrival.

"What's next?" Nick asked as I tore into a cupcake. I might not dream of normal meals, but chocolate and coffee were a combo I found irresistible.

"We've enough fuel for a mission," I said. "After we deploy these guns back on Ophir, I'd like to carry on with what Anino started. Though he tricked us, I think I speak for everyone when I say Anino had a righteous cause."

"Most of the comm crystals he left have some sort of activity on them," Nick said. "One is persistent and I'd like to check it out. It could be a dead end, but it's sending a periodic signal requesting assistance."

He was, of course, referring to the ninety-three quantum communication crystals Thomas Anino had given his life to protect. Each crystal represented a failed exploration mission where Belirand had abandoned a ship and its crew. Belirand had the technology, but was unwilling to retrieve their people, stating each mission's failure to meet 'corporate objectives.' The deeper we dug into Belirand, the more we discovered what this giant corporation was willing to do to protect its bottom line and keep its secrets.

"I think we should leave *Strumpet* on Ophir," I said. "If we leave the command codes with LeGrande, we can be assured it will be in good hands. We can't afford to sail *Intrepid* with such a short crew. It's dangerous."

"*Intrepid*?" Ada asked. "I thought she was *Peace Bringer*."

"I renamed her. It's not written in stone, though. If you have a better idea, I'd be okay with a vote."

"I think it fits," Marny said. "You're right. We can sail three ships poorly or one ship well. I'd prefer the latter."

"Should we recruit?" Tabby asked. "You know, from Ophir? They'd be green, but anyone is trainable."

"We could open it up," Nick said. "I'm not sure how many of *Cape's* old crew I want, though. Some of them hold grudges about being stranded on Ophir. Could cause hard feelings."

"With Moonie and Jonathan, we have seven. I'd like at least twelve. We should get LeGrande's take on it," Marny said. "At a minimum, three gunnery mates would help."

"So minimum three and a maximum of five?" I asked.

"I'd say as many as ten," Marny replied. "But yeah, minimum three."

"All right, plan is: set up the guns, recruit locals from Ophir, leave LeGrande in charge of *Strumpet*, and check out Nick's signal?" I asked.

"We feel we should warn you about this mission," Jonathan said. The side conversations that started after I summed up our plan stopped and all eyes turned to him. "As you know, the four settled solar systems that represent humanity are all relatively close in terms of the overall universe. Each system settled by humanity is located along the Orion-Cygnus arm of the Milky Way and all within four hundred parsecs of each other. The location of the signal Master James refers to is in the Dwingeloo galaxy. The Aeratroas region is home to four hundred twelve inhabited systems occupying a roughly tubular shape only three hundred parsecs long with a diameter of a hundred parsecs."

"I'm not following how that's dangerous." Ada posed the

question we were all thinking.

"They're really close together," Nick said. "Close enough that some of them would be aware of each other."

"Precisely, Master James," Jonathan said. "There is a concentration of these planets at the heart of the Aeratroas region. They've formed a confederation and established laws related to trade and acceptable treatment of sentients."

"How concentrated?" I asked.

"One hundred twenty-three planets within a radius of thirty-eight parsecs." Jonathan answered.

"What's the confederation called?" Ada asked, sitting on the edge of her chair.

"As no one speaks a human language, it is very much up for interpretation. Perhaps the most succinct answer being The Confederation of Planets." Jonathan said.

"This confederation. Are they the danger?" I asked.

"No. Master Anino found them to be agreeable, as I believe Belirand does. A simple registration process and an agreement to abide by their laws while within their territory is all that is required to trade within The Confederation. Most species simply want to trade for items they require for survival or aesthetics. The danger comes from a small, but dangerous minority of sentient species. Where we are planning to travel, that minority is represented by the Kroerak."

Jonathan flicked instructions to the holographic display in *Strumpet's* ready room and a biped that looked like something between a human and a blue cockroach with big ugly bug-eyes, antennae and short pincers for hands appeared. "This is a Kroerak warrior. They're fast when compared to humans, have an exoskeleton which is a natural armor that rivals your steel, and most importantly, cannot be reasoned with. As a species, they have little respect for other sentients. Beings they deem to have any value at all, they enslave."

"Do you have information about their tactical capabilities?" Marny asked.

"Some," Jonathan replied. "We're sending it to you now."

Marny nodded her thanks.

"What of trading in this Confederation?" Having currency in a new system could be critical.

"Metals are in high demand, especially zero-g formed nano-crystalized sheet and beam," Jonathan replied.

My eyes glazed over for a moment as an idea hit me. It was nuts, but my current company was all of that and then some.

"Jonathan, have you ever TransLoc'd an asteroid?"

"What?" Tabby sounded scandalized.

"The Co-Op is one forge from making nano-steel. It was Big Pete's dream; he even cleared the shelf for it," I said. "So is it even possible?"

"You can't sail a rock," Tabby said.

"We did once when we moved it closer to the claims. Besides, TransLoc isn't about speed, it's about the fold-space wave." My simplistic position might be ignorant, but I wasn't ready to give up on the idea.

"It is possible, but why wouldn't we simply purchase the necessary equipment and transport it?" Jonathan asked.

"How long would it take to purchase, transport and set it up? There's no platform or materials near Ophir. We push that rock out there, we'll have a ridiculous amount of iron and the means to smelt it. Add a nano-crystal steel forge and we're in business." I felt like I was losing the battle, but I had one more shot in me.

Jonathan turned the full length of his gaze on me. Sometimes I could swear I saw every single one of its residents in those eyes. "We had not considered bringing iron to Ophir. The engines required are similar to what we had on *Mastodon*, of which we have two replacements that no longer have a purpose. We foresee two problems. First, we would need to leave a supply of Aninonium with whoever is tasked with retrofitting the asteroid - the volume of which would be extremely valuable and highly sought after by Belirand. Second, Thomas Anino's company is under constant surveillance. Moving the engines would require a level of deceit we are not capable of."

"How would the asteroid be navigated?" Ada asked.

"A simple AI could be configured. It's not like we're worrying about the ban on autonomous vehicles," Nick said.

"Break out your checkbook, Jonathan. I know just the guy," I said, looking at Nick with a grin.

"Berandor," we said in unison. He was the perfect choice, with his advanced degree in propulsion systems. Just as importantly, he didn't mind working on the grey side of the law.

"You'd trust Berandor with enough Aninonium to send the Co-Op from Descartes to Ophir?" Ada asked. We all knew and even liked Jake Berandor, but that much temptation might be more than he could resist. Not only that, I wasn't completely sure we wanted Jake to become aware of the element's existence.

She was right, but I wasn't out of ideas yet.

"So, why not pay the Lichts to load the Aninonium? They're beyond honest. I'd like to run Mom over there anyway to say goodbye to her friends and pick up a few personal items," I said.

"That works," Nick agreed. "Would you mind if I tagged along?"

***

Two hours later, *Hotspur* dropped from hard burn as we approached the Descartes asteroid belt. We'd left *Intrepid* behind, but had taken advantage of her sensitive long range scans which hadn't picked up any large ships in the vicinity.

Hail Licht family claim.

"Liam Hoffen, as I live and breathe. We hadn't expected to hear from you so soon." The voice belonged to Annalise, wife of Frimunt and the head of the Licht family household.

"We were hoping to drop in for a visit, Annalise," Mom answered.

"Of course. I'll tell the boys. I'm sure they'll to want to see you," she said.

"We'll be there shortly," Mom said and terminated the comm.

Fifteen minutes later, I circled the ruined Co-Op. MacAsgaill's jackboot, Ahmed Mussa, had obliterated the habitation domes on the topside of the shoe-shaped rock, doing little to the mostly iron-cored asteroid. I was shocked by the damage. My cheeks grew hot as the horrific events of my father's murder rushed back at me. The strike had been cowardly, my father not even knowing who his enemy was. Then again, most of my anger was inwardly pointed; guilt at not having sufficiently warned him.

The bottom of the asteroid, or sole of the shoe, was still piled high with ore owned by Loose Nuts. The refining equipment stood covered, not having been utilized for months. Under orders from MacAsgaill, Mussa hadn't fired on the equipment; his entire purpose had been to destroy my family. It was something I would never let myself forget.

"He'll get his," Mom said, laying her hand on my arm. "Seeking vengeance will hurt you, Liam."

"I know. That's not where I'm at." It was a lie; nothing could be further from the truth. I would have my vengeance on MacAsgaill and Belirand and would give no quarter when the time came.

I veered away from the Co-Op and sailed over to Mom and Dad's claim. All of their equipment had been cleaned and neatly arranged. I suspected we had Frimunt Licht to thank for that. He was a man of few words, but had been a good friend to my dad. It was a final show of respect that he had arranged Dad's homestead so everything was in order, as if it were waiting for him to return.

"I was thinking," I said, interrupting the solemn moment. "Once we relocate the Co-Op, we should call it Petersburg Station, as a tribute to Dad."

Mom didn't respond. When I looked over, she was quietly wiping tears from her face. "I think he'd like that." Mom said when she was finally able to talk.

A few minutes later, I set *Hotspur* down on the shelf I'd helped clear in front of the habitation dome where Mom and Dad had lived. They'd been splitting their time between their claim and the Co-Op. I wondered what would have happened if they hadn't been at the Co-Op when Mussa arrived. Would Dad still be alive or would MacAsgaill have pursued them both back to the claim? It was the sort of question that drove a person nuts.

Nick stayed behind on *Hotspur* as I followed Mom into the dome and waited while she gathered small items in a bag. Mining families rarely had many possessions other than equipment due to the transient nature of their lives. Mom collected the few things both she and Dad would have considered keepsakes. I watched as she wiped fresh tears from her eyes and looked around one last time. I hugged her and we walked out of the dome together and back to *Hotspur*. Once aboard, Nick wordlessly lifted off and sailed toward the Licht family claim.

"Have you been eating enough, Silver?" Annalise worried out loud as she inspected Mom, much like she would a daughter. Mom had always been thin, as most spacers were. With new eyes, I recognized that Annalise was right. Mom had lost a few kilograms - ones she didn't have to spare. "You have to look after yourself, dear. I'm not there to do it for you." I found it comforting to hear my mom being scolded by the caring woman as I was led away by Selig and Ortel.

"You don't want to get in the middle of all that. Once she gets going, it can take her hours to slow down," Ortel said. I swore he'd grown four centimeters since I'd last seen him. At sixteen stans, he was nearly as tall as his older brother Selig. For brothers, they couldn't be more different. Selig was reserved like their father and responsible to a fault. Ortel was quick to speak and had an easy smile.

"Liam!" I was pushed forward into the family's living space by the two smaller boys, Ulran and Merley. I grabbed them and used my grav-suit to float the three of us to the ceiling. "Hey, what's that about?" Ulran asked. "No fair!" Merley complained, pinwheeling his legs.

"New tech." I lowered us slowly to the ground.

"That's cool!" I couldn't tell which of them had said it.

We rough-housed for a few minutes, finally settling back onto couches. I noticed Wilma, the youngest daughter, and Milenette looking into the room from the hallway. I'd forgotten that the Lichts had taken in the two orphans from Grünholz. I looked around and found Milenette's brother, Priloe, leaning against the wall, observing, standing next to a thin girl I didn't recognize.

"Hey, Priloe. How's mining treating you?" I asked.

"I miss Big Pete," he said plainly.

The statement hit me like a hammer to the gut and I saw loss in his eyes. Big Pete had opened up a new world for him and Belirand had closed it down just as quickly. Only through the kindness of the Lichts was he allowed to stay and help on their claim, but even I could see that allowing Priloe and Milenette to stay could only be a short-term arrangement. There would be too many mouths to feed and not enough O2 to go around without more paydays. Without Big Pete, the mining colony was foundering.

"Me too, my friend. Me too." I nodded as we shared the moment. At twelve stans, he was older than most seventeen stans I knew. Growing up on the streets with a kid sister to fend for did that to a person.

"What are you guys doing on Descartes? Are you getting the Co-Op up and going again?" Ortel interrupted as his father, Frimunt entered the room.

I stood out of respect and as Big Pete had taught me, shook his outstretched hand.

"Nick has a proposal and wants to run it by your Dad and Selig," I said. I knew leaving Frimunt out of the discussion would cause problems, even though Selig was old enough to make his own decisions.

"Run along, boys," Frimunt said.

"Really, Dad?" Ortel asked. He was old enough to make his own decisions and I understood why he chafed at being lumped in with the wonder twins.

"You may stay," Frimunt agreed. "It is time your voice is heard in family matters."

Ortel crossed his hands over his chest and looked down at Ulran and Merley. "Move on, squirts."

It appeared that both boys knew they couldn't successfully argue with Frimunt and cleared out. Frimunt, a man of few words, simply waited for the room to empty.

"Mr. Licht, Selig, We're moving the Co-Op," I started.

"That's nuts," Ortel said. "Moving it where?"

"Away." I said. "And we need help with a few things, like helping a man who'll be coming out later to install big engines on it."

"What about Big Pete's claim?" Ortel asked.

"Let them speak," Frimunt admonished. His voice was firm, but understanding.

"Mom still owns the claim. She'll keep it for now," I said.

"And the *Kestrel*?" Selig asked referring to the ship we'd purchased with the sole purpose of moving ore from our own Descartes claims.

"For your help, we'll transfer *Kestrel's* ownership to your family," Nick said. "Belirand has made it so we won't be able to come back here for quite a while."

"It'll be sad to see the Co-Op go," Selig said. "But I'm willing to help and you don't need to leave *Kestrel* behind."

"But we need it," Ortel interrupted. It wasn't news. We all knew the *Kestrel* was their only way of delivering ore to market and without it, they'd pay Belirand most of the profits to arrange for delivery.

"Ortel." Frimunt warned again. "*Kestrel* is not our ship."

"But you have been good friends," I said. "The offer stands. We have no use for *Kestrel* and would appreciate knowing it has a good home."

Selig held his hand out and we shook.

"I'll have our lawyer, Mr. Ordena, contact you with details," Nick said, also shaking Selig's hand.

"Frimunt, could we have a word, alone?" I asked.

He said nothing but waited for his eldest sons to leave. I hadn't said anything to Nick yet, so he was looking at me with interest.

"We're looking for crew for our ship, Frimunt. Ortel will be seventeen in a month. I'd like to offer him a position. It'd be hard work, likely dangerous. I won't make the offer without your blessing," I said.

"Peter would be proud of the man you've become, Liam

Hoffen." Frimunt was the only one I knew who referred to Dad by his given name. "You may talk to my son, but first I must speak with Annalise."

We stayed with the Lichts for another hour, sitting with them for a meal. Annalise initially objected to the idea of Ortel leaving the family claim, but after talking with Frimunt, she finally acquiesced. Both parents knew Ortel had no desire to live his life on a mining claim. When I asked, he jumped at the chance to sail on *Intrepid*. I smiled as I studied the young man. He was the same age I had been when pirates first attacked Colony-40, which was just over seventeen stans.

It was a tearful goodbye as we loaded onto *Hotspur* and made our way back to *Intrepid*.

"I gotta be honest," Ortel said as we transitioned to hard burn, having snaked our way free of the asteroid belt. "When I woke up this morning, I sure didn't see this coming."

SCRUFFY LOOKING

"How do you think the kid is doing?" Tabby asked, referring to Ortel, as we jogged through the long passageways of *Intrepid*. She'd donned a weight pack and was carrying an extra forty kilograms of mass. Even so, I was breathing harder than she was. Ortel was back on *Strumpet* with Nick, Marny and Ada and I was curious how he was fitting in.

We'd entered fold-space twelve hours previous and would sail for another eighty before reaching Ophir. While *Intrepid* was fast in local space, her engines did nothing to overcome the effect mass had on fold-space travel.

"Makes me wonder," I said with a laugh. "Which will Marny hit first? Physical training or ship etiquette and systems?"

Tabby grinned at me. She knew exactly what Marny was capable of. "Think about it. Marny is on a ship with only Nick and Ada as possible workout partners. That kid is in trouble. She'll grind him into paste, then sit him at a gunnery station and run him through battle simulations. Speaking of, ready for some sparring?" We slowed to a walk and pushed through the hatch that led through the crew mess to the gym.

"Sure," I said, although I meant anything but. I was still wearing med patches from our last few bouts and anticipated a new round of thorough pummeling.

She patted my back. I hate to admit that I flinched when I saw her hand come up. We were in her territory now and I would never compete with that body. She tried to encourage me with, "You're getting stronger." It might be a true, but I understood her statement for what it was. She was concerned for the beating my ego was about to take. As a slower, weaker opponent, combat in a boxing ring didn't offer many options for overcoming my shortcomings.

"Thanks, but I doubt Ortel is the only one who is looking forward to you and Marny being on the same ship again," I said.

I'd caught her off-guard and her laughter was unrestrained. It was one of the many things I enjoyed about being with her. When she smiled, the whole universe lit up.

An hour later, it was time for me to be back on watch and Tabby to get some rest. I'd sacrificed sleeping next to her for spending a shift together while we were both awake. The headaches I'd been battling lately made me suspect I wasn't applying the right dosage for the mild concussions I'd self-diagnosed, so after watching her walk away, I stepped into the upright medical scanner in sick bay.

"*Prosthetic replacement recommended.*" I'd been focused on my new injuries and was surprised at the full body scan the Medical AI performed.

"Out here in the deep-dark that isn't possible. What do you have for this headache?" I asked the AI.

"*Dispensing medication now. Please apply as indicated.*" The screen showed two semi-circular patches that were to be applied behind my ears. "*Intrepid is sufficiently equipped to replace your amputated foot, Captain Hoffen. Medical oversight is recommended.*"

The relief from the freshly manufactured med patches was immediate and welcome. "Thank you." Thanking an AI for its help wasn't a regular habit, but my mind was suddenly occupied with the possibility of having my foot back. The prosthetic had become part of my life, but even though I'd become accustomed to its fit, it was a poor substitute for a truly manufactured limb.

I made my way back to the bridge and palmed my way through the hatch.

"Captain on the bridge," Mom said.

"As you were," I responded, mostly out of habit. Marny required bridge entry protocols on *Sterra's Gift*, but we'd dropped many on *Hotspur* out of practicality. Still, after months of practice, the habits were hard to shake. Technically, bridge staff were to come to attention when I entered and I wanted to avoid that as much as possible.

We exchanged helm transfer protocols and I took my place, then lost myself in thought for two reasons: the possibility of the medical procedure I'd just heard about and the bliss at having my headaches well treated for the first time in several days.

"Marny sent along real coffee," Mom said, interrupting my reverie. "I was going to brew a new batch. Would you like some?"

"Sure," I agreed.

"Moon?" She turned to Jonathan's replacement. He was slow to respond and the reflection on his eye of a vid playing on his HUD gave him away.

"What? Oh. That'd be great, thanks," he replied.

"What are you watching?" I asked once Mom and Jonathan had cleared the bridge.

"Just a vid I picked up while we were in system," he said.

"We need to be careful with that," I said with just a touch of warning. "If Belirand catches communication between you and your family, it could be bad for them."

He stopped the vid. "Understood."

"I wanted to talk to you about a few changes we'll be making once we return to Ophir," I said. "We'll be picking up new crew and need to establish a more formal system of rank."

"Does that mean you want me to clear out of the captain's quarters?"

"You're good until Ophir, but that'll be part of it."

"So, when do I get my share of *Intrepid*?"

"What do you mean?"

"I've helped you take two ships. What's my take?" he asked.

He had me there. With the exception of Moon, we were a close-knit group, working on a single objective. We didn't really think much about pay.

"Good question and one I haven't given much thought. You get that our mission is to provide aid to the people Belirand abandoned, right? I'll be honest, I'm not sure how we'd pay you."

"If I heard things right, you're looking to bring on more crew. Is that going to be your sales pitch? Come with us, save the universe

44

and go broke?" Moon Rastof had a smile on his face, but the tension in his voice was significant.

A whistle broke the moment, alerting me to Mom standing at the door with coffee and cupcakes. I waved her in.

"That smells amazing," I said, accepting both from her tray. I still hadn't taken time to explore the ward room.

"Moon?" She held the tray for him.

"Thanks," he grumbled. When she turned back she gave me a questioning lift of her eyebrow.

"Thanks, Mom," I said.

"I set up a course for you on ship handling. It's four hours, but you should work through it until you get a ninety-five percent or better," she said over her shoulder as she left the bridge. I chuckled and shook my head. It wasn't like I'd planned to sit on my hands for my entire shift.

"Is this the pay you're going to offer? All the coffee and cupcakes you can eat?"

"You've made your point, Moonie. But don't hang this on anyone else. You're angling for something. What is it?"

"By my count, you have over seven hundred million credits in ships, mostly due to my efforts," he said around the bite of a cupcake. "All I really want is a way home and enough money to stay below Belirand's radar. I'm thinking hard currency, like gold or platinum. Sixty kilograms of gold would do it."

The math wasn't hard. "You're looking for a buyout of two million Mars credits?"

"It's a steal for seven hundred million in ships," he agreed.

I nodded thoughtfully. I was annoyed because he'd ambushed me, but he had a point. Any crew we brought in deserved to know what was in it for them. I could sell them on lofty objectives, but my experience with people was that they needed more.

"We don't have those kind of resources readily available, but at the same time, you're entitled to some sort of compensation. I'll bring it up with Nick," I said.

The guy was not going to give up. "Surely, you've pulled precious metals on that asteroid you're floating back to Ophir."

"Maybe. Wait, how'd you hear about that?" I asked. "You haven't been in those conversations."

"You guys aren't exactly quiet when you're exercising," he said.

"You've been eavesdropping?"

"You were talking in a public space. It's well established that's not eavesdropping."

If I hadn't been so tired from exercising, I'd have considered throttling him right there. He was right, by normal conventions. Speech in public areas wasn't protected for privacy. Being a spacer, however, I'd learned that to get along well with others, you respected people's privacy as much as possible. This was a lesson in human relations that I didn't like learning.

***

"He said that?" Tabby asked. Her eyes flashed with fury.

I'd kept most of the conversation with Moonie to myself for several shifts and had reached a point where I couldn't keep it in anymore. I'd updated the ship's privacy protocols and made it so a person couldn't listen in on public conversations if the involved parties weren't in their chain of command. I wasn't willing to admit to Tabby that Moonie had likely seen her very naked entry into the public showers on more than one occasion.

"Yeah. Some of it's valid, but I don't think we'll be dropping him at Mars anytime soon. He could reasonably expect prize money for the ships. Two million isn't that far off, either. We wouldn't have either ship without his help."

"I'll give him his gold. Right up his..."

"So a weird thing happened to me the other day while I was getting scanned by the medical AI," I interrupted.

"Why were you getting scanned?" She jabbed, catching my chin and I blinked away the pain I'd become used to. The real irony was she didn't recognize the cause and effect.

"Been getting headaches, but that's not the thing," I said.

All of the cocky flooded out of her and she sagged. "Frak. I've been hitting too hard, haven't I?"

"Like I said, I'm looking forward to Marny being on board. But listen to this; *Intrepid* has a med-tank that can replace my foot. It's already started manufacturing a new one."

My words stopped her cold and she dropped her guard. I was sorely tempted to punish her, but I knew better. She wasn't above paying me back if I got her with a cheap shot.

"That's incredible, how long will the surgery take to reattach?"

"If you and Mom would suck up my last two shifts, I could have it finished before we're out of fold-space."

"Done. No way does your mom say no to that," Tabby said. "Have you told her yet?"

***

I strained to see, but my eyes were covered with small goggles. The feeling of a respirator tube being withdrawn from my throat caused me to gag and I dry heaved as medical suspension fluid drained from the tank. When the fluid level lowered sufficiently, my back came in contact with the soft mesh that kept me from touching the back of the tank. Slowly, the tank rotated until I was in a fully upright position. I naturally favored my right foot, as I was used to taking showers without my prosthetic.

Warm fingers tugged on the opaque goggles. "Close your eyes. We've turned down the lights, but it's still going to be really bright." Tabby's voice was nearly a whisper. "I'm just going to pull these off, okay?"

The tube had dried my throat so I couldn't talk so I nodded my head. Gently, she removed the goggles and stroked my cheek. "Give it a try, love. Open your eyes."

I did as she suggested and saw that the medical bay was crowded. Seeing Nick and Marny, I realized we must have already dropped from fold-space. I'd missed out on at least one event of the smeary colors. Worth it.

"What happened? Did we drop out early?" I croaked.

"Program had to run a little longer than expected because of more damage on your leg. Apparently, you've been stressing it

47

too much," Tabby explained. "We've been orbiting Ophir for about a day."

"Wiggle your toes, Liam," Ada said. She was leaning against my mother, with her arm wrapped around Mom's waist. They both stared at me intently; Mom's eyes red and puffy.

Seeing a foot at the end of my left leg was both strange and familiar, but when I envisioned wiggling my toes, nothing happened. I looked up at Tabby. I wasn't sure what I was doing wrong.

"It might be easier if you put it on the deck," Tabby said, trying to reassure me. She was the only one who knew what I was sensing ... or not sensing. "I recall needing to feel feedback before things started working," she said.

I did as she suggested, putting my arms out to her, and attempted to step forward with my right foot. The feedback from my new extremity was initially more than I could take, but then it all started making sense. I'd grown up with a normal foot and those memories took over. With hands on my family's shoulders, I limped around the room, each step more solid than the previous. It felt like I'd sat on my foot, put it to sleep and was having to walk it off until circulation resumed.

"Sweet!" I said.

"Think you could make a meeting on Ophir?" Nick asked. "The council has a proposal for us."

"About what?" I asked. Such was my life, not even a few minutes to celebrate the restoration of a completely new foot, but then I wouldn't trade it for anything.

"About recruiting crew for *Intrepid*," he said.

"How's that?"

"Long story. I'll explain on the way down," Nick said, handing me a towel.

Twenty minutes later, we found ourselves in the chamber of Yishuv's Town Council. Captain LeGrande approached with a broad smile. She'd gained five or six kilos since I'd last seen her and no longer looked like the refugee she'd been.

"Greetings, Katherine," I said.

"Captain Hoffen, so good to see you. I understand your fleet has grown."

"It has indeed. Have you had a chance to visit *Cape*?" We'd landed *Hotspur* next to *Strumpet* just outside of the city's walls, *Intrepid* being too large for atmospheric entry.

"Who gave her that name?" she asked.

"That was Moon Rastof. Last act before we abandoned her back in the deep-dark," I said.

"He has an odd sense of humor."

"Has Nick talked to you about using her as part of Yishuv's defense?" I asked. "We expect to retain ownership, but she was once yours and you seem to be the natural choice to put her to use."

"We'll probably take you up on that," she said with a nod. "I'll put it before The Council in our next meeting. We won't want to muddy the waters today."

"What's this meeting about?" Nick asked.

I was pretty sure I knew what they were thinking. "The Council doesn't want to approve recruiting without concessions?"

"I know it sounds crass, but try to look at it from the perspective of the settlement. Our young people are our greatest resource," Captain LeGrande replied. Rather than seeing herself in exile, Katherine LeGrande had become invested and I appreciated her for that.

"What are they asking for?" I asked.

"Let's call the meeting to order, Mr. Hoffen, and we'll discuss it. Katherine, please join us." Councilwoman Peraf, an ancient old biddy, approached us from behind. I'd never been in a conversation with her where I didn't want to bash my head into a wall.

A hand on my shoulder caused me to turn from the old woman as she shuffled away. The hand belonged to Councilman Bedros, who I'd never completely figured out. His quick smile and easy conversational style made him easy to like, but he always seemed a little shifty. We shook hands and he made his way to the table.

The final person to enter was a small woman, Eliora; her

diminutive size in sharp contrast to her position as the captain of the small settlement's protectorate.

"Captain."

She nodded as she shook my hand and took her seat.

"The Council is called to order. Councilwoman Peraf presiding as chair." Peraf placed the ornate and primarily ceremonial quantum communication device on the table in front of her. It had been the very item that had gained our attention and brought us to the planet in time to save hundreds of citizens from an attack by the native Ophir.

"The agenda for today is to discuss a petition by the principals of the Loose Nuts Corporation to allow for recruiting of citizens of Yishuv to join them as crew members," Peraf announced. "We will hear your proposal, Mr. James."

Nick stood up. "Our proposal is simple. Informally, we'll continue to supply Yishuv with technology and material and we'd like the opportunity to openly recruit your citizens to join us. We propose a recruitment period of a single tenday and would like to hire the best three or four candidates."

"Surely you understand our young people are needed on Yishuv. How else are we to rebuild?" Peraf asked.

He smiled patiently, a response I'd grown used to when asking questions I should already understand the answers to. "The technology we've already supplied has both saved this proud city and serves to provide ongoing protection. Without your citizens being decimated by the indigenous population, your settlement will continue to thrive."

"We need more," Bedros said simply. "It is not that we don't appreciate all you've done for us. Quite the contrary, we recognize that without it we would have been lost. But just as we're starting to make headway, you ask for our most precious resource."

It was the second time I'd heard the words 'precious resource.' The Council had already cooked something up and were just laying groundwork.

"Let's skip to the bottom line," I said. "We need people. Without them, we won't be able to help other settlements like Yishuv.

What's it going to take?"

"You're out of order, Mr. Hoffen," Peraf scolded. "You will wait for the chair to recognize you."

"While your customs are unfamiliar to me, your actions aren't. I'm a trader at heart and recognize a good old-fashioned shakedown when I see it. Name your price," I said.

"Well..." Peraf huffed. She was either a good actress or she was really offended.

"I believe leniency for cultural differences is reasonable here," Bedros said smoothly. While I didn't know much about him directly, I knew the type. He was the guy who told you to go to hell and made you think it might be a pleasant trip. "To answer your question, Captain Hoffen, we require livestock."

He might as well have said he wanted Leprechauns for as much as I understood his words.

"Are we in the middle ages? Did you just propose to trade people for sheep?"

"Sheep, goats, cows and chickens to be more specific. Three breeding pairs of each. You see, the Ophie slaughtered all of our animals and we need to replace them. I've taken the liberty of laying out the pens in the hold of your ship, *Hotspur*, and you appear to have more than adequate room." He flicked a plan to me and he had indeed laid out pens that would fit. He'd clearly adapted to modern technology.

I shook my head in astonishment. "You've got to be kidding me."

"We're setting an orbital station above Ophir," Nick said, his voice still quiet and patient, though he'd returned to his seat. "We'll want to recruit for that as well. No more than ten in total."

Bedros looked between the members of The Council and got subtle affirmative nods.

"And we want three recruits before we deliver the livestock. We're short-handed otherwise," I hastily amended.

"Done." Bedros said.

"All in favor?" Peraf asked.

The entire council raised their hands in agreement.

"Motion is passed." She slammed a gavel on a small block of wood.

I looked at Nick and then to Tabby. "Did we just become sheep herders?"

TRAINEES

"How do you want to go about recruiting?" I asked the assembled group.

Captain LeGrande had joined the meeting with my senior staff. *Strumpet* was sitting just outside the gates to the battle-hardened settlement of Yishuv and we'd chosen to meet in one of her several conference rooms.

"Word is traveling through the settlement," Nick said. "I've received multiple inquiries already."

"I'll second that," Katherine LeGrande added. "Several of my old crew are interested."

I'd invited *Strumpet*'s previous captain to join us because she'd have insight into who amongst her original crew might be suitable for our mission. I also had a proposal I wanted to pitch to her at some point.

"What positions are we hiring?" Ada asked. "And do we have a way to pay them?"

"We're hopelessly under-crewed on *Intrepid*. If we were attacked, we'd have to run," I said. "I have some ideas about pay, but it's hard without a currency."

"Identify the mission, Cap," Marny said. "With that it'll be easier to identify experience level."

I briefly considered the woman who wore so many hats in our small organization. Six centimeters shy of two meters and heavily muscled, Marny out-massed any two of the rest of us. She was both a fierce warrior and as loyal a friend as I could hope to have. To say I had a secret crush on her wasn't quite correct. I tried to hide it, but my fascination with her amazing physique had been outed so many times, it was a running joke. There was just something about how such a big woman could move so gracefully... I shook my head as it wasn't a productive line of thinking. All eyes in the room were on me and so I pushed on.

"Nick and I have been working with Jonathan to map out the failed Belirand missions. Nick, would you show what you've found?"

Display Milky Way, Dwingeloo galaxies. Highlight Ophir, Tipperary and Dwingeloo, Nick said.

Above the glossy conference room table a holo projection appeared, starting with a top view of our galaxy then zooming out to show the two galaxies Nick had requested.

"As you already know, the four publicly settled human systems are all located in Orion-Cygnus." Nick drew a circle on the arm of the Milky Way we occupied. As he did, four stars grew significantly and pulsed. "You might notice that Ophir is on the very edge of the Orion-Cygnus arm. As you might not know, fold-space between galaxies is extremely efficient. It has something to do with no mass between the galaxies, allowing for bigger folds. The point is, while great distances are involved, it doesn't take substantially more time."

"What's that to do with the other Belirand missions?" Ada asked.

"I've taken the liberty of animating the failed or abandoned missions and their galactic locations in chronological order," Nick said.

Start animation.

The hologram zoomed the galactic image down to a familiar topical, solar system view of Sol, with Earth at its center. Automatically, I searched for the asteroid belt between Mars and Jupiter where Colony-40 was located. Nick had thoughtfully provided a blinking icon where our home had been. He knew me so well.

"The first missions appeared to be random," Nick said as glowing yellow arcs emerged one-by-one from Sol, zooming further and further out to include the relatively close systems in all different directions. "As we know, vids from these first missions were publicly available which, of course, turned into a public relations nightmare for Belirand."

"Right, because those crews died from asphyxiation or starvation while the world watched," Ada added.

"What's this got to do with recruiting?" Tabby asked, impatiently.

"Give me five more minutes," Nick said. Tabby nodded, but he had less than five before she pressed again. "It was about this time Belirand discovered the first inhabitable system - Bethe Peierls - and built the TransLoc gates. Now watch as they continue."

We all watched as the arcs were more or less random until the discovery of New Pradesh and finally Tipperary. Right after this point, the Ophir mission failed and then the very next mission jumped across from the Milky Way to the Dwingeloo galaxy.

"Up to this point, we only know of twenty-five failed missions," Nick said. "Take a look at these next twenty."

"They're clearly searching for something," Jonathan observed as the mission indicators dotted across a small section of the Dwingeloo galaxy in a well-organized grid pattern. "We believe they were searching for The Confederation of Planets or The Kroerak Empire and we believe they eventually found both."

"Not that this changes anything," I said. "Our mission is as clear as ever. We follow Belirand's trail to find human populations that need aid. What is just as obvious from all of this is the strategic importance of Ophir. We already know that fold-space between galaxies is significantly more efficient than within galaxies, making Ophir's position at the edge of the Orion-Cygnus arm of the Milky Way critical for staging missions."

"If it's so strategic, why did Belirand abandon Ophir?" Tabby asked.

"The only explanation I can come up with is they found a better location," Nick answered. "But that's just a guess."

"Regardless, defending Ophir just became a top priority," Marny observed.

Captain LeGrande smiled wryly. "And I thought you just invited me for my sage advice."

"We're concerned with what Belirand will do once they

discover we're in the Aeratroas region," I said. "That and we're not sure how they'll deal with our acquisition of *Intrepid*."

"You also have a new problem," LeGrande said. "The Council of Yishuv is considering asking you to leave and not return. Some believe you bring more danger than value."

"That's gratitude," Tabby spat. "I suppose they'll wait until we fetch their cows, though."

"They're not wrong," Nick said. "With us continuing to drop into this system, we're painting a target on Ophir."

"In three more centuries, Yishuv will be right back where they started," LeGrande said. "This colony was seeded with more than twice as many settlers as they have now and roughly the same technology. This generation and the next few will live well and grow, but in time, technology will fail and people will become complacent. Yishuv will not succeed if they wall themselves off. What we need are the means to repel a Belirand strike force."

"I'm glad you see it that way, Katherine," I said. "Because we believe you're the right person to lead that initiative."

"Me? My experience is as a ship's captain. What do I know about defending a planet? We have exactly three guns on the planet's surface and they're hundreds of stans old."

"No ship is going to attack Yishuv directly with her current defenses," Marny said. "They'd be more likely to bombard from space. You must have an orbital defense platform."

LeGrande tipped her head, considering Marny's words. "Do you have a solution for this?"

"In three tendays, we'll place a mining platform in orbit. What we need is someone to command *Strumpet*," Marny said. "It wouldn't need to be a full-time operation."

"What would Yishuv get out of this?" LeGrande asked.

"Aside from protection?" Tabby asked.

"I hear you and I agree. But I need a way to sell this to Yishuv's council. Like it or not, they recognize their strategic importance," LeGrande answered.

"Do they get that we're putting our necks on the line for desperate people, possibly in as much trouble as they were in?"

Tabby asked.

"They do. They're just looking out for their own best interests," LeGrande answered. "They need to see a benefit to Yishuv, otherwise this will be a lot harder."

"Steel sheet and beam to start with," Nick answered. "Eventually, nano-crystalized steel. I just forwarded a copy of a proposed trade agreement with Yishuv that places a value on the services we're requesting and the value of the material we can provide."

"Perfect," LeGrande said. "To be clear, *Strumpet*'s mission would be to defend Yishuv and the new orbiting platform."

"There may come a time when we need your help against Belirand. We'd like to be able to call on you if that happens," Nick said.

"I accept. I'll command *Strumpet* on one condition," she answered.

"What's that?" I asked.

"We're renaming her. I'm not sailing around in a French whore."

***

"Merrie, Amon, what are you doing here?" I asked.

Tabby, Marny and I had set a table in the hold of *Hotspur* and were interviewing possible crew candidates. The arrival of the energetic, young engineer and her blacksmith husband was unexpected. We'd put out a call for general crew and had been interviewing mostly young candidates, maybe sixteen to twenty stans. Merrie was hardly general crew material.

"We want positions on the orbital platform," she said.

In the two days since we'd talked to Captain LeGrande, while we'd had a lot of interest in the crew positions, we hadn't advertised any needs related to Petersburg Station which would arrive in three tendays.

"What do you think Yishuv's council would say about that?" I asked. "I can't imagine how they'd feel about losing their top engineer and blacksmith."

"You'd be surprised," Merrie said. "With the arrival of *Cape of Good Hope*'s crew, there are more than enough technically minded people on planet. And try to find work as a blacksmith with an industrial replicator two doors down. Amon has been relegated to farm work."

"Do you know what we're doing on that platform?" I asked.

"Not completely, but I suspect you're harvesting the ore from an asteroid that is more than sixty percent pure with the dual objective of making a livable habitat and manufacturing steel materials for trade. You're sitting on eight kilo-tonnes of sifted ore that needs processing, while there's a thousand times that much material still to be harvested. Further, I believe you're looking to construct a nano-steel manufacturing plant, which would require the use of an industrial replicator, much like we have in Yishuv."

Tabby and I exchanged a glance and I barely suppressed a bark of laughter. Merrie's cheeks reddened and she pushed back from the table.

"Wait," I said. "It's not what you're thinking."

Amon, who still hadn't said anything, grabbed her hand, stilling her for the moment.

"I don't think it's such a ridiculous notion," Merrie said, hotly. "And I'm tired of being cast as a dumb local."

"Merrie, I can honestly say that there is no member of my crew who consider you a dumb anything. What Tabby and I found surprising is that you seem to grasp the essential function of Petersburg better than most of us."

"Oh," she said sheepishly. "Does that mean you'll consider our application?"

"Top of the list, Merrie, but it will have to wait until we return with the livestock. Yishuv Council has capped us at three recruits and we need them as permanent ship's crew. Once we return, we plan to staff Petersburg Station with four full-time residents," I said. "I'm comfortable offering you two of those four positions."

"We accept," Merrie said, thrusting her hand out.

"What if Yishuv Council throws a fit?" Tabby asked, shaking

Merrie's proffered hand.

"Leave that to me." Merrie smiled and led Amon away.

Marny waved in the next recruit in the short line that had formed. We'd interviewed over twenty possible candidates and had another twenty to go. Most of them seemed woefully inadequate for much of anything on a ship. They were simple farmers, apprentice woodworkers, bakers and laborers.

By the time the Herschel star was low in the sky over Ophir, the three of us were mentally exhausted and Tabby was becoming more of a liability than a help.

"What are we going to do?" I asked, palming the security panel to close the hold door. "None of those kids have any business on a ship."

"You're looking at it wrong, Cap," Marny said.

"How's that?"

"There are only three on that list I wouldn't consider. The rest are a recruiter's dream," she said.

I stood flatfooted, looking at her incredulously.

Tabby, on the other hand, had climbed to the top of the bay and was standing in the boxing ring, looking down at us. "Can we have this conversation while I hit someone?"

Marny chuckled. "You need to exercise that new foot, Cap."

I'd all but forgotten about my new foot.

"Or what? I'll want to hit people?" I asked as I followed her up the ladder to the inverted exercise area we'd installed in *Hotspur's* hold. One thing that had improved almost immediately had been my ability to climb a ladder.

"You're thinking of these recruits as officers. We need people who will follow orders and not get overly creative. Mark my words, some of these people will surprise you once they get their sea-legs."

"Do you have three in mind?" I asked, pulling an elliptical running machine from the floor.

"Aye, I have six," she said. "I've sent their names to both of you."

Tabby lunged across the ring at Marny who caught her attack

and rolled back, tossing Tabby behind her into a padded barrier.

I pulled up the top three names and was surprised by the amount of detail Marny provided with her recommendation for each of them. Zebulon, Mark-Ralph and Baker. We'd talked to each of them for less than five minutes, but she'd observed much more than I had. I recalled that Zebulon had an easy smile and had been part of the tree cutting crew. Having grown up planet-side doing manual labor he was bulky. Mark-Ralph was average height by spacer standards which made him short on Ophir, but like Zebulon, he was bulky due to manual labor as a farm laborer. The next name on the list was Baker. I scrolled through the interviews back to Baker's. Brick layer, average height, jet-black hair and not overly talkative. I remembered that her hands were scraped up and calloused from what I imagined was constant contact with the tools of her trade.

After listening to all three of the interviews again, my concerns weren't alleviated. They seemed like nice enough people, but had zero experience in low gravity environments and had not grown up with technology. I just didn't see how it would work out.

I wanted to talk to Marny and Tabby about the recruits, but they were in mid-furball. As I watched, I was grateful to no longer be on the receiving end of Tabby's angst. Marny was able to absorb the pounding and also hand out her fair share, but it was clear that Tabby had the capacity to finish Marny if she wanted to. Finally, after twenty minutes of all-out brawling, Tabby relented, bumped her gloves on top of Marny's and bowed.

"What about these three?" I pinched the three names I'd chosen from the top of Marny's list and flicked it to her.

"Aye, Cap. They look like winners to me," she said.

"What in the plains of Mars are you seeing?" I asked. "They're all laborers, without a lick of low gravity training or technology."

"Aye, Cap. We'd have work to do. But you'd be surprised what can be trained in a short period of time. What you're missing is that each of these fine young recruits has worked hard for a living, defended their homes from an invasion, and when asked to step back into danger to help their fellow human beings, were first in line. That's not the sort of thing you can train," she said.

***

Marny approached *Hotspur* with four recruits jogging behind her in two-by-two formation. I had to admit, they already looked more like spacers, now wearing the dark-blue vac-suits we'd adopted as uniforms aboard *Intrepid*. Marny had required officers to change their suits so the right shoulder was gold with a narrowing slash from the shoulder across the chest ending in a point at the ribs. She'd argued that crew would need a sense of individual identity and the ability to quickly recognize officers.

"At ease," I said as they jogged to a halt in front of *Hotspur's* loading ramp. With the exception of Ortel, each had a backpack slung across their backs, presumably carrying the possessions they most wanted to bring with them. Marny had limited them to thirty kilograms. Zebulon seemed to be breaking her rule as I noticed the neck of a stringed instrument sticking out above his head. Marny had coached me on how to interact with the crew, especially on our first several interactions. As captain, I was expected to be mostly out of reach.

"Trainees report," Marny commanded.

"Seamen Baker, Zebulon, Mark-Ralph and Licht reporting for duty," Ortel replied. Marny had assigned him as team leader for the small squad, his experience as a spacer critical for the first phase of their training. I hoped his age wouldn't become a hindrance as he was the youngest by several stans.

"Welcome aboard." I caught Ortel's eye and gave him a nod. "It takes a special kind of person to leave the safety of their home and place themselves in the path of danger for the benefit of others. Each one of you, for whatever reasons, made that choice today. Such is the legacy of the crew you're joining. More rational people might ask to quantify the pending danger so they could weigh those risks against the possible gains. You haven't done this. It also takes a special kind of crazy to join us on this mission. If you were to ask me, I'd say you're all nuts, which puts you in good company as I welcome you to Loose Nuts Corporation.

"Any questions before we get going?" I asked.

"How dangerous could this be? Aren't we just picking up livestock?" The question had come from Zebulon, the tree cutter with shoulder length blond hair. His easy smile felt mocking to me.

Marny raised an eyebrow at me. She'd warned me about a question answer session and I'd ignored her.

"The most powerful corporation in the known universe has labeled us as enemy number one. To make matters worse, we just stole one of their prized warships. Best case, they're just really pissed now and will be gunning for us even more than before. At worst, they've shared this theft with every civilized nation in humanity and we're now on the shoot-first-talk-later list for every one of them," I said. "Add to that, my gunnery crew has never seen the inside of a ship, much less fired a ship's weapon. Your question was insightful, Mr. Zebulon. I'll leave it to you to decide what you've learned from the answer, however."

PRIDE GOES BEFORE FALL

"Ada, would you set a course for Jeratorn?" I asked.

"How close in?"

"Two hours on sixty-percent burn," I said.

"Copy that," she answered.

"Jeratorn?" Tabby asked. "I thought we needed cows and pigs."

"I assume we're persona non grata on any civilized planet, so we're going to have to deal with an intermediary. Beth Anne Hollise runs a successful smuggling operation from Jeratorn," I said. "I'm hoping for a contact."

"Why not Berandor?" Tabby asked. "At least we can trust him."

"Jake asked us to cool it for a while. There's a lot of heat around our names right now," Nick said. "I don't like talking to Hollise anymore than you do, but Jeratorn won't check our ship's identification as long as we pay their docking fees. It's a good option."

"Navigation is complete. I'm showing one hundred thirteen hours in fold-space," Ada announced.

The bridge was currently crammed with people. I hadn't laid out a watch rotation and people wanted to know what we were up to. I chastised myself for not doing a better job of setting expectations. Somehow, my job had turned from septic repairman to chief communicator. It wasn't exactly what I had in mind when we'd started, but things rarely were.

"All hands. This is Captain Hoffen. We transition to fold-space in five minutes," I announced.

"Ada, after Nick double-checks the numbers, would you lay it in?"

"Yes, Captain, they're in and waiting for your approval," Ada answered. I found the navigation orders she'd crafted on the screen in front of me. Nick had signed off and a count-down was silently ticking away. I approved the orders and watched as the timer showed on the forward bulkhead.

"I'll put together a watch schedule and get it out shortly," I said.

"Captain," Ada caught my attention. "I've proposed a two-person watch schedule per Marny's recommendation. She's asked that we rotate the new crew into the watch."

I opened the schedule she'd sent. The addition of the new crew made it easier to run the four-four-six configuration of shifts we all preferred. With the new crew members, we'd actually have enough down-time where we weren't just running for sleep every time we came off shift.

"My name isn't on here," I said.

"Marny said that's how it has to be and if you have a problem with it, talk to her," Ada said.

"You need to accept this," Mom, who was standing next to the doorway to the ready room, offered. "A captain is available to all shifts. It's why your quarters are so close to the bridge."

Without further warning we shifted into fold-space. I closed my eyes, which didn't help, then shook my head, trying to clear the swirl of color behind the lids of my eyes. I wasn't sure what I thought about being out of the watch schedule, but I'd have to live with it. When transition finally ended, I opened my eyes and made room on my forward display to show current and upcoming watches. Ada and Nick were on current watch and it looked like Tabby and Baker were up next.

"I'll retire for now," Mom said. She, no doubt, had a shift coming up later. "Liam, when you get a chance, I'd like to run over some things with you."

"I'll walk with you," I said. "It looks like Ada has things well organized."

"Best to remember that, Liam," Ada said as we cleared the bridge door and it had already started to close.

"Do you know where you're going?" I asked. Mom had turned forward and was walking fast enough that I had to hustle to keep up with her.

"Never be seen moving from one location to another lackadaisically. Crew pick up on a captain's attitude and will unconsciously adopt her stance," Mom said. At least now I knew what she wanted to talk about. "My berth is just around the corner."

We were about to round the bend that would take us to the port side of the ship when we ran into Marny and Seaman Baker. Marny turned sideways and pulled her hand up in a salute. Baker mimicked her. Mom continued forward, turning her shoulders to make room, giving a quick salute. I followed her example, watching Baker as I did. The woman's face, ruddy from working outside, looked unusually pale. I suspected she hadn't enjoyed transition to fold-space any more than I had.

Upon reaching the port passageway, Mom turned left to head aft. From previous exploration, I knew that to take the passageway forward would lead us down to Deck-3 where the crew were housed. Three doors down, Mom palmed open the door to a reasonably spacious room, three meters wide by four meters deep. She'd configured her bunk to a single size along the starboard bulkhead and a couch on the aft bulkhead.

"Is all that saluting necessary?" I asked.

"Better to start with it and back down than to try to add it later. Marny and I talked about it at length and we believe that since we're likely to experience combat, we want to observe a higher level of discipline than most civilian ships."

"What did you want to talk about?" I had things I wanted to start researching, although I knew I had several days to accomplish those tasks.

"Standing orders," she said.

"What's that?"

"Orders you create that organize the crew. For example, mess schedules. Will all crew eat together or officers eat by themselves? What about exercise? Is it mandatory or a suggestion? Certifications. Do you want officers and crew certifying on ship's systems? That sort of thing," she said.

"I guess I'd like people to eat together at least once a day, maybe have officers have breakfast together," I said.

"That's doable. I'd propose you gather all available personnel for evening meal at 18:30 to 19:00. That will offset with the watch change. We can set the first meal at 06:30 to 07:00. The meals we have aboard are heat and serve or meal bars. Currently, the crew is small enough that officers and crew alike should set food out. Once we get a few more crew, we can rotate that responsibility. I'll send you a schedule," she said. "As for certificate training..." Mom pulled up a list, fifteen long, of items she wanted to get through with me. Ninety minutes later, I finally escaped only by making the excuse that I needed to use the head.

"Captain on the bridge," Marny announced when I entered again. She'd placed a stool next to Baker's workstation.

"As you were," I said after a message with those words exactly popped up on my HUD from Marny.

"Where'd you go?" Tabby asked. "You've been gone a while."

"Mom wanted to go through a list of standing orders she thought I should implement."

"Like what?" Tabby asked.

I gave her the top four examples I could recall.

"Those sound reasonable," she agreed.

"Did Silver say anything to you, Marny?" I immediately felt bad that I'd interrupted her conversation with Baker.

"Aye, Cap. Perhaps you could implement the orders around meal preparation, times and locations first. That would give us a means to solicit input on the remaining items," Marny answered.

"Sounds like a good plan," I said. "Baker, what did you think of transition to fold-space?"

She looked to Marny, who nodded, then back to me. "It was ... colorful, Captain."

"Everyone keep their lunch down?" I asked.

"Mark-Ralph did, sir," she answered, her cheeks turning scarlet.

"Nothing to be done about it," I said. "I'm still trying to get used to it." Then I asked, "What do you think of our ship? Be honest."

"Air smells funny and everything is so clean. There's no dust," she said.

"Oh, there's plenty of dust, but the ship's air-scrubbers filter it all out," I said. "You'll have to ask Nick to give you a tour of the mechanical plant."

"I'd like that, sir," she answered.

I settled back into my chair to organize the tasks I needed to accomplish. Not having a watch responsibility was going to give me more free time than I was used to and I wanted to make sure I took full advantage of it.

"Marny, one more thing and I'll let you go," I said.

She gave me a reassuring grin. I think she enjoyed watching me struggle with the mantle of leadership. "Fire away, Cap." I was jealous at how confident she was in her role.

"I assume you're organizing martial training. I'd love a chance to spar with our new recruits. I'm tired of getting my head caved in by Ms. Masters."

"Aye. I was planning to talk with the two of you about that," she said looking at Tabby and then back to me. "Our trainees are required to spend one hour out of every twenty-four engaged in physical activity. Top on that list is yoga for strength and flexibility and one of the martial styles."

"Sure," Tabby said. "I'm in. I'd even be willing to set up a schedule."

"Count me in for yoga and kick-boxing." I said to Tabby.

"Already have you down."

***

"I want to spar with Masters and this yoga is stupid." Mark-Ralph was about as bendable as a tree and I understood his frustration. We'd need to spend time researching modified exercises that didn't require as much flexibility.

"Stick with it, Mark-Ralph, it will take some time. If you don't stretch, you're going to pull something."

"I've never had trouble winning a brawl, ain't that right, Big Z?"

"You handed out your fair share," Zebulon answered noncommittally. Unlike Mark-Ralph, Zebulon had taken to the yoga forms. His flexibility wasn't great, but he wasn't fighting it.

"Put *you* down a few times," Mark-Ralph pushed.

"Let's not get ahead of ourselves, Ralphie," Zebulon said casually.

"Don't call me that. I hate it when people call me that."

"Good job, Baker," I interrupted, not wanting to let things get out of control. I'd learned that Baker kept mostly to herself, but watched everyone. "And for the record, Mark-Ralph, you don't want to spar with Ms. Masters."

"Are we speaking as equals here?" Mark-Ralph asked.

"If you keep it respectful, we are," I said.

"Well, respectfully, I don't think you or Masters stand a chance against either Big Z or me. I'm not sure about Baker. And personally, I'd rather look at Masters than you," he said.

"Is that how you feel about things, Zebulon?" I asked.

"Seriously?" he asked and I nodded. "I think Commander Masters is hot as hell."

I mentally face-palmed. The only thing he'd taken from the conversation was a comment on Tabby's looks. A grin flitted across Baker's face, gone as quickly as it had appeared.

"That wasn't the question," I said, trying to keep exasperation from my voice. I was losing the group and knew for a fact that Tabby was spying on us from the bridge. I'd never live this down if I didn't regain control. I stood and opened a locker that contained the safety gear, tossing gloves and head protection to each of them.

"What was the question?" Zebulon asked, the slightly mocking tone back in his voice.

"In space combat, just like hand-to-hand, agility is key. And you're right, Mark-Ralph, your extra strength and mass are definite advantages. At some point, all the agility in the universe isn't going to allow a ship the size of *Hotspur* to take on and defeat a dreadnaught. Much like me trying to arm-wrestle you."

Mark-Ralph hopped to his feet with his gloves in place. "I won't need the helmet. I don't give you much of a chance of getting to my head."

"Join me in the ring, Seaman," I said, pulling on shin guards but nothing else.

Zebulon and Baker hung on the ropes as Mark-Ralph crawled through. I ran, placing my hand on the top rope and swung over. Mark-Ralph started to turn as I landed one foot on his thigh and wrapped my other leg around his neck and shoulders. He tried to stand, but my inertia had already sent us spinning into the middle of the ring. I grabbed his head and used my leverage to pull my other leg around, locking my ankles in front of his chest. The two of us fell to the mat and I released, rolling on my curved back and popped to my feet. Mark-Ralph clumsily tried to gain his feet, stumbling forward while throwing a sloppy punch which I batted easily with my hand and danced away. I considered kicking him in the butt on the way past, but I needed to teach a lesson, not completely humiliate him.

"That's not fair. I wasn't ready," he sputtered, turning on me.

"I clearly saw you in the ring," I said. "No harm, though. Let me know when you're ready." He turned and firmly planted his feet on the mat. His body tensed as he prepared to rush me. It was more warning than I ever got from either Marny or Tabby, his hips and feet broadcasting his intended path.

Like a bull, he charged, arms wide, no doubt intending to wrestle me to the ground. His speed was such that I had a few moves I could utilize. I chose to reverse my clockwise dance and slapped his outstretched hand downward as I passed. He changed direction and tried again. This time I grabbed his hand and used his momentum, rolling back onto the mat and throwing him with my leg into the ropes behind.

"What kind of bullshit is that?" Mark-Ralph sputtered as he used the ropes to stand back up.

"You're right. I had you on the ground. I should have finished you," I said.

"Hardly a fair fight." His hands were down as he approached again. "You're not even hitting me." The muscular man was breathing hard from exertion.

"Remember the *Hotspur* and the dreadnaught?" I asked. I

stepped in, slipped his right jab with my forearm and landed a quick combination on his face. I didn't want to hit him too hard as I wasn't wearing gloves and he wasn't wearing face protection.

"You're trying to confuse me. It won't work. Once I get a hold of you, this fight's over," he said and barreled forward.

I'd positioned him perfectly and jumped up, spinning my padded heel into the side of his face. I winced for him as I felt the contact. I'd tried to pull the kick, but also wanted to make my point. Between his momentum and my heel in his face, he dropped like a rock.

"Shit," I said as I landed next to him. "Grab the med kit, Baker." I'd knocked him out cold.

"Where? I don't know where it is," she said, panicked.

"Slow down and look at your HUD. The AI is highlighting it," I said in as calm a voice as I could manage. I wasn't overly worried about Mark-Ralph, but I hadn't intended to drop him on the mat, either.

Zebulon had entered the ring and was leaning over with his hands on his knees. "You really clocked him."

Baker slid a med kit onto the mat and looked at me expectantly.

"Open it up and ask your AI what to do next," I instructed.

She opened the kit and my HUD immediately highlighted the diagnostic scanner. I'd used a med kit often enough that I didn't have any questions on what came next, but it was a perfect training opportunity. I watched as her shaky hands pulled the scanner out and laid it on Mark-Ralph's temple.

"It says to apply a P-1 to his right temple," Baker recited what I was also reading on my HUD.

"Best to get after it," I said.

She looked from me to the kit and then pulled a P-1 patch out and applied it more-or-less where the AI instructed.

"What now?" she asked.

"We wait. The patch contains nano-bots - basically tiny robots thousands of times smaller than a grain of sand. They'll go turn the lights back on," I said.

"Did you have to kick him so hard? ... Sir," Baker asked, accusatorily.

"I'd have preferred he wore protective head gear." I wasn't about to defend my actions to her. From my perspective, things couldn't have worked out better.

"What the hell does kicking me in the head have to do with *Hotspur* and a dreadnaught?" Mark-Ralph mumbled, trying to sit up.

"Hold on there, killer, give the bots another minute. You took a pretty good hit there," I said, laying my hand on his shoulder.

"No, seriously. I don't get it," he said.

"Would you say you're physically stronger than I am?" I asked.

"I'd bet on it, Captain."

"Me too," I answered. "How about mass? I bet I give up forty kilos to you."

"Sounds right," he agreed.

"So, by your estimation, you're both bigger and stronger?"

"Yes."

"Sound familiar, Baker?" I asked, looking at the dark-haired woman. She didn't answer other than to nod her head. "So how dumb would it be for me to stand toe-to-toe with you and trade punches, Mark-Ralph?"

"It'd be a fair fight, Sir," Mark-Ralph wasn't quite ready to give it up.

"When *Hotspur* ran down the Red Houzi dreadnaught *Bakunawa*, we weren't looking for a fair fight. What we were looking for was a way to kick 'em in the head. If we'd tried to stand toe-to-toe with the big beast, we'd have been shredded within seconds. Somehow, we not only survived, but we captured the ship. Now, I've sent the video logs of that mission to the three of you and I'd like you to review them in your down time."

"You got lucky," Zebulon said. "No way you do that to someone who's expecting it."

"I'll give you points for stubborn, Zebulon. How 'bout you pull on that safety gear and we give it a go?"

Ten minutes later he held his arms up in surrender. I'd taken a few of his better punches - his long arms difficult to avoid - but I'd given way better than I'd received. Having already rendered one of Marny's crew inoperable, I'd pulled my own strikes back to eighty percent. Zebulon had some idea of defense and an even better understanding of his own strengths. In the end, however, he'd died the death of a thousand cuts, or in this case, hundreds of painful, but not debilitating, strikes to any open surface I could find on his body.

"You're impossibly fast," he said, sweat running down his face.

"Is everyone from Ophir as hardheaded as you two?" I asked. "I'd have thought watching me take down Mark-Ralph would have been enough. How about it, Baker?"

"No, sir. I never got into many scraps," she said.

"That's not what I heard," Mark-Ralph said. "I heard…"

"Seamen! Attention!" I hadn't heard Marny's approach and snapped to attention with the rest and then tried to act like I hadn't. I'd heard Marny's angry, ten-hut voice before, but I'd been totally surprised by it this time.

"Seaman Mark-Ralph. Tell me you weren't about to spread gossip about your squad-mate Baker."

"Uh, no ma'am. Well, yes ma'am, I was," he answered. I was both proud of and terrified for him in that moment.

"Ma'am, may I speak?" Baker asked.

"No, you may not, Seaman Baker," Marny snapped. "Squad, that's twenty laps. How you talk to your own in crew country is your business, but you will *not* denigrate your squad mates to an officer. Now get moving." Marny pointed to the door. One of the great features of *Intrepid* was the passageway layout. A person could run all the way around the ship. The entire trek, if you were to run down through Deck-3, was two-hundred twenty-five meters.

"I didn't see you come in, Master Chief," I said, picking up the safety gear and returning it to the locker. I was still getting used to Marny's new rank. It seemed to fit her nicely.

Marny chuckled. "Aye, Cap, I believe I recognized that."

"Sorry about your recruits. I really didn't mean to knock Mark-

Ralph out," I said.

"Mr. Zebulon will have quite a headache tomorrow. I saw him teetering on his feet a couple of times. Why didn't you put him away?"

"I didn't want him to think I got lucky. I wanted him to realize who was in charge," I said. "Otherwise, I didn't think they'd pay attention when we actually started training."

"From what I saw, you've already started the training." She laid her arm over my shoulders as we walked from the exercise room and I wondered how she might have handled things differently. The sound of the trainees rounding the corner on their first lap caught my attention and I took off after them. Mark-Ralph might have been the one to get us in trouble, but I'd participated. I might as well share in the discipline.

RELOCATION

I awoke to a quiet alarm chiming in my ear. Tabby and I had hit the sack six hours previous and it was going to be a big day.

"Where are you going, lover?" Tabby ran her hand down my chest and onto my stomach. She wanted me to stay in bed to keep her warm and wasn't above getting frisky to achieve it.

"You have to get up too. We're transitioning from fold-space in an hour," I said.

Lights, Tabby requested, jumping out of bed. I watched as she wriggled into a suit liner followed by her grav-suit. I recognized too late that I should have played along a little longer. "Who's got watch?" she asked.

"Ada and Moonie are just coming on," I said, pulling my grav-suit from the suit cleaner.

I looked around the captain's quarters that were starting to feel more like home. It wasn't overly spacious with the bed pulled out into a two-person configuration, but the room also had a small desk built into the port bulkhead. We'd taken to displaying the ship's port feed on the built-in vid screen, although I could easily switch to bridge, engineering or just about any number of different compartments with a single command. The only other furniture, other than storage compartments, was an L-shaped couch. There were a number of possible configurations, but neither Tabby nor I were particular about such things. Perhaps the most luxurious appointment was the private head which I certainly appreciated.

"Did Nick decide whether he or Jonathan is going over to Jeratorn?" Tabby asked.

"It'll be you, me, Nick and Ortel," I said.

"Ortel?"

"Marny wants him to have time in a gunner's chair," I said.

"You think he's ready? Jeratorn is rough," she said.

"Were we?" I asked, pushing my way into the passageway that cut in front of our quarters and over to the officer's wardroom. I tossed a high calorie meal bar to Tabby and poured coffee for us.

"How heavy are we loading?" she asked as I palmed my way through the security panel and onto the bridge. A familiar whistle warned the bridge's occupants that I'd arrived.

"Captain on the bridge," Marny announced.

"As you were," I replied reflexively. "And I'm not sure, Tabby."

"Cap, the team is gathered in the conference room," Marny said. She was standing in the workstation that spanned both the bridge and the gunner's nest. While I could see through to the gunner's nest, a sound deadening wave prevented the gunner's mates from overhearing bridge talk and vice-versa. As it was, she had Zebulon, Baker and Mark-Ralph all running drills.

I followed Tabby into the conference room that joined with the bridge, finding Ortel, Nick and Jonathan looking at a holographic image of Jeratorn.

"Is that current?" I recognized the three interconnected towers from our previous visit. The docking bay, which ran horizontally about a third of the way up the forward-most tower looked wider than I recalled.

"Up to date, within a tenday," Nick answered. "We were just going over the publicly listed shipments." It was something we used to do when we were interested in making money. There had always been a premium on shipping in and out of Jeratorn due to the infrequent visits by Mars Protectorate.

"What's the premium running?" I asked.

"Forty-five percent over standard," Nick answered.

I whistled. It was up fifteen percent from when Red Houzi had been secretly running the station.

"I hope your Beth Anne Hollise isn't off vacationing," Tabby said. She was annoyed that we were dealing with the shapely pirate. I wasn't sure which part bothered her the most, the voluptuous woman's shape or the fact that she was an unrepentant pirate. "Or this will have been a wasted trip."

"Won't be a complete waste. Their prices on precious metals are good," Nick said. "We have six hundred fifty thousand Tipperary credits that we've converted to three hundred thousand Mar's credits. We'll be converting that to platinum."

"We've identified three possible mining groups that we believe will have a sufficient volume of platinum," Jonathan said. "We believe it would be wise for Loose Nuts to convert their outstanding credits to something more portable, given the current, pending litigation."

"The mission is simple," I said. "When we exit fold-space, we contact Hollise to see if she can help us find a source for the livestock."

"I still don't understand why you think she can help," Tabby said. "Don't you have better connections through Anino's mega corporations, Jonathan?"

"We need to do this quietly," Nick said.

Tabby sat back in her chair, arms folded across her chest, as we continued to work through the smaller details.

"All hands. Transition from fold-space in five minutes." Ada's voice came over the public address system.

"That's our cue," I said. "Ortel, on me."

"Give 'em hell, Cap," Marny said as we emerged from the conference room and exited the bridge.

"Keep the lights on," I replied, then led our group through the passageway to the airlock that would take us to *Hotspur*.

"Normal space in 10... 9... 8..." my AI warned. I closed my eyes and braced myself by placing my hand on the passageway's bulkhead.

As expected, transition sucked, but I wasn't about to show that to Ortel. Once it was over, I opened my eyes and cycled the airlock. "Everyone in," I directed.

Our first stop on *Hotspur* was the armory. I handed Ortel an armored vac-suit and AGBs.

"Put these on," I said, nodding toward the berth deck's main head. "Then meet us on the bridge."

I stepped back into the armory and Tabby handed me my favorite heavy Ruger blaster pistol which I strapped into a clipless thigh holster. If I expected combat, I'd have chosen a chest holster, but I wanted to appear less provocative when dealing with Hollise. For herself, Tabby chose to strap a short-stock blaster rifle on her back and holstered a flechette to her hip. Nick chose a thin laser pistol that would be illegal on most stations.

Establish ship-to-ship communications bridge with Intrepid, I directed as I slid into the port-side pilot's chair and looked out the armored glass screen onto the familiar star field.

"Greetings, Liam. How's our girl doing?" Ada asked.

I scanned the status displays. We'd left *Hotspur* in a warm state and she'd awakened quickly. "We're green. I'm releasing docking lines in five... four... three..." *Hotspur* shuddered and drifted away from *Intrepid*. I nudged the arc-jets to give us more separation until I was confident we were well clear.

"We'll see you at the rendezvous in forty hours," Ada said as *Intrepid*'s large engines spooled up and she slid forward.

"Roger that, Ada, stay safe. *Hotspur* out." I closed comms. As I did, I heard the lift arrive and turned to see a much bulkier looking Ortel.

"You're by me," Nick said, indicating the gunner's station that Marny normally occupied. Ortel nodded, his face flush from exertion and possibly the fact that he had all of our attention.

"Nick, have you pinged Hollise to see if she'll be able to meet?" I asked.

"Message is away," he said. "We'll see what she says."

"Ortel, I understand you're doing fairly well in the gunner's chair. We're going to set out a few targets so you get a feel for *Hotspur*. You good with that?" I asked.

"Yes, sir," he replied. It wasn't as if I intended to give him a choice.

"Nick, you're on bottom turret. Tabby, you have missiles and rear turret. Ortel, you have the two top turrets," I said.

"Two?" he asked.

"We'll link 'em," Nick said, leaning over to Ortel's workstation and indicating how to change the setting.

"Everything on *Hotspur* uses energy, so go easy on it. Once the batteries are done, we're either losing speed or firepower. Trust me. In battle, we don't want to lose either," I said, ejecting five blinking targeting dummies along an arced path.

At five hundred kilometers I turned and accelerated hard toward the dummies. I didn't want to spend a lot of time on the exercise, but I wasn't about to have a crew member on board who had never even used the equipment.

"These are all yours, Ortel," I said as I rolled *Hotspur* lazily away, making the shots more difficult.

"I don't have a shot," he said as he sprayed empty space.

"Don't think so linearly," Tabby said. "You're lined up on the second one perfectly."

Before he could reorient, I flipped the ship and accelerated hard on an oblique angle which only gave him a line on the final target. He caught on and sprayed blaster fire all around the target, catching it after a moment.

"One," he counted under his breath.

I pulled over hard and lined him up for an easy kill and he took it, still over-spraying. But a kill was what we needed. I reversed our direction and pushed back through the target field, giving him different looks at the targets, never making it easy, just possible. By my count, he was about twenty percent accurate. It took several minutes and forty percent of the battery to finish off the rest of the targets.

"Whoo hooo," Ortel exclaimed as he dispatched the final target.

"Not bad for your first live fire," I said. It was hard for me to say, but it was the right thing to do. Tabby gave me raised eyebrows and I didn't need to be a mind reader to wonder what she was thinking.

"I just got a response from Hollise. We're a go," Nick said.

All hands, prepare for hard burn. We'd dropped into Sol space twelve hours from Jeratorn on hard burn. Compared to fold-space, transition to hard burn was a joy. A momentary flip-flop of the stomach as inertial and gravity systems kicked in and then you were done; no color smearing and no jittering star fields.

The trip to Jeratorn was uneventful, as was to be expected in hard-burn.

"Jeratorn, this is *Hotspur* requesting permission for twenty-four-hour berth," I radioed as soon as we dropped from burn.

"*Hotspur,* state the nature of your business," a man's voice said.

"Speculative trading interests," I replied.

"Understood. You're clear on Concourse-C, berth fourteen," the man instructed. A twelve-hundred credit charge appeared on my screen requiring approval. It was twice what I'd have expected to pay on Mars.

"Copy that." I accepted the charge and closed the comm.

As we sailed past the outlying structures on the way to the station, evidence of the conflict we'd engaged in over twelve months before was still evident. Jeratorn had been rebuilding, but was not fully recovered. It was well after 2000, but I was still surprised by just how few ships and sleds were moving about.

"That's huge," Ortel said as we closed on the three towers that made up the station. I'd forgotten he had little experience with space structures.

"Sure is," I said. "Now remember, your job is simple. Don't let anyone aboard. If anyone even gets close raise one of us on the comm. If you have to, pull out from the station. You should only fire on someone if you don't think you'll survive otherwise. Got it?" We'd been over the conversation several times and I was responding mostly to his apparent nervousness.

"Aye, Captain," he replied.

I swung *Hotspur* around and slid her into our berth backwards.

"Think he's going to be okay?" Tabby asked as we processed through the airlock onto the station's new concourse.

"He's just nervous," I said. "First time he's been left in charge."

"I hope he doesn't do anything stupid," Tabby said. I hoped she hadn't just jinxed him.

Our destination was the Welded Tongue bar, which wasn't difficult to find. The last time we'd been here, we had a stand-off with a few of the locals, but it had worked to our benefit. I wasn't a bit surprised to hear the noise coming from the open double doors as we approached. The rusty, metal tongue sculpture hanging above the doors was a familiar sight. As we turned the corner to enter, we were stopped by two armed security guards.

"You'll have to check your weapons," the taller of the two said, holding his hand up, almost placing it on Tabby's chest. I winced at the nearly critical mistake.

"We're here to see Beth Anne and we're not checking our weapons," Tabby said.

"Then you're not here to see Beth Anne," the other, beefy looking man, replied.

I stepped forward, getting between Tabby and the guards. "Cool down. We don't need trouble. What my friend here is saying is we'll check our long guns, but we're keeping side-arms. That work for you?"

"No." The first said, pushing me into Tabby. Tabby tried to get around me, but I cut her off.

"We'll wait out here, in that case," Nick said. "Beth Anne is expecting us and I know she's the forgiving type so we'll just let this play out." He pulled Tabby to the other side of the hallway.

"Frak, let me just drop these meatheads," Tabby said.

"Who are you calling meat..." The first started across the hallway.

"Boys, girls, no need to get riled up." A sultry figure stepped from behind the shadows of the doorway and placed her hand on meathead-one's shoulder, her voice purring like only one person I knew.

"Xie." I whispered. "What are you still doing here?"

"Is that any way to greet the woman who saved your life, Liam Hoffen?" She sidled over and wrapped her arms around me, drawing me into a kiss before I knew what was occurring.

"What... Stop," I sputtered, pushing her away.

"And Mr. James. Lover. Oh, how I miss traveling with my young adventurers. Could it really be Tabitha Masters? The one-armed girl in the chair? Restored to full health? And to think, you have me to thank for that as well," Xie continued. "Beth Anne said you were coming today and I couldn't believe it. Yet here you are."

"Perhaps the hallway isn't the place for this conversation," I said, interrupting Tabby, who I was sure was ready to say something less than flattering. Either that or preparing to hand out a beating.

Xie smiled pleasantly. It reminded me just how remarkable she was at masking her feelings. Deep down, I had conflicted feelings about her. She'd both endangered me when the chips were down as well as saved my entire crew under similar circumstances. I did not believe she was a lost cause and I think she knew it, although this was one of the forbidden topics between Tabby and me.

"This way, then," she said as meatheads-one and two moved out of the way.

"I guess we'll just keep the guns." Tabby couldn't resist rubbing it in their faces as we passed.

I saw Beth Anne as soon as we entered the crowded bar. The woman was as beautiful as I remembered. Long medium-blonde hair and a voluptuous body that was extraordinarily uncommon for a spacer. Her smile was as dangerous as Xie's and for all the same reasons.

"Liam Hoffen and Nick James. So good to see you," she said graciously, crossing the room, her white scarves flowing out behind her. She gathered us in for hugs and I hated myself for enjoying it. "And who is this beauty you've brought along? Could this be the warrior princess I've heard so much about?" She grabbed Tabby's hand and held it up, inspecting her like she might a slab of meat. "My dear. If you ever find you've joined the wrong team, please know I will always have a place for you."

Tabby pulled her hand back abruptly. "That won't be necessary."

Beth Anne smiled indulgently. "Of course. I've been rude. Please accept my apologies. Bernd, bring brandies to the VIP room, please." An unusually good-looking man dressed in tight, silky clothing smiled and nodded.

We followed Beth Anne and Xie Mie-su to a room that had

couches around the outside walls.

"Please, sit," Beth Anne requested as we entered.

"Not without UV light," Tabby growled quietly.

"Thank you for seeing us," Nick said, once Bernd had dropped off the drinks and the doors had slid shut.

"I like a mystery as much as the next gal," Beth Anne said, "but it's been – what - nearly a stan-year and you show up out of nowhere? You wouldn't believe the rumors that are flying around about you."

"It'd be best if we could stay out of the land of rumor," Nick said. "I'll put our cards on the table as best I can, however."

"That would be refreshing in my line of business," Beth Anne said.

"We've run afoul of Belirand," Nick started. "So much so that we are not currently welcome at spaceports that perform strong identity checks."

She blinked. "I would not have expected you to lead with that."

"I wouldn't want to insult you. I know you have sources," Nick said.

Beth Anne nodded. "Xie told me that I shouldn't underestimate you all. How is it that I might help you?"

"First, we need someone who can fulfill this." Nick swiped what I suspected was the livestock deal to her.

"Cows and sheep?" Beth Anne asked, chuckling.

"Remember how we can't go to most space ports?"

"Right. That does present a problem, but that's not my usual smuggling material. What is your second request?" she asked.

"We would like to purchase precious metals," Nick said.

"That's considerably easier," she said. "We'll take five percent. How much do you need?"

"That depends on how much the livestock transaction will cost," Nick replied.

"How much time do you have?"

"We'll be gone in six hours," Nick said.

"Give me thirty minutes, I'll have an answer on your livestock," she said and abruptly left.

"Red Houzi wasn't enough, you needed to piss off Belirand?" Xie Mie-su looked at me after Beth Anne had left the room.

"Not a lot of difference, as far as I can tell," I said. "Although, Belirand gunners hit a fair bit harder."

This earned a genuine laugh from Xie. When we'd first met, I'd been so sure of the world; confident in my estimation of just how bad the Red Houzi were and how righteous the law abiding corporations were. Xie had seemed so awful to me then. Now that I was an outlaw and Xie had saved my life, those lines had blurred.

"I'll drink to that," Xie said, raising her glass. I leaned forward and clinked my glass with hers, which earned me a dirty look from Tabby.

Forty minutes later, Beth Anne joined us again.

"I have a deal for you, Nicholas, Liam and Tabitha," she said. Something was amiss, her tone of voice had changed and instinctively I knew we were in the shite again.

"Give it to us straight, Beth Anne," I said.

"Oh, don't be dramatic," she said, her lips tight. "I have cargo I need delivered. That delivery will be my broker's fee. You will exchange three kilograms of platinum for your livestock at this station in ten days." She pinched and delivered coordinates on the outside of the Kuiper belt.

"There's no station at that location," I said.

"It's there and it's called Freedom Station and is run by a man known as Bard Sanderson."

"He can get livestock?"

"He has your livestock now."

"What's the hitch?" I asked.

"No hitch. You make the delivery, pay Bard his platinum and you'll be on your way with your livestock," she said.

"What's the delivery, Beth Anne?" Nick asked.

"Ah, yes. That would be Bernd, Xie, me and as much of the Welded Tongue as we can pack in six hours," she said.

That sat me back in my seat. "Is it that bad here?"

"Jeratorn has not been able to recover since the Red Houzi tried to steal the refinery. Up until then, as bad as the pirates were, they did not completely strangle trade. They were smart enough to allow most traders to pass unharmed. The bandits we now have strike at everything that moves; the station is dying," she said.

I stood up. "We should get to work."

BANDIT FIELDS

"Those are sure nice looking runabouts," I said. We'd been loading from Beth Anne's private warehouse for several hours and *Hotspur*'s hold was just about full. "Either of them do atmospheric entry?" Both oval shaped craft were in good shape and were made for hauling up to eight people comfortably.

"The bigger one is good for atmo," Beth Anne said. "Why? You want to try to strap them onto your hull? I've already run the numbers; it won't work."

"Wouldn't you like to have one at Freedom Station?" I asked. I'd already sussed out from idle conversation that she was nervous about moving under Bard Sanderson's control.

"What do you have in mind?"

"Fifty-fifty. If I can get them both there, you take the smaller, I get the larger," I said.

"Done," she agreed. "The platinum is on the way. We need to move. Once it's on board, we'll have a target on our backs."

"Have Bernd get in your runabout. We'll provide instructions after that," I said and turned. "Ortel, on me." My AI redirected the comm to Ortel and I saw the flash of red hair as he turned. "Ortel, manufacture straps for those runabouts and tie them together, set 'em on this course with as big of a punch as you can, then go lights out." I flicked a navigation vector at him.

"Unmanned?" he asked.

"That's right," I said.

"What if someone finds them?"

"How? They'll be lights out," I said.

Ortel raised his eyebrows at me, but didn't say anything further.

A familiar shape caught my eye as Beth Anne's bouncers from

the night before struggled to negotiate the heavy, steel tongue sculpture to the top of a stack of crates.

"Nicely done, boys," she said. "As promised, once we shove off, I'll turn control of the bar over to your more than capable hands." Wordlessly, they turned and left.

"Think they can make a run of it?" I asked.

"With fifteen kegs of beer and forty liters of bottom shelf liquor?" Beth Anne looked skeptically at me. "I suppose it's possible if they don't drink all of their profits. If I were a betting woman, which I am, I'd bet they go broke within three months."

"Liam, we have company," Tabby held her short-stock blaster rifle loosely at her waist. I turned to see the approach of six people, a man in a vac-suit and cape in the lead. He was followed by five armed guards; the one in the center pushing a grav-cart that held two small steel chests with sophisticated locks.

"Close it up," I ordered raising my finger in front of me and twirling it quickly for effect. The loading ramp started closing as Xie scrambled out and joined Tabby, Beth Anne and me. "Nick, I need you on security perimeter. Bernd, Ortel, we're about to leave."

"Copy," Nick replied. The lower turret on *Hotspur* twitched slightly; Nick reassuring me that he was on it.

"Beth Anne, are the rats jumping ship?" The caped man had long black greasy hair and hadn't shaved recently. It appeared he was in a poor mood.

"Don't mince words, James, tell me what you think," she replied. Her words might have been harsh, but she had upped the seduction quotient.

"How do you expect to clear the Bandit Fields? I hate to see my beautiful platinum in the hands of those rats," he said.

"We all have our jobs, James," Beth Anne replied.

"Open up," I said, pointing at the carts. "I need to verify mass and purity."

The man Beth Anne identified as James nodded to the one pushing the grav-cart, who palmed open the two chests. It was quite a sight to see that much platinum in one place. The refiner had chosen a common form we referred to as fingers, which massed at twenty grams apiece. If pure, they were each worth five hundred Mars credits. I held out one of the bags I'd replicated the night before; they were designed to work with my suit.

"Is this necessary?" James asked, annoyed.

"For all I know, we're looking at nickel. We're not buying three hundred thousand credits of platinum, unverified," I said.

We proceeded to dump the contents of the two chests into the bags, arriving at fourteen kilograms of ninety-five percent pure platinum. It had been watered down with nickel, but not so much I'd kill the deal for it.

"Looks like you're taking a haircut, unless you brought another kilogram along," I said.

"I don't think so," James replied. As he spoke, his armed guards leveled their guns at Tabby and me. The lower turret on *Hotspur* spun menacingly, aiming directly at them.

"James, don't be a grouch," Beth Anne stepped between us, resting her hand on his chest seductively. "We both know it's your boys out in the Bandit Fields. What's another kilogram to recover?"

"I say we waste 'em and be on our way. If they want to play rough, that is." Tabby leveled her blaster rifle at James' head.

James carefully reached into a pocket in his robe and drew out a translucent pouch of platinum fingers. "As you say, Beth Anne. We'll recover these later."

I added the contents of his pouch to the bag I was holding and we totaled to the exact number we'd agreed upon. I shook my head at the unnecessary drama. The man who'd wheeled the platinum in held a signature pad out to me.

"Your men need to leave before I sign this," I said. "I'll not be signing with a gun to my head."

"Nor will I," James replied. I wanted to point out that he'd started it, but it felt like a juvenile response.

"Tabby," I said. She lowered the rifle but didn't move.

James waved off his guard and once they were ten meters away, I signed the pad and lifted off with the bags of platinum in tow. Using my grav-suit, I negotiated to the starboard airlock on *Hotspur*. Once inside, I stowed the bags in the armory and quickly made my way to the bridge.

"Are we ready to kick some bandit ass? And what's she doing here?" Tabby asked as she sprinted through the bridge, looking at Xie, who was seated on the bridge couch.

"Today, our objectives align, Masters," Xie said.

"Don't try to play that crap with me," Tabby said with a snarl. "Liam, I don't trust her."

"As you shouldn't," Xie agreed. "Today, I want to live, though. I'll submit to bridge restraints if you wish."

"That won't be necessary," I said. "Tabby, we're all on the same side and I need you focused on getting us out of here."

All hands prepare for departure.

"All right, kids. I'd recommend strapping in. Ortel, you ready for this?"

"Aye, Captain," he replied. "Locked and loaded."

Hotspur had been designed as a blockade runner and I couldn't imagine how anyone could possibly stop us from escaping. I eased away from Beth Anne's private warehouse and my question was immediately answered as Jeratorn's main gun ripped a furrow across our once pristine bow.

Silent running, I shouted and tipped the stick downward so we would spiral beneath the station and out of the reach of the top mounted gun. Unfortunately, to move much further we'd have to come within range of the smaller, but just as deadly bottom gun.

"Tabby, take that station gun out." I'd no more completed the sentence and two missiles rocketed forward and exploded, destroying the gun. I accelerated away from the station, using it as a shield for as long as possible.

"Liam, we're venting. Silent running is worthless. We've got to get that plugged," Nick warned.

"Frak," I said.

"I've got it," Xie jumped up. "Where are tools?"

Project Jeratorn cannon range. Show all possible cover.

The overlay on the holo display showed a narrow corridor of

possible safety and I hit it hard. As I reached the edge of our protected space, *Hotspur* was once again punched, this time aft, and we cartwheeled.

Exhaust emergency airlock and starboard airlocks.

"Liam, you have to correct," Tabby said. I couldn't have agreed more; the cartwheeling was overwhelming, but I watched the holo as we tumbled seemingly out of control.

"No. They're pirates, they want the load." I strained to stay conscious as the inertial systems attempted to adjust for our crazy cartwheeling through space.

Finally, after what seemed like hours, we cleared the range of the station's main guns. I tipped the stick into the direction of our spin and continued adjusting until we achieved level flight.

"Xie, report," I requested. She'd been the only member of the crew who hadn't been strapped in for the last ten minutes and I felt horrible for her.

"Liam, bogeys on approach," Tabby warned. I turned my attention to the four cutters headed our way.

"Tabby, weapons status?" I asked.

"Two missiles and batteries are full," Tabby replied.

"Nick, give me a system's report. What's broken?"

"Starboard engine has a ventral leak. You have ten minutes max on her," he said.

"Weapons?"

"We're go," he replied.

There were two lessons I'd learned in one-on-multiple combat. First, some pilots were better than others, but anyone could knock you out. Take out the weak first instead of getting distracted by the hotshot. I located the pilot who was sailing the weakest looking boat and tucked in behind another ship; he was about to learn a hard lesson. I painted him on the targeting display as priority one and the second smallest as priority two.

Hail approaching ships. "This is Captain Liam Hoffen, *Hotspur.* I'm about to drop two of your number. Nothing you can do about it, so I recommend pulling off now and salvaging what you can."

"Fire missiles on targets," I directed, muting the comm.

As soon as the missiles were away, I turned into the first ship I'd marked and followed the missile in, painting his escort as primary target. As expected, the two smaller cutters turned as soon as they recognized they'd been weapons locked, but it was too late. I could imagine their confusion; their ships were barely worth the value of a missile and the thought we'd expend one on them seemed almost wasteful.

To the pirates' credit, the loss of the two lesser ships didn't deter the larger cutters one bit. From my perspective, however, cutting in half the number of turrets pointing at us was a giant win.

"We're coming around for another pass," I said.

"Liam, two more coming at five thousand kilometers," Tabby said.

"Frak!" I nosed over and lay hard into a roll, feeling guilty about Xie. She was either getting tossed around in the tween deck or worse. The problem was, there was nothing to be done about it.

As I'd expected, the cutters weren't in good repair. These pirates were pack hunters, relying on numbers much more than skill. I ran up on the closest ship, which attempted to juke out of my way, and lined him up perfectly. Ortel's whoop of excitement was followed by an explosion. Three down.

I turned into the approach of the fourth ship and he stitched a perfect line across our well armored bow. Ortel returned fire, missing with the turrets on what felt like an easy shot. I gritted my teeth. I should have expected some failure, but had gotten caught up in our early success. I dropped *Hotspur*'s tail and gave chase. We'd lost speed from our starboard engine and I was having difficulty catching him as he raced toward his reinforcements.

"We won't have the starboard engine once we reach them," Nick warned.

"Are we close enough for aft blaster?" I asked.

"Do it," Nick said.

I flipped us over and Nick fired the heavy blaster that sat just above the loading ramp. The gun had very limited adjustments available and it took precision on both our parts to achieve a good alignment. It was also something we'd become reasonably good at.

I watched with grim satisfaction as the cutter quietly exploded and Ortel whooped in celebration. I knew, at some point, he'd realize we'd killed today. That knowledge would eat at him, as it did me. There was nothing to be done about it. It was a game of survival and we had no other choice.

"We need to find Xie," I said.

"On it," Tabby said.

"Why don't you take the helm," I said. "If I can get us sealed up, we can go quiet."

She nodded in agreement. I hustled down the stairs to the main portion of the bridge and laid my hand on Ortel's shoulder. "Nice job today," I said.

He looked at me with a wide grin, the thrill of battle still coursing through his veins. I'd seen it before; he'd have trouble sleeping when the time came.

Locate Xie Mie-su. Estimate medical status.

"*Bilge, Section-A. Subject is unconscious. Multiple broken bones and perforated lung suspected,*" the AI replied.

I grabbed the heavy med kit and jumped into the bilge access in what used to be Nick and Marny's bunk room. Xie's small body lay across the keel of the ship, blood bubbling from her mouth as her unconscious body fought for survival.

Next to her was a hull patch that she'd just missed deploying. I prioritized and ignited the patch, allowing it to bond with the hull. "Nick, are we sealed?"

"Checking," he replied.

Pulling the med scanner from the kit, I placed it on the back of Xie's neck. My HUD lit up with medical diagnostics, most of which looked bad.

"We're sealed," Nick said. "Going silent."

"Understood," I replied as I peeled Xie's suit back and applied med patches as directed. I'd broken three of her ribs. Two of them had pushed through her right lung and one had broken the skin.

I'd rolled Xie onto a back board and was doing the grisly work of closing her skin back up when Tabby ducked into the bilge.

"Seriously? You finally get a moment by yourself and you take her shirt off?" she asked.

Xie, still unconscious, moaned in pain. "Almost done, Xie. You're with friends." I tried to soothe her.

"Look at all of these scars," I said. Xie's torso was covered, far worse than anything I'd ever seen.

"She really took one for the team today," Tabby said. "Pisses me off, too. I had a solid grudge going."

I laughed, despite the situation.

"Cutters still looking for us?" I asked.

"Yeah, there are five of them out there," she said. "No wonder Hollise wanted out. Her boy, Bernd, is up there crapping steel pipes. I don't think he'd be much in a fight."

"Help me get Xie to the bunk room." The back board had a grav-lifter beneath it, but Xie wasn't much more than forty kilograms and in 0.6g we could easily lift her. I set the med scanner to warn if her condition worsened and warmed the bunk room. I wanted to take time to clean all the blood off, but we were still in enemy territory and my first responsibility was to the crew.

"How's she doing?" Beth Anne asked.

"Not great," I answered. "Although, I've seen her in worse shape."

Nick stepped out of the pilot's chair once I took the helm.

"Any word on *Intrepid*?" I asked.

"I think we're in for a show any moment now," he replied.

"*Intrepid*?" Beth Anne asked.

"You might want to come up here," I said. "Once they arrive, it's going to go pretty quickly."

"What do you mean?" she asked.

"See for yourself," I said as the much larger *Intrepid* sailed into the combat zone. Like *Hotspur*, *Intrepid*'s engines were equipped such that she could accelerate and decelerate equally without flipping, like *Sterra's Gift* and the cutters were required to do. If it hadn't been so tragic, it would have been comical as the five ships all flipped and fired up, pointing away from the gleaming warship that had come to our aid.

"Incoming hail, Intrepid."

Accept hail. "This is, Liam. Go ahead," I answered.

"What's the play, Commodore?" Ada asked. The title was a new one. I knew the crew had been talking about using it when we were in fleet formation, even though I'd been opposed to it. Apparently as 'Commodore' I didn't have a lot of say in such things.

"Let 'em go, Ada. Hopefully we've thinned the herd enough to help Jeratorn," I said.

"You certainly did not lead with your best cards," Beth Anne said. "Remind me to avoid playing poker with you. You're all over the board. First, you start with missiles on the smallest craft, then you leave a frigate at home."

"If I'd known about the bandits, I might not have come at all, Beth Anne," I said.

"A reasonable point," she said.

***

"Hey there," I said as Xie's eyes opened.

"Hey yourself," she replied noncommittally, looking around the medical bay of *Intrepid*.

"How are you feeling?" Her charts showed she was healing nicely. Xie had been in the medical tank for nine days, the entire time we'd been underway to Freedom Station. She was at the point where she could heal with patches, albeit more slowly.

"Were we captured?" she asked, looking around.

"No. Why?" I said, not sure why she was asking until it dawned on me. "Oh, the tank? We've been doing some upgrades. Remember how I said we're having a tiff with Belirand?"

"Yeah?"

"Well, we decided that since we weren't friends anymore, it'd be okay if we borrowed one of their frigates. Plus, they did destroy a bunch of our stuff," I said.

"And they're okay with this?"

"I don't think they're any more pissed than they were before," I shrugged weakly.

"You seem to have a polarizing effect on people," she said.

"Like you don't?" I asked. "Although that little stunt you pulled on *Hotspur* got Tabby's respect."

"That's why I did it," she said.

"You want to come up to the bridge? There's a suit liner on the table and a vac-suit next to it. Sorry about yours, I had to cut it off."

"Get a good look?" Xie asked.

"I did. I especially liked the ribs sticking through your skin," I said.

She scrunched up her face, losing the sultry look she was going for and we both laughed.

"I'll be outside the door."

A few minutes later, Xie joined me in the passageway outside of the medical bay, looking much better than when I'd pulled her from the bilge of *Hotspur*.

"This way," I said as we walked to the forward observation room. "I understand that Freedom Station is quite something to look at."

"That's what I hear too," she said.

"You'll have a nice view here," I said as I led her into the room where Beth Anne and Bernd were already seated in comfortable observation chairs. "If we run into any sort of trouble, make sure to fall back to a designated safe room. This is armored glass, but still."

"Where are you going?" Xie asked.

"Got a ship to sail," I said. "It's good to have you back, Xie." I made my way back to the bridge.

"Captain on the bridge," Marny announced.

"*Hotspur* crew loaded?" I asked.

"Roger that," Ada replied.

"We're sure that starboard engine is solid?"

"It is, Captain," Jonathan answered.

I wasn't thrilled. I'd been convinced to stay on *Intrepid*, while

Tabby and Nick were aboard *Hotspur*. Tabby and I were equally skilled as pilots, but I always took the helm if I was aboard. Tabby wanted her own commission and I could hardly blame her. When it came to *Intrepid*, I would trust her to Ada - that was, until I didn't. I guess we'd see how that worked out.

"Dropping from hard burn in three... two..."

"Captain, I have multiple bogeys," Ada said. My tactical projector showed Freedom Station twenty thousand kilometers away, just as we'd planned. A blockade of fifteen ships, most of them small, lined up fifteen thousand kilometers from our position. The blockade wasn't our problem. Four Belirand ships - two cutters, a fast frigate named *Ferez* and *Intrepid*'s sister, *Justice Bringer*, sat in the space between us.

"Battle stations," Marny said.

"Launch *Hotspur*," I said. "Tabby, I want you to go stealth until you can take out that fast frigate. You copy?"

"Copy that," she answered.

Unlike *Hotspur*, *Intrepid* could take quite a lot of plinking from two cutters. What I wasn't sure of was just how much of a stomach Belirand captains had for losing ships. Today, I figured we'd find out.

FREEDOM STATION

"Captain, we have an incoming hail from *Justice Bringer*," Ada said.

"Captain, before you receive that, you should know they're attempting to take over our systems," Jonathan said.

"Understood. *Accept hail.* This is Hoffen, go ahead," I said. Jonathan would either stop them or they wouldn't. Worrying about it would do me no good.

"Captain Hoffen, the ship you are currently in possession of and call *Intrepid* has been illegally seized. Surrender now." The face that appeared was none other than Admiral Lorraine Tullas.

"Lorraine. I see you've upgraded from *Fist of Justice*," I said. "Or is she still in the shop?"

"Cut the small talk, Hoffen, we're tracking your sloop right now and if she gets any closer we'll open fire," she said. I suspected she was bluffing, but it might be possible her sensors were reading *Hotspur*.

"I didn't see you as a fair-fight type of gal," I said. "Are you sure you want to get into this today?"

"If you didn't notice, you're outnumbered."

The velocity of her fleet was increasing as they sped toward our position with *Justice Bringer* at the point of a V-shaped formation.

Mute. "Hard burn, Ada. Tullas won't budge and she's going to attempt to rake us as we pass. I want to pass between her and *Ferez* and rake *Ferez* as she does." *Unmute.*

"I'm not sure why we're having this chat. You and I both know you're not looking for us to surrender. Your goal is to disable our ship with those codes you're sending and then space the lot of us." I said.

"I'd have hoped we could end this peacefully," Tullas responded.

"I've seen what you believe is peaceful, Lorraine. Dying peacefully in the deep dark is still dying. I'll give you this chance now to leave. You have no business here," I said and cut comm.

I drummed my fingers nervously on the arm of my chair. Once again, I was in the open field of battle, tilting at my enemy, ready to drop my lance and unseat my opponent. Mankind had progressed so little in the few millennia since horses were the preferred conveyance of knights into battle.

"Missiles are aloft," Jonathan reported.

"Gunners, pick 'em up," Marny ordered calmly. Both *Ferez* and *Justice Bringer* had launched missiles bringing the total to nine in flight. At least they'd launched them early. I supposed they'd done so with the hope of being ready for a second salvo before we passed. I smiled as I heard a whoop from the gunner's nest as one after another, missiles were picked off.

"Counter-measures," I ordered. The gunners had done a great job of picking off five missiles. Even with their success, four would make it through.

"Roger that, Captain," Jonathan replied.

Predict location of missile strikes. The AI showed a spread along the front side of *Intrepid*, reminding me that I'd just dropped Beth Anne and Xie in that very location not fifteen minutes previous. I hoped they'd taken my warning to clear out if we ran into trouble, as it was too late now. There always seemed to be some contingency I should have considered more seriously, but didn't. When people's lives hung in the balance, it was maddening.

The ship shook as counter-measures launched and missiles exploded near the hull as well as on the hull, but there wasn't time to become distracted.

"Executing close pass now," Ada warned as she rolled *Intrepid* onto its side, passing *Justice Bringer* on her starboard. The pounding we were taking from *Justice Bringer*'s guns was fantastic, but we were handing out the same punishment to the much smaller ship, *Ferez*.

Up to this point, I hadn't seen *Hotspur* and was surprised when she momentarily appeared just above our bridge, following *Ferez* no more than a kilometer behind. Both her missiles launched from nearly point blank range and the top two turrets erupted in a constant stream. Coupled with our barrage, it was more than *Ferez* could withstand and the light frigate exploded.

"Flip. Combat burn!" I commanded.

Ada was already on it.

"Marny, everything you have on *Justice Bringer*." Tabby's maneuver had been brilliant in terms of obliterating *Ferez*, but *Hotspur*'s close proximity to *Justice Bringer* would make her easy to find. When *Hotspur* went dark, all *Justice Bringer*'s guns had to do was pick at empty space. *Intrepid* was well past the cluster of ships and we couldn't hope to provide *Hotspur* any cover for at least twenty seconds.

As expected, *Justice Bringer* replied in kind, stitching space, searching for a fleeing *Hotspur*, while Marny poured missiles and blaster fire into their, likely uninhabited, crew section. The difference between Tullas' first attack and ours was that her gunners weren't knocking down our missiles but allowing them to tear through their ship. Tullas wanted so badly to take out *Hotspur*, she would sacrifice her crew and ship to do it. I watched as the damage mounted while *Justice Bringer* searched wildly for *Hotspur*.

"Frak, Tabby and Nick got another one!" Ada squealed. I looked up to see that one of the two cutters following *Justice Bringer* had been obliterated. Initially, I wondered if it had been friendly fire, then I saw the familiar transponder. I should have known Tabby would go for a point instead of running for cover. It wouldn't work a second time - although it wouldn't have to. We'd closed the gap and would provide the cover she needed very shortly.

Hail Justice Bringer, I ordered.

"We're a little busy here," Tullas replied tersely.

"Stand down, Tullas. Call it a draw," I said.

"You just destroyed two of my ships - murdered two entire

crews."

"Want to make it an even four? You attacked my fleet, unprovoked, in open space. You are the aggressor, as you always have been," I said. I knew my face was hot from anger, but this woman's insistence on our destruction was over the top.

"Are you mad?"

"You want to finish this?" I asked. "You are bested, Lorraine. You know it and I know it. Look around. Your ship has major damage and your numbers have been cut in half, while we've given better than we received. If you'd like to continue to stand toe-to-toe, we can take passes at each other until one of us is no longer able to move, or worse."

"Cease fire," she commanded.

"Cease fire," I ordered.

"We have more ships, Hoffen," she said. "I'll hunt you to the corners of the universe."

Mute comm. Ada cut in. "Captain, there are ships approaching," Ada warned.

"Belirand?" I asked.

"Freedom Station," Ada answered.

Unmute. "I suggest you take a different approach with Freedom Station, Lorraine. Hoffen out." I closed the comm.

Locate Beth Anne Hollise. I prayed she hadn't actually stayed on the observation deck.

"*Beth Anne Hollise is in the civilian bunker,*" my AI replied.

"We're being hailed by Admiral Jorge Penna, Freedom Station," Ada announced.

"On forward screen. Greetings, Admiral Penna," I answered.

"Please state your business, *Intrepid*," Admiral Penna requested. He was a middle-aged, good looking, brown-skinned man with an accent I couldn't quite place.

"My apologies for the drama, Admiral Penna," I said. "I would like to request permission to enter Freedom Station's controlled space. We're here on a delivery mission and are unsure as to how Belirand might have located us this far out."

"Are you in need of immediate assistance?"

"No, we are functionally intact," I answered.

"I'm sending stand-off coordinates and require that you accompany my escort," he replied.

"Would you allow me to retrieve my sloop?"

"Certainly. Penna out," Admiral Penna cut the comm.

"Captain, incoming hail from the *Marcos Pontes*." Ada informed me.

"On main bridge comm," I said. A woman with similar brown skin as Admiral Penna appeared on the forward wall vid screen.

"Greetings, Captain Hoffen. Welcome to Freedom Station. I'm Lieutenant Wilmarie Fuentes. If you'd accompany me to a standoff zone, Admiral Penna would like a moment to de-escalate things with *Justice Bringer*," she said.

"Roger that. *Intrepid* out," I terminated comm. While Freedom Station had launched twenty-two ships in total, most of them were too small to be considered in a real fight. Penna was in one of two light frigates and Fuentes was sailing one of three schooners. Beyond those five ships, I didn't believe any of the rest of them would be able to damage *Intrepid*.

"Mister Rastof, would you start a physical assessment of damage to the ship? Feed your information to Jonathan, please."

"Aye, aye, Cap," Moonie answered and hopped up, exiting the bridge.

"Captain, *Hotspur* is secured and crew aboard," Jonathon announced.

"Ada, please communicate with Lieutenant Fuentes that we're ready to get underway."

"Aye," Ada answered. *Send acknowledgement to Marcos Pontes. We are ready to comply.*

Intrepid slowly turned, following a navigational path uploaded to us by Lieutenant Fuentes. On my tactical screen, Marny highlighted several large cannon emplacements nestled in a sparse asteroid field we'd be resting near. I expected some level of defense by Freedom Station. Admiral Penna was ensuring the fight between us and Belirand was over by bringing his cannons into the mix.

"That's quite an array, Marny," I said.

"Aye, Cap. Confirms a suspicion I had ever since I heard the name Bard Sanderson," she said.

"What's that?"

"Sanderson family was a big-time defense contractor back on Earth. The kid, Bard, took over and when he discovered extensive corruption, shut it down. Rumor was he took off for the stars and formed a commune with more credits than you could shake a stick at," she said.

"You know anything about that, Jonathan?" I asked.

"Bard Sanderson is indeed the son of a wealthy industrialist. There is little public information about Freedom Station, other than it does not respect Ordwall conventions and is therefore banned as a public trading hub," Jonathan answered.

"How many cannons are we looking at?" I asked.

"Enough to take down a frigate," Ada quipped.

"Aye, Ada, and I doubt we're seeing them all," Marny agreed. "Most defensive installations like this have cannons that are dark until there's a need, making them impossible to target. We'll want to play nice here."

Just then Tabby and Nick entered the bridge. I caught Tabby's eye. It was hard to let her fight without me and when she returned, that point was driven home. The look of spent exhilaration in her face was enough for me to realize that there would be no getting around her desire to do just that.

"Nice job on that cutter. You had all of us fooled," I said as I met her at the door and pulled her in. I didn't care who was watching. I'd had to deal with her getting shot at, so they could deal with this. My hands lingered on her hips as I looked into her face. She was alive with excitement.

"Nick's idea. He knew you'd be looking to give us cover and *Justice Bringer* would be playing hunt-the-wumpus," she said and then whispered in my ear. "I want to do bad things to you."

"Liam, incoming hail from *Alcântara*," Ada interrupted.

I grinned at Tabby and turned away. I hated the idea of losing whatever she had in mind, but we were on a mission. Knowing her, it was a good bet she wouldn't lose too much of it.

"On forward screen." I was starting to appreciate the forward bulkhead's large bank of integrated vid-screens. The workstations were set lower into the deck, giving us all a great view of whomever we were talking with. In this case, Admiral Penna reappeared in his impeccably tailored uniform. The bridge of the *Alcântara* looked identical to that of *Strumpet*, giving me some idea as to its manufacturer. Judging from the interior, it was older, but still well maintained.

"Greetings Captain Hoffen. Lieutenant Fuentes communicated your desire to trade with Freedom Station. Is this your intent?" he asked.

"Yes, Admiral. We're transmitting those details now." I nodded to Jonathan. We all watched as Penna reviewed the order we had.

"Seems like a lot of tension for livestock," he finally summarized.

I chuckled. "Admiral, I believe you may have a knack for understatement."

"You are welcome to proceed to the station. Would you like to assign the salvage claim of your two wrecks?"

"One moment, please?" I asked. *Mute.*

"Jonathan?"

"Freedom Station's governmental process is self-described as pro-liberty. It is somewhere between the extremes of anarchy and socialism," Jonathan stated.

"You can't get much further apart than that," Nick replied.

"Respectfully, we disagree," Jonathan said. "They are not exclusive concepts, rather they are orthogonal ideas. In this case, socialism is only applied to basic needs: housing, food, air, water, medicine and defense. A person has the right to defend themselves, but if obviously attacked, the government might step in. It seems poorly defined as presented in publicly available information."

"Information overload. I need to answer Penna's question. What's he asking?"

"Belirand attacked us," Nick interjected. "According to their laws, we own those wrecks and they have value. He's asking if we want to assign them to someone to be salvaged. He's helping us."

Unmute. "Thank you, Admiral Penna. We would like to assign those wrecks. Do you have a recommendation?"

"I do." Penna looked to his side. "Wilmarie, tell Scooter Beers he has the wrecks."

"Aye, aye, Admiral," Lieutenant Fuentes replied, her face appearing on the forward vid-screen. "We've also cleared docking twelve for *Intrepid*. With your permission, I'll transmit a navigation plan now."

"As efficient as you are deadly, my dear. Please do," Penna replied. "Captain Hoffen, as for the matter of straying into our controlled space without invitation, I am dismissing this as an unavoidable. It is our belief that any entity must be given the latitude to defend themselves. Clearly, you were not the aggressor here, as Belirand arrived well in advance, lying in wait for your arrival."

"Your generosity is appreciated, Admiral," I responded. "Hopefully, I'll have a chance to buy you a drink on station."

"Perhaps," he replied and terminated comm. A moment later, with his light frigate *Alcântara* in the lead, *Marco Pontes* on its wing, and the rest of the Freedom Station fleet forming up quickly behind, they snappily sailed away. I smiled. They were obviously a proud lot.

"We have a course, Liam," Ada prompted.

"Ahead, slow. We don't need to give anyone the jitters," I said.

"Aren't we going to talk about the elephant in the room?" Tabby asked.

"Which one?" I asked.

She rolled her eyes. "How'd Belirand know we were coming here? Someone aboard this ship told 'em."

I sighed. She was right and I was trying to ignore it.

"That seems like the most obvious answer," Nick agreed. "Jonathan and I are looking into it. There will be telltales if it came from the ship."

"My money is on Xie Mie-su," Tabby said.

"That would be a neat trick," I said. "She was in the med-tank up until a few hours ago."

"Look at that," Ada interrupted and flung *Intrepid*'s forward view onto the forward and top vid-screens. The screen resolution was so high it appeared as if she'd opened up our view directly to space.

Involuntarily, I gasped. Freedom Station wasn't at all what I'd expected. In my mind's eye, I'd pictured a boxy, metallic structure like Baru Manush Station or possibly a watermelon shaped asteroid- turned-station, like Colony-40. But Freedom Station couldn't be compared to either of those. In front of us lay a kilometer wide, ten-kilometer-long strip of farm land. The strip was bent in an arc with bright lights that shone down from strategic locations. Beneath the land was a combination of asteroids, steel girders and finished space station. Bard Sanderson had dropped an oasis into the desert of space and it was of a magnitude I had difficulty coming to grips with.

"Is that thing moving?" I asked. It appeared to be rotating around an unseen fulcrum.

Nick tossed a diagram to my HUD and understanding of the magnitude of the station struck me. The strip was only half of the station. The other half, a more standard looking station, sat opposite, attached by cross members and an elevator system that transported residents between the two sides.

"They're using rotation for gravity," Nick said. "It's very efficient."

"And they've enclosed the farm side in armored glass?" I could see it was the case, I was just having difficulty believing it.

"If you have manpower and access to the machinery, it's not unreasonable." Nick defended the idea. "I'm sure it's segmented to protect against asteroid strikes. With all those cannons, nothing very big is getting through."

"Our docking instructions put us dead center between the two big pieces of the station," Ada said. "According to my instructions, it's called The Collet. Otherwise, its Dirt Side and Star Side."

I shook my head in acknowledgement. "Nick, can you reach

out to Scooter Beers and find out when he'll have a value on the wrecks? We'll need local currency for repairs and crew shore leave," I said.

"On it," Nick said.

"Marny, would you and Ada work out bridge watch and shore leave? We won't know when we're leaving until we know if someone here can affect repairs and we can afford them," I said. "Ada, you have the bridge. Ping me when we're docked."

"Roger that, Liam," she replied.

"Tabby, you're with me," I said.

"Oooh, where are we going?" Tabby asked suggestively as we stepped from the bridge. For a moment, my mind jumped to where hers already was, but I wasn't really in for a five-minute event. I would prefer to enjoy more time together. I didn't answer her, but led her forward to the Civilian Bunker, which had been locked down shortly after hostilities had started.

I palmed open the door to the room. Beth Anne and Xie looked up expectantly. "We're on approach to Freedom Station. I've restored your communications if you'd like to make final arrangements for arrival. Beth Anne, I believe you were going to introduce us to the livestock handler?"

"Were those Belirand ships?" Xie interrupted.

"Right, like you don't know," Tabby spat.

"Having Belirand follow us to Freedom Station would provide me with no benefit," Xie said smoothly. "Not to mention, I was attempting to repair the ship we were sailing when I was injured."

"Who knows why you do anything," Tabby said.

Xie nodded. "An understandable suspicion. In this case, I recommend casting a wider net."

Beth Anne stepped forward, clearly annoyed by the exchange. "I've already received a comm from Mr. Jackson. He is most interested in meeting with you and starting work on the livestock pens on *Hotspur*." She flicked instructions to me. Freedom Station had to account for the change in mass with all of Beth Anne's material being moved onto the Star Side and the livestock and feed being removed from Dirt Side. We were to check in with the station at every step of the way.

I couldn't imagine the conversation Marny was about to have with Zebulon and Mark-Ralph. They were about to become baby sitters to twenty-five tonnes of livestock, after having left Ophir to escape just that. But then, for all my running away from being a miner ...

RED SHIRT

"Which part of crew don't you get, Ralphie?" Ortel asked as we loaded onto *Hotspur*.

"I said, don't call me Ralphie!" Mark-Ralph shoved Ortel into the bulk-head. The crew's antsy behavior had been brewing for a while and a change of pace, even if it was loading livestock, would do them good. "I didn't sign up to be a farmer."

"If you boys can't work things out, I can cancel crew shore leave," Marny said. "I've a new conditioning routine I've been wanting to work on."

"No, Master Chief," Ortel quickly replied. Mark-Ralph shot Ortel a dirty look, but didn't reply.

"Company, halt," Marny ordered. "Cap, go ahead. It appears I have a discipline issue to work through."

"No, Master Chief," Mark-Ralph quickly amended.

I led Beth Anne and Xie up to the bridge, along with Nick and Tabby. Marny had already explained she would keep Mark-Ralph, Zebulon and Baker on the berth-deck while we sailed Star Side to offload Beth Anne's cargo.

"Will you set up another bar?" I asked Beth Anne casually as I slid into the pilot's chair.

"We'll see. Most of the goods I trade aren't illegal here, so I won't need a front," she said. "I won't be able to require a premium, but then I won't have to go to the same lengths to move them, either."

"Are you concerned about security?"

"For the first few weeks, yes. After that, I should have things figured out. Xie will be a big help," she said.

Establish comm with Freedom Station, I instructed.

"Freedom Station, go ahead."

"This is *Hotspur*. We're requesting permission to dock with Star Side to offload cargo for Beth Anne Hollise," I said. I pinched the original instructions we'd received from the station on organizing.

"Wait one," the man replied. I slowed *Hotspur*'s approach. "Please hold fifteen minutes. We're transferring mass."

"Roger that, Freedom Station. Fifteen minutes. Waiting on your word," I cut the comm. "Nick, have you heard from Scooter Beers yet?"

"His team just made it out to the first wreck. Would you believe Tullas just left two survivors behind?" he said. He waited a beat, then continued. "Beers said there's a good trade on slaves."

"Frak. Are you serious? We can't let him keep slaves on our account," I said.

"I already told him." Nick chuckled at my emphatic response. "He said the salvage looks decent; plenty of armor, which is in demand. *Ferez* might even have an engine left. If that's the case, this might not be a total loss."

"That'd be a first," I said.

"Says the man sailing a stolen frigate," Beth Anne said.

"Spoils of war, my dear," I replied. "Don't forget though, Tullas only has to win once and we're done. That's why she's willing to hit us so hard."

"There's more going on here than you've let on," Xie Mie-su interjected. "Your behavior is irrational. Stealing a ship from Belirand, purchasing livestock at exorbitant prices from a non-terrestrial source. It's almost as if … I'm not sure what you're doing, but it's big."

"Trust me Xie, you don't want to look down that rabbit hole," I said. "Belirand has a special brand of justice they like to apply for people in that realm. And you've just seen a small part of it."

"I've been an outlaw for as long as I can remember, Liam. I've never seen someone move as quickly from the bright-shiny-hero column to the enemy-number-one column. Moreover, there has been nothing about this on any of the grey news feeds. And believe me, they've loved covering you so far," she said.

"Surely they won't be able to cover up this battle," Beth Anne said.

"We'll know in forty minutes, give or take," Xie answered.

Beth Anne smiled. "You really don't like mysteries."

"*Incoming hail, Freedom Station.*"

"*Hotspur.* Go ahead," I answered.

"You're clear for docking at M-143, instructions embedded." The woman's voice was all business.

"Copy that." I pulled the instructions from the comm-stream, dropped them onto our nav-computer and sailed in. The 'M' level, or mezzanine, was just below the main commerce level. It was a new setup for me. I was to sail in and allow the station's grapples to pull us in.

"Hold on," I said as we approached.

"What the frak!?" Tabby asked as long arms unfurled and reached for us. "Do you want me to take 'em out?"

"No!" I laughed. "No. That's just how they do it."

"They need positive contact with the ship," Nick explained. "We're enough mass that they need to balance out the opposite side once we're part of this side of the station. It would be a problem for them if we detached abruptly."

"You really should warn a girl," Tabby said, giving her head a quick shake. She patted the console in front of her. "Any chance we'll be able to pick up missiles? I hate this empty feeling."

"I'm feeling pretty good about it right now," I said. "Although, I can't imagine what they'd have done if we'd shot their grappling arms."

"I asked first," Tabby said.

"Tabbs, you've the helm." I stood. "Try not to shoot anyone."

"I'll do my best."

We'd agreed that Jonathan and Tabby would stay aboard *Hotspur* while we unloaded Beth Anne's cargo. I couldn't help but think she'd gotten the better end of the deal. She'd successfully brokered a free ride between Jeratorn and Freedom Station that would have cost tens of thousands of Mars credits under normal circumstances.

It also wasn't lost on me that we were being yanked around by the Ophir council, expending time and effort to fetch livestock for them, when we could be out working on our mission. Of course, when I'd brought this up with Nick, he'd argued that the livestock were very much our mission. Without them, the people of Ophir would have a difficult time surviving and we wouldn't have a safe place for refugees. To which I'd argued the Ophir council would eventually balk at receiving refugees, as it threatened their status quo. The conversation generally fell apart at that point … I hated it when Nick was probably right.

"You in there?" Nick asked, having arrived at the armory where I was equipping myself.

"Yeah, sometimes I get lost in how we ended up at this point," I said, palming open the door.

"It's not easy doing the right thing. If it was, everyone would do it," Nick said, handing me my favorite heavy Ruger pistol, which I strapped across my chest. I'd be carrying a reading pad instead of a blaster rifle and wanted to have my pistol immediately accessible.

When we arrived in the hold, it was crowded with both people and cargo. "Cap, dock master just arrived," Marny announced.

I joined her and looked out the armored glass peep hole. A well-armed, vac-suited gang of six awaited. Standing in front was a man with a reading pad. Notwithstanding his armed escort, it looked like any other docking bay.

"Here we go." I palmed the security panel to lower the docking bay ramp. Those few moments we waited for the ramp to finish lowering were tense as we considered each other. Once it finally did, I approached. "Greetings, Freedom Station."

"Captain," the man answered, holding out his reading pad. It was a familiar gesture, which I mimicked and transferred a physical count and mass of each of the containers we'd be transferring to Beth Anne's new home.

"Vince? Vince Ferrante?" Beth Anne stepped forward from the hold. As she did, the well-armed gang behind the dock-master tensed up, rifles lowering to a more readied state. I didn't have to look back to know that my crew had done the same. I had no doubt she was familiar with some of the people on the station, but it hardly seemed the right moment.

The dock master nodded in acknowledgement. "Beth Anne Hollise, I'd heard you might be showing up here. This is all yours?"

"Not all of it," she said, sliding smoothly next to my arm. "I seem to remember stuffing a case of Jeppeson Scotch into one of these crates just for you. That is, if you're still drinking it."

"I see. I'll make sure the boys are extra gentle today." He smiled greedily. "Stand down, fellas. Ms. Hollise is on the up and up." It occurred to me that 'the boys' he was referring to were Freedom Station's equivalent of stevedores. It also occurred to me that if anyone were to know how to handle someone like this, it was Beth Anne Hollise.

"Just unload the crates anywhere," Beth Anne said, walking into the loading bay. "I've already negotiated to have them transported to their new home. Come along, Bernd. Xie will oversee it from here." With that, she sashayed from the loading bay, her overly thin assistant in tow. Every eye watched as her voluptuous figure disappeared into the oversized airlock at the back.

"Uh, right," Ferrante turned back to me. "Ready?"

"My life just gets easier once this is done," I agreed, which earned me a chuckle.

For all of the posturing, unloading *Hotspur* worked just like it did anywhere else. Stevedores directed stevedore bots that had long forks jutting out from an arc-jet propulsion unit. The forks had the capacity to either grip or simply lift crates, depending on the gravity of the environment. In this particular case, a gravity generator was providing a .4g field, directly in line with the floor of *Hotspur*. I suspected that once we were undocked, the docking bay would revert to station normal, but that wouldn't be my issue.

"How will you pay for the livestock transaction?" Vince Ferrante asked once we were done offloading the cargo.

"Platinum?" I proposed.

He nodded subtly, which I took as communication with his AI.

"I've been given authorization to collect for the pens. I'll need fifteen hundred grams."

I gritted my teeth. The price we'd been given was twelve hundred grams and I had to decide if I wanted to be taken advantage of. At a difference of three thousand credits, it was a dangerous precedent to set. If word got out that we were an easy touch, we'd have people lining up. On the other hand, Ferrante had real power and I had no idea how far I could push him.

"That's a pretty substantial tip," I said.

"Lot of mouths to feed." He glanced over his shoulder to his armed group. At least now I understood why they were along.

"Thirteen hundred seems more in line with what I'm thinking," I said.

"Sixteen hundred," he answered.

I looked back into his eyes and saw only a cold stare. He was definitely not messing around. I sighed. "You're right. We've gone to a lot of trouble to get here. What's a few grams of platinum, given all that?" I asked and then paused for effect. "I'll tell you what. We've been pushed around by a lot of assholes and we're pretty much done with it. So, here's how this is going to go. The next number I give you is my final answer. You give me another number and we'll do this hard. Wouldn't be the first time for my crew, won't be the last. Thirteen hundred fifty grams and you need to start loading right now." I stared back at him, not blinking. We had even odds, having brought all of our crew.

Finally, he nodded his head grudgingly. "I can work with that. But you owe me a drink."

"Deal." I didn't extend my hand.

Loading of the pen material only took fifteen minutes. I handed Ferrante a bag of platinum fingers after contacting the seller, verifying it was acceptable to do so.

"Nicely done, Cap," Marny said once *Hotspur*'s loading ramp retracted and we were back in a pressurized environment.

"I thought we were gonna toss 'em a beating," Zebulon said.

"I'd have thought you'd had enough of that on Ophir," Baker replied dryly.

A glowering look from Marny cut off Zebulon's reply.

"*Hail Freedom Station*," I requested.

"Go ahead, *Hotspur*." It was the same woman I'd talked to last time.

"We've successfully offloaded our cargo and taken on our new load. We're ready to detach and move Dirt Side."

"Copy that, *Hotspur*. Please allow the station to fully eject your craft before moving into position on Dirt Side," she replied. In her message, a minimum safe distance was communicated. It would take several minutes before we'd be on our way.

"What was that standoff all about?" Tabby asked.

"Dock Master wanted three hundred grams of plat to finish delivering the pen material," I said. "Pissed me off."

"We believe you handled the situation correctly," Jonathan interjected. "To have acted otherwise would have made you and your crew targets for the inhabitants of the station."

"Doesn't seem to bother Beth Anne," I said.

"Beth Anne Hollise trades influence," Jonathan replied. "Her strength is not physical, but rather a carefully crafted façade of connections. It is implied that to inflict harm upon her would invoke the wrath of more powerful individuals."

"Whatever it is, she's good at it," I said.

"Here we go," Tabby said as *Hotspur* was gently flung from the Star Side. Skillfully, she arced our path and caught up with Dirt Side. As she did, I received docking instructions, which I flicked to her, the process of which looked much like what we'd experienced on Star Side. We docked a level below the grassy area. Of course it wasn't reasonable that we'd be parking on the grass, but I'd hoped.

"How will we seal the ship, sir?" Mark-Ralph asked when I arrived. "Livestock won't survive vacuum."

"They have a cowl," Nick replied. "It's part of what we're paying for."

I looked through the armored glass and received a thumbs up from a much less well-armed group of farm hands. As soon as the loading ramp was down just a meter, a smell I'll never forget assaulted my nose. It was sickly sweet, somewhere between bilge goo and rotting fruit. It took everything I had not to gag and I raised my vac-suit just for the purpose of not becoming further exposed to the odor. I shook my head, wondering if this was how *Hotspur* would forever smell.

"I'm to take possession of the construction bot." A woman stepped forward, offering her hand. I shook it and then bumped reading pads with her, exchanging a list of what we were expecting to load. "I think this is the first time we've sold livestock," she observed.

I flicked instructions to the construction bot, which had easily built the pens in the short time we'd taken to sail between Star Side and Dirt Side.

"You'll want to stand to the side," she said, directing me out of the way as eight four-hundred-kilogram bovine rushed from a tunnel within the station and were directed into the pens. I hadn't initially understood the design of the pens, but as each animal was loaded, their handler expertly slid a gate across their rump, making a new channel for the next to be loaded.

"How long can they survive confined in here?" I asked. "And I'm Liam Hoffen."

"Juanita Ferrante. I've sent instructions for med-patches for each of the species. We'll keep them out of it for most of the trip. They can make it a near indefinite amount of time as long as you have sufficient food and water. It's not great for them, but they'll survive."

"Ferrante. Any relationship to Vince Ferrante?" I asked.

"Guilty. Husband," she replied. "Good man, a little hard around the edges."

I raised my eyebrows. I wasn't about to get into it with her.

"Is there local currency on the station? I'd like to get my folks shore-leave."

"There's a chit you can get at the exchange," she said.

"How many chits does a burger and three beers cost, do you figure?" I asked.

She thought about it for a moment, "Beer will set you back

three chits each. Protein burger will cost twice that unless you pay for a real beef burger, which is twenty. So, conservatively, twenty chits if you tip - which you should."

"Much appreciated," I said. At eleven crew we'd need to hand out enough chits for two on-station meals, making it five hundred chits. I wondered how conversion from platinum to chits would work.

"There you go," Juanita finally said after the last of the chickens was loaded onto a higher shelf. "You'll want to collect those eggs. They'll keep laying 'em if you do."

"Hey, we're going to be here for a few days, any chance you have any workers who'd like to help us with the livestock while we are?" I asked.

"What are you paying?"

"What do I need to pay?" I asked.

"Eighty chits a shift would do it," she said.

"If I make it a hundred twenty, would you oversee and pay them?" I asked, still not knowing how much a chit was going to cost me.

"Make it one-sixty and we'll bring our own feed and keep your hold clean," she said, holding her hand out to shake.

Once the loading ramp had closed, the noise and smells were overwhelming. I wanted to talk to Nick, but nodded my head toward the door to the berth deck instead.

"How'd we get talked into this?" I asked Nick once we were behind closed doors. "And what's a chit going to cost us?"

"They're about twice a Mars credit. Expensive beer and burgers, but then you're about as far out as people get in Sol," he explained.

"Mark-Ralph." I placed my hand on the man's shoulder, causing him to flinch. "I don't for a minute blame you for not wanting to raise livestock."

He smiled for the first time. "Actually making me a little homesick, Captain. That's a good looking bull you bought. I thought we'd never see the like on Ophir after those damn Ophie killed our last. For the record, you get used to the smell."

I laughed. "Not in this lifetime. I think there are beers in the fridge, Marny. Your crew worked hard."

"Way ahead of you, Cap," she said, handing tall-necked bottles out to the three Ophir natives.

"We really getting shore leave?" Zebulon asked.

"That's up to the Master Chief." I stepped onto the lift next to Nick and we disappeared onto the bridge.

"Any word from Beers on salvage and repairs?" I asked.

"They've already started repairs," Nick said. "Beers needs another thirty. If we want the Belirand crew he captured, we need six kilograms of platinum."

"How about missiles?"

"That's with a reload," Nick said. "If you're trying to figure out what we'll have left, we're down to twenty-five hundred grams after we buy chits for shore leave."

I wanted to ask what the captured Belirand crew were costing me, but I didn't need that much temptation.

"I was hoping we'd have more for our trip across to the Aeratroas region," I said.

"One step at a time."

"Tabbs, negotiate with Freedom Station and take us back to *Intrepid*. I feel soiled."

***

I kicked my chair back so I could lean against the wall of the bar. If there was one thing Freedom Station didn't want for, it was bars. Ada, Tabby, Nick, Marny and I had left Mom and Jonathan in charge and found the least rowdy establishment we could.

"So, was this really what you had in mind when you said you'd find Ophir's livestock?" Ada asked.

"Not really. I just figured with enough hard currency we should be able to figure it out," I said.

"The thing I want to know is why we haven't heard from Sterra or Buckshot Alderson," Nick said. "Do you think Belirand has such a tight lid on this that even Mars Protectorate doesn't know what's going on? And what about Xie's report to the grey news feeds?"

"Miss me already?" Xie cooed as she approached. I found it uncanny how she always knew when she was being talked about.

"No," Tabby replied. "I thought we already dropped you off."

"I'm here to volunteer," Xie said, ignoring Tabby. "I understand you're looking for crew."

Tabby's response was immediate. "No frakking way."

"You think I can't figure out what's going on? The only account I could find about the battle got pulled from the feeds almost immediately. Belirand must have eaten the story. And that ship you stole? No one's heard a single word about it. Be real interested to see what would happen if you showed up over Puskar Stellar with it. You wouldn't make it out alive. You're buying breeding pairs of livestock. Doesn't take a genius to put this together. You've either broken into the TransLoc gates or you have tech that takes it one step further."

"Stop," I said.

"Why? Making you nervous?" she asked. "If I'm figuring this out, others will. You know me, Liam. I saved you on the *Bakunawa* when I didn't need to. Take another chance."

"Liam. Don't," Tabby said.

"We'll take you on under one condition," I said, ignoring Tabby. "If you betray me or mine, I'll space you myself. If you're coming along, you're swearing fealty. Understood?"

"Agreed."

"Cap. We have another problem. We have crew in a fight," Marny said.

"Okay guys, back to the ship. That includes you, Xie," I said. "Marny, Tabby, you're with me."

The scene we entered was pure chaos. Baker, Zebulon, and Ortel were standing with backs to each other over Mark-Ralph's body. Marny hadn't allowed them to carry anything larger than flechette pistols, although I noticed Baker had a nano-blade drawn. Five men, some I recognized from the stevedore crew that unloaded us earlier, stood with weapons drawn.

"Sit rep, Baker," Marny barked as she plowed her way through the unruly crowd.

"Mark-Ralph is down," Baker replied.

I noticed a hand and a prodigious amount of blood lying next to Mark-Ralph's prone body. A blood trail led off toward the bar exit. Whoever lost their hand had made a hasty retreat.

"It's Ferrante and his crew. They don't like how you treated them at the docks," Zebulon added hastily.

"So you attack my crew?" I pulled my blaster and turned toward the stevedore crew. I'd read enough of the station's laws to know there would be no sheriff showing up to mete out justice. As long as the station itself wasn't attacked, inhabitants were encouraged to settle disputes amongst themselves. "Where's Ferrante?"

Initially, I didn't see where the shots came from and was grateful to Anino for the grav-suit's capacity to absorb light weapons fire. My suit's helmet stiffened and my HUD targeted the individual who'd shot at me. A quarter of a second later, that idiot was targeted by Marny's tactical program and before I returned fire, Tabby had responded. The fins of three flechette darts quivered in the man's chest as he fell in slow motion to the deck. I had to get things under control or there would be more bloodshed.

"STOP!" I yelled. "We're in armor and this is a blaster." I spun around, brandishing my Ruger, looking for anyone else who might take a potshot.

"Situation to your right, Cap," Marny said over the tactical channel.

I spun and watched as the crowd parted from the opposite side of the bar. It was as if a plow had rolled through and I wasn't overly surprised when Admiral Penna emerged. He was shorter than I'd expected, but that wasn't unusual for me and people of power. For some reason, I always made them taller in my mind.

"Your man was provoked, but he escalated the situation," Penna proclaimed.

"I'd like to withdraw and get my man to our medical bay," I

said. "Do we have a problem here?"

"You do not and we are not as lawless as you seem to believe. Ferrante will be punished for his attack on your crew. On behalf of Freedom Station, I apologize. We would very much like to keep Loose Nuts as a trading partner," he said.

I leaned down to check Mark-Ralph. He was dead.

"Ferrante is on the deck, Cap. Tabby's darts weren't fatal," Marny informed me over our private tactical channel.

I walked over to where Ferrante lay. His bleeding arm had been cuffed by a med-patch. I pulled the darts from his chest, rousing him, and lay an emergency med-patch onto the torn skin. "Get up. You have taken from me and now I claim you," I said.

"Captain?" Admiral Penna asked with a note of warning in his voice.

"Is it not your law, Admiral?" I asked. "Blood for blood?"

"It is… But this man has a wife," he said.

"A lovely woman," I agreed. "And what of Mark-Ralph's family and his responsibilities?"

"You are a hard man, Captain Hoffen."

SHANGHAI

"We're not done talking about Xie," Tabby said as we worked our way through cluttered passageways on the Star Side of Freedom Station, heading for the elevators.

"Understood." My heart was still racing from the quick decisions I'd had to make back at the bar. Xie Mie-su was far from my mind. I was half pulling, half dragging Ferrante along behind us.

My tactical display lit up with two targets following behind at ten meters.

"Zebulon, Baker, take this one to the ship and drop him in the brig. Have Silver provide medical," I ordered. *Establish comm, Nick James.* "Nick, I've got crew coming up the elevator. Can you provide an escort once they get topside?"

"Yup. Marny has us on standby," he answered.

"Marny, we need to make a stand. If we let these guys run us out of here, we're never coming back," I said.

"Are we coming back, Cap?"

"Not running today. You with me?" I asked.

"Never a question," she answered. I felt a tug on my finger where my engagement ring sat. Tabby and I had rings that shared a quantum crystal that could be excited simply by touch. She was communicating her support of my decision, no matter what.

The number of targets behind us had grown from two to five. My tactical display prioritized them and also highlighted potential cover in case a firefight broke out. I stepped forward with Tabby and Marny on either side.

"Far enough," I said. "Go home or we'll let this play out."

"You think you can take on the entire station?" One of the men stepped out from a dark storefront.

"I don't see an entire station. All I see is a handful of thugs who picked a fight and lost," I said. "It's over; leave it alone."

"You don't get it. Who do you think we are? We run the docks, cannons … everything. You think you've won? You're dead. You just don't know it," he said.

"I'll be sure to pass that along to the Admiral," I said.

"He can't be everywhere. Mistakes happen."

"Glad we worked that out." I turned back to the elevator. My HUD would warn me if a weapon was raised in my direction. "Nick, do you have the crew?"

"They're just getting off the elevator," he replied.

I wasn't surprised that we hadn't made it more than a few meters down the passageway when my HUD blinked red on the lead figure. He'd drawn a weapon and the three of us responded in kind. As for me, it was an easy move to unclip my Ruger from the chest holster, turn and align the targeting reticle. The man's first shot plowed into my shoulder and burned; a much heavier load than those used in the bar. My shot ended up firing wild.

According to my HUD, four out of five of our pursuers were actively targeting me. I made a tactical decision to seek cover as two more rounds punched into my armor. Fortunately, the suit was better able to absorb these shots - or perhaps it was the adrenaline.

As with most combat in space, gun fights in hallways are pretty quick events. I've read about the stupidity of showing up to a gun fight with a knife. While that does sound like a bad idea, there's a close corollary. Don't show up to a gun fight without armor and communications, especially when your opponent has both. So, much like my battle with Tullas, the attackers had focused all their efforts on a single target, in this case, me. While I'd taken the brunt of the opening salvo, these geniuses had all but ignored Marny and Tabby. They left my teammates, who were the two most offensively devastating in our group, complete tactical freedom.

"Cease Fire!" A disembodied voice erupted from every surface of the passageway. My HUD showed the command had been broadcast from Freedom Station Security Services.

I still hadn't taken a shot, but nodded affirmatively to Tabby and Marny, complying with the station's request. Tactically, three of the five who'd attacked us were down, but they still appeared to be moving. I was impressed with my team's moderate response. I had intended to do some damage.

"You will not move from your positions and you will put your arms on the ground," the woman's voice announced.

I sighed as I placed my weapon on the ground. I'd read enough of Freedom Station's laws to know that disobeying a directive wasn't an option.

"What's going on, Liam?" Nick asked.

"We got jumped. We're being detained. I'll update you when I can," I said.

"Understood."

It took several minutes before Lieutenant Wilmarie Fuentes rounded the corner, accompanied by ten uniformed security personnel. I was surprised to see that she was both responsible for security as well as Captain of Freedom Station's second largest ship. Although, I knew from experience, that on a remote station people had to wear multiple hats.

"Captain Hoffen, you appear to be having quite a night," she said as she approached, offering her hand. Mentally, I sighed with relief. If she was shaking my hand, it didn't seem like she'd be looking to put us in the brig.

"To be honest, I'm not exactly sure how we've gotten on the wrong side of this group," I said.

"A question we'll spend some time getting to the bottom of. Jens, take them away," she said. "I assure you, this is not representative of Freedom Station. It is true, we enjoy our freedoms and do not desire much oversight by our government. We also do not allow the type of lawless behavior you've seen this evening."

"If you learn anything from them, I'd be interested," I said.

"It is the least we can do," she said and turned away, motioning to the remainder of her guard to follow.

"Cap, you think she came along so we wouldn't Shanghai those boys?" Marny asked as we approached the elevator.

"Is that a thing?" Tabby asked.

"Illegal procurement - better known as kidnapping? Yes, more than you would expect," Marny answered. "North American Navy lost more than a few sailors to pirates that way."

"Do we need to set out a guard tonight?" I asked as we stepped onto the elevator that would take us to The Collet and *Intrepid*.

"Scooter Beers' people are working around the clock and have significant ship access. I'll post an interior sentry to keep track of their movement. You hired a local to care for the livestock; I believe that's Ferrante's wife. I've temporarily revoked her access. I'm not counting on good behavior there."

"What are you doing with Ferrante?" Tabby asked.

"Good conversation to have on *Intrepid*," I said as we stepped from the elevator. I had no doubt our conversations were being monitored.

It would have been a long walk to the end of the concourse if Tabby hadn't been so keyed up. As it was, she made us double-time it and we arrived in short order.

"Captain! Master Chief." Ortel stiffened as he stood at the end of the pressurized catwalk joining *Intrepid* to Freedom Station. He'd changed into an armored vac-suit and was holding a blaster rifle. It momentarily gave me flashbacks to when I'd first boarded the *Kuznetsov*. It was obvious he was enjoying the moment.

"Well done, Ortel," Marny answered. "Is everyone aboard?"

Ortel's confidence cracked. "I'm not sure."

"Aye. It's one of the responsibilities of this particular watch. We have to know who's aboard and who's ashore at all times. No harm, this is a training cruise. Take a minute and see if you can find the information. Cap, go ahead. I'll work with Seaman Licht."

"Thank you, Marny," I said. As I passed Ortel, I clapped him on the back in a friendly gesture. We might be adopting a formal reporting structure, but that didn't mean I had to lose who I was. I hadn't even gotten to know Mark-Ralph and now he was dead. Never again.

"I can't believe you let Mie-su come along," Tabby said as we walked toward the medical bay.

"I don't know how to explain it, but I need you to give me some room on this. It's not that I trust her implicitly; it's just that I feel like I understand her. She's like Celina. Life crapped on her and she did what was required to survive. We owe our lives twice to Xie," I said.

"She tried to kill you and Nick."

"I get it. I just can't discard her," I said.

"I don't know if I love you more or if I want to break your neck," Tabby said. "You have a blind spot where women are concerned."

"I certainly hope not." I pushed her shoulder, spinning her into the passageway's bulkhead just outside the medical bay. She was annoyed and defensively blocked my approach. There was little I could do if she wouldn't allow it, but there was always the matter of how hard she wanted to resist. I pushed her arms away and slid inside her defenses. "Some of my favorite people are women and I'd hate not to be able to see them." I gave her my best lecherous look.

"You're an ass," she whispered huskily, turning her mouth onto my own. It'd been days since we'd shared a moment of intimacy and I felt the strain of it.

"Cap, we've a problem," Marny's voice sounded through my earwig.

"Go ahead, Marny," I said, closing my eyes, accepting the responsibility.

"Moonie isn't aboard."

"What happens when you ping him?"

"No response. Technically, he's still on leave, but he should have his comm unit available," she replied. "We could send a search party."

"Contact Freedom Station and let them know we're looking for a crew member. And no, we're not doubling down tonight by going back out," I answered.

"Aye," Marny cut the comm.

"What's that?" Tabby asked.

"Moonie is off comm and still on station," I said.

"Figures."

"Let's do this," I said and palmed my way into the medical bay. I found Mom seated in a chair, laser pistol clipped to her waist with Zebulon standing guard in full armored vac-suit. Vince Ferrante was resting on an incline table, his vac-suit open with a thick med-patch where Tabby had shot him three times and then ripped the darts from his breast bone. He glared at me as we entered.

"Thanks, Mom," I said.

"He's not very happy," she said, then gave me a once over. "What's wrong with your shoulder?"

For the moment, I ignored her question. "Give me a reason not to drop you in the deep dark." I crossed the room to stand next to the restrained man.

His glare said everything. "You'll never leave here alive."

"Your gang is in the brig. They made their move and failed. The thing I don't understand is why all the anger. You and I didn't know each other thirty hours ago and now you're gunning for me and mine. What's more, I gave you a couple hundred grams of platinum you didn't earn," I said. "Clear up for me how we got to this point."

Ferrante leaned forward as if to speak and instead spat on me. Tabby, quicker by twice than either of us, caught him in the jaw with a right cross.

"Stop," I rested my hand on her arm. "Don't get pulled in."

"Disrespect has to cost him something," she replied.

"He's just the messenger," I said. "One more chance, Ferrante. Tell me who sent you."

"Frak off."

"Lean forward," I said, placing my hand on his back. He resisted, choosing instead to push against me. "I'm not going to hurt you, Vince." It was to no avail, however, he just thrashed around, pushing harder.

Suspend medical treatments. Apply tranquilizers to render patient immobile for transport.

"Zebulon, would you take Mr. Ferrante down to the brig. Tell Marny what's going on," I said as Ferrante collapsed onto the table. "He's to come to no harm."

"Copy that, Captain," Zebulon replied, easily lifting the spacer-born Ferrante over his broad tree-cutter shoulders.

Alert me if Ferrante's medical condition worsens.

"I don't like you getting shot at," Mom said when the door finally closed. "Now, off with your suit."

I pulled back the shoulder of my vac-suit where the charred wound looked a lot worse than it felt. I was fairly sure it was because the suit had administered a dose of anesthesia and I was about to hate life.

"It looks worse than it is."

"Pretty sure that's not true," Tabby poked her finger into it and got my attention immediately. "Does that hurt?"

"Tabby. Stop," Mom came to my rescue.

"Just wanted to see how deep it went." Tabby laughed.

"Try this," Mom placed the medical sensor onto the wound. I watched the readings on my HUD. It wasn't great, but a good old fashioned patch or two would do the trick. Tabby located the correct one and applied it.

"Liam, sorry to interrupt. Juanita Ferrante is here looking for Vince," Nick said, connecting via comm.

"Not unexpected. Invite her to the civilian conference room and I'll be right there," I said. "No show of force if we can avoid it."

"She has Lieutenant Wilmarie Fuentes with her," Nick replied.

"Understood." As I pulled my vac-suit back on, I explained the situation to Mom and Tabby.

"What are you going to do?" Mom asked.

"Listen to what they have to say, I guess."

The civilian conference room was so designated because it was *Intrepid*'s largest and nicest, rivaling *Strumpet*'s fit and finish. Baker stood outside the door in an armored vac-suit with a flechette pistol at her side. I wondered if she had any training with it, but at a minimum, she looked impressive.

"Lieutenant Fuentes, Juanita." I held my hand out in greeting. "This is Tabby Masters. You've already met Nick James. I know it's been a long night for everyone; how can I help?"

Juanita's eyes were puffy and her nose was red. She'd obviously been crying. I understood the feeling. Her life had been turned upside down and I recognized my role in that. No doubt, Vince wasn't all bad.

"What do you intend to do with Vince?" Wilmarie asked.

"He killed my man. When asked who hired him, he refused to answer. I have no choice but to take him with us," I said.

"Do you intend to kill him?" Juanita asked.

"So far, he is unrepentant and believes *Intrepid* will be stopped before we leave Freedom Station," I said, not answering.

"I brought your platinum back, at least as much as we had left," she said and laid it on the table. It was less than a hundred grams and it broke my heart. I bit the interior of my cheek so as to not give in to the raw emotion.

I pushed the platinum back to her. "This is not about money, Juanita. It's about the survival of more people than you can imagine." It didn't escape me that I sounded like Tullas, justifying my actions in the name of the greater good. "I can say that he will be treated humanely."

"Would you allow Juanita to accompany Vince?" Lieutenant Fuentes asked. "I vouch for her character."

I looked at Nick. Of all the crazy things I'd expected to hear, I hadn't anticipated this.

"As crew," Nick replied. "She'll earn passage, just like everyone else."

"I can't say it will change Vince's outcome, but perhaps you can talk sense into him," I said.

"I accept," Juanita replied. "Thank you."

Before she could say more, Fuentes stood up. "The night is young and I've my own brig-full to deal with."

"What now?" I asked after seeing the two women off the ship.

"I've watch in four hours. I should probably get some sleep," Tabby said.

"Scooter Beers will be here at 0600 to inspect the repair progress and we're getting a load of missiles about the same time," Nick said.

***

Scooter Beers was an affable man on a mission, which I appreciated. Upon arrival, he tossed me a map of the repairs his team was affecting to the hull. He immediately flitted off in an open sled that he straddled. It was nothing more than arc-jets and a bench seat and I idly wondered if the sled was how he'd received his nickname. I struggled to catch up to him, laying hard into my grav-suit.

"I've not seen this type of repair bay before," I said as we approached the first section that was currently being worked on. Armor was being set onto the ship by a device that was fixed to *Intrepid*'s hull.

"About the only way to do it without a full shipyard. It's a Chinese design, don't see 'em too much with Mars and the North Americans. But those Chinese are clever; don't waste a lot of energy building unnecessary structures. See over there?" He pointed to a similar machine lifting a pock-marked piece of armored hull. "We're able to remove the damaged armor while fabbing a replacement. Be close to good-as-new when we're done. Only better if you were in orbit over Mars. But if you could do that, I'd guess you wouldn't be here," he said, winking at me.

"Ballpark amount … what do you have wrapped up in this gear?" I asked.

"Each one is four billion yen, give or take," he answered. "That's all purchased new, of course."

My HUD immediately converted that to Mars credits which put it at forty million credits. I whistled to myself. "You get a lot of call for these kinds of repairs out here?"

"This is a big project for us. Got to say, you have the boys and girls all in a titter. Most of them never worked on a big warship like this," he said. "Not me. Bard plucked me from a contract on the moon. I saw this - and much bigger - day in and day out. Mind telling me what's got Belirand's panties in a wad?"

"Let's say there's a disagreement on registration."

"That'd do it." He laughed as we arrived at the last repair. "Looks like we're well ahead of schedule. Two hours and we'll be out of your hair."

"That's quite a bit ahead," I said.

"Let's say I got a call from the Admiral requesting we give you our best service."

"Appreciate the help."

"My pleasure."

I moved around to the other side of the ship, cycled through the airlock next to the cargo hold and made my way to the bridge.

"Nick, you get the latest from Beers?" I asked as I entered the bridge.

"Yup. Just updating things now," he said. I turned to Moonie, who was also seated at a bridge workstation. "Moonie, what happened yesterday?"

"Sorry, Captain, I pulled my earwig out when I was sleeping. Bad habit; won't happen again," he said.

"Make sure it doesn't. If we'd needed to move out, you'd have had a permanent new home," I reprimanded, not believing his explanation for a nano-second.

"Ada, any word from Juanita Ferrante?" I asked. "She should have reported for duty."

"Marny checked her in this morning," Ada answered. "I assigned her to oversee the livestock in place of Mark-Ralph." Ada's voice choked at the end at the mention of his name. I mentally kicked myself. I needed to give the crew a sense of closure regarding Mark-Ralph. We couldn't just let him die with no words being said.

"Marny, how many missiles are we down?"

"Full load, Cap," she said.

"How about the two Belirand prisoners?" I asked.

"They're sharing a cell next to Ferrante," Marny answered. "Have you given any thought as to what you're going to do with any of them?"

"I figure the Belirand crew can live on Ophir," I said. "As for Ferrante, I'm going to get him to tell me who paid him to come after us. I owe Mark-Ralph that much. Beyond that, I don't know."

Two and a half hours later, Nick arrived back on the bridge with an announcement that couldn't have been more welcome. He'd inspected the final repair and *Intrepid* was once again ready to roll. It would take weeks for the one reno-bot we had to repair all of the internal damage, but with our limited crew, it would be merely inconvenient.

Hail Freedom Station.

"Go ahead, *Intrepid*."

"This is Captain Hoffen, requesting a departure vector," I announced.

"Copy that, Captain. Catch you next time." The man's reply was professional and a navigation path was embedded with his message.

"All hands, this is Captain Hoffen. We're about to get underway; please prepare for departure," I announced.

"Ada, the helm is yours once we're green," I said.

"Copy that, Liam." She switched the vid screens to the exterior view we all preferred. Freedom Station was an odd little piece of the universe and I wondered if we'd ever find ourselves back here.

I avoided looking at the cannons as we passed them. If Ferrante's predictions were right, we'd deal with it. We couldn't be held hostage by the ravings of a madman and if those cannons targeted us we were done.

"We're out of range," Marny finally announced and I let go of a breath I didn't know I'd been holding.

"Set course for Ophir," I said.

"Already plugged in," Ada replied.

"I guess we now find out what livestock feel about fold-space," I said.

STOWAWAY

"Liam?" My earwig chirped with Xie's voice as we finished the transition to fold-space.

"Aye, Xie, welcome to fold-space," I replied.

After a long pause she finally got back to me. "Belirand will hunt you with every last credit in their accounts. You are beyond crazy."

"Welcome to the biggest lie perpetrated on humanity," I said. In the background, I heard the sound of chaos erupting.

"I must go," Xie said, terminating comm.

Locate Xie Mie-su. Put on bridge projector. The forward projector changed to show the hold of *Hotspur* where Xie, Juanita and Zebulon were all struggling to maintain order with the animals, all of which looked to have simultaneously defecated upon entering fold-space. I didn't blame them; I felt the same way.

"Juanita, are you surviving down there?" I asked.

She looked up at my voice, astonishment apparent on her face. "Captain, what happened? I've never experienced anything like that in space flight."

"Long story. Will the livestock survive?"

"Depends on how often that's going to happen," she said. I felt bad for her, as her suit was filthy with a brown-green viscous fluid.

"One more time in a hundred ten hours, but then we'll be to our destination," I said.

"That's a long trip to be cooped up like this," she worried. "But I imagine they'll survive. A little warning would have been appreciated."

"My sincerest apologies," I said and cut the comm. I glanced over to where Ada sat and noticed that she'd turned back rather quickly to her navigation station. It wasn't lost on me that Tabby was nowhere to be seen during transition to fold.

"You're busted, Chen," I said.

"What? I told them we'd be transitioning," she said, feigning innocence.

"Quite a coincidence that Xie happened to pull livestock duty on *Hotspur* for transition," I said.

"No coincidence," Ada said. "Just laying out ground rules."

"No more special ground rules or hazing, okay? Xie is a member of the crew and we have to play nice," I said.

"Understood."

"Would you schedule an all-hands service for Mark-Ralph?"

"What about Juanita?"

"I'll give her some time with her husband," I said. "I'm hoping her presence will bring him around."

"Sure, I just don't think having her at the memorial makes sense," Ada said. "There could be hard feelings."

"Let's schedule for 1800 dinner tonight. I don't see a problem locking the bridge down for a short time."

Ada nodded. "We'll make it work. Marny put on fresh supplies at Freedom."

"Thank you. I'm out for a while."

"Understood. I know the crew will appreciate having a memorial," she said.

"We owe it to Mark-Ralph."

My next stop was the brig. We'd rescued the two abandoned Belirand crew from being sold as slaves. With any luck, they had information and were ready to talk. Marny had chosen to use three of the four isolation rooms in the brig, as opposed to keeping our three prisoners in either of the two much larger general population cells.

I knocked on the door before entering the first cell. A woman, a few years older than myself, with considerable bruising on her face considered me from her bench. "Are you Hoffen?" she asked before I could say anything.

"I am. And you are?"

"What does it matter? You killed my crewmates," she said. "You're going to kill me too."

"Is that why I didn't let them take you as a slave on Freedom Station?" I asked.

"I don't know, was it?"

"You're welcome to be grumpy at me, but it won't help your situation. What do you need to make your travel more comfortable?"

"Basic med-patch would be nice," she complained.

"I can arrange for that. How'd you know we were going to Freedom Station?" I asked.

"Above my paygrade," she answered. "We got the call, met up with *Justice Bringer* and you know the rest."

"How about the other survivors? What's their story?"

"They say you're worse than any pirate. We'd be better off dead," she said.

"Pretty horrible so far, eh?"

"Hasn't been great."

"If you recall, you jumped us, not the other way around. You should get your facts straight. I'm offering you a shared cell with the other Belirand crew - if you tell me both your names and ranks," I said. "If you lie, then you can stare at the walls in here. The truth will get you entertainment pads and a shared cell. Incarceration is a hundred times better with someone else to talk to."

"Melanie Webber, Fire Control technician, third class," she said. "Your other prisoner is Braden Webber. No relationship. He just made Boatswain second class. He doesn't know anything either. Belirand doesn't share mission details with low level people like us."

"You know something. You didn't ask about transition," I said.

"Sure. Done plenty of that," she said.

"I'll give you an hour of entertainment pad for every story you record about visiting an alien planet," I said. "That is as long as your story checks out."

"How you going to verify it? I could tell you about purple

unicorns named Maggie Grant and you'd never know if I was telling the truth," she said.

"You're on a ship headed into the deep dark. Your life depends on the good will you establish," I said. "My point is. Don't lie. I'll show good faith and upgrade you to the general population cell and get you a med-patch."

"I thought you were going to check out my story," she said.

"It's not a long trip." I handed her a reading pad and a med patch and closed the cell door. "You start recording stories; we'll see about getting you something interesting to watch."

I knocked on the next cell door and repeated the interview with Braden. Turns out, they were either amazing liars or really were as far down the pecking order as one could get. According to Braden, the chaos aboard *Ferez* right before it was destroyed was incredible. Apparently, *Ferez*'s captain hadn't been told to expect a real battle. Running into a full-up frigate and then a sloop had been well more than they'd expected.

"Let the crew know if you're uncomfortable. If the request is reasonable, we'll do what we can," I said after placing Braden into the general population cell with his crewmate. "You'll understand why we can't allow you to roam freely, though."

Melanie looked at me skeptically, but shrugged when I didn't demand anything further. "Where are you taking us?"

"Planet Ophir," I said.

"Where's that?" Braden asked.

"Look it up," I said and walked off, immediately annoyed by his lack of knowledge about the damage his company had wrought in the universe.

I knocked on the final door and pushed it open. I wasn't surprised when Vince Ferrante rushed the door. I was ready for it and diverted his energy into the wall. He was in no shape to be grappling and I easily pushed him to the ground. "I'm just here to talk, Vince."

"We both know how this ends," he said.

"Juanita is aboard."

His chest fell and he looked at the floor. "You're a monster.

Everything they said is true."

"Nothing they've said is true, as far as I can tell, but I very well could be a monster. I will, however, let Juanita eat dinner with you tonight, then we'll talk. I'll tell you what I told her, though. You keep holding out on me and you'll never get off this ship alive. You're endangering my crew and I won't have it. Think about that while you're having dinner," I said and held my hand out to him to help him from the floor, which of course he slapped away.

"Frak off, Hoffen."

I finally made it back to my quarters and was pleased to see that Tabby was already in bed and the lights were low. I dropped my suit to the ground and slid in under the sheets next to her. She didn't completely wake up, but accepted my presence all the same. It was initially hard to ignore her lightly clothed presence, but neither of us had been getting much sleep and we were more than happy to leave it at spooning. At least, that's what I thought. Apparently, Tabby's alarm was set to leave-enough-time-to-get-frisky mode and my waking dream was beyond fantastic. I wasn't a journal keeper, but if I was, this would have gone down as my favorite way to wake up.

"Now, that's how we do it on the big ship!" Tabby smacked my naked butt on her way to the shower. I lay face down on the bed, wondering if my presence at dinner was really required. "Are you really going to make me soap myself?" I heard from the shower.

It was a good point and I rushed to join her. I'd seen entirely too little of her in the last several days and the invitation was too much to resist. I tried not to be obvious about it, but I suspected we had more than a little of a skip in our step as we joined the crew in the large mess hall.

A whistle sounded and the din of many people speaking dropped as the crew turned toward Tabby and me. "As you were, my friends. This is a celebration of Mark-Ralph." I raised a glass, grabbed from the table in front of me. I had no idea whose glass it was, but I needed to divert attention away from me as quickly as possible.

"Maybe say a few words, Cap?" Marny prodded. "Then we'll eat. Jonathan and I put quite a feast together."

"Of course, but someone's going to need a new glass," I said, which earned me a small laugh from the group.

"Together, we've traveled a long distance. Some longer than others. The danger we've all faced coming to this point in space ... is significant. As a company, we've embarked on a mission of critical importance to the survival of many of our fellow humans. We've agreed to not turn our backs on people in need, but to come running with arms outstretched. For Mark-Ralph, this ended tragically, but he died a hero. And it is as a hero he shall be remembered. Mark-Ralph - who we early on discovered should never be called Ralphie - was a farmer. Just hours before he died, he confided that he didn't mind the gentle beasts we'd purchased from Freedom Station. The wistfulness with which he looked across the green fields of Dirt Side told me something about him. While his soul needed to wander, his heart was firmly attached to his home, Ophir. So raise a glass to our friend and hero, Mark-Ralph. Drink with me and celebrate our friend. We'll take him back to his home and give a proper burial so he can watch over the new herds of Ophir." I swallowed a long drink of what turned out to be water.

"Did you find out why he was killed?" Baker asked.

"I haven't yet, but I'm determined. If I can, I'll share it," I said. "That brings to mind another point I wanted to make and that's just how proud I was when I entered that bar and saw my newest three crew members guarding their fallen mate. You might not have understood what we saw in you – the qualities that would make you good recruits - but I guarantee the rest of that bar did. Baker, you care to give a guess what they saw?"

She looked at me with concern, like I'd put her in the spotlight one too many times.

"That'd be a team, Cap," Marny answered for her.

"Aye, Master Chief. That's what they saw all right," I said. "Now I know we've all seen Mark-Ralph eat and I sure know we've heard him complain about letting the food get cold. So I say we get to it!"

For twenty minutes we enjoyed the spread put in front of us by Marny and Jonathan. We ate fresh beef steak along with potatoes, vegetables and loaves of fresh bread that were crusty, but with a soft interior. I'd learned to enjoy the small moments and while alarmed, wasn't particularly surprised when Mark-Ralph's wake was interrupted by the sound of rumbling beneath our feet. A concussive wave like we'd hit a rock rolled through the deck. Those of us who'd lived through something like this before knew what was coming next as our vac-suits snapped into place and automated hatches snapped shut.

Status, I ordered as Ada and Moonie jumped from their seats and sprinted from the mess.

"*Decompression event on deck three*," my AI replied.

Show location. My heart sank. There was exactly one location where it would matter and when it appeared on my HUD, I knew it was no accident.

"Marny, on me. Nick, we're going to need a hallway sealer," I said. "Tabby, can you help Nick?"

"On it," he replied.

I flicked the schematics I'd already pulled up to Nick and Tabby.

"Sorry to cut it short, folks. Let's get this cleaned up. Our mission can't be ignored for even an hour, it would appear," I said.

It took almost thirty minutes for us to work our way into the breached sections of the brig. An armored plate had given way to the interior pressure and our three prisoners as well as Juanita Ferrante had been sucked out into vacuum.

"Too convenient," Nick said as we watched a replay of the hapless Ferrantes being sucked out through the opening, their bodies lost to fold-space, their fate both romantic and horrible at the same time.

"Did we have repairs there?"

"Checking," Nick answered. "No, nor did we take a strike."

"Who?" I asked.

"My best guess would have been one of Beers' crew. We'll need to go through our data streams," Nick said.

"The timing is convenient," I said.

"What do you mean?"

"I was hoping Juanita would put pressure on Vince to tell us what was going on," I said. "Someone wanted to stop that. With both of them in the cell, the timing was too good."

"You're thinking it was someone onboard," Nick said.

"Who else would have known our schedule?"

"Beth Anne arranged for travel to Freedom Station before we took off. People on Freedom Station knew we were coming. They could have easily communicated with Belirand," Nick said. "If the attack came from someone on the station, it would explain Ferrante and his crew."

I sighed. I wasn't satisfied. Nick's was the simplest explanation, but for whatever reason it just felt off. "How would they know where our brig was located and that we'd keep Ferrante in there?"

"They had access to schematics," Tabby said.

"The only people not at dinner were sucked out into space," Nick said. "If there is evidence, we'll find it."

"Unless that evidence got sucked into space too," I said.

"True."

***

"All hands, prepare for transition to normal space," Ada announced over *Intrepid*'s all ship comm system. We'd adopted a primary transition stance, which put Tabby, Nick and Ortel in *Hotspur* with Moonie, Ada, Marny, Jonathan and me on the bridge of *Intrepid*.

"Three... Two..." My mind flitted to Zebulon and Baker, who were tending the livestock during transition. No doubt, they would be dodging a literal shite storm in a second.

"We have two sensor contacts at fifty thousand kilometers," Ada announced. As she did, the forward video displays switched to tactical mode, showing *Intrepid* and the two objects; the first was huge, the other resolved to a light frigate. It appeared our experiment with moving rocks had been successful.

"I'm reading Petersburg Station and a light frigate, *Dulcinea del Toboso*?" Ada announced, although it came out more like a question.

"*Hotspur* has separated," Jonathan announced.

"Mark both as friendlies," I responded and establish comm.

"Liam, we're heading straight for Ophir. We have animals down," Tabby announced.

"Understood, Tabbs. Ada, make way for Petersburg Station," I said, my breath catching in my throat as I said it. I hoped I'd be able to get beyond that feeling every time I approached the Co-Op where Big Pete had died.

"We're being hailed by *Dulcinea del Toboso*," Moonie said.

"On main," I said. "Greetings, Katherine. I wasn't expecting to see you out and about."

"I could say the same to you, Liam," Captain LeGrande replied with a big smile. "I trust your mission was successful."

"How long has the Co-Op ... Petersburg, rather, been in orbit?" I asked.

"Arrived thirty hours ago. We were just headed up to check out a signal we're receiving," she said.

"From the asteroid?" I was confused. "There's nothing on there but equipment."

"Merrie, send the signal to *Intrepid*," LeGrande said.

"Jonathan, can you make anything of it?" I asked after we'd received it.

"There appear to have been passengers," he replied. "We believe they are in need of medical assistance."

"Ada, get us over there as quickly as you can. Mom, meet me in the cargo bay. We'll take Beth Anne's shuttle," I said, grabbing the bridge's emergency medical kit.

"Baker, grab a rifle and go with 'em," Marny ordered.

I caught up with Mom, who had come from her cabin and was already jogging down the starboard passageway. Together, we took the ramp down to Deck-3 and pulled to a stop in front of the cargo-hold's air-lock.

"Just a second. Baker's on her way," I said.

"What's going on? Aren't we orbiting Ophir?" she asked. She'd just woken up.

"Did you sleep through transition?" I asked.

"Hardly. It woke me up. I just got off watch," she explained.

"The Co-Op asteroid is orbiting Ophir and there's an emergency signal," I said. "Jonathan believes someone hitched a ride and they need medical assistance."

"Of all the stupid things," she exclaimed as Baker slid up behind us, out of breath, but wearing an armored vac-suit and holding a blaster rifle. I raised an eyebrow at her quick change, but didn't question it. I palmed the security panel on the airlock. The cargo bay was pressurized, so we passed through with minimal fuss.

"I'll fly," Mom said, pushing me aside as we climbed into the shuttle that was designed to hold six comfortably or eight snugly. "I remember how you like to push these small crafts."

"Hear that, Baker? Even the captain answers to his mom," I said.

"Darn right, you do," Mom replied.

Link comms Intrepid, bridge. I ordered. I wasn't getting buried further.

"Moonie, can you cycle the air out of the hold? We're loaded up," I said.

"Copy that, Captain," he replied.

"We're closing in on Petersburg Station, Liam," Ada said. "Once you get the green from Moonie, go ahead and take off."

"Roger that," I said. "Mom has the helm."

"I think she gets motion sick," Ada said and I could swear I heard snickering as her voice cut out.

I ignored the jab and found the data-stream Jonathan was sending. The distress signal was originating from the flat side of the shoe-shaped asteroid, near the central elevator shaft that led down into the ruined habitation area. I flicked the information to the shuttle's main vid-screen.

"If someone was going to stow away on the Co-Op, that'd be

GIVE NO QUARTER

the best place to do it," Mom said.

"But who?"

"All I can say is, I better not know him," she said firmly. I was missing something and felt like I was in trouble.

A moment later the doors of the cargo hold slid open and light poured into the hold. The sight of Ophir was beautiful. Unlike Grünholz, the planet was considerably more arid and didn't boast nearly as much cloud cover. Regardless, the site was breathtaking.

Gently, mom lifted the small craft from the deck of Intrepid's cargo hold and scooted out. Pride welled up in my chest as we rounded the bow of Intrepid and Petersburg Station came into view, back-dropped by Ophir. "Look at that," I murmured.

"Pete would have loved seeing this," Mom said as she accelerated, pinning us into our chairs.

"Someone set up habitation domes." I stated the obvious as she set the shuttle down. "And they didn't have a clue what they were doing."

"If he's alive, he's so dead," Mom said.

"What? Who?" I asked.

"Just get out," she said, pushing on my backside impatiently.

I opened the shuttle's door as quickly as the atmo-reclamation system would allow and jumped out of her way. Mom and I bounded across the top of the station to the habitation domes. Baker followed more slowly, struggling in the low gravity. I marveled at how quickly Mom moved. Something was definitely going on.

The airlock on the habitation dome was only good for a single person and there was no way I was getting between Mom and whoever she was after. As I waited for her to cycle through, I noticed that the dome was short on O2.

"Oh, geez," I said when I finally entered. Before me were three kids, one of whom was already in Silver's arms. The other two were on the receiving end of a lengthy and brutal tongue lashing, something I hadn't heard in over ten stans and had hoped to never hear again. I held my hand up to the window of the airlock and muted my external mic. "Baker, you don't want any part of

141

this. Why don't you hold up a moment?"

"Aye, Aye, Captain," she replied.

"What's the situation?" Ada's voice came over the comm.

I patched her into my current external data-stream, adding Nick, Tabby and Marny to the subscribers. It would save more explanations later. I filled them in on the drama.

"Priloe and Milenette stowed away?" Ada asked. "Who's the other kid?"

"Not sure. We're not to the question and answer portion of this sortie just yet," I said.

THREE STEPS FORWARD

I'd set *Hotspur* on the downhill side of the lake that provided water for the Yishuv settlement.

"Tell me again why our cleaning bots can't get this?" I complained as I slogged into four centimeters of sludge left behind by the animals.

"Too much material," Nick replied over the comm link. We'd split duties. He was up on Petersburg Station organizing Merrie, Amon and Ortel as they worked to undo the damage wrought by Belirand. I was to clean out *Hotspur* and fulfill our contract with the Yishuv Council.

"How long does Silver stay mad?" Priloe asked sheepishly, not bothered by the slop which coated the entire hold and was now dripping from the ceiling.

"Give her a few days; she'll cool off," I said. "I'm doing you a favor today."

"This isn't so bad," he said. "The gang used to make me crawl through the privies of homes we broke into on Nannandry. That stuff smells a lot worse."

I laughed and handed him a heavy bundle. "You and Demetria drop this pump in the lake so it has at least a meter and a half of water on top, then stretch the hose back to the hold."

I pulled at the loose pieces of the animal cages we'd assembled on Freedom Station. We were in for a fairly ugly afternoon, but I wasn't about to leave my ship to amateurs.

As for the girl we'd found with Priloe and Milenette, so far, we'd learned that she was abandoned by Oberrhein when they'd been run out of Descartes. Priloe, Ulran and Merley had discovered her trying to survive on an old claim. She was still hoping someone was coming back for her, although it sounded like that was another story entirely. I didn't mind putting the two of them to work, especially considering the amount of work I had available.

"What now?" Priloe asked, handing the hose to me.

"Now," I said, handing the two of them long-handled brooms, "we clean."

By the end of the afternoon, we'd cleaned out enough of the gunk that we were able to sit back on the rocky hill and allow the construction and cleaning bots to take over. At first, the cleaning bot exited the hold every four minutes, ejecting a new batch of biological material that closely resembled what the three of us had all over our suits.

"We should jump in the lake," Priloe said.

Demetria objected immediately. "We'll drown."

"No way! Besides, we'll just wade in," Priloe said, looking to me for confirmation.

"He's right. Your vac-suit will hold the water out; just close your mask," I said.

It was well past sundown when we finally closed up the hold and accompanied the construction bot back to Yishuv. It would be another twelve hours before the cleaning bot would complete its job.

I couldn't help but be impressed with the changes to Yishuv. When we'd first arrived, the settlement had been constructed using primitive building supplies employing a mix of worn technology from ages past in key locations. With the influx of the highly tech-savvy Belirand crew from *Cape of Good Hope*, as well as the donation of an industrial replicator from Anino's company via Jonathan, the settlement was improving quickly. Perhaps the most notable features were the presence of a city-based AI, smart fabrics, and responsive surfaces.

"What do you think of our new Municipal Center plans?" Councilman Bedros clapped me on the back, catching me from behind.

"I don't believe I've seen them," I replied.

"We broke ground two tenday ago," he said, flicking plans of a modern, three story building at me.

"Nice looking building, but that's a lot of glass and steel," I observed. "Do you have manufacturing capacity?"

"Indeed, it is beautiful. I was hoping to talk to you about sourcing zero-g panels from your new station," he said. "Not that I have any idea what I'm talking about."

I laughed. "Given time on your industrial replicator, we could probably facilitate that."

"We'd want future discounts on the product of your kilns." Clearly our meeting wasn't by chance.

"As long as we receive future discounts on the products of your livestock," I shot back.

He stopped and considered me for a moment. "I'll have to keep my eye on you. I wasn't sure if you were serious just then. I assume you've heard that we've lost one of the cows and two of the sheep."

"Unfortunate," I said. "But not unexpected. It was a difficult journey."

"There are those on the council who would like to change our deal as a result," he said.

"You mean, the deal where we are allowed to finish recruiting after putting our lives on the line to bring back livestock so you can eat food that's more palatable?" I couldn't withhold the hostility from my voice.

"It is not helpful that Mark-Ralph was killed," he said.

"Your council has remarkably short memories," I said. "Councilman, we have a deal. We kept our end of it and you will keep yours. I will not be summoned to your council as if I were a schoolboy to be scolded. Tomorrow our recruits will report for duty. After that, I would love nothing more than to negotiate how Petersburgh Station could supply nano-steel and zero-g panels for Yishuv."

To his credit, Councilman Bedros did not immediately speak, but considered my words, looking at the ground as he did so. "I previously learned you are not one to mince words." He slowly looked up at me. "You must understand that while your crew has brought salvation to Yishuv, you have also brought much change and a perception of new danger. From what we have learned of Belirand, if they choose to destroy us, they would not find it difficult. Unlike you, we have no means to defend ourselves."

"Setting yourselves against my company will not change how Belirand treats you," I retorted.

He nodded. "Perhaps not, but we'd like to be part of the process that decides how to move forward."

"We have no desire to shape how Yishuv grows," I answered.

"That is not what I'm referring to. Let me be plain spoken. We would like to approve the missions you're embarking on," he said.

I'm sure my cheeks flushed and I was glad for the darkening sky that hid my visceral reaction. "One step at a time, Councilman. Let's get those recruits delivered and we can work out a contract for building materials."

"And if we refuse to deliver the recruits?"

"If you default on our contract, it will change the relationship between Loose Nuts and Yishuv in a negative way. If you're asking for details, I don't have them. I suspect you've considered a number of scenarios ..." I looked at him for confirmation. A short nod was all I needed. "I'd suggest you're thinking short term, in that case. My guess is that you've taken measures to protect the industrial replicator and the recently delivered livestock just in case we try to make a move on them. Is that about right?"

"I don't think this is an appropriate discussion ..."

Even with the darkening sky, I could see I'd struck home. "You've misjudged us. We value the lives of the people of Yishuv too much to threaten those resources. No, the threat is that when we recover new refugees we will seed a new settlement as far away from Yishuv as we can place them and we give that new settlement the benefit of our trade and technology. Simply put, Yishuv becomes irrelevant to us."

"I will see to it that the volunteers are not delayed. There is no reason for us to grow apart," he replied smoothly. "Shall we proceed to the municipal building site?"

I nodded and followed along with him. Thirty minutes later I slumped into a chair in the corner of one of the revitalized settlement's many cafes. "Liam, what are you up to?" Tabby's voice came over my comm. She and most of the non-Ophir based crew had spent the day working on Petersburg Station, moving the defensive guns into place and setting up habitation domes.

"Just finished up. *Hotspur* is out of action until tomorrow 0500," I said. "Are you guys coming down?"

"That bad, eh?" she asked.

"I need a shower and a suit cleaner. How did things work out today with Merrie and Amon?" I asked. I'd wondered how the young couple who'd been Yishuv's engineer and blacksmith were adjusting.

"Funny to watch. Neither of them have experienced zero-g, so that was entertaining. They're smart though and Amon is strong like Marny, though not as flexible. Ohh... you'll never guess! It sounds like Ortel wants to stay on the station and run the mining operation. Did you put him up to that?" Tabby asked. It felt good to just hear her go on about things for a while and I took a pull on my beer.

"First I've heard of it," I said. "I wonder if the idea of being crew wasn't working out for him. Did Nick say anything?"

"Said he wanted to discuss it with you, but that he thought it sounded interesting," she said.

"How did things go with Xie?"

"We're not going to be friends, Liam, but she certainly worked hard today, just like everyone else. Oh, there's Nick now. Looks like we're headed out and we'll see you down there soon," she said. "Your mom wants to have a chat with Priloe back on the station."

"Good. They need to work things out," I said. "My guess is she's not sailing with us anymore. I can't see her bringing Priloe along and I can't imagine her leaving Milenette behind."

"She as much as said that today," Tabby said. "Didn't want to speak for her, though."

***

"Get up!" Tabby placed her foot squarely in my back and pushed. I'd been ignoring my 0430 alarm and it was now 0445. I'd promised to go running with her before we met with the new recruits.

"Have mercy." I rolled from bed and pulled on my clean grav-suit.

"What's that smell?" Tabby asked as I opened the ramp. The funky smell from the remnants of the material we'd flushed out the previous day was wafting back into the now very clean hold.

"Right, let's move the ship up next to the gates," I said, closing the hold back up.

After moving the ship, we set out for our run and by 0545 we were back, showered and had coffee brewing.

"There they are." Tabby pointed at a single file line of people slowly jogging our way.

In the lead was the slim figure of Baker, closely followed by Zebulon and five more I recognized, but couldn't put names with. Marny was jogging beside them. The contrast was striking and it wasn't between Marny and the rest. The disparity was between Marny, Zebulon and Baker and the other five recruits. Something in the present crew's bearing was simply different.

"Company, halt," Marny ordered as they came even with Tabby and me.

"Welcome to Loose Nuts; Burford, Cary, Divelbiss, Hill-Clark, and Kerwin. First, if anyone wants to turn back, this would be a good time to do it. I'm hoping you've had a chance to talk with Baker and Zebulon and get a good feel for what we're about. If this isn't for you, no hard feelings," I said. "Anyone feel like they've taken a bad turn here?" No one in the group spoke up.

"You've about twelve hours to figure that out. After that, we'll be underway and you'll be part of the crew," I said. "Once you step aboard *Hotspur*, you're under Master Chief Bertrand's command. Anything to add, Marny?"

"Aye, Cap. If you'd run us over to the back gate, Yishuv set out a significant cache of supplies," she said. "Compliments of

Councilman Bedros."

I smiled. He had either been listening last night or was a really great politician. I'd take either if it set us up with fresh supplies.

"Give me an all-clear when you're ready to lift off. We'll be on the bridge. For the rest of you, welcome aboard," I said and turned back to the forward door that led to the berth deck.

"Cap, give us fifteen minutes," Marny instructed as we set down next to the back gates.

"Roger that." Tabby and I watched Marny work with the new recruits and organize the stevedore bot to load the hold. It was unusual for Marny to miss a deadline and, sure enough, fifteen minutes later we sailed through the upper atmosphere of planet Ophir on our way to raft-up with *Intrepid*.

Catwalk extended, Marny disembarked with her recruits and Tabby and I then sailed on to Petersburg Station, coming to rest on the flat side. Much work had already been completed and I was surprised to see the refinery had already churned out several tonnes of iron ingots.

"They're waiting for us inside," Tabby said, motioning to the habitation domes that had sprung up like so many toadstools in a damp bilge. I followed her to the central-most dome and the smell of something baked hit me straight away.

"What is that?" I asked.

"Apparently, Amon is something of a baker," Tabby said. "He says it comes from being a blacksmith."

In the main room were Mom, Nick, Katherine LeGrande, Jonathan, Ortel and Merrie. "There you are," Mom got up and gave me a hug. "Everything go okay picking up your new recruits?"

"Sure did," I said. "Marny just transferred them to *Intrepid* a few minutes ago for orientation."

"The recruits are probably the first thing we should talk about," Nick said.

"Oh?"

"Katherine says Yishuv is getting pushy about ownership of *Dulcinea*," Nick answered, not really following his own topic.

"The Council believes that since the original crew is now part of Yishuv, they have rights to the craft," she said. "I explained to them how maritime law with regards to derelicts has worked since the beginning of time and they were unmoved."

"Nonstarter for me," I said. "I don't mind leaving her behind for defense, but I also need to be able to count on her in a pinch. I'm not giving her to Yishuv."

"I agree," Nick said. "As does Marny."

"Katherine?" I asked. "How do you feel about this? You're part of Yishuv's council now."

"I resigned this morning. There are too many strong-headed people and I've had enough of that for one lifetime," she said.

"That's interesting," I said, noncommittally. There was no way that Nick wasn't a million kilometers ahead of me in this conversation. "Mom, rumor is, you're not coming with us to the Aeratroas region."

"Liam," Tabby swatted my arm, annoyed. "I told you that in confidence."

Mom smiled at Tabby and turned to me. "I am not. I won't abandon Milenette and Priloe twice. Not to mention Demetria."

"And Ortel? What about you?" I asked. "Might as well get it all out on the table."

Ortel squirmed in his chair while looking at the floor. He was obviously uncomfortable with what he had to say next. "I thought I wanted to be a sailor. But there's so much need here for mining. At home, I was just one of the boys, even though I knew every piece of equipment as well as anyone could. Here, I have something to add. I'd like to help run the mining operation, train miners, and organize it. This asteroid has forty stans of work on it alone." The stan he was referring to was a stan-year of work for one miner and from what I recalled, his was a low estimate.

"What's all this have to do with my recruits? I think you all have this figured out and are waiting for me to connect the dots. I think I see most of it; someone want to just give it to me straight?" I asked.

Nick chuckled. From anyone else, it might have sounded

patronizing, but he knew I'd been working on other issues. He was also smart enough to anticipate the decisions I would think made sense. "Sure. Ortel, Amon and - to a lesser degree - Priloe and Demetria mine the asteroid while Merrie runs production and fabrication. Silver is in charge of the station and Dulcinea, with Katherine second in command. They need three of our recruits and an engineer," Nick summed up.

"What are the recruits for?" I asked.

"Exploring this solar system in *Dulcinea*," Nick answered. "We can't expect them to sail her without crew."

"You're all good with this?" I asked, looking around the room. It made sense, but it felt like three steps forward, two steps back.

"We've all had a part in crafting it," Katherine LeGrande answered.

"I'd like to get Ada's take." I said.

"I'm here, Liam," Ada answered through comm. "I'm on watch on *Intrepid*, but I've been involved in the negotiations. Your biggest problem is an engineer."

"Tabby?"

"I'm in. Engineer is easy, Ada, as much as I hate admitting it. Moonie is the best choice. He knows the ship," Tabby said.

"That leaves us short an engineer," I said.

"We have another one," Nick said.

"I know. I just can't stand the thought of her on the bridge," Tabby said.

"You wouldn't dare," Ada chimed in.

"Xie?" Mom asked. "I wouldn't trust that woman..."

"I have," I said. "Look, I know she's done some crappy things in the past and she paid for that. I trust Xie Mie-su."

"Have you forgotten that someone has been selling us down-the-river to Belirand?" Tabby asked. "And Xie had plenty of opportunity to do that."

"I think you're forgetting who was unconscious in the medical bay on our trip to Freedom Station. A trip she earned because she was trying to save my ship, might I add," I said.

"You can't keep treating her like a second-class citizen and ask her to serve on the bridge," Nick said. "Keep her as crew and don't talk to her if need be." It was unusual for him to get involved in squabbles and I was surprised to see him come down on Xie's side, since she'd both vamped him as well as shot him on our first trip together. To be fair, he'd also shot me on that same trip.

"You could leave Mie-su here," Katherine said.

"No way," Tabby said. "If she is bad, I'm going to be there when we catch her."

"Tabby. That's hardly right," I said.

"Look pal, you're jamming her down my throat. I don't have to like it."

"But we can treat her respectfully," Ada said. "Right, Tabbs?" I could remember a time when Tabby had been jealous of my relationship with Ada. It gave me some hope for Xie.

"I can do respectful, especially if we can spar," she growled.

"I'll talk to Moon," Nick said. "I'd like to consider the assignments as rotations more than permanent positions, though, so we'll need to look for another engineer to recruit."

"Speaking of. Did we find out what happened to our armor panels next to the brig?" I asked.

"Everything was lost in the decompression," Nick said. "We were able to repair the damage. Whoever caused the problem wasn't looking to permanently hurt the ship."

"How long before you're back in the main portion of the Petersburg Station?" I asked, looking at Mom.

"Ortel?" she asked.

"The missiles made a mess of things, but as you know, they fired on an iron rock. Some of the material was simply vaporized, other material was slagged. I'd guess we're looking at three tenday," he said.

I nodded. "Nick, could you talk Bedros into meeting us on *Intrepid* before we leave? I think he'd like a tour of things and I promised I'd negotiate manufacturing a kiln with Yishuv's replicator. We could certainly use the glass for the station," I said.

"On it. Would you like a case of whiskey I put aside as a bartering chip?" Nick asked.

"I'd take a bottle or two. That'd be a great touch," I said. "Mom, how many of those iron ingots can we take without cutting into your sheet needs?"

She looked to Merrie. "That's more Merrie's call."

"Take what you need. I've worked out a schedule with Ortel. Clearing the rooms will generate the ore we require. We really need that armored glass kiln manufactured on the industrial replicator, though," she said.

"I fail to see why Yishuv is insisting on controlling the replicator as they are," Jonathan interjected. "It was a gift from the Anino Corporation."

"Leverage," I answered. "It gives them the ability to get things from us."

"But Loose Nuts has demonstrated nothing less than complete generosity," Jonathan said.

"Not true," Nick said. "We are unwilling to share our ships."

"We accept your point," Jonathan said. "Not all human behavior is interesting."

I laughed. "I couldn't agree more. Would you like to negotiate with Bedros for an armored glass kiln?"

"We would not," he answered.

PLANET K-A0223B

"Let's keep things simple," I said. It was 1600 and Merrie, Councilwoman Peraf, Councilman Bedros, Nick and I had been negotiating for an hour and a half in the civilian conference room aboard *Intrepid*. "We need these parts manufactured." I flicked the list to Bedros, although I knew he already had it. "It will take three tenday to complete and we'll provide the metals. In return, we'll supply the glass, steel sheet and nano-beam for your municipal building."

"How is that a reasonable trade?" Peraf asked. I rarely wanted to hit people for just saying things, but this old woman had punched my buttons one too many times. "The industrial replicator is more than sufficient for manufacturing building materials."

"The industrial replicator, while extremely versatile, is not suited to repetitive tasks, such as creating glass, steel sheet and steel beam," Merrie explained patiently. "The parts list I've provided would be used to create manufacturing equipment that will allow us to produce armored-glass, light-weight steel sheet, nano-crystalized steel beams and more. For three tenday of production on the replicator you will receive over forty tenday of goods."

"If that's the case, then we should be doing this in Yishuv," Peraf said, crossing her arms.

"Doesn't work that way," I said. "These parts must be manufactured in zero-g. That is the value of Petersburg Station."

"I'm sure there are other options," she harrumphed.

"You have as many options as you can dream up, Councilwoman Peraf," I said. "None of which are relevant to this negotiation. Like I explained to Councilman Bedros, if you simply

154

don't want to work with us, just say so and we can part ways. Otherwise we need cooperation. Every deal we've offered weighs heavily to the advantage of Yishuv, yet every conversation turns into an argument."

"It's simple, Captain Hoffen. You took our ship," Peraf said. "What will you take next?"

I looked to Bedros for help and he shook his head, looking at the table. I could tell he was embarrassed. "We are stronger together than we are apart, Peraf," I said, standing. "We'll leave the two of you to discuss our proposal. You are under no compulsion to accept and we will return you to your homes upon request. Please understand. When *Intrepid* leaves orbit the deal will no longer be valid."

"When will that be?" she asked.

"We accept," Bedros interrupted, standing with me and offering his hand. "I hope you will forgive us, Captain Hoffen and esteemed members of Loose Nuts. We are used to bickering over limited supplies and making decisions about how best to reallocate dwindling resources. We are having difficulty adjusting to this time of unparalleled growth. We recognize your generosity and hope that someday we will be able to repay it both in action and in word."

He smiled as he caught the look of shock in my face at his words. For a moment, I didn't have words to respond with. Fortunately, Peraf filled in for the both of us.

"You fool. You'll sell us down the river." She stood and walked to the door, which opened for her, although it was blocked by Zebulon, who was wearing an armored vac-suit. "Move, you tree cutting idiot."

To his credit, he didn't move.

"Mr. Zebulon, would you escort the Councilwoman to the shuttlecraft?" I asked.

"Aye, aye, Captain," he replied.

"Don't judge her too harshly," Bedros said apologetically. "We're all playing catch up."

"When will you be able to start manufacturing the parts?" I

asked. I wasn't about to let go of the conversation.

"I believe we have other priorities that also require attention," he replied.

"Five tenday from tomorrow," I replied. "After that, every day delay will cost two percent of the materials that we would otherwise deliver. If all parts are not delivered by the end of the seventh tenday, we will consider the contract to be void."

"That sounds harsh," Bedros answered. "What of a schedule for delivery of materials from the kilns and presses?"

"You will receive seventy percent of our manufacturing capability until fulfilled," I said.

"How will we hold you to this?"

"What other customer do we have?" I asked.

"I'm going out on a limb here, Captain Hoffen, but on behalf of Yishuv, I agree to your terms."

"In that case, there's just one thing to be done," I said.

"Oh?"

I nodded to Nick who had already produced a bottle of aged Scotch Whiskey.

"Oh! Very well, then."

"Merrie, are you comfortable with the shuttle?" I asked. I hadn't seen if she was capable of flying Beth Anne's craft.

She gave me a sly grin. "I'm not sure what all the hubbub is about. Is there more than directing the AI where to go?"

"Busted," I laughed. "But don't pass that around or I'll be out of a job." I escorted her and Bedros down the passageway to the catwalk that would take them to the shuttle.

"Nicely done," Nick said once they were through the airlock. "Ada thought you were coming across the table on the old lady."

"Ada was watching?"

"We were broadcasting on the bridge," Nick said. "Apparently, they had a pool on if you were going to go off on her."

"Who set that up? You guys are horrible!" I said as we entered the bridge to the sound of applause. I shook my head, mostly in embarrassment.

My eyes came to rest on Moon Rastof and it caused me a

moment of confusion. "Captain?" he asked.

"I was under the impression you were transferring to Petersburg Station for this rotation," I said.

"That was the plan," he said. "But I talked to Jenny Caton. She was second engineer on *Strumpet*."

"Sent you a comm," Nick said quietly behind me.

"Right. Welcome aboard, in that case," I said sitting back into the captain's chair and listing the personnel assignments. There was a never-ending set of things I needed to keep track of. I was surprised that I felt disappointed to see we'd transferred Zebulon to *Dulcinea* and that he'd left on the shuttle with Merrie. Baker and three of the four new recruits were staying aboard.

I started reading through the different reports that demanded my attention. An hour later, I looked up, believing I'd addressed the most critical issues. I was pleased to discover that even with Moon remaining on staff, Xie had been upgraded to the engineering watch rotation.

"Tabbs, can we get Xie into the exercise training rotation also? She's an expert at Aikido," I said.

"Oh, hells yes," Tabby replied.

I wasn't sure I wanted to know why she thought it was such a good idea, but I'd certainly learned a lot from training with the woman.

"Liam, we're thirty minutes from departure. Marny requests we lock down all external access ports and retract the catwalk," Ada said.

"Agreed. Let's orbit Petersburg at five kilometers," I said. We'd been sitting at zero delta with the station and I wanted to give Mom and Katherine the heads-up that we were on the move.

"Copy that, Liam," Ada replied.

"All hands," I announced once we started moving. "First, I'd like to welcome our newest crew members: Burford, Divelbiss, Hill-Clark and Kerwin. You're no-doubt wondering what you've gotten yourselves into and I for one appreciate your leap of faith. Second, now that we've pushed off, I'd like to share details of our mission. We have contact with another base that the Belirand

Corporation abandoned. It will require the longest jump in fold-space we've ever made and we'll end up in the Dwingeloo galaxy. Just as with the jump to Ophir, we have no idea what we're getting into. We only know that a mission was abandoned and we're going to see about rendering aid. The trip will take two hundred forty-three hours and we will be entering a system with the designation K-A0223B. Hoffen, out."

"Ada, the helm is yours," I said.

"Copy that, Liam, the helm is mine," she replied.

I hated the wait and busied myself reviewing the upcoming watch cycles. Baker and Tabby had the first watch after we transitioned. We'd settled on a two-person watch, with one officer and one sailor. Neither Marny nor I were given regular watches - for different reasons - and this provided five rotating watches, with each watch lasting four hours.

With ten minutes remaining, Marny entered the fire-control room, followed by our new recruits who all looked exhausted. Baker caught my eye and smiled. No doubt Marny's initiation had been tough.

"Greetings, Master Chief," I said as she sat in the workstation that connected the fire-control room to the bridge. "How are your recruits faring?"

"Good effort today," she said. "I believe they'll sleep soundly."

"Count me in for exercise rotation," I said.

"I have you and Xie scheduled for 0600, Cap," she replied. "Want to work on close quarters grappling tomorrow against larger opponent? If we run into that Kroerak species, I believe it will come in handy."

"Xie's the master, but I'm game," I said.

Ada broke into our conversation. "Hailing Petersburg Station, this is *Intrepid*."

"Petersburg Station, this is Hoffen, go ahead," Mom answered.

"Silver, we're about to break orbit on the station," Ada replied.

"Copy that." Mom showed up larger than life on the immense vid-screen that covered the forward bulkhead and most of the domed ceiling.

"We'll see you in a few tenday," I said. "Good luck digging out."

"Stay safe, Liam."

"Love you, Mom," I said and closed the comm.

"Transition to fold-space in thirty seconds," Ada warned over the ship's public address.

"Oh geez," I said to myself and sat back into the chair. Eyes closed or open didn't seem to matter and I braced myself for the unpleasantness. At least I didn't have to worry about livestock.

***

The next morning came plenty early and I decided to run with Tabby before our Aikido training with Xie and the recruits. When we arrived in the gym, the recruits were already assembled in a line, Marny nowhere to be seen. They snapped to attention as we entered and I remembered my first run at this.

"At ease, everyone," I replied. "I'm sure the Master Chief has been instructing you on our relaxed version of military conduct. It will take some getting used to, but there's value in it and it's not optional. If you believe someone's taking advantage of rank, I'd like you to talk to me about it. If you have a problem with me, Master Chief Bertrand is a good first stop. With that out of the way, tell me who you are and what your profession on Ophir was. Let's start on the starboard side."

I purposefully looked to the starboard side of the line. My HUD showed the man's name as Burford.

A medium-sized man with dark hair and a well-groomed beard stepped forward. "Everyone calls me Burf. I was in sanitation, worked on septic systems."

"Welcome, Burford. Glad to have someone aboard who feels my pain," I said. "How are you finding life aboard ship?"

"Pain, sir?" he questioned. "As for life aboard, the Master Chief was rather hard on us yesterday. I'm not used to quite so much running."

"It will get easier; I promise. And I'm the resident expert in all things septic," I said smiling. "And you?" I looked at the next in line.

Burf stepped back and a giant of a man stepped forward. My HUD had his name as Divelbiss.

"I'm Divelbiss," he nodded his light brown head politely. Like Burf, he had a paunch that Marny and the AI would be shortly taking care of. "I worked in forestry service and odd jobs."

"Any nickname?" I asked.

"Nope. Just Divelbiss," he replied.

"Welcome, Divelbiss. And next?"

"Jenny Hill Clark." A small, thirty-stan woman stepped forward as Divelbiss stepped back. "I worked with Baker as a mason."

"Three names? That's unusual for Yishuv, isn't it?" I asked.

"It is," she agreed. "Just something my family has always done. Most people just call me Jenny."

"Welcome. And finally?"

"Kerwin." The man was about my age and I could tell he didn't like military discipline. "I didn't have a permanent job. I was a floater, I guess. Was trying to get into the protectors."

"Care to elaborate?" I asked.

"Nah."

"Alright then. Welcome aboard," I said.

"Any brawlers in the group? Folks who like to mix it up?" I asked. I looked down the line. I wasn't overly surprised to find that this group didn't have quite the same aggressive nature as our first.

"I'm a brawler," Xie Mie-su announced from the entry to the gym as she sauntered in, gaining everyone's attention.

"Recruits, I'd like to introduce you to Xie Mie-su. She'll be your trainer for today's session," I said.

"Figures," Tabby grumbled under her breath.

"Divelbiss, you're a nice hunk of a man, aren't you? Join me on the mat, will you?" Xie purred.

"I'd join that," I overheard Kerwin murmur.

"Ms. Mie-su, I believe you had a volunteer," I said. "Kerwin has requested to join you as well." Kerwin shot me a look of concern, unsure what to do now that I'd overheard his obviously inappropriate statement.

"Two for the price of one. How can a girl resist?" Xie didn't miss a beat. "Yes, of course, Mr. Kerwin, please join us. Today we will learn about falling and if you are very lucky, you will understand what it means to fall poorly. Once you learn what it means to fall poorly, we will start to learn how to fall less so."

"You're talking in riddles," Kerwin said as he approached.

"We shall simplify. Place me on the deck, gently or with force, this is your decision," she replied. Kerwin looked back at me, as did Divelbiss.

"Don't look at me. I've struggled to drop her to the deck with a blaster pistol," I said.

"I don't want to hurt you, now," Divelbiss said as he approached and tried to grab the much smaller woman.

"Do not worry about such things." Xie danced around him. It was at this moment Kerwin chose to charge. Having worked with Xie for many hours, I saw the train wreck well before either of the recruits. I winced for them both as she gracefully accepted Kerwin' charge, rolled onto her back and flung him into the approaching Divelbiss. It happened so quickly it looked quite random, but I knew better.

"Impressive," Tabby said in a low voice as she observed. "She was manipulating Kerwin the entire time, but had us watching Divelbiss. Her timing was exquisite."

"Almost sounds like you're warming up."

"Don't push it."

It was a well-worn recipe for training. First, get their attention with an outrageous demonstration, then work to break down bad habits and form new ones. Just as with Zebulon and Baker, our recruits were unskilled in any form of martial art. We had to start from the ground up. By the time we reached K-A0223B, they'd have slightly better skills than they did now, but I wouldn't make the mistake I'd made with Moon Rastof. I wouldn't put them into combat before they were ready.

"Nice job, all," I said once we'd used the time Marny had

allotted. "Hit the showers. I'm sure you all know your schedules."

"Xie, do you have a moment?" Tabby asked as the group started breaking up. I tried not to spin around right away, but I was intensely curious.

"Of course, Tabitha Masters," she replied, much of the normal silkiness in her voice missing.

"Are you open to training with me?"

In a hundred stans I wouldn't have guessed this would come from Tabby.

"I am not sure, Tabitha. Your speed and strength are formidable. Some might think you're looking for an opportunity for additional hazing of an undesirable crew member," Xie replied smoothly.

"As appealing as that sounds, no. You are tremendously skilled and I would like to learn from you," Tabby replied.

"Let us get a measure of each other," Xie replied.

Without warning, Tabby lunged for Xie at full combat speed. Xie, expecting the strike, raised her arm to intercept, but lacked sufficient strength to deflect. I knew what was coming next, Tabby would follow with either a knee or a left-hand combination, expecting the block. The real damage would come from the second blow. Xie, however, accepted the strike, recognizing the futility of struggling against it. Instead, she held onto Tabby's outstretched arm, rolled onto her back and used her momentum to flip Tabby over. It was a move I'd been on the receiving end of too many times to appreciate. Unlike me, however, Tabby turned in mid-air, twisting just enough to land on her side instead of her back. The loud thwack on the floor reverberated through the gymnasium. She popped to her feet coming up to face Xie, who was already standing.

Xie pulled her hands together as if praying and closed her eyes, nodding to Tabby as she did. "Most impressive, Tabitha Masters. You fall like a stone in heavy gravity, but lose no advantage. Your speed is even more than I expected after your surgery. There is much Aikido would offer you. I am a poor teacher, but am willing."

Life aboard ship settled into a comfortable routine. In fold-space, there are few exterior dangers and we primarily focused on preparing for the mission ahead. With a new class of recruits, training jumped to the forefront and our days were split between exercise, systems training, combat training and meal preparation.

Beyond responsibility to the crew, we also spent time in the bridge conference room planning our upcoming mission to the K-A0223B system.

"Why would anyone try to colonize that moon?" I asked. "Between its rotation, its orbit around the gas planet and the planet's orbit around the star, it would barely support life. The temperature ranges are minus five to sixty and that can happen within a tenday."

"If Belirand wanted to establish a foothold in the Aeratroas region, it would be a perfect location though," Nick replied.

"It belies a certain naiveté regarding the Kroerak, however," Jonathan added. "K-A0223B is well within their territory."

"Do you think we could run into a Kroerak patrol?" Marny asked.

"We believe it to be unlikely, although possible. Even the Kroerak would find this system to be of minimal value unless there was a colony," Jonathan replied.

"We should be prepared for hostilities," Marny said.

"In the case where we encounter no other large ships, I'd like the initial ground team to include myself, Tabby, Nick and Xie," I said. "I'd like to bring you, Marny, but I'd feel more comfortable with you sitting behind *Intrepid*'s guns, just in case."

"What about Jonathan?" Tabby asked.

"Our physical presence isn't required to gain information in the same way yours is. We'll send a probe with you," he said.

"You're not questioning Xie?" Ada asked, turning to Tabby.

"We're working out our differences," Tabby replied.

"Oooh, so that's why she's been wearing med-patches..."

I looked between the two women and tried to determine if it was something I needed to deal with. In the end, I decided that Xie wouldn't appreciate me stepping in.

"I'm sending Divelbiss and Clark," Marny said. I wasn't surprised at her choice, even though they were about as far apart as two sailors could get. Where Jenny Hill Clark was small-framed, Divelbiss was the largest crewman we'd had aboard. Both of them were relatively easygoing and Marny had been pleased with the progress they'd made in the last ten days. I suspected this assignment was Marny's reward for rising to the challenge.

"We're thirty minutes to transition," Ada reported. "Liam, I assume you're staying on the bridge until we know if there are hostiles in-system?"

"That's right, Ada," I said.

We stood and I pulled Tabby in for a quick kiss. "Be safe."

"I'll do my best," she said and ran her finger under my chin as she turned to walk away.

Back in the captain's chair, I checked the myriad statuses that had already been checked by so many. It was a nervous habit, but certainly didn't hurt anyone. Mostly, I was trying to take my mind off the transition from fold-space.

"Three … two … one …" I breathed out and tried to quiet my mind as the universe around me went nuts. I had decided to attack my issue with transitions head on, using breathing techniques I'd researched. I wasn't entirely successful, but I survived.

My first look was at the tactical display. It would take a few moments for *Intrepid*'s high resolution scanners to fill in the details of nearby space and then reach out tens of thousands of kilometers at lesser and lesser resolution, searching for anything that resembled a threat. I finally let go of the breath I'd been holding when the only thing to appear was the beautiful gas planet and its eight orbiting moons.

"Captain, we're clear and dropping probes," Marny announced.

We'd decided to manufacture and drop information gathering probes. They wouldn't be immediately useful, but if we ever got back this way, we'd be able to retrieve them.

"Roger that. I'm making my way to *Hotspur*," I said.

"We've got your back, Cap."

I fought adrenaline which attempted to propel me at a sprint down *Intrepid*'s passageway to *Hotspur* and settled instead into a jog. Once outside the ship, I had an unimpeded view of the poorly named gas giant. The raging storms and massive swirls of gas were beyond gorgeous and I wondered how anyone could simply assign a number to something so wondrous.

"Looking sharp, crew!" I chirped as I passed Divelbiss and Jenny Hill Clark who were both seated on *Hotspur*'s bridge couch. They were quite the odd couple in their armored vac-suits. Divelbiss made the couch and Clark look like toys. I'd heard the term gentle giant before and knew it applied to Divelbiss, but any sane person would be very cautious before assuming that about him. "Ready for this?" I asked, patting Nick's shoulder as I passed.

"What's got you so fired up?" Tabby asked as I slipped into the pilot's chair next to her.

"Been waiting for this moment for a few months now. Light it up!" I said.

At first, we fell gently away from *Intrepid*, but as soon as we'd established a safe distance, Tabby fired the engines. I listened while she negotiated navigation with Ada over a shared channel.

"Let's take the last ten thousand in stealth-mode," Nick suggested.

"Understood," Tabby agreed.

The moon we approached grew in our view screen. It was large for a moon, half again larger than Earth's own. It would have natural gravity of about .2g. Large patches of green dotted the surface, although there were more red-brown patches than anything. I searched for signs of open water and wasn't surprised when I didn't find them.

"I'm locked in on the signal," Nick said. "Do you have it, Tabby?"

"Roger that," she replied. "We're ten minutes out."

"There's atmosphere?" I asked.

"Not enough," Nick said. "With suits, you'd be good. There are low levels of oxygen but too much ammonia."

"I have a visual," Tabby said. She'd dropped into the valley of a mountain range that had been formed by volcanic activity. The glint of sun reflecting off metal caught my eye immediately.

"What is that?" I asked.

"They built something into the side of that mountain," Nick said. *Hotspur*'s forward holo zoomed in on a forty-meter-tall, twenty-meter wide steel and glass wall that was built into the rock face of the mountain. A weathered Belirand Logo emblazoned across the front provided ample evidence that we'd found the right spot.

"I'm setting down," Tabby said.

The wide rock apron in front of the building was strewn with fallen rock and it appeared there had been substantial damage to the building. Tabby chose a relatively clear spot and spooled down the engines.

"I'm picking up a lot of debris," Nick said. "The structure has taken a lot of damage, although it's not clear what from."

"Doesn't speak well for survivors," I said. "I want you to stay on *Hotspur*. I've a bad feeling and want the turrets manned." I was adjusting our original plan, but the situation had also changed. "The rest of you are with me."

A light wind gently buffeted us as we exited the ship and for a moment I searched the barren landscape, looking for any sign of life. As we approached, my stomach tightened at the scene of destruction before us. The heavy front doors had been ripped off and lay on the ground several meters from where they'd originally hung. Thick armored glass windows on the first level were broken through or completely missing.

Involuntarily, I pulled my blaster rifle around, pointing it into the darkened structure as we picked a path through the debris field.

"We're going in," Tabby said as she bravely walked through the ruined opening. I followed behind. "Frak," she cussed quietly.

"Oh, man," I said as my eyes adjusted to the darkened interior. Dozens of vac-suited partial human remains littered the once highly polished marble floors.

KNUCKLE SANDWICH

"Tabby, sweep left. Xie, sweep right. We'll meet at the back. Jenny, I want you to hold this door," I said, turning to the woman who, twelve days ago, had been a bricklayer. "All that means is you stay here and sound off if anything weird happens."

"And you should avoid shooting at us," Tabby said.

"What are you looking for, Captain?" Xie asked.

"Some explanation for the bodies," I said. A short burst of static over the tactical channel communicated that Tabby was acknowledging and headed out. Xie followed suit in the opposite direction.

With Divelbiss close on my six, I crossed over to where the largest concentration of corpses lay. The first remains were mostly contained within their vac-suits. A mummified woman of indeterminate age had fallen, holding an older model blaster pistol.

"Jonathan, you have any way to read the data-stream on this woman's suit?" I asked. Jonathan was still on *Intrepid* but they'd upgraded the sensors on my grav-suit to provide a richer remote experience.

"No. It appears that suit's memory was purged," he replied.

"Why would they do that?"

"To keep the captors from gaining information the suits contain," he said.

"I'll check a few more," I said and moved to the next.

"Divelbiss, help me," I said as I pulled on a body.

To his credit, Divelbiss leaned down and grabbed the shoulders of a large corpse as we tried to roll it over. The sight that greeted us was horrific; the legs of the man had been severed and his chest cavity appeared to have been carved out.

"I'm going to be sick." Divelbiss stood up quickly and stumbled away, running for the door, tripping over body parts as he did.

"Breathe!" I said as I jumped up and followed after him. "Deep breaths!" I caught up with him just as his face plate fogged with a light brown paste. I placed my hand on the side of his helmet and cycled his mask open. We couldn't survive for long in the moon's light atmosphere, but we could certainly open up for an emergency. He looked at me in horror as atmo rushed past his ears and the suit attempted to balance the pressure differential. His mask slammed closed with the majority of Divelbiss' breakfast splattered across my shoulder.

"How'd you know to do that?"

"Spacer trick," I said. "Jenny. I need you to step in. Divelbiss, switch out and take the door."

"Aww Captain, I got this," he complained.

"Not a demotion, Divelbiss. You get your legs back and I'll need you back in here," I said.

"What do you need, Captain?" Jenny Hill Clark arrived as Divelbiss walked back to the door.

"Keep on my six. I've a grisly task and I need someone keeping a heads-up," I said. I walked back and started working through the corpses.

"Looks like these are all security forces, at least those who had intact uniforms," I said as Xie and Tabby approached from the back of the room, having swept through the rest of the level. "Thirteen in all. Whoever attacked them didn't even bother to take their weapons."

"What happened to their stomachs?" Tabby asked.

"The signs suggest Kroerak," Jonathan replied. "They would have fed on them before departing. The Kroerak have no use for human weapons."

"Liam, we need to find what's generating that signal," Nick said. "We're getting a low power reading on the third level."

"Over here," Tabby said. She'd located a stairwell.

"We're Oscar-Mike, Divelbiss. Fall in," I said, waving him over. The five of us entered the stone stairwell and jogged up to the third level. "Hold this position, Divelbiss. I want to know if anything moves in this stairwell."

"Roger that, Captain," he replied. What he didn't know was that I'd been dropping security discs along the way that would warn us of the same. I figured he'd had enough excitement for his first outing.

The space we entered was a fairly standard Belirand office

level. That is, other than the fact the lights were off and every piece of furniture had been thrown violently in one direction or another.

"What's that?" Clark asked as we worked our way through the office wreckage. She was pointing to a corpse.

I was about to dismiss her when I realized she'd picked up on a detail I'd missed. It wasn't a partial corpse, but rather a very small humanoid. It had an oversized cranium that was, indeed, somewhat frog-shaped. "Hold up, Tabbs," I said as I approached. "Jonathan, is this a Norigan?"

"It is, Captain. We would want to bring the body with us if we can," he replied.

"Understood." The body was just as Jonathan had described. A translucent film, which I suspected was a vac-suit, covered the body of the small alien. I reached across and pulled the eyelids closed on its large, bulbous eyes. "Sorry, little fella. Wish we'd met under better circumstances. Divelbiss, you want to come grab this guy for us?"

"What about all the people?" he asked as he caught up to us.

"We'll give them a proper burial," I said. "But our Norigan friend needs to go home if we can make that work."

"Sure. That's good," he said as he knelt and gingerly picked up the small body that was probably only a tenth of his mass.

"Take him back to the ship and put him in a body bag," I said.

"Nick, how close are we to the power source?" Tabby asked.

"Fifteen meters," Nick replied.

Tabby continued leading us through, picking the most direct route she could, finally ending at a closed door. It was an unusual feature in the building so far, as most entryways had been torn down, presumably by Kroerak.

"What's the play?" Tabby asked.

"Clark, watch our six. Try it, Tabby," I said, pointing my blaster rifle at the door.

"Locked," she said.

"Stand back." I toggled my rifle to a breaching configuration. I missed the good old days when we had fully mechanized, armored suits. Tabby and Xie moved away from the door as I fired. It took several shots, but the mechanism finally gave way. I stepped forward, kicked the handle and the door swung in, falling from its ruined frame.

Tabby and Xie flowed into the room and the three of us scanned for problems. The only issue we came up with was that the room was completely empty.

"Frak," I said. "Nick, there's nothing here."

"Where are all the people?" Tabby asked. "There had to have been a couple hundred people for a settlement this big. We've seen two dozen, tops."

My stomach tightened again. There weren't any good answers to her question.

"You're still four meters short," Nick said.

"How can that be? I'm looking at rock face," Tabby said. The office had been built into the side of the mountain and for aesthetics, the rock face had been left uncovered.

"Jonathan, use your sensors. Can you pick up on any cracks, hidden doors or anything?" I asked.

"We're not detecting anything," he responded.

"What about the balcony?" Jenny asked from the door.

"There's no balcony," I replied. "We'd have seen it when we arrived." I recalled that the face of the building had been completely flat.

"Then, where does that door go?" she asked, pointing to the glass at the front of the building. It wasn't anywhere near the rock face, but it was also a door to nowhere.

"Nowhere, right now," I said. "Good eyes." I walked over to the broken out armor glass and pushed off from the floor. In .2g, my grav-suit didn't have to work too hard to lift me out and I slithered through the window. Indeed, on the face of the building were broken off supports for a balcony, which I followed to the side.

I followed holes in the rock face that I suspected were supports for a ladder. It didn't take long to discover an airlock door hidden beneath a screen of fallen rock.

"Tabbs, I've got something," I said.

"On my way. Xie, Clark, hold this position," she ordered. She soon joined me and we were looking at a well-hidden door in the side of the mountain. The rocks were easy to move in the low gravity and we soon had the door uncovered.

"Ready?" I asked. Tabby nodded and I spun open the old-fashioned, manual airlock door.

"This could be a mistake," Tabby said as she closed us inside and I started to work on opening the other side.

Two men in Belirand vac-suits sat, perfectly preserved, in comfortable chairs at a small table. A bottle of liquor, long since consumed or evaporated, stood next to a deck of cards, and a communications array sat on a shelf next to the table with the quantum crystal still in its cradle. A makeshift signal generator was scratching out the message Nick had picked up. I grabbed the pink quantum crystal and as I did, noticed a small note had been tucked beneath it. I pushed both into a pocket for later consumption.

"Jonathan?" I asked, but didn't get an answer. Not surprising. I suspected the reason the room had gone undetected was due to the material in the mountain blocking all other power signals inside the small room.

"We'll need to bring all of the equipment back for Jonathan and Nick to examine," I said.

"Copy that," Tabby said, spinning open the manual airlock. It was a small room and there was no reason to keep ourselves locked in with the well preserved sentries.

"Liam! We lost contact with you and we're picking up movement in the stairwell." Xie's hushed voice came over the comm. I checked tactical on the HUD, hoping it was Divelbiss returning from the ship. No such luck, he was still near *Hotspur*, although moving at a high rate of speed toward the building.

I dropped the equipment I'd picked up and leaned on my grav-suit, accelerating from the hidden room's airlock. A quick check of my HUD told me that two blips were converging on Xie and Clark's position at a high rate of speed and would get there before we would.

My suit's tactical comm channel thrummed with the muted sound of automatic blaster fire. They'd made contact with something and it wasn't friendly. I dared a glance through Xie's visor and saw two Kroerak warriors temporarily halted by a relentless hail of blaster fire from the two women.

"It's not getting through," Tabby said, as we landed on the ground and opened fire. Our blaster fire was punishing, even pushing the two and a half meter tall Kroerak backward, but it was as if we were firing into the very mountain itself. The first time I'd seen a three dimensional picture of a Kroerak, I'd thought they looked like a cockroach that stood on its hind legs. It was still an apt description. Standing three meters from one, however, made it significantly more terrifying, especially when it seemed invincible.

At the moment, we were at a stalemate. We were pouring fire into the Kroerak so they couldn't move forward. The problem was, that while a blaster rifle has an incredible energy reserve, it's not infinite. We were quickly running out of time.

"Clark, Mie-su, fall back to the windows," I said. "Don't let off the pressure."

"No AGBs," Xie started to say, but was interrupted by an explosion at the door. The two Kroerak warriors were thrown to the side and Divelbiss tried to use the confusion to charge through the door. He even clipped one of the bugs along the way, causing it to spin, but the Kroerak's reflexes were too quick. It jammed its pincered hand into Divelbiss's side and tossed the one-hundred-twenty-kilogram man to its partner as one would toss a meal bar. A spray of blood followed Divelbiss as the pincer was withdrawn.

The second Kroerak caught Divelbiss, snapping its jaw menacingly before biting down on his left arm, severing it just below the elbow. My AI muted the big man's scream.

"We have to shoot him," Xie pled. "We can't let them eat him alive."

Divelbiss stopped screaming long enough to incoherently mutter, "Rit ded bch," as he punched his free hand into the snapping proboscis of the Kroerak.

She was right. I raised my gun to put down the big man.

"No! Wait." Tabby stopped me just as the bug snapped down on Divelbiss's outstretched arm. Time froze and then the big man was thrown backward as the bug exploded from the inside.

"All fire on the remaining. Tabby, get Divelbiss out of there!" I said. Without hesitation, Tabby jetted forward and picked up the broken man, retreating out the windows behind us.

Even with three blaster rifles, we made no progress against the Kroerak. I had no trouble understanding why the Belirand post had been overrun. Our weapons were nearly useless.

"Xie, Clark, I need you to trust me. You're going to jump out of the building when I tell you," I said. "We're only twenty-five meters up and .2g. You read me?"

"We can't leave you, Liam," Xie said. "One rifle won't hold it."

"We have less than a minute. Get going. That's an order," I said.

"Frak," Clark answered and dove out the window. It was a lot to ask from a heavy worlder.

"I hope you know what you're doing," Xie said as she followed.

The Kroerak, no longer pinned by three blasters, pushed forward, clawing toward me. "Nick, I hope you're lining up for a shot," I said.

"Yup. Way ahead of you. Probably best if you make your exit," he said.

I jumped up and pushed back through the broken window. The Kroerak would have no leverage to jump at me without climbing out onto the building. I gambled on the bug doing just that if I stayed close enough. I marveled at the Kroerak's strength as it tore through the façade of the building and hooked its pincers into the nano-steel sheet. Just as it was about to spring, Nick's warning forced me to move. Jonathan had informed me that the joints of the Kroerak's hind limbs were most powerful at extending and they had difficulty with lateral movement, so I dodged to the side. Just as I did, Nick lit the office with four powerful blasts from *Hotspur's* top turrets. The Kroerak might be able to resist rifle fire, but the turret blasts easily slagged the fearsome bug, not to mention leaving a sizeable hole in the once proud building.

"Tabbs, what's the status on Divelbiss?" I asked.

"Not great. He's stable, but lost a lot of blood and his system is shocking bad. I have patches on him, but we need to get him to the medical bay ASAP," she replied.

"Nick, we're headed your way. Marny, I need a better plan for these Kroerak. Our blasters had no effect on them," I said as I swooped down and followed Clark and Xie onto the ship.

"Aye, Cap," she said. "Talking it through with Jonathan and Nick right now. We can discuss once you're up here."

"Frak, wait one," I said.

"What!" Tabby yelled. "We gotta go."

"Can't leave comm gear. Give me three minutes." I jumped back out of the airlock. We'd come this far and couldn't afford to lose the information on the equipment.

I pushed against the grav-suit and sailed up the front of the smoking face of the Belirand outpost. The electronics equipment and comm gear was right where we'd left them and I scooped up what I could carry, slinging my blaster rifle over my back. It wasn't as if a single gun would do me any good against the Kroerak anyway.

Back at *Hotspur*, Xie waited, holding the airlock door open for me, allowing me to glide in and deposit my prizes on the floor.

"He's in, Nicholas," Xie purred, giving me a wink and pulling the door closed. Her response felt overly informal for the situation, but I supposed it was a step up from 'lover' as she was used to calling him.

We moved the equipment into the berth-deck and found Divelbiss laid out in Nick and Marny's old bunk room. The med-patches had him unconscious. I felt a twinge of guilt, knowing that I'd endangered him for a pile of electronics.

"Help Nick," Tabby directed. She seemed pissed and I imagined I knew why. We'd already lifted off and Nick was more than capable of sailing the ship, but he'd be more comfortable with company. I turned from the room and saw Clark sitting at the mess table. It had been a tense situation and she didn't seem as upset as I might have expected.

"You did well out there. I guess you all saw plenty of action on Ophir," I said.

"More than a lifetime's worth. I guess you just never get used to it, though."

"He saved us, you know. Divelbiss broke the stalemate; he saved lives today," I said.

"Is he going to be okay?"

"I think so. The med-tank on *Intrepid* is first-class." I stepped onto the lift and raised up to the bridge-deck.

"You doing all right?" I asked Nick, in the port-side pilot's chair.

"You can take it," he said, gesturing to the open chair.

"Hope we don't run into too many Kroerak," I said.

"Any fight you walk away from, right?" Nick asked.

"Tell that to Divelbiss."

"He'll be okay," Nick said. "Took guts - what he did."

"I just want to know what he was saying." I sailed us next to *Intrepid* and accepted the rigid docking collet and catwalk.

We were met at the airlock by Baker and Kerwin, who were pushing a grav-cart style gurney. I followed them to the medical bay where Tabby continued to work on Divelbiss. "I've got it," she said, still giving me the cold shoulder.

"If he wakes up, I want to know right away," I said.

She nodded. "I know."

"Jonathan, did Clark find you with the equipment?" I asked over comm. I'd tasked Clark with bringing the electronics to Jonathan when we'd docked with *Intrepid*.

"She did, Captain," he answered. "We've got it set up in the bridge conference room for security purposes. I think you're going to want to meet us in here."

"Do you have Nick?"

"He's here," Jonathan replied.

"I'm on my way."

The familiar whistle as I entered the bridge helped to calm

nerves I hadn't realized were quite so on-edge. I breathed deeply and exhaled.

"Liam. What's on your suit?" Ada asked as I crossed the bridge to the conference room. I looked down and realized I hadn't cleaned up since Divelbiss' reaction to seeing the violated corpses.

"Best we not talk about it," I said and walked into the conference room. "What'd you find?"

"You wondered where all the people had gone," Nick said. "This outpost wasn't just attacked. It was raided. The Kroerak were taking slaves."

"Where?"

"We have a location. The Norigan was actually at the outpost warning them of the imminent raid. Belirand totally ignored them," Nick said.

"How do you know all this?"

"They've been sending it in that message for one hundred seventy-five stans. It was an encrypted message. I thought it was just junk," Nick said. "The key was on that note you recovered."

"Let me listen," I said.

The message was short, hitting the points already communicated by Nick. One hundred forty-two outpost staff had been abducted, presumably set to slavery, the location of the slave planet encoded in the message.

"Why would the Kroerak let that be public information?"

"You've seen 'em," Nick said. "Who's going to do anything about it?"

"Liam, Divelbiss is awake," Tabby called over the comm.

"I can think of someone," I said and walked out. It was unfair for me to be pissed at the messengers, but just because we didn't know how to defeat these bugs, didn't mean we were going to give up on whoever remained of the expedition. My mind wandered as I thought about how much time had passed. Was it possible any of their descendants were still alive? If so, what condition would they be in - that is, if they hadn't just been used as food. The very thought made me sick.

"There he is," I said, trying to sound upbeat as I walked into the medical bay. Divelbiss was lying back on a bed, not looking so hot. The medical AI was prepping him for the tank and it was easier if he was awake, although not impossible otherwise.

"Heya, Cap," he replied, groggily.

"I'm sure Tabby informed you that you're in for a ride in the tank," I said. "If there's anyone who knows about tanks, it'd be her."

"Really?"

"Probably not the time, but when you get out, you might ask her. I think you're one of the few people who might have earned that story," I said.

Tabby rested her hand on his forehead. "Frakking aye you have," she said softly.

"I gotta know. You said something right before you jammed your hand into that bug's mouth; what was it? We were having trouble picking out between... well let's say there was a lot of other noise."

He grinned a big, dopey I've-been-given-too-many-drugs grin. "I was just explaining to the bug that I was right-handed."

DIGNITY

"Did we figure out where those Kroerak came from?" I'd reassembled the team after helping Tabby put Divelbiss into the medical tank. He'd be out of action for ten days, but he'd live.

"They were on the second floor," Marny said. "It appears they have the capability to enter some sort of deep hibernation."

"And we woke 'em up? Are there others?" I asked.

"We're not detecting additional Kroerak," Jonathan said. "Unfortunately, we didn't see the two we know were there until you saw them approach. They clearly show few signs of life while hibernating."

"That makes operations planet side difficult," I said. "Our blaster rifles didn't do much beyond push them back. I don't feel good leaving all those corpses just lying out in the open, though."

"There's a fuel depot half a kilometer away," Nick said.

"No chance there'd be bugs there," Ada quipped sarcastically. "Who'd set up an ambush at a fuel depot?"

"Agreed," Marny added.

"Jonathan, what are we missing? Why were the blasters so ineffective?" I asked.

"When you refer to them as bugs, you are not specifically incorrect. Their anatomy and function is more similar to that of insects than humans. The Kroerak warrior, which is what we have encountered, has a hard exoskeleton. That is to say, they do not have bones like many humanoids. The exoskeleton has several properties that have allowed the species to rise in dominance. Specifically, the ability to absorb electrical energy, not to mention strength that rivals steel," Jonathan said.

"What about nano-blades?" Tabby asked.

"We would expect the charge around the nano-blade to be

absorbed by the carapace," Jonathan said.

"You said it rivals steel," Marny said. "How closely?"

"The data we have is imprecise."

"We need to recover that body," Nick said, nodding at Marny.

"What are you thinking?"

"I've been analyzing the fight," she said. "The Kroerak are fast on a straight line, yet lack side to side agility, which is confirmed by Jonathan's analysis of their ligaments. We need to adapt our training to take advantage of this. You have to ask yourself – why did Divelbiss' attack work so well? His first grenade, which landed next to the Kroerak, almost knocked them off their feet, but otherwise they were unfazed. When he jammed a grenade down one's throat, it was lights out, because once something got inside the exoskeleton, that hard shell contained all of the damage," Marny said.

"That was one in a million," I said. "Don't get me wrong. Divelbiss was brave beyond belief, but we can't count on that."

Nick smiled and gave me a look I'd come to know. They had already solved the problem and were just letting me know. "You'll like this," he said.

Marny stood, pulled a long barreled gun from the floor next to her, and laid it on the table. "I had Moonie manufacture this. It's an old design I used back in the Amazonian war," she said.

My HUD displayed the specs of a Colt 42816 slug thrower with an optional integrated under-barrel grenade launcher. Missing from the table was the backpack full of explosive ordnance that would power the weapon. It was similar, albeit smaller, than the weapons of the mechanized suits we'd used to breach the *Bukunawa* dreadnaught. What I wouldn't give to have those mech-suits back at this moment.

"Bulky," I observed.

"If it'd drop one of those bugs, it wouldn't matter," Tabby said.

"Cap's right. If you wear this, you lose agility and we can't be certain they'll do the job," Marny said, "Perhaps the most important problem is we only have enough material to fill two packs, and that's only if we're willing to decommission one of our missiles."

"Do it," I said. "But decommission two missiles and make four ammo packs. If we get into this, who knows what we could run into. I don't want to be short."

"Why aren't we bringing Mars Protectorate in on this?" Ada asked. "I'd have thought Commander Sterra would have already contacted you, especially after we absconded with *Intrepid*."

"I've been wrestling with that, Ada. It's something we all need to wrestle with," I said. "Belirand's - or at least Tullas's - position is that, for the good of humanity, we can't let everyone know interstellar travel is possible. They believe big scary aliens will find Sol and obliterate us all if we do. I hate to take her side in this, but imagine what an army of Kroerak could do if unleashed on Mars."

"Isn't that an argument for talking with Mars Protectorate?" Ada asked, sitting forward in her chair. "Sol can't defend against what they don't know."

"Humanity is horrible at holding onto secrets," Nick said. "Once the cat's out of the bag, Sol will be reachable by everyone."

Ada shook her head. "It feels preposterous that this has become our secret to hold. I'm all for being on the front line setting things right, but Belirand is getting away with murder and someone else needs to know about it. What if Belirand eliminates us before we tell anyone? No harm, no foul?"

Ada had said what none of us had been willing to and I nodded my head in agreement. If we died out here we'd just be gone.

"Your argument presumes that Mars Protectorate doesn't already know," Jonathan said.

"Are you saying they do?" Ada asked. She'd already said more than she wanted and was having trouble stepping back from the conversation.

"We have no information to add regarding Mars Protectorate. Master Anino long held that the North American Alliance unofficially sanctioned Belirand's covert operations in the Dwingeloo galaxy. He was unable to substantiate this with anything more than conjecture," Jonathan said. "Overall, most of us find your argument compelling; given a belief that Mars Protectorate is a benevolent government."

"It would be war," Nick said.

"What would?" Tabby asked.

"Mars and NaGEK relations are already strained. Belirand uses the TransLoc gates as a noose to restrict trade between the systems, not to mention how they've attempted to almost completely lock out the Chinese," Nick replied.

"That's my point," Ada said. "We have no business holding onto this information. We're citizens of Mars, operating under a Letter of Marque from the Mars Protectorate. Does it really matter that we're outside of Mars territorial boundaries? Do you really believe this information isn't going to get out?"

"It isn't fair," I said.

"What!?" Ada asked, still hot from having been called out.

"Putting all that smart and sexy into one body," I said.

"What ...?" Ada asked, her pinched face turning into a smile.

Tabby backhanded me, knocking me and my chair over. "I can't believe I ever let you sail with her and Marny by yourself."

"Ada makes a compelling case." Marny gave us a quick smile, but held onto the matter at hand. "At a minimum, we need a dead man's switch to send a message."

"I trust Commander Sterra," I said, picking my chair up and rubbing my arm. "What do you think, Nick?"

"I say yes to the dead man's switch and I could go either way with Mars Protectorate. I just don't think they're going to do anything in a timeframe that will affect us. Worse yet, they might attempt to prevent us from moving forward with our mission." He paused to think, then said, "I guess I'm not opposed to talking with Sterra."

"Marny, how long before we can have the Colt 816s replicated?" I asked.

"Moonie will have the ammo packs in four hours," she said. "I'll let him know we want a total of four and configure them so they use the same interface as the mechanized armor we trained on."

"I appreciate that you're not rubbing my face in the fact that I sold our suits," I said.

"Water under the bridge, Cap."

"Liam. You, Tabby and Nick need to rest," Ada said. "Your suit's a mess and you can't just keep going. You have to be running on empty."

"Not sure I can sleep, but a shower does sound good. How about six hours and we'll finish things up planet side?"

"You want to tell me why the cold shoulder?" I asked Tabby when we final got back to our quarters.

She turned away from me and slipped into bed. "I don't know what you're talking about."

I slid in next to her and laid my arm over her shoulders. She didn't shrug me off, but didn't respond otherwise. I was too tired to push and woke in the same position, five hours later. I realized I'd been an idiot. By asking Tabby to deal with Divelbiss, she'd no doubt come face-to-face with her own horrific injuries when the cruiser she'd been assigned to, *Theodore Dunham*, had been obliterated by the Red Houzi dreadnaught *Bakunawa*.

I ran my hand down her right arm as I watched her sleep. She looked so small next to me, vulnerable as she slept. "I'm sorry. It was a hard day," I whispered as she slept.

"I can't believe you went back for the electronics," she said. I hadn't realized she was awake. "Divelbiss could have died."

"I had to make a call, Tabby. I feel like it was the right one," I said.

She rolled over so that we were face to face. "I know. It makes me wonder how well I really know you. What if it were me lying on the deck of *Hotspur*?"

"I'd move the universe for you," I said, staring into her eyes in the dim light of our quarters. "If you want to hear me say that I weighed Divelbiss's life against the mission, I did."

"Doesn't that bother you?" she asked.

"Why do you think I came back to the ship first? I was so wrapped up in dealing with our wounded I let go of why we were even here. I had to know what those men had willingly given their lives for in the vault," I said. "I couldn't let their deaths go. We opened the vault, what if there were more Kroerak?"

She stared back at me, searching my face, then finally reached over and brushed my hair back. "You've really grown into this whole captain thing. I guess I'm just playing catch up."

I reached my hand down to the small of her back and pulled her in as tightly as I could. I needed to be close to her. As our legs intertwined, I closed my eyes. The knot in my stomach that I hadn't even acknowledged having, released as I drifted back to sleep.

A warm kiss on my forehead brought me awake. Tabby was already dressed in her grav-suit, her copper hair neatly braided into a ponytail. "Coffee is on the stand," she said.

I sat up. Next to the coffee sat my earwig. Apparently, she'd decided I needed more sleep. I hoped we hadn't lost whatever element of surprise we might have had, but pushed the worry aside and picked the device up. I'd only been asleep for an additional two hours.

"Thanks," I said, taking a drink of coffee.

"Moonie needed extra time to finish the ammo packs," Tabby said. "Apparently, he ran into some problems. Good thing Jonathan was around to fix it."

"What kind of problem?"

"You'd have to ask Moonie or Jonathan," she said. "I figured you could use the extra sleep. About yesterday ..."

I grabbed her hand and pulled her to me. "Air out the airlock," I said. "We talked it through, as long as you're still okay with things."

"I checked on Divelbiss," she said. "Good thing he's taking a round in the tank. He has serious liver damage."

"From the Kroerak?"

She grinned. "No. According to Kerwin, Divelbiss helped one of the locals grow something they called moonshine. It's an alcoholic drink. Very potent. I guess he was also one of their better customers."

I chuckled. "Seems like our medical scans should have caught that."

"They would have eventually," Tabby said. "Otherwise, he's making good progress."

"Who's going planet-side today?"

"Marny is pissed. She really wants to, but realizes she can't leave *Intrepid* behind. There's no one who can man the gunnery stations without her in command. It'll be same as last time, except we're taking Kerwin instead of Divelbiss. Crew is already loaded in *Hotspur*," she said, handing me a fresh vac-suit liner. I enjoyed the sensation of being able to easily slide my replacement foot into the material. It was nearly impossible to distinguish from my original and I wiggled my toes, enjoying the moment.

"Do you need to be alone?" Tabby asked, giving my foot a sardonic grin.

Ignoring her jibe, I pulled my grav-suit on and we headed out of our quarters, aft to *Hotspur* and our awaiting crew.

"Welcome aboard, Mr. Kerwin. Clark, I hope you got some rest," I said, as Tabby and I stepped onto the lift that would take us to the bridge-deck. Jenny Hill Clark and Kerwin were seated in the galley wearing armored vac-suits.

"Think we'll see any bugs?" Kerwin asked. "I'd sure like to get a shot at 'em."

Jenny shook her head almost imperceptibly. They differed by at least fifteen stans and their responses showed.

"Let's hope not. Two of them nearly wiped us out last time," I said.

"I just want a shot at 'em," he said, fidgeting with his blaster rifle. I didn't have a chance to reply as his enthusiasm was cut off by our arrival on the bridge-deck.

"Why the blaster rifles?" I asked.

"Not enough of the new 816s," Tabby said. "Marny equipped the blaster rifles with three shot, under-barrel grenade launchers."

"Were we ever that young?" I asked as we detached and pulled free from *Intrepid*.

"Maybe you were," Tabby answered.

"Have we had any other movement on the pucks since we left?"

I asked.

"None," Nick said.

"How do you want to do this today, Liam?" Xie asked. She'd been quietly sitting on the bridge couch waiting for us to get settled.

"Focus on the vault room first while the construction bot is working on a mass grave. I'd like to recover DNA from as many of the victims as possible since their suits were wiped. I'd like to be able to let someone know who we found," I said.

"I volunteer to take Kerwin up to the vault if you desire to start on the main building," Xie said.

I had to tamp down a surge of distrust. On the face, it was a good distribution of work.

"How would you get Kerwin up there?" Nick asked.

"We must all learn to fly with AGBs at some point," she said. "It would appear his day has come. The lower gravity is a perfect learning environment."

"Take a grav-cart with you," I said. "Worse case is you load him on it and bring him back."

"As you wish, Liam," she said smoothly.

"And just when I think we're making progress," a message from Tabby showed on my HUD.

"You'll need to equip one of the 816s," I said. I'd originally thought we'd only bring two into the field, but with us splitting up, I didn't want her to be at any disadvantage.

I landed in roughly the same spot we had the day before. From what I could tell, nothing had changed that couldn't be explained by wind. "Three hours max, Nick," I said as Xie, Tabby and I descended to the berth deck where Kerwin and Clark stood, waiting for us.

"Kerwin, you're with Xie. Clark you're with Tabby and me." I led us into *Hotspur*'s hold.

The Colt 816s had been neatly arranged on grav-carts. The ammo packs were big enough that I was concerned their mass would be unwieldly. It wasn't that they would be difficult to lift in .2g, but extra mass will throw you around at the wrong time. I wasn't interested in that experience while fighting for my life. I shrugged myself into a pack and my HUD displayed a familiar status display. I nudged the weapon into safe mode and switched my ammo manufacturing to armor piercing, explosive rounds and sent a recommendation to Xie and Tabby.

"Remember. If you make contact with Kroerak, I want you to make all possible haste to the ship. Do not engage if you can avoid it," I said.

"Frak," Kerwin cussed quietly.

"Are we going to have a problem?" I stepped in front of him.

"No, sir, Captain," he said dejectedly.

"Don't worry Kerwin, you'll get your turn. My job is to keep you alive so you can," I said. "You don't want anything to do with these Kroerak in the open field. Believe me."

"We'll be back before you know it," Xie said.

"Jenny, have you ever run a construction bot before?" I asked.

"No, sir," she replied.

"It's not hard, palm the interface panel and set up a link, your AI will do all of the work," I said. "We need a grave that's two meters deep, three meters wide and eight meters long. Tell it to find a nice soft spot within line of sight of the ship and get to digging."

"Can do."

"Once you're done, stay on the ship until we come back for you. I don't want anyone running around by themselves."

"I've interfaced, sir," she said.

"Oh. Nice job, then."

"Like you said. It's not very complex."

"Nick, we're headed out," I said. "Clark, chain those grav-carts together and bring 'em along. I want Tabby and me to keep our hands free, just in case." I'd always had trouble telling people to do work I could just as easily do and Clark was no exception. I appreciated that she took the direction easily and just set about the task.

Tabby and I entered the first level and quickly cleared it. The scene was just as gruesome as when we first arrived. When we entered the second level, it quickly became obvious that we'd made a huge mistake by not clearing it the day before. The Kroerak had set up a nest on this level. The office furniture was gone and the floor covered in a dark, muddy material I was sure I didn't want to smell. In the center of the mud were two pods, torn open, looking like broken eggs. The insides looked perfectly suited for the Kroerak to rest within.

"You getting this, Jonathan?" I asked.

"We are. We have never seen anything like it. Most likely, you're looking at a hibernation chamber," he said. "The material on the floor and walls appears to be a combination of dirt from the surrounding mountain and organic material from the outpost victims."

Tabby and I sidestepped around the center pods, sweeping our gun barrels and bright lights around the room, looking for any other features worth noting for Jonathan. We found nothing.

"It looks like there were just two. You agree with that?" I asked.

"That is a reasonable assessment. We believe they were using the humans as a food source. Very efficient," he observed. "Oh. Our apologies, Captain. That was insensitive."

"Appreciate the information," I said.

We continued to sweep the floor, but found nothing else. Apparently, the Kroerak didn't like the idea of walls and had knocked down everything, making our job easy. The third floor was just as we'd left it and I leaned down to check out the remains of the Kroerak Divelbiss had taken out. The grenade had removed the top third of the bug, but most of its lower body remained.

"Over here, Clark," I said and pulled the Kroerak onto a grav-cart. "We'll take that with us."

She looked at me skeptically.

"Wouldn't you like to know what will penetrate that carapace?" I asked, to which she nodded agreement.

The rest of the morning wasn't anywhere near as much fun as we loaded corpses onto grav-sleds and laid them to rest in the grave dug by the construction bot.

"What's the point?" Kerwin finally asked as I leaned over to recover DNA from the Kroerak's final victim. We'd had good luck in locating records for the deceased. A woman's portrait showed on my HUD. Dark hair, shoulder length and an easy smile. I didn't know if I was causing myself more pain by seeing the pictures of the Kroerak's victims or not. Her name – Thren Blively.

I gently removed a silver necklace from around her neck and placed it in a bag next to the other jewelry I'd found.

"Of getting DNA?"

"This whole thing. Why bury them?" he asked. "These guys are the enemy." He nodded at the bag where I'd placed the jewelry. "Is the crew getting a cut of that?"

"No cut, Kerwin. It won't be sold and I don't see these people as enemies. Do you think Thren Blively chose to be left behind on K-A0223B's moon so she could be eaten by Kroerak?" I gestured to the woman's corpse that lay on the grav-cart in front of me "She's as much a victim of Belirand as anyone at Yishuv. We bury her because she's a person and we should give her the dignity that was denied her for two centuries."

DONE PLAYING

"Do we have a name for the system where the slave planet is?" I asked, slumping in the captain's chair on the bridge. We'd pulled away from planet K-A0223B's moon after loading a full hold of fuel. Nearly twice as much had been left behind, but it was useless to us.

"K-A0292X. Not much information otherwise," Ada said. "We're only forty light years away, though."

"Seriously with the names?" I asked. "I'm never going to be able to tell these things apart."

"What do you want to call them?" Ada asked.

"How about we call K-AO223B – Thren's Rest and the moon can be called Divelbiss' Right Hand?" I said.

"Who's Thren?" Nick asked.

I flicked the portrait I had of the last woman I'd buried onto the forward vid-screen.

"Was she one of the deceased?" Marny asked. "Cap, you're in dangerous territory here."

"No. I'm good. I just don't like that they've been forgotten."

"Thren's Rest then," Ada agreed. "I'll put an application into Mars to have both of them renamed if we ever get back to civilization."

I smiled. "Forty light-years. Kroerak have FTL travel?" I asked.

"They do," Nick said. "But just barely. If I have Jonathan's calculations right, forty light-years will take them two stans."

"Ugh," I said. "Hate to think of these guys having FTL."

"Yeah, that's better than anything we've developed back home," Nick said.

"Wait," I said, sitting straight up. "Could they reach Sol? This is a big deal."

"Jonathan and I already talked about that," he replied. "It's not practical. Norigan drives aren't efficient enough for a trip that long. The fuel required would be five orders of magnitude greater than the payload."

I wasn't particularly surprised that Nick had done the math. I was, however, confused on one point. "The Norigans gave these drives to the Kroerak? Why would they do that?"

"I don't think it was a willing partnership," Nick said with a sour grimace.

I shook my head. We had other issues to deal with. "Ada, what's the jump to get to the slave planet's system?" I asked. I'd already forgotten its real name. "I'd like to drop near the planet, but no closer than eight hours on hard-burn. Anyone care to add to this?" I asked.

"Aye, Cap, that should give us sufficient reaction time," Marny said. "If we were to sit at that distance for an hour, our scans would give us quite a lot of information about the planet and the system."

"Nick?"

"Yup, we're in agreement," he said.

"Three ... Two ... " Ada counted us down. I forced my eyes to remain open and embrace fold-space. Nausea threatened to have its way with me, but fortunately the actual effects of transition only lasted a few seconds.

"We'll arrive above the planet's ecliptic," Ada explained. In a normal system where there was a lot of ship activity, just about everything happened within the ecliptic plane.

"Copy that, Ada," I said.

"That's our cue then," Tabby said, standing up from her station.

I turned to her. "Who are you taking as a gunner's mate?"

"Sending Baker this time," Marny said. "I've also asked Xie to help out in the gunner's nest. With Divelbiss down, we're short-handed."

An uneasy silence filled the bridge as we continued through fold-space. I probably should have had something reassuring to say, but that's just not where my head was. I wasn't at all sure what we were getting into and I appreciated the few hours I'd have to process everything we'd faced. Marny was right, seeing the faces of the corpses wasn't necessarily the best idea. At the same time, it was better than just remembering their desiccated and dismembered forms.

"Transition in thirty seconds." Ada's warning broke me from my thoughts.

Anticlimactic was by far the best description of our transition into the system we knew as K-A0292X. The star was a yellow sun, very close in size and color to Sol's sun. We already knew planet K-A0292X-2 was in the second orbital position and our AIs worked quickly to fill in the displays as sensors gathered information.

Five planets orbited a single star, the second and third both in the goldilocks zone where life was possible. The third, however, was a large gas planet and unlikely to support human life on the surface. Two smaller moons orbited the second planet and both appeared to be big uninteresting balls of rock. I knew from secondary education that moons were essential for planetary life as they often took asteroid and comet hits destined for the planet. Similarly, a big gas planet provided a celestial shield.

The second planet was now of primary interest. Fortunately, we were closest to it, so details filled in quickly. The most important information, so far, was that there appeared to be zero modern communication structures. My heart sank as I considered the implications, including the possibility that the planet wasn't inhabited at all and our trail had run cold.

A familiar whistle broke my train of thought and I looked over to Marny, who was the current officer on deck.

"Cap, Jonathan is requesting entry to the bridge," Marny answered my unasked question.

"Roger that," I said.

"Quite a significant system," Jonathan said as he entered.

"It appears abandoned," I said.

"Certainly of most civilizations that come to mind. But little is known of the Kroerak," Jonathan said. "Put in human terms, we see quite a lot of evidence of a pre-bronze age civilization."

"You see evidence of human activity?" I asked.

"To attribute this information to humanity is perhaps optimistic. We are seeing activity by sentient beings that include agriculture," he said.

"From these scans?" I allowed myself to feel some hope.

"Yes, Captain Hoffen. The resolution is sufficient to identify land patches that have been cleared for growing. Ada Chen's positioning has allowed us to identify light sources that we do not believe are formed naturally," he said. As he spoke, the forward vid-screen showed fuzzy square patches of ground. On a second display, dots of light spread across a region that I had no size reference for.

I wasn't sure what I'd been expecting, but this certainly wasn't it. "I suppose we should check it out in that case. Marny, any reason not to start a burn toward the planet?"

"I'll negotiate a plan with Ada," she replied. "So far, we're not picking up any bogeys."

I busied myself with the details filling in with regard to the planet. The data showed a slightly richer oxygen environment than a human would need, 0.95g and a climate that was warm and humid, at least where Jonathan had detected agriculture. There was surface water, although not to the same degree as Earth, and there were active storms. All in all, from a human perspective, it was about as perfect a place as I could imagine. I was still cautious, knowing that was how initial settlers had seen Grünholz. First impressions really should be discounted.

The trip toward K-A0292X-2 remained relatively quiet, at least for the next several hours. It was when we were five thousand kilometers from the smaller of the two moons that things really got interesting.

"Cap, we've got a problem," Marny said.

A red outline showed on the horizon of the moon as a battleship-sized ship broke free from orbit.

"Ada. Combat burn, evasive," I ordered and pulled on my combat harness.

The ship didn't look like any I'd ever seen. It resembled a badly misshapen, flattened potato with stumpy, organic growths across the surface. Even more peculiar was its flight orientation. The monstrosity was sailing horizontally, or sideways. It wasn't as if, in space, shape had as much of an impact on performance as it did with atmospheric ships, but form often intimated function. In *Intrepid*'s case, we were long and narrow, created for a hit-and-run type mission. I couldn't imagine what this giant flying spud's function might be, although I had a suspicion I wasn't going to like it.

"Should we separate?" Tabby called on the tactical channel.

"Not yet," I said. "I want to see what's going on. If we start taking fire, make your best call."

"Roger that," she replied.

The AI warned us of the upcoming combat burn and I briefly felt sorry for anyone who hadn't taken the opportunity to strap in. *Intrepid* was running heavy with *Hotspur* strapped onto her belly and if we needed the extra punch, we could separate.

"Jupiter, that thing is ugly," Moonie said as the ship cleared the horizon and made way for us. There was no question it intended to intercept us on our path to the planet. For a ship that out-massed us by a factor of twenty, it was making good time.

Show delta-v.

Ada couldn't completely arrest our forward momentum toward the planet, but she did have options that would send us across the opposite side of the moon and away from the spud-ship racing toward us. Maneuverability was one of the joys of the frigate and the arcs on her navigation map showed we could easily swing aside and cross behind the moon. Our attacker would lose all advantage once we did, but they could still take some shots at us before we reached cover.

"Incoming fire," Marny announced.

The unidentified ship had fired a barrage of fast moving projectiles from the knobby-looking out-growths. Their timing had been perfect; their window to fire, shrinking.

"Separate, Tabbs," I said. "Take evasive!" It would be a

dangerous maneuver while we were in combat burn.

My order wasn't necessary. Tabby and Nick had already seen the hail of projectiles and peeled away from *Intrepid*'s underside. The gain in acceleration was significant as the two ships separated.

Ada seemed to surf the wave of destruction, spinning the ship at the last moment, utilizing the forward section once again to shield the more valuable engines. The ship shuddered from the impact of projectiles.

"Hull status, Moonie," I said.

"Still holding. If we hadn't been running all out, it would have been a different story," he replied.

"What were they?" I asked.

"Basically, they were spears," he replied. "Just really fast moving. If we make it out of this, we'll be able to collect some. Sensors show we have a number of them stuck in our hull."

"Nick, status."

"We're good. We jumped in behind you when the wave passed," he said. "So much for arriving unannounced, eh?"

"Yeah, frak," I said. I checked our delta-v with the enemy. We were still running at a full combat burn and our delta-v was ratcheting up quickly. "Ada, we can probably back it off some. They won't catch us anytime soon."

"Give me one more minute?" she asked and flicked a prediction curve onto the forward display. We were still within reach of another salvo of projectiles.

"Roger that," I said.

***

"What do we do now?" Tabby asked.

We'd gathered the command team in the bridge conference room.

The ship we'd come to believe as Kroerak had given up chase after an hour. We slowed our retreat and they were staying visible. It seemed a clear message – Stay Away.

"I want a look at that planet," I said. "There's no way they can land that ship. I say we take *Hotspur* in and check out a few of those spots Jonathan located. Have you any updates on the initial scans?"

"Our sensors show a significant agricultural civilization, mostly restricted to the southern continental landmasses," Jonathan added.

"Define significant," I said.

"Our best estimate is several thousand sentient beings spread out over ninety thousand square kilometers," he answered.

"Why would they be so spread out?" Nick asked immediately.

"It is by design," Jonathan said.

"How do you know that?" I was skeptical. I'd seen much of the data from the sensors and they were making assumptions I didn't feel were supported.

Jonathan flicked a map to the conference room's vid-screen wall. A perfectly laid out grid of dots appeared, overlaid with a topographical map I hadn't seen before. "We have the benefit of a constant feed from the sensors. This civilization was planned by an advanced species with a view from space. This level of precision would be impossible for the technology we've been able to detect from the planet's inhabitants."

"Just what I need. Another Nick in my life," I said sarcastically. Jonathan looked at me quizzically, but I wasn't about to explain. I understood it was my job to sound like the idiot in the room, but it wore on me some days. "You're implying the inhabitants aren't Kroerak."

"A reasonable assumption. In our estimation, the only reason a more advanced species would go to the trouble of planning such a technologically inferior civilization would be if they wanted to control that population."

"I don't understand what the Kroerak gain," Ada said.

"Humans reproduce more frequently than most sentients," Jonathan said. "You also have one of the strongest drives for survival of any species we've encountered."

"To what end?" Ada asked. "I thought you said you didn't

know if those settlements were populated by humans."

"It is a sensitive conversation," Jonathan said. "But we believe there is sufficient evidence that we are looking at human populations."

"Sensitive? Say what you think is going on," Ada said, starting to get annoyed. "Shading the truth has no place here."

Nick leaned forward, breaking line of sight between Ada and Jonathan. "What Jonathan is trying not to say is they think the people are the product of the agriculture, you know... like livestock."

"That's ridiculous," Ada said, slapping the table. "There have to be a million better animals you can raise for that purpose."

"Is it?" I asked. "What animal is better at adapting? Look at the population of Earth and Mars for that matter. Given time, we fill the space available."

"I'm going to be sick," Ada said quietly and sat back in her chair.

"They'd have to take precautions against them organizing," Marny said. "The larger the population, the more danger the Kroerak would have."

"What could pre-bronze age people do against Kroerak warriors?" Tabby asked. "That's got to be why they're so spread out."

"Any reason to expect Kroerak sentries?" I asked.

"Yes. We believe they are strategically located," Jonathan said, highlighting five locations. "There is evidence of transportation paths between these hubs." A pentagon shape formed as lines were drawn between the newly highlighted security installations.

"So we pick a settlement that's as far from those spots as possible," I said.

"We recommend one of these," Jonathan said, highlighting three settlements at the edge of the map he'd constructed.

"Done," I said. "Ada, while we're gone, you're in charge. If we don't return for some reason, you need to get out of here and tell someone. Our lives aren't nearly as important as this information."

"Don't talk like that, Liam," she said. "Besides, I'll have Marny."

"Not this time," Marny said. "I'd like to come along, Cap. We'll not be mixing it up with that ship and you'll need me on the surface if things turn south."

"Are you sure?" I asked.

"Aye, Cap. If Ada does end up in a slug-fest, Baker and the crew will do what needs doing," she said. "I don't mean to take anything away from them, but it'd be hard to miss that big ugly."

"Any naysayers?" I asked, looking around the table. Ada looked uncomfortable, but she bore the responsibility I'd placed on her.

"Just like old times, eh?" I asked as the four of us walked aft.

"Quick stop," Marny said, opening the door to the armory. She handed Tabby and me heavy pistols. They were thirty percent bigger than the largest flechette I enjoyed carrying.

"What gives?" I asked as she closed the armory and we continued aft.

"About as illegal as they come," she said. "These are true slug throwers and you can reload with the 816 ammo pack. Never hurts to have another option."

I wasn't sure about this. "We don't even know if the 816s are going to break the Kroerak shells."

"Don't get ahead of yourself," Tabby interjected. "We don't even know if there are Kroerak or if there are even any humans down there. It's been one hundred seventy-five years since they were taken from Thren's Rest."

I strapped the pistol into place and watched as Marny strapped on the ancient katana blade she'd received from Anino. "Why are you bringing that?"

"Only weapon I've tried that's sharp enough to pierce Kroerak exoskeleton. Nano blades don't work," she said.

I dropped my head. "My goal is to avoid fighting."

"Aye, Cap, as is mine," she said as we worked our way through the airlock of *Hotspur*.

Engage silent running, I commanded arriving on the bridge. *Disengage docking clamps*. I pulled back on the flight stick and gently separated from *Intrepid*.

"Happy hunting," Ada transmitted, knowing we wouldn't be able to respond. "Come back in one piece please. We're counting on you."

"Nick, lay in a course that takes us as far around that damn potato as we can get," I said. Normally, when sailing silent, we didn't have much in the way of sensors, but with *Intrepid* periodically broadcasting updates, we had no trouble keeping track of the large ship.

"Yup."

A navigation path appeared on the forward vid-screen. It would take us five hours to reach the planet as we had to lose all of the speed Ada had been gaining in the opposite direction. Such was travel in space.

While the trip was tense, it turned out to be uneventful and we reached the planet's atmosphere on the opposite side of our enemy's ship.

"Either they aren't tracking us or we're too small for them to be concerned," Tabby summarized as I pushed *Hotspur* into the atmosphere. Regardless of the circumstances, I enjoyed the sensation of flight as *Hotspur*'s wings caught and we glided along with the air currents.

The first part of our plan was to make a high altitude fly-over and map the settlements Jonathan had mapped from long distance. At fifteen thousand meters, we were close enough that our passive sensors were able to resolve previously muddy detail.

"Not much of a civilization," Tabby said as we inspected the video of mud and stick, round-topped houses. The size of the openings were the right size for humans, although none had yet entered our sensor's field of vision.

"The Ophie are more advanced," I added. "How could people as technologically superior as Belirand be pushed back so far?"

"I'd guess it isn't by choice, but we don't know those are human settlements," Nick said.

"Let's get loaded up. Nick, you have the helm," I said. "We'll jump from five thousand meters."

"Agreed," he replied. "Be careful, Marny."

"I've got it, little man." She mussed his hair and walked from the bridge to the lift.

I'd done a lot dumber things than jump out of a perfectly good spaceship and so the idea didn't strike me as particularly bad as we lowered the ramp and one by one, jumped out. It was in this environment that Anino's grav-suit was at its most efficient. With the strong gravitational fields of the planet, the suits easily counteracted the free fall.

"I've found a spot to set down," Nick said over point-to-point communications. "Twenty kilometers north. Looks clear."

"Be safe, little man," Marny said as the three of us formed together in free fall. We'd done enough jumps with mechanized suits that we preferred to stay within a few meters of each other as we fell. The grav-suits allowed for considerably more control over the arc-jet based mechanized suits and we were counting on a safe landing.

"I'm getting movement," Tabby said. My HUD showed a human figure carefully moving between two of the dwellings. The figure's movement was slow, finally stopping. In response, Marny slowed our descent and flipped the tactical view to infrared. Half a meter in front of the figure, a pin-prick of red widened into a saucer shape, about a hand's breadth in width and quickly turned orange and then yellow.

"I'm guessing no indoor plumbing," I said, wryly.

"Break for the ridge," Marny instructed. The plan was for us to hunker down on the ridge in the foothills of the mountain range that ran along the eastern border of the settlements.

"Copy that." We'd gathered as much information as we could during our fall and landed under a shelf of rock. Visually, we were hidden from satellites, even though we had seen no evidence of them. Marny was all about taking maximum precautions and making as few assumptions as possible.

"I'll set the sensors and then I'd say we'll want to get comfortable." She reiterated the plan we'd worked up.

As it turns out, comfortable and rocky ledges aren't particularly synonymous and I wondered how I was going to make it through the entire day as we settled in, waiting for the system's star to rise on the alien horizon.

"More movement," Tabby said. We'd had several glimpses of movement, but never a full sighting. At five thousand meters, our sensors easily dialed in on the village of five mud-covered dwellings.

"That's a human," she added unnecessarily as a poorly dressed, rail-thin woman exited, carrying a clay pot. We watched in fascination as the woman carried the pot to the edge of the village and dumped the contents onto the dusty ground, using a tool to cover the material.

"That's not," I said as a meter-tall creature with short, spindly legs, hunched back and large frog-shaped head exited next. Its blue and green coloring and oversized, black eyes sitting atop its head were a perfect match for the Norigans that Jonathan had shown us. As the woman approached, they communicated with a series of hand signals.

"Norigans," Marny said. "Living with humans. Wonder what that's about."

"Look at him," Tabby said as a dark-brown skinned man exited the same hut. We watched as he joined the Norigan at a central fire pit where the two worked together to restart the glowing embers into a small fire. The girl we'd first seen, joined them after filling a pot with water and handing it to the much larger man.

Marny handed meal bars to me and Tabby. "Breakfast time."

In all, there were fourteen villagers. The tall brown-skinned man, the Norigan and the boy we'd seen relieving himself the night before were the only non-female residents. If there were more Norigans, we didn't see them. As they moved through the day, they set to work in the terraced hills around the village, growing what my AI believed to be a plant similar to rice. A few other well-tended plants grew along the edges of the watery terraces.

"No kids. No old people," Marny observed. "And almost no men."

We continued to spy on the villagers. It was like watching an old documentary vid depicting life as it was before civilization, only these weren't actors.

"No sign of Kroerak," I said as the sun finally set behind the mountain, leaving us in darkness.

"What would be the point?" Tabby asked. "They're barely surviving down there."

"Looks like they're turning in for the night," Marny said. "We're a go in five minutes." We were on a communications blackout and had set a time table with Nick.

"Marny, you'll set up on top of that hut?" I asked, just recapping the plan. She would stay outside as Tabby and I attempted to introduce ourselves to the village residents.

"Aye, Cap," Marny agreed as we glided across the rocky plain that separated us from the village.

Landing gently next to the dwelling, I turned up my light amplification as I stepped into the door frame of the pathetic dwelling. I was hardly prepared for what we were presented with. On the ground lay a huddled mass of sleeping humans, covered by little more than dirty off-white blankets. Toward the front, the broad, blue and green frog-shaped Norigan's head rested intimately over the bare chest of the well-muscled brown-skinned man.

The young boy, who couldn't be older than eight stans lifted his head from the center of the pile and looked at me. The keening wail he made next was a sound of despair I would remember for a very long time. I held my hands out in an attempt to quiet him, but he was having nothing to do with it.

A number of things happened next, most significantly, however was that the man quickly moved the Norigan's head to the side and with remarkable grace, jumped to his feet, pulling a crude bone knife from a belt as he did.

"Whoa," I said, holding out my arms defensively. Apparently, this was not the right answer as he pounced immediately. I was in no-man's land. We were here to rescue them and were instead being attacked. In hindsight, perhaps approaching the tiny village while they were lying down was a bad idea.

Before I could react, I was on my back in the dirt, unwilling to pull my pistol and fire; unwilling to fight. I needed a better plan. Fortunately, Tabby didn't have any issues with a plan. A quick side-kick tossed the man to the side, which was apparently a breach of some sort of protocol. We were jumped by two women, who immediately came to the man's aid. It was a proverbial dust-up. However, with Tabby under attack, I was no longer willing to sit back, although I still wasn't interested in lethal force. I felt horrible, pushing back the women and children. They weren't overly strong and were clearly fighting for their lives. After a few minutes of scuffling, Tabby got her arm wrapped around the man's neck and held his bone-knife to his throat.

"Your helmet, Liam," Tabby said.

I held my hand out to the man who'd initiated the attack while I pulled my helmet off. "Do you speak English?" I asked. He narrowed his eyes, but didn't respond. It was a longshot that we still spoke the same language.

Translate to Norigan, I directed and looked at the Norigan who'd stepped forward to hold the man's hand. "We're here to help, Norigan. Tell them to back down."

"Why would you attack if you are here to help?" The Norigan asked.

"You have incoming," Marny said over the comm. "A group of eight approaching the dwelling you're in."

I looked at the tactical display. Marny had identified them as yellow targets which indicated they weren't Kroerak at least.

"Copy that, Marny," I said quietly.

"I am Captain Liam Hoffen. We come from Sol and have a faster-than-light capable ship," I said. "We desire to provide transport away from this planet to a place of safety."

The Norigan looked up to the brown-skinned man and exchanged a series of hand-gestures.

"Clear the doorway, Liam," Tabby said, pulling the man back into the room, though still holding him.

"Sendrei believes this is a test from the bug-gods," the Norigan answered. "He says we will resist you."

A woman, no older than Marny stepped into the dwelling and looked first at me and then to Sendrei. An animated exchange of non-verbal communication ensued, at the end of which, she ducked out quickly.

"Liam. We have a runner," Marny warned. "What do you want me to do?"

"Not sure. It could be a problem," I said.

"Frak!" Marny said. "We're going to have trouble. She lit some sort of pyre. Nick, we're going to need you. Tabby, Liam, I've got fifteen Kroerak inbound, twenty seconds."

"No test, Norigan. Make a choice, come with us and live or stay here and starve. Convince them," I said and scooped up my helmet, sprinting as Tabby pushed the man away from her and followed.

The sound of gunfire spurred us forward and I found Marny standing her ground, her 816 on full automatic fire. If I'd hoped that the guns would simply mow them down, I was sorely disappointed. The armor piercing rounds bit deeply into their thick shells, causing chunks to fly off, but the amount of time it took to tear through a single bug was too much.

Surprise was on our side as the Kroerak were certainly not expecting a full out blast in the face. I switched over to grenade loads and blooped out three at the front of the chaotic line that approached. I knew from our previous encounter that I wouldn't kill them, but knocking them back might buy us much needed time.

Switching back to automatic fire, I joined Tabby and Marny. For a while, we reached a sort-of equilibrium. We were losing ground, but we'd also cut down half of their number. The problem was they'd surrounded us and I for one was running out of ammo at an alarming rate.

"Ten seconds," Nick said.

Two Kroerak turned from the remaining seven. It didn't take a genius to realize they were headed for the soft targets.

"Hold this ground," Marny demanded and bolted skyward. I smiled and took the easy shot, as the Kroerak I'd targeted was distracted by her skyward launch.

"Frags, Tabby!"

She was more than happy to oblige and plastered the remaining bugs with grenades. I toggled the focus-fire target to the first Kroerak to stumble and we chewed him up.

"Bug out!" Nick yelled. It was hardly a standard command but with the remaining Kroerak at danger-close we gladly rocketed up to safety. A second later, *Hotspur*'s bottom turret illuminated the night with a blast that incinerated the last Kroerak.

Tabby and I jetted back toward the dwellings where Marny had lodged her katana into a bug. She was, so far, successfully dodging the attacks from a second.

"No auto-fire," Marny commanded. "The civilians have no idea about lines of fire. You'll kill 'em with friendly fire."

Still in the air, I pulled the pistol she'd provided and aimed it between my feet as the bug charged. First, I'd like to say that I was quite surprised at the kick of the weapon. I was barely able to hang on for the ten shots I fired and struggled to maintain my position. Second, while I didn't kill the beast, I did cause it to stumble.

"Aaiieeee." A blur from the side was the only warning any of us had as the brown-skinned man, Sendrei, landed atop the bug, burying Marny's katana behind its head. The Kroerak stopped moving and fell to the ground, dead.

"We got a shite-storm coming in three minutes," Nick said. "That was just the warm-up band."

"I've marked a landing-zone, Nick," Marny said. "Tabby, when that bird hits the ground, I want you in that ship on those turrets."

I half-sprinted, half glided back to the first hut where the Norigan stood watching.

"The time for decision is now. A Kroerak army is coming," I said to the alien. "We will take you to safety or you will stay here. Bring nothing, we will provide whatever you need. But you must hurry, your lives depend on it."

"Nick's on the ground," Marny said. "We need to go!"

I lifted off. It wasn't difficult to tell from what direction the army was approaching. A cloud of dust rolled behind a column of heavy, ground-based vehicles. I was mystified as to how we were unable to detect the technology of the Kroerak from our ships, but I could certainly detect it now as they lit up my grav-suit with a targeting laser. Heavy projectiles were next. To my relief, the frightened humans and Norigans were shuffling onto *Hotspur*.

"Marny, help me," I said, grabbing the husk of the fallen Kroerak that still had Marny's katana embedded in it.

"I like where your heart's at, but I'm not sure we have time," she said, but joined me anyway.

Hotspur's hold was plenty big for fourteen people, especially when empty. Put a dead Kroerak at one end and you gain a lot of open space in between.

"We're in, Nick. Go," I said as I palmed the security panel to close the loading ramp. It was none too soon, as the dust of our enemy closed in on our position. As it was, Nick would have to fly close to the surface to avoid whatever they might have that could hit us at range.

"We're missing one," the Norigan approached me and reported. "It was the human boy."

"Frak. Where?" I asked.

"He is still in the hut," the Norigan answered as I threw myself out of the closing door.

"Keep going. I'll figure it out."

"We're done playing," Tabby said. "Stay low, Liam."

Hotspur spun and rocketed away from my position. Projectiles streaked into the air and the whooshing sound of ground-to-air weapons drowned out everything else as launchers released their payloads. *Hotspur* rolled out of the way and I could only wonder how the people in the hold were faring. Moments later, two missiles streaked forward from *Hotspur* and the thunderous sounds of impacts were followed by twin fireballs rising a hundred meters from my position.

I ran into the hut, found the child cowering in the corner and scooped him up. I knew my actions weren't going to reduce his fears, but this wasn't going to be a great place to hang out for quite a while to come.

LIVESTOCK

"Liam, they've set up heavy projectile launchers," Tabby snapped as I approached *Hotspur*.

I glided through the exterior airlock door that stood open for me and responded. "Let's get out of here."

"Hold on to something. They're coming in fast and I'm going to hit it hard," she said.

It was all the warning we would receive. A moment later, the boy and I stumbled into the aft bulkhead, thrown by the excess of inertia. The roar of the atmosphere rushing by and the rapid thwupping of our turrets firing were a stark warning of just how close the enemy was.

The boy's bright blue eyes shined through his muddy, tear-stained face as he looked at me questioningly. His fear had given way to resignation more quickly than I'd have expected. He moved his hands sharply, rested for a moment and then repeated the same movements again.

Interpret hand signals.

"Not enough information," my AI replied.

The atmosphere rushing by the skin of the ship slowed well after the thwupping of the turrets ceased.

"Are we clear?"

"Aye, Cap," Marny replied. "We're clear of the ground forces and fifteen thousand kilometers from their orbiting ship. We shouldn't stick around, however. It doesn't appear our technology is well suited to detecting Kroerak. There might be more surprises."

"Negative. I want to try one more village, Marny. I'm going to see to our passengers," I said.

I pulled off my helmet and gloves and lay them on the passage floor. The boy had scurried back against the airlock door, cowering as far away as he could get. I approached and then crouched next to him. His bright blue eyes stared at my hands.

"Just like yours," I said in a gentle voice as I fidgeted my fingers. "Would you like to join your family?" I placed my hand over his and while he flinched, he didn't panic further. I tried to pull him to me, but he was having none of it. I'd need help.

I opened the aft hatch in the passageway that led into the hold and was met by Sendrei who held Marny's katana. His posture wasn't overtly threatening, but he was no doubt looking to gain some control of the situation.

"Sendrei does not trust you," the Norigan said from behind him.

"Why does he not speak?" I asked.

"The Kroerak removed his tongue," the Norigan replied. "He wants to know why you came to the village and caused such great problems. I will translate."

"My crew has come a long distance to undo a great wrong done to Sendrei and his people."

"You are not of Bell-eye-rand?" It only took a split second for me to interpret the Norigan's pronunciation.

"No," I said. "There will be time for questions, but I have a small boy in the passageway. Will you ask Sendrei if he will help me bring him inside?"

"You wish to sell us?"

"No. I told you, we're here to help. Now, the boy!" I wasn't willing to be drawn back in.

The Norigan turned to Sendrei, who'd been watching us intently, its three-fingered hands almost a blur as it seemed to communicate much more than my simple request.

"Sendrei will go," the Norigan finally replied through the translation of my AI. Sendrei lowered Marny's katana just enough to reduce the implied threat.

It seemed a simple matter, only requiring us to step through the hatch into the short passageway and retrieve the boy. Without the ability to communicate, however, I was reduced to hand-waving and pointing. I regretted not bringing Jonathan along to help with translating, although I knew that even now the sentients would be analyzing the hand movements and we'd soon have some basis for language.

When Sendrei finally looked through the forward hatch that led to the airlock where the frightened boy sat curled in the corner, he grunted and looked back into the hold. A poorly covered woman timidly rushed forward, keeping her head bowed as she passed, rushing to the cowering child. I blew out a hot breath of tension. The condition of the pair was pitiful, their hair tangled and muddy, their emaciated forms showing near starvation. Scrapes, bruises and welts on their skin testified to violent living conditions.

"Have them come back into the hold," I said to the Norigan.

Sendrei turned to me as he gestured to the Norigan.

"Sendrei would like to know if we are to be sold back to the Kroerak," he asked plainly.

I considered the man in front of me. His dark brown skin was scarred just as the woman's, but he carried himself with pride.

"You understand me," I said. I watched his eyes as he listened, looking for a hint of recognition. "How is that possible after so many generations." A slightly lifted eyebrow communicating his comprehension. It was all he was willing to give. "To answer your question, no. We do not trade in people's lives. You already believe that or you wouldn't have gotten on our ship."

"The Kroerak would have destroyed the village," the Norigan said. "Your arrival provided but a single choice."

I nodded at the Norigan's information, but stayed focused on Sendrei. "I'd like you to consider putting that sword down. Right now, my security officer, the woman who first used it, is watching and you're making her nervous. I'm her friend. The sword is false comfort if she believes you mean me harm."

Sendrei nodded his head affirmatively.

"The man you're talking to is Lieutenant Sendrei Buhari," Nick informed me over the comm. "He's from Earth. Obituary says he died in a training accident twelve years ago."

"Belirand employee?" I asked, which got Sendrei's attention.

"North American Navy," Nick replied. "Graduated Annapolis Naval Academy. Served aboard the Destroyer - *McCain*."

"What the frak, Nick?"

"I don't know. I've got Jonathan looking too, but we're sure you're looking at Buhari," Nick said. "I've manufactured a reading pad with a virtual keyboard. Get him on the network."

I pulled my earwig away from my head and offered it to Sendrei. "My suit provides sufficient comms, Lieutenant. You are welcome to the ship's guest facilities. Our first priority is the immediate needs of your people."

The man looked back at me and the internal struggle was evident as he finally decided to accept my offering. He slid the earwig into position.

"Cap, I'm coming in," Marny said.

"You hear that?" I asked Sendrei. He nodded affirmatively.

The forward hatch in the passageway slid open and Sendrei tensed. In response, the small boy started whimpering again.

"Lieutenant. You'll place the sword into this cloth," Marny said, holding out an oilcloth I'd seen her use to clean the blade in the past. "I will not have armed guests aboard my ship. You have my word as a Marine that no harm will come to you."

Sendrei made no attempt to hide that he was reading information being displayed on his HUD. I imagined after twelve years of being away from the technology, he'd lost some of the subtlety associated with reading from the HUD. Once he finished, Sendrei drew himself up taller, standing stiffly and placed the sword into the oilcloth Marny held. Once he released the sword, he pulled his hand into a sharp salute, which Marny answered.

"Amazonian War was a long time ago," she said. "But you know that." As she spoke I realized that the two of them must have been in the service at the same time. With sword stowed, she handed him the reading pad Nick had no doubt just manufactured.

"Our galley and mess are open as are the two heads on this level. It might be worth some instruction on the use of a ship's head," I said, nodding to a gaunt woman who was squatting in a corner of the hold.

"Liam, we're receiving a hail from the planet," Tabby said over my suit's comm. In that I was no longer wearing my earwig, Sendrei heard what she said and looked at me with concern. He started scrawling on the reading pad in front of him.

"*They will demand our return.*" Sendrei's typed message showed on my HUD.

"It's not something we're willing to negotiate," I replied.

"*They will use the other villages as leverage.*"

"Good information," I said. "You're welcome to listen in."

Sendrei gave quick hand signals to the Norigan and then nodded. "*Blue Child will work with Sergeant Bertrand to help settle the people.*"

"The Norigan's name is Blue Child?" I asked.

"*Yes.*"

"Understood. And be careful with rank designations. Master Chief Bertrand runs quite a lot of this show," I said.

"*No offense intended.*"

"I've got this, Cap," Marny said.

"Never had a doubt." I led Sendrei forward to the lift that would take us to the bridge.

"*Accept hail,*" I said as I passed Nick and gestured for Sendrei to sit on the bridge couch. "*Hotspur,* go ahead." I slid into the open pilot's chair next to Tabby. Not wanting Sendrei's presence on the bridge to be known, I refused video transmission. We did, however, accept the incoming video stream from the planet. My vid-screen showed a middle-aged man wearing a Belirand uniform. He was clean shaven, hair neatly trimmed.

"Greetings, crew of *Hotspur.* I am Ambassador Bassef Turenik. With whom do I have the pleasure of speaking?" The man's demeanor was gracious, if not friendly.

"Captain Liam Hoffen."

"Oh. It is my pleasure indeed, then. I was told there was some possibility we would see you here on Cradle," he said. "My counterparts in the Kroerak Empire would like to inquire as to your intent in their system. It appears you have entered uninvited and there are suggestions of impropriety."

"I'm not following," I said. "Are you saying Belirand is working with the Kroerak?"

"A delicate matter to be sure, but my communication is more in reference to the illegal removal of breeding stock from nursery forty-nine," he said. "I'm formally requesting that you return to Cradle so that the property which you have stolen might be replaced. I'm also requesting that you turn yourselves over to the Kroerak authorities to answer for your crimes against this great and powerful nation."

"And if we're reluctant?"

"They will, of course, expend the necessary resources to achieve the same objectives, as will Belirand Corporation in cooperation with NaGEK. I'm afraid, Captain Hoffen, there is little you have to say about this. Running will simply ensure the destruction of you and your crew," Turenik said.

"That's pretty much been our S.O.P. for the last several months, Ambassador," I said.

"Your belief in noble gestures is heartwarming, but you are missing information. The Kroerak Empire will likely destroy the current stock in retribution for your actions, should you not comply," he said. "Simply put, you are killing the very people you would save."

"Oh. You completely misunderstood me," I said.

"So, you will turn around?" he asked, brightening.

"No. That, you got right. You mistake our actions as noble. We're simple slavers who have access to FTL drives that are better than anything the Kroerak have. We're just here picking low-hanging fruit. Your mighty Kroerak Empire needs to keep the barn door shut if they don't want the animals getting out," I said. "We have open orders for seventy slaves, so I'd say hang on to your panties, it's going to be a long night. Now, if you'd like to make a bargain, we could probably be talked into taking it easy on the bugs. But I'd recommend keeping them away from our operations. We've more than a few crew with itchy triggers."

"Nick, are you picking up where this is coming from?" I asked, muting the conversation.

"Northern hemisphere," he said. "But there's no obvious civilization there. I suspect they're underground."

"Captain Hoffen. I sense a bluff on your side. I'm looking through a briefing by Admiral Tullas who says you're a zealot who sees himself as a great crusader for truth," he said. "You will turn yourselves in or we will destroy the remaining nursery stock."

"We? Am I to understand you've joined the Kroerak Empire?" I asked. "Believe what you need. If you wipe your stock, that's your business. Let me know if you change your mind on the other." I cut the comm.

"Frak, Liam. That's cold," Tabby said.

"Just words, Tabby," I said. "There's no way we're turning anyone over to the Kroerak. If that means I just doomed thousands of people, then I'll have to live with that. I'm not giving back the people we've rescued. But I needed to make them at least question if killing all those people was worth it. Go silent and fly over another village. I'd like to see if they're still open for business."

"It's a risk," she said. "If the bugs are up and running around, we're no match for their ground forces."

"Seriously? We have missiles," I said, raising my voice to overcome the increased noise of the atmosphere as we dove toward a second village.

As Tabby brought us in closer, I ran through the data stream of the ground assault that had run us off. The Kroerak were not just simple bugs, but rather had substantial, if not unconventional looking vehicles and weapons. Akin to our grav-carts, the vehicles ran on some sort of anti-gravity mechanism that didn't appear to be able to escape the surface of the planet by more than a few meters. These gliding platforms moved quickly and carried loads of projectiles that appeared to be little more than spears, much like the weapons launched from their space-born battleship. On replay, I could see that these spears were launched at supersonic speeds. Simple and deadly. The physics was easy. It doesn't matter what you throw at something, if it's going fast enough, it will either pass right through or transfer all of the energy into the surface it comes into contact with. It was a lesson spacers were rarely given the chance to learn more than once.

"There's a larger force incoming," Marny said as we landed at the fifth village. With Sendrei and the other villagers aboard, we'd successfully convinced sixty people to load and were now approaching a dangerous level of overcrowding. I hated the idea of leaving anyone behind, but we'd barely made a dent in the population.

"Define larger," Tabby said.

"They've scrambled air-borne ships from the north. We have to leave, Cap," she said. "They'll be here in twenty minutes or less. We're out of time."

"Frak, okay, let's get out of here," I said.

"*Incoming Hail,*" my AI announced as we lifted into the upper layer of the atmosphere.

"Accept," I answered. It had been a long night and the inadequacy of rescuing dozens while thousands remained behind weighed heavily on me.

"Your victory is fleeting," the Ambassador started out immediately. "You are now an enemy of the Kroerak Empire."

"Show yourself, Kroerak," I said. "Stop hiding behind your puppet."

"As you wish," Ambassador Turenik replied and the camera panned wider to show the desk where he sat within an underground cavern. A vividly colored alien with a reflective metallic carapace that sparkled in blues, greens and golds stood to the side. Symmetrically shaped, the Kroerak had four upper limbs and side-pinching mandibles with spikes that looked like they would push food into its mouth. Its size was smaller than the warriors and I'd guess it massed about the same as the Ambassador.

"What do you wish to discuss, Liam Hoffen?" The bug's English was perfect, even though its mouth moved mysteriously as it formed the syllables.

"Do you have a name?"

"Not one you could comprehend, Liam Hoffen. You may refer to me as Overlord of Cradle," it said. "Admiral Tullas will be displeased to hear of your breach in protocol. I believe she finds it distasteful to capture more breeding stock."

"Tullas will not be bringing you more people for slaughter," I said. "I'm ending your arrangement."

"You are such a delightful child, but you must know Admiral Tullas will do as we require," the Kroerak replied. "I've always enjoyed young humans. So full of hope and naiveté. You possess but a single piece of technology that we desire. Once we have it, we will enjoy visiting your home-worlds."

"You seem intent on antagonizing me. Is there a point to this conversation?" I asked.

"There was a time when Admiral Tullas resisted us as you do today. I was hopeful you would learn from her example and join with us. With our leadership, humanity could be so much more than mere livestock."

"Not while I draw breath, cockroach," I said and closed the channel.

TRIAGE

"Intrepid, come in," I called over the comm. There was no sense trying to hide our location as we'd burned as hard as possible through the atmosphere to escape the Kroerak airships. Aboard *Hotspur*, we had sixty-five souls, leaving little more than standing room. The ripe smell of the refugees was almost too much to take as our atmo handling systems strained to keep up.

"Liam, what's your status?" Ada's face appeared on the holo projector between Tabby and me.

"We're overloaded and *Hotspur* is struggling," I said. "Nick is projecting critical O2 levels in thirty-five minutes."

"Wait one," Ada replied. "There. Execute that burn-plan."

The plan she sent had a significant dog-leg. It was a good maneuver if the Kroerak battleship gave chase. A heavy ship would very likely overshoot. I accepted her plan and *Hotspur* slowly changed direction.

"We have other issues, Liam," Ada said. "We received a message from Yishuv. Belirand showed up with a fleet. According to Councilman Bedros, they're under siege."

"What about Mom?" I asked. My heart raced in anticipation of what might be.

"Comms are down between Petersburg and Yishuv. Some of the *Cape of Good Hope* engineers are attempting to establish line-of-sight laser communications," she said, "but they haven't been able to reach anyone yet."

"Frak," I said. "Understood. We can't do much about it now and these refugees are in tough shape."

"What do you need from us?" Ada asked.

"We'll have a better assessment by the time we raft up. Hoffen out," I said, closing the comm.

Hotspur surged ahead under Tabby's direction. She'd avoided hard-burn to allow Ada and me to communicate but her impatience was palpable.

"We're going to spike on CO2 if we don't offload soon," she said, pointing at a gauge on the forward vid-screen I was all too familiar with.

"Understood. Ping me when we get close. I'm going to help Marny."

She grabbed my wrist as I spun out of my chair and started down the short flight of stairs to the deck of the bridge. "Silver's going to be okay, Liam. She and LeGrande have been planning for this."

"All Mom has is a light frigate," I said. "Tullas has at least two justice class frigates and a normal frigate if she brought everything we've seen so far."

"True. But even a destroyer wouldn't be stupid enough to get close to the cannons your mom has," Tabby said and released my arm.

I picked my way through the crowded bridge. On one hand, I felt good about having rescued so many, but on the other, sixty from an estimated population of ten thousand was a drop in the bucket. A sense of hopelessness threatened to overtake me as I mentally calculated how many trips would be required to rescue the inhabitants of the planet.

"Cap, good," Marny said as I slid through the crush of people on the berth-deck. "This is Jester Ripples." She gestured to a Norigan, who, in addition to the blue and green coloring of Blue Child, had brilliant yellow bands with red streaks flaring back from around its deep black eyes.

"Jester Ripples, it is my honor to meet you." I smiled and held out my hand as if to shake. Jester Ripples, however, took it as an invitation. He pulled up onto my arm and seated himself on my hip with his spindly legs cinching on my waist. My discomfort at hugging was being put to the test.

"Don't fret, Liam Hoffen. Today is a great day." The Norigan's speech was translated by my AI; the sound of its higher pitched voice like a child, babbling in my ears. His wide, semi-circular mouth opened only slightly when communicating. He stroked the hair on the side of my head with his three-digit hand. The radiating warmth surprised me as much as the intimate gesture had.

"Cap, would you take Jester Ripples to the hold and start triaging?" Marny asked, handing me a medical scanner and a mesh bag full of meal bars and water pouches. I couldn't believe she said nothing about the fact that I held an alien in my arms. "Blue Child and I are working our way through the mess and will head up to the bridge once we're done here."

"Copy that," I watched water pouches being handed between the mostly female passengers.

"Your technology is quite sophisticated," Jester Ripples chattered at me as we slid past the berth deck's occupants.

I raised my eyebrows and nodded. "I understand it isn't on par with the Norigans."

"Your ships and weaponry are significantly more advanced."

"Tell me, are there Norigan males and females like there are humans?" I asked.

"Certainly," Jester Ripples answered. "Blue Child and I are both male. A mistake, certainly, by the Kroerak."

I held my scanner up to the first person I approached in the hold. The woman shrank back from my attention and covered her head as if expecting to be struck. Jester Ripples reached out and stroked her brow, gently pushing her hand to the side. The quandary was evident in her face; she clearly trusted the colorful Norigan, yet was terrified of me.

"It's okay," I said in a soothing voice as I placed the scanner on her chest, just below the collarbone. She jerked backward at the touch of the device but did not resist.

"No patient data found. Subject is fifteen stan-years, in her first trimester of pregnancy, and suffers from dietary deficiencies and parasites. A treatment plan is available," my AI said.

Retain plan. We're triaging approximately thirty patients, organize accordingly.

219

"Next patient," my AI responded.

Jester Ripples climbed down and held his hand up to me. "I assume you wish to place your device on each of the inhabitants of this space."

"We call it a cargo-hold. And yes." I removed the device from the woman's chest and gave her a reassuring smile, which was mostly lost as she avoided eye contact. I held a meal bar out to her after ripping the wrapper open. "Would you communicate that this is food?"

Jester Ripples pulled the meal bar from my hand and signed to the woman by pinching the fingers of his free hand together and pushing them toward his mouth. Timidly, she accepted the bar but refused to eat.

I moved to the next woman and decided to take a different tack. I opened another bar and nibbled a small amount from the end then handed it to her. I was surprised when she took it from me roughly and bit into it. Her face contorted in disgust at the sweet, but dry bar.

"Everyone's a critic," I said with a laugh and handed her a water pouch, which I opened to allow a small amount of water to freely flow out. Less timid than the first woman, she looked suspiciously into my face, but also accepted the water. "Please?" I held the scanner toward her chest. Initially, she shook her head no, but didn't stop me as I put the device in place.

"Fourteen stan-years. Nutritional deficiencies. Recent pregnancy unsuccessful in reaching full term," the AI read off. I worked to keep the anger from my face. I was starting to understand why the ratio of men to women was five-to-one.

"Give the bag to Selfia and she will help you," Jester Ripples said by the time we'd made our way to the fourth woman. "They're all watching and know what you're doing."

I had yet to catch a pair of eyes looking at me or paying us the slightest bit of attention. I wasn't about to argue, however, and held the bag out to the woman in front of me after removing the medical scanner. She, like two of the others I'd scanned, was pregnant. She accepted the bag, keeping her eyes on the floor as she did.

"Would you ask if anyone is hurt?" I was moving more slowly than I'd have liked. "Perhaps bring them forward."

Jester Ripples communicated my request and a corridor of people opened up, showing a tall, older woman with skin even darker than Sendrei's. A relatively fresh wound showed across her face, down her neck, and disappeared over her shoulder. From casual observation it had missed the artery in her neck by very little.

"Shite," I muttered under my breath, picking up the bundle of med-patches I'd brought. As I approached, a woman of small stature stepped between us and placed her hand up to stop me. She was the first who was willing to look me in the eyes and I felt the challenge she issued. She pointed at my left hand, which held the medical scanner.

"You want this?" I asked, holding the scanner up, to which she nodded and pointed again at my hand. I tried to give it to her, but she thumped her fingers on her chest, still staring at me defiantly. I looked from her to the wounded woman and back. The hold had grown quiet.

"What's this, Jester Ripples?" I asked. My only interpretation was that she was preventing me from tending to the wounded woman.

"She is concerned that your device will harm her friend, Bliez. The woman in front of you is Flaer," he said. "It is a name she shares with a small, furred predator on Cradle. She is also a healer and has been forced to not participate in the harvest."

I placed the medical scanner on the woman. The AI's diagnosis was poor. She had a long list of curable problems, but left to her own on the planet below, wouldn't have lived long. Unlike the other women, she was neither pregnant, nor had she been recently.

"Forced?" I asked. "Wouldn't that be a good thing?"

"Not when another is required to take your place," Jester Ripples responded.

I held the scanner out and once again pointed to the wounded woman. Without hesitation, she took it and placed it on the woman's chest.

"Infection present, immediate response is recommended," my AI replied. My HUD highlighted no less than three med-patches as an initial treatment. When I moved to apply the patches, Flaer grabbed my wrist. For such a small, frail woman, I was surprised by her grip strength.

"Flaer, this is important," I said quietly and resisted her pull. I placed the most critical patch on Bliez's neck and continued laying the other patches along the length of the deep wound. Seconds after their application, the woman sighed, no doubt in relief from what must have been great pain.

"Any more?" I asked, turning to Jester Ripples.

"Yes, there are several injuries," he replied. "They will come to you now that Flaer has accepted your treatment."

I turned to see a man hobbling toward me, his foot wrapped in a dirty rag. Two more women stood behind him. Both had obvious injuries, one to her arm, while the other appeared to have something wrong with her back.

"Cap, we're five minutes out," Marny's voice came over the comm. I hadn't finished with my task and couldn't imagine half an hour had passed so quickly.

"Set the catwalk up," I said. "I'm not done yet. Are we clear of Kroerak?"

"No. They're forty minutes from our position and still closing. We'll need to be quick," she said.

"Gah," I closed the comm channel.

"Flaer." I looked for the small woman and found her tending to someone who was in tears. She looked up, recognizing her name. "Jester Ripples, please translate for me."

"We're about to dock with our larger ship. The Kroerak are chasing us and we must move quickly. She needs to help coordinate the transfer to *Intrepid*. This ship cannot process the carbon dioxide that's building up," I said.

Jester Ripples fired off a series of hand signals.

"What would you have her do?"

"We must walk through a tunnel. It will be scary, but my people are on the other side and will make you safe," I said. "I would have Flaer encourage them to move quickly."

After a few more exchanges he finally replied, "She understands and will help."

"We'll go through this hatch," I pointed at the forward hatch. It went against my spacer training to put un-suited people in a cat-walk, but there was nothing to be done about it. "Marny, we're ready. Who do you want to go through first?"

"Sendrei will lead a group from the berth-deck," she said. "He's been in a frigate before and understands the layout. You're next, but I want to keep the hatch to the hold closed until Sendrei's group is clear - to keep confusion to a minimum."

"Copy that. Just give us the signal; we're queueing up," I said. Technically, we only needed to move half the people off *Hotspur* to fix the CO2 issue, but my goal was to transfer them all. Without vac-suits, it would be next to impossible to move the remainder once we entered fold-space. The transfer would have to be quick; we needed to get to fold-space as soon as possible.

From my suit's HUD, I watched the progress of Sendrei's group as they turned from the berth-deck and out into the cat-walk. Sendrei carried a woman who appeared to be in bad shape, but even so, they made good progress.

"Go, Cap," Marny finally said, once the last of Sendrei's group made it to the middle of the catwalk.

I pulled the hatch-door open and looked at Flaer. "With me," I said and beckoned.

Whatever Flaer had said to the inhabitants of the hold must have been inspiring because I actually had to slow down the leaders who surged forward, ready to run.

"Welcome aboard, Captain," Kerwin said. "Nice of you to bring a group of lovelies along. This trip just keeps getting better."

"Stow it, Seaman," I growled. "These women have endured enough."

"Aww, don't be like that," he said. "They can't understand me."

"But I can," I said and turned back down the catwalk, using my grav-suit to fly along the edge past our confused guests.

"Last group," Marny said as I passed Jester Ripples.

"Is the cargo-hold empty?" I asked him.

"I am the last," he said as he continued forward.

Blue Child led the final and smallest group.

I checked the approach of the Kroerak battleship. They were just under ten minutes to firing range. It would take three of those minutes to collapse the cat-walk. We were going to make it, but not with a lot of time to spare.

Marny brought up the end of the group. "We're missing one," she said.

"Go ahead and close up," I said. "I'll find him."

"How do you know it's a him?"

I smiled and shook my head.

***

Explaining transition to fold-space to a group of people who hadn't even experienced travel by vehicle was a futile exercise. In the end, we simply explained that everyone was going to feel sick for a few minutes, but it would pass. As expected, more than a few of our passengers, who'd already felt nauseous for most of the day, became sick. Fortunately, we were prepared.

"They're all pregnant?" Ada asked, disgusted.

"Thirty-eight," Tabby reported. "We lost one of the babies. There was nothing that could be done. Most of the women had parasites and a variety of infections. Bliez's face and neck are healing nicely, though. She is so good with the other women - very gentle - and she's a hugger, just be warned." Tabby raised an eyebrow, knowing I wasn't overly comfortable with random hugs. If I could hold Jester Ripples, I could manage this woman.

"How are we coming on vac-suits and liners?" I asked. We'd been in fold-space for five of our ten-day journey and our replicators had been cranking out personal hygiene and clothing items for most of that time.

"Making some progress," Nick replied. "The bigger problem is they don't understand the need. We've started some training, but it's slow."

"I spoke with Bedros this morning," I said. "For a short time, they established contact with Petersburg. Mom and LeGrande are alive, but they don't know much more. Tullas moved a ship to block the line-of-sight communication. As you might expect, Councilwoman Peraf is looking to negotiate with Belirand."

"Was Bedros able to stop her?" Nick asked.

"For now. He convinced her to wait until we showed up and see who comes out on top. Apparently, they've had scouting parties from Belirand testing out their defenses," I said.

"If Tullas brought a tactical team, they might be able to breach the colony," Marny added. "At least Yishuv has several Marines from *Cape of Good Hope* who should have anticipated that."

"What's our play at Ophir?" Ada asked. "We don't have much chance against Belirand's justice class Frigates."

"It's not as uneven as you think," Marny said. "Remember, we nearly took out *Fist of Justice* with a light frigate and *Mastodon*."

"Our plan is to assess," I said. "I hate the idea of combat with passengers aboard."

"I do not believe you will be given a choice," Jonathan added. "Belirand is in place precisely to prevent your passengers from surviving."

"You don't sound like any pacifist I know," I replied.

"That's not a strictly accurate description," Jonathan said. "Most of us feel humanity is too quick to resort to violence. In this instance, we believe our survival is more likely with a measured, aggressive response."

"Have you checked on Divelbiss?" I asked Tabby.

"He and Sendrei Buhari are waiting to join us in the crew's mess once we're done," she said.

"What's next?" Ada asked. "Let's say we get through this with Belirand."

I sighed and gave her a sad face. "What have we done to my sweet, optimistic Ada Chen?"

"There are only so many things we can un-see, Liam," she said.

"Like how Kroerak use women as livestock. How can we survive in a universe like this?"

"We stand in the way, Ada," I said.

"How?"

"I've prepared a comm to be sent to Mars Protectorate if there is any danger of *Intrepid* being destroyed," I said. "When we do make it past Tullas and her thugs, we're going to set up a meeting with Admiral Buckshot Alderson and we're spilling the beans."

"Really? I thought you were against the idea," she said. "What changed your mind?"

"You and ten thousand slaves on Cradle," I said. "We don't have the capability to save ten thousand. Mar Protectorate does."

"What makes you think they'll get involved?"

"Commander LaVonne Sterra won't turn away from this," I said.

"What if she gets shut down?"

"We'll start with her and Alderson. He might have some bluster to him, but in the end, he does things for the right reasons," I said.

"He might sing a different tune if it means war with NaGEK," Marny said.

"You heard the Kroerak. They're coming for Mars and Earth eventually. They won't want to sit on this for very long," I said. "We have to trust someone and I say Commander Sterra has earned that."

"Agreed," Nick said quietly.

Ada rolled her neck. "Now all we have to do is survive."

"One day at a time," I said.

"To that end," Marny said, "the survivors from Cradle have put together a special celebration feast in our honor."

"Now?" Ada asked.

"They're waiting for us," Tabby said as she opened the bridge's conference room door, showing an empty bridge.

I stood and walked out with Ada, wrapping my arm around her shoulder. "I'm sorry this is hitting you so hard, Ada. Without us, many of the people we're about to eat dinner with wouldn't be alive in a couple of years. We have to look at the good we can accomplish and not focus on the evil that's been done. If we're successful, we could very well put an end to Belirand's tyranny."

"It's just so hard to leave all those people behind," she said.

"I promise you, I'm not giving up on them," I said.

"You mean it? You're not trying to hand this off to Mars Protectorate?"

"I might be willing to ask for help, but just try to get me to walk away," I said.

She wrapped her arm around my waist and pulled closer to me. "Mom would be proud that this is where I ended up."

"I bet she wouldn't be a bit surprised," I said.

Tabby fell back to walk with us. "What are you two up to back here? You might make me a jealous woman, Ada Chen."

"Don't ever let this one go," Ada replied. "I won't give you a second shot at him."

I looked from Ada to Tabby and raised an eyebrow.

"Stow it, Hoffen. I already know what you're thinking and it ain't going to happen," Tabby said.

Before I could respond, we turned the corner to the crew's mess. As expected, music was playing, but two men I didn't recognize stood at attention on either side of the door.

Recognition and understanding registered as I held my hand out to the two plus meter tall Divelbiss. I shook my head in wonder at his transformation. Where he'd been soft around the middle before he entered the tank, he was now trim and fit. His arms and hands had been completely restored. I might not have recognized him if not for the broad smile I associated with the big man.

"Well met," I said and stuck my hand out to shake. "Tonight we'll tell the story of how Mr. Divelbiss fed the Kroerak and saved us all. Without your sacrifice, we might never have made it this far."

"Aww, heck, Captain. Frakking bugs just pissed me off," he said.

"Remind me not to piss you off," I said as I moved out of his way so he could greet the rest of the command crew.

The man on the other side looked so different in an *Intrepid* vac-suit and with a clean shave, I struggled to accept that I was looking at Sendrei Buhari. Where Divelbiss's transformation had been dramatic, Sendrei's was incomprehensible.

"Mr. Buhari," I said extending my hand. "Welcome aboard."

"It is my honor," he said in a rich baritone voice as he smiled broadly.

GIVE NO QUARTER

"Thank you for joining us." I looked around the officer's mess table at all of the officers of *Intrepid*, including Moonie and Xie. I'd also invited Sendrei, Flaer and Ganesh, the respective leaders of the three villages we'd successfully rescued, as well as the Norigans - Blue Child and Jester Ripples. "In twelve hours, we will transition from fold-space into local space near the planet Ophir. I believe you've all had a chance to review the information we have on this planet and the free settlements of Yishuv and Petersburg."

"It seems a dream," Flaer intoned in the dialect with roots in the language spoken by most people of Earth and Mars.

"The Ophie natives are of concern," Ganesh, a man of twenty-five stans said quietly.

"Yishuv is well defended," Marny offered.

"We do not know if they will welcome us," Bliez responded. "Why would they share their resources?"

"It's true, we can't speak for Yishuv," I said. "But resources are not as scarce as you experienced on Cradle and we will speak with Yishuv's Council on your behalf."

"We don't want to be ruled again," Flaer said. "We would like to settle in the location Jonathan identified and we will learn to defend ourselves from the Ophir natives."

"Is that a consensus?" I asked looking from Sendrei to Ganesh and then back to Flaer and Bliez.

"Yes," Sendrei answered.

"Five hundred kilometers and a mountain range separate this location from the closest indigenous population," Jonathan said. "It is an ideal location at the confluence of two mountain rivers where they join a great lake. The mean temperature, fertile land

and natural defenses are ideal for human habitation, especially if seeded with technology and biological resources."

"Biological resources?" I asked.

"Seeds for planting, livestock, that sort of thing," Nick answered.

"We will not raise livestock for consumption," Flaer said stolidly. "No species has that right over another."

"A decision you will make for yourselves," I said. "You don't have to decide right now and I'd recommend talking with the people of Yishuv before making your final decision. We'll support you, regardless of the choices you make."

"But that's not what we're here to talk about, is it?" Buhari asked.

"You're right, Sendrei," I said, which earned me a sharp look from Flaer. "Belirand Corporation awaits our arrival at Ophir."

"They will seek to return us to Cradle," Sendrei said flatly.

"We think that's likely," I replied.

"Why did you withhold this information?" Flaer asked, still hot from her impassioned speech about livestock.

"Flaer, don't be rude," Ganesh whispered harshly. "Is it not enough they rescued us?"

"To be returned to Cradle? I'd rather die," she said.

I placed my hand on the table to stop the conversation. "If it is within our power, we will not allow Belirand to return you to the Kroerak."

"You're telling us because it might not be within your power," Sendrei summarized. "How large of a force awaits?"

"We don't know," Nick said. "We've had only sporadic communication and what we received has had little tactical value."

"Then why are we here?" Flaer asked.

"Do you speak for your people when you say you'd rather die than return to the Kroerak?" I asked.

"Without hesitation," Flaer answered. "The last nine days, living as free women … if they are our last, it is enough. We will not live as slaves again."

"She speaks for us all in this," Ganesh agreed. "A fire has been lit and we will not allow it to be put out."

Ada spoke up quietly and firmly. "Then, we'll see that you have a chance to live free."

The table grew quiet as the finality of their decision sunk in.

I slid a small box across the table to Flaer. "There's one more thing."

"What's this?" she asked, levering the top open and pulling out a silver necklace.

"We recovered jewelry from your predecessors who lived on the moon of a planet we named Thren's Rest," I said. "Flaer, the necklace you're holding belonged to your ancestor, Thren Blively." I flicked a collage of pictures onto the vid-screen built into the forward bulkhead. "That's her in the middle."

"I don't understand," Flaer replied in a much quieter voice than usual.

Ada stood up from her chair and walked around to where the small woman sat staring into the box of recovered treasures. "May I?" she asked, gesturing to the necklace.

Flaer handed the silvery rope to Ada, who gently placed it around the woman's neck.

"Look there," Ada said, placing her finger on the still picture of Thren Blively on the vid-screen. "Her daughter was also on the mission and was one of the original people brought to Cradle."

"It's the same necklace - but how?" she asked it a small voice.

"These items were recovered from the site where we believe the Kroerak first encountered your people," I said. "You share this ancestry with a few others in your group. Our ship will be able to help you identify who. Perhaps you'd like to share the information with them before we arrive at Ophir."

"Yes. Very much," she said, fingering the small green stone that hung from the necklace.

"Cap. I'd like to request that Mr. Buhari be added to our crew as a weapon's officer," Marny said, changing the subject.

I was glad for the shift in topic. While I enjoyed returning the jewelry, I was more than happy to move on to less emotional topics. Sendrei certainly looked the part, but he'd been out of action for ten years. "Your call, but the timing makes me wonder how that would work. We're about to get into a major battle here and Sendrei has been out of it for quite a while."

"A reasonable precaution," Sendrei replied.

"Aye, that it is, Sendrei," Marny replied. "What Cap doesn't know is that you saw combat on a ship larger than *Intrepid* and spent more time in a gunner's nest than anyone aboard, myself included."

"Is that right?" I asked him.

He gave a slight shrug of his shoulders and acknowledged my question. "We saw plenty of combat. My specialization was missile systems and I was in charge more than I was actually in the seat."

"How much time in the seat?" I asked.

"Actual combat hours? Ninety-two on turrets, one-hundred forty-seven throwing rocks," he said. "That was over the course of eighty-two enemy engagements."

"Ninety-two hours?" Ada asked. "Four days? I don't understand."

"Don't be fooled by the numbers, Ada," Tabby piped up. "He's being modest and reporting actual combat hours. Most engagements in ship-to-ship combat are over within twenty minutes. You could add up the actual combat hours of everyone on this ship and not hit that. With the exception of Marny, of course."

"Ohhh," Ada said, mirroring my own surprise.

"I'd say check him out on simulations," I said.

"Way ahead of you, Cap," Marny said. "Sendrei approached me a few days back with that very idea. His scores are triple that of the rest of the crew, but his real value is in missile targeting."

"I don't understand."

"Different ships have different vulnerabilities," Sendrei answered. "For example, *Intrepid*'s real strength is in her engines and the fact that there are no critical systems in her bow. Yet when I reviewed your encounter with *Justice Bringer*, more than sixty percent of her missiles strikes were forward, a natural consequence of two ships passing on attack runs."

"Marny?"

"Sendrei reviewed our combat data-streams and pointed out a number of tactical changes we could make when engaging Tullas," she said. "The information is invaluable."

"In that case, I'd say welcome to the crew, Mr. Buhari," I said. "As for the rest of you, try to get some rest. Once we reach Ophir, we'll be in the thick of things."

As much as we enjoyed each other's company, the prospect of combat in a few hours had us all on edge and the officer's mess emptied immediately.

"Captain, I need to talk to you." Moon Rastof caught my arm as Tabby and I were taking our leave.

"Okay if Tabby joins us?" I asked.

"I guess," he replied glumly.

"What's on your mind, Moonie?" I asked. It hadn't escaped my notice that Moonie had become more and more withdrawn as the trip progressed. The once ebullient man was merely fulfilling his shifts and refused to interact with our guests. I could only imagine how he felt, having worked for Belirand and seeing the chaos wrought by his previous employer.

"Can we find somewhere quieter?" Moonie asked.

"What's this about?" I asked as I led him toward the civilian conference room.

He closed the hatch behind him. "I don't really know how to say it."

"I know how you feel, we've all had to face some ugly truths in the last couple of weeks," I said.

"That's part of it, but I've done something that I can't undo," he said. "I'm afraid it's too late."

"Not you," Tabby said. "It can't be you. How could you? I thought we were friends."

He sighed as he leaned forward, resting his elbows on the table and holding his head in his hands, refusing to look at me. "We *are* friends, Tabby. I'm so sorry," he said.

"Be clear, Moonie, what did you do?" I asked.

"I was the one who told Tullas about our trip to Freedom Station," he said. "That's why she was waiting for us."

My chest tightened. I couldn't fathom why he'd do such a thing. "Why? How?"

"When we arrived in Sol and I picked up messages, there was one from Tullas. She promised me a position in Protective Services Division if I gave up our plans," he said.

"That's ridiculous. She could have killed us all." Anger and frustration filled my voice.

"She said it was the price I had to pay for my part in all this," he said. "It sounded fair."

"It sounded fair to betray your shipmates after Belirand abandoned you in the deep dark?" I asked, wanting nothing more than to throw him across the room. "Don't you get it? Tullas and people like her have been turning people over to the Kroerak and for what? Technology? A pass through their systems? Are you really willing to betray the entire human race?"

He just shook his head which rested in his hands.

Tabby lit into him. "We took you in, Moonie. Gave you a place. How could you do this?"

"I know, I know, I know," he said, still staring at the table. "There's more. She knows we're coming and I gave her the coordinates where we'd be exiting fold-space. They're ready for us."

"How?"

"An agent passed me a quantum comm crystal when I was on Freedom Station," he said.

"Xie?" Tabby asked.

"No. I don't know who it was," he said. "Mie-su almost caught me, though. She was following me around. I thought sure she'd ratted me out," he said. "She threatened to kill me."

"Why'd she do that?" Tabby asked.

"She said she knew I was up to something and I'd better not be making a move against the ship," he said. "Please don't tell her."

Tabby squinted her eyes and shook her head in confusion. "I

stuck up for you, Moonie. I said I couldn't imagine you'd be the rat. Now, you want us to save you? Frak off. You don't have to worry about Xie because there won't be anything left of you to worry about."

"Did you kill the Webbers and Ferrantes?" I asked.

"I had to. I couldn't take the chance that Vince Ferrante would give me up or that he'd told his wife," he said.

"Why tell us now?" I asked.

"She wants to talk to you," he said.

"Who?" Tabby asked.

"Tullas," I answered before Moonie could. "Give me the crystal, Moonie."

"You have to promise you won't kill me," he said.

I laughed, humorlessly. "You've given away our position and that's an act of mutiny. Now, you're bargaining for your life? Give me the crystal or I'll put you in a room with Xie and ask her to find it for me."

His face blanched as he dug in the belt of his vac-suit and produced a small, pink, quantum crystal.

Establish comm, Marny, I instructed the AI. "Marny, would you join us in the civilian conference room?"

"Aye, Cap," she replied, the door opening almost immediately.

I caught Tabby's eye. It wasn't much of a tell, but a raised eyebrow was all I needed. She had looped the command crew into our conversation.

"Would you ask Xie to escort Mr. Rastof to the brig?" I asked.

"You can't. You promised," he said, looking at me in horror.

"Make sure he's given the same cell where we kept the Webbers," I said and turned to Moonie. "I made you no promises. You haven't given me anything, so you'll have to work things out with Ms. Mie-su."

"Wait. There's more," he said. "Promise me you won't let Xie get to me."

"We'll see. What do you have?" I asked.

"They plan to disable *Intrepid* when you arrive. I've re-established Belirand's control circuits," he said.

"Jonathan, shut that down," Tabby said.

"Not this," he said. "It's programmed to run after we transition out of fold-space. Jonathan won't have time."

"I have a promise for you," Tabby said. "You show Jonathan what you've done or I'll ask Xie to go slow."

Nick entered the conference room as Marny escorted Moonie to the brig. He placed a quantum comm receiver on the table and looked at me expectantly. "At least we have that resolved."

"I have a bad feeling about this," I said as I dropped the crystal Moonie had given me into the device.

"She can't be trusted," Nick said.

"That's an understatement," I said as I pressed the transmit button.

"Ahhh, Mr. Hoffen, finally our little game of cat-and-mouse comes to an end," she said. I was glad I couldn't see her face. "I take it you've talked with Mr. Rastof?"

"We have," I said. "What do you want?"

"I believe the phrase 'nothing new under the sun' comes to mind," she said. "You will surrender when you arrive in system. You are badly outmatched as I've brought *Stark Justice, Hammer of Justice* and *Justice Bringer*."

"Doesn't it bother you?" I asked. "Selling out humanity to the Kroerak?"

"I assure you that is not what has occurred," she said. "I've bought much needed time and waylaid a Kroerak invasion. You, on the other hand, insulted the Kroerak Empire and have undone centuries of peace between our species."

"I've set a dead man's switch on a message to Mars Protectorate, outlining Belirand and NaGEK's culpability in enslaving civilians. You stand in direct violation of international law," Nick said.

"We have stopped all outgoing communications within the Ophir star system," she said.

"And yet, you're talking with us," I said.

"We're using a quantum communication crystal," she said. "They don't suffer from the same limitations as do ordinary communication systems."

"Good thing we have a direct line to M-Pro," I said. "Or didn't you know that they hand crystals out to all their privateers?"

A long pause followed and when she finally started up again, her voice was low and angry. "Now, you listen here, you worm," she growled. "Do you really want to start a war between Mars and NaGEK? What would be gained? We have to be united when the Kroerak finally arrive."

"Not my problem, Tullas," I said. "You crossed the line. Why should anyone believe you have humanity's best interest at heart? Your best bet is to clear Ophir's system before we arrive and figure out how you're going to retrieve those ten thousand souls on Cradle. Either way, we're done talking." I pulled the crystal before she could reply.

***

"Transition to normal-space in thirty ... twenty-nine ...," Ada announced.

I gripped the arms of my chair. I couldn't afford to be distracted by the transition. The lives of my crew and likely the people of Yishuv depended on us making it through the next thirty minutes alive.

"We have contact," Ada said sharply before we'd completely cleared transition.

"Evasive," I said. "Tabby, separate!" My orders were mostly unnecessary as we already had a plan for the first few moments.

The forward vid-screen jumped to life, showing that indeed we'd arrived, flanked by the Justice class frigate *Stark Justice* and *Intrepid*'s sister, the frigate *Justice Bringer*.

"All fire on *Justice Bringer*." I reinforced the order I'd already given.

Locate Hammer of Justice, I requested from the AI. The forward vid-screens showed an immediate view of combat and I was unable to locate the third ship. The holo-projector in front of my chair zoomed out and then back in on a bulky, justice class frigate positioned sixty-thousand kilometers away from our current position, just outside the range of Petersburg Station's heavy, defense guns.

"Incoming hail, Justice Bringer," my AI announced.

Accept. "What is it, Tullas?"

"I wanted to make sure you were watching your mother's position. Captain Mussa is about to finish the job he started in Tipperary, and then Captain MacAsgaill and I will put an end to this ugly chapter in our history. Captain Mussa, you are clear to breach," Tullas said.

For a moment, time stood still as *Hammer of Justice* turned toward Petersburg Station and accelerated, a flight of missiles launching as Mussa slipped inside of the station cannon's perimeter. I couldn't breathe as I willed the guns to respond and obliterate the enemy.

"Ten seconds to impact." I could hear Tullas's AI informing her of the missile's progress.

All around me, I heard the impact of missiles on *Intrepid's* hull and the warning of a hull breach in a forward section. I was unable to make heads or tails of the action.

The missiles impacted the gun emplacement at Petersburg and the cannon exploded brilliantly. My mind raced. Would Mussa try to pick off all of the guns or go straight for the kill shot on Mom. We'd disabled Belirand's ability to override the cannons, so why wasn't Mom shooting?

"Number two engine, offline," Xie Mie-su reported. "We're taking heavy fire."

"Your hubris was your end, Mr. Hoffen," Tullas chided, as a second flight of missiles streamed from *Hammer of Justice.* *"Seven seconds to impact."*

Dulcinea del Toboso sailed around the asteroid, positioning itself between Mussa and the station with its turrets firing steadily. "Fire your missiles," I whispered. "before it's too late."

"What's that, Hoffen?" Tullas asked as the second of three defensive turrets exploded brilliantly.

"We can't escape their crossfire," Ada complained as she rolled

Intrepid over, attempting to weave out of the trap set by *Stark Justice* and *Justice Bringer*.

"Surrender now," Tullas demanded.

We might have had a chance if we hadn't started in the kill-box.

"It's too late for your mother and the traitor, LeGrande," she said as a barrage of missiles launched from *Hammer of Justice*. Their targeting showed on my holo-projector and they were headed straight for *Dulcinea del Toboso*. That woman talked too much.

I watched in shock as the smaller ship was shredded by an impossible barrage of weapon's fire and missile explosions. An iron band seemed to form around my heart as I considered the loss of the heroic Captain LeGrande.

A moment later, a fourth flight of missiles was launched from *Hammer of Justice* as it slid around the ruined hulk of *Dulcinea*. My breath caught in my throat when, finally, the last defensive turret burped to life. The powerful cannon had no difficulty dispatching the incoming missiles and then oriented on *Hammer of Justice*, which was now too committed to the station's defensive perimeter to pull away. Round after round from the remaining cannon tore into the vulnerable ship, each more devastating than the last. I almost felt pity for the crew as they attempted to limp from the kill zone, but the arrogant Mussa had overcommitted and no one would escape today. There would be no mercy given by my mother and when the firing finally ceased, all that remained of the stubby frigate was debris.

"Frakking aye! Now mine this, bitch." Tabby's voice rang out over the comm as *Hotspur* came into view in local space. Twin missiles streaked forward, targeting the center of *Stark Justice*. I knew from experience that two missiles were not enough to rip open the heavily armored ship, so I wasn't surprised Tullas had allowed Tabby to make her bombing run. Tullas was keeping both her ships focused on *Intrepid*.

"Number one is at twenty-percent," Xie announced.

"All fire on *Stark Just...*," Marny never finished the command.

My comm with Tullas cut out and *Stark Justice* shuddered, bright pin-points of light spilling from the middle of the ship as if someone had poked it with a hundred small needles. Gas and debris spewed from the ship as her engines and weapon systems spooled down. "Finish her," Marny's voice rose as our turrets tore through the small openings, widening them like a welding laser on a habitation dome.

"Hard to starboard," I demanded. "How many missiles do we have left?"

"Six remaining," Marny replied.

"Focus on *Justice Bringer*'s engines," I said.

"With pleasure," Marny answered.

While a frigate was designed to run, it was always a poor decision to turn tail in a battle when starting from a dead-stop. It appeared Tullas was going to try it anyway. *Intrepid* was in bad shape, but the destruction of two ships in her battle-group must have shaken Tullas's confidence.

Hail Justice Bringer.

The comm opened, but I didn't receive a reply.

"Admiral Tullas, you need to cut your engines," I said. "Otherwise, we'll shred you on the way out and you'll never get home."

"I would expect nothing less," Tullas answered.

"I'm not going to let you run this time, Tullas. You came for my family again," I said. "You've murdered your own and for what?"

"What I did, I did for humanity. You've brought ruin to our species, Hoffen. At least I won't have to live to see that," she said.

"Surrender, Tullas," I said.

"You'd like that. No, we'll be going now," she said. "I know you well enough to know you won't fire on a ship full of people who won't fire back."

"Cap? She's presented her engines and we're point-blank." Marny stated, muting our comms.

"Give no quarter, Marny. It's time to end this."

LIBERTAS

"Cease fire," I ordered as our missiles ripped into the spine of *Justice Bringer* and her engines went dark. Sendrei had provided a targeting solution that focused on disabling the ship rather than destroying it.

"Xie. Ship status?"

"Engine one is offline. I'm in the process of shutting down engine two. We lost atmo in a few forward crew sections. The majority of our armor on starboard and port sides along the waterline is ruined. We'll need to get a repair crew out there shortly or we'll have more decompressions," Xie reported.

"Tabby, give me a status," I requested over our tactical channel.

"One hundred percent," she said. "Tullas only had eyes for you."

"What in Jupiter's name did you do to *Stark Justice*?"

"We took a page from the Kroerak," Nick said. "Neither of those ships were moving, beyond just trying to keep pace with *Intrepid*. We just got a nice super high speed run at them and dropped our load of iron ingots out of the hold. *Intrepid*'s guns did the real work."

"You'll have to watch the data-streams, little man," Marny said cheerfully. "You must have hit something internal. That ship was ready to go when we lit her up."

"Jonathan, how are our passengers? Any casualties" I asked. My stomach knotted as I considered the question.

"Negative on casualties," he replied. "There is considerable anxiety and two women appear to be completing their gestational cycles."

"They're delivering their babies!?" Ada asked. "Are they okay?"

"Yes, they appear to be within the last ten percent of their cycle," Jonathan replied. For all the strides in normal conversation he'd made, I was having trouble following what he was saying.

"Liam." Ada looked at me, her face fraught with worry. She'd taken a special interest in the women from Cradle and it was hard on her to think of them in distress.

"I relieve you, Ada," I said, shortcutting our normal formality.

"I stand relieved." She jumped from her station and bolted out of the bridge.

"Tabby, Nick, we need to look for survivors," I said. My primary status screen was overlaid with a search pattern of the combat arena. Every piece of material larger than the end of my finger was being tracked and scanned.

"We're on it," Tabby replied. "Jonathan is coordinating."

Establish comm with Petersburg station.

"Liam?" Mom answered right away. "Sit-rep," she demanded. You could take the officer out of the military but the opposite was harder.

"Still assessing, but overall we're whole," I said. "LeGrande. I'm so sorry."

"We're showing you have significant loss in engine function and multiple hull breaches," she said.

"Aye. We lost an engine and another is on life support, but we've no casualties. Please report *your* situation," I replied.

"No doubt you saw the loss of the defensive guns," she said. "That was planned. We had to draw *Hammer of Justice* in far enough they couldn't escape. The station is one hundred percent. *Dulcinea del Toboso* was unmanned. Jenny Caton rigged a remote navigation device for us. Sorry about your ship, but we had to ensure that *Hammer of Justice* was completely destroyed."

"MacAsgaill?" I asked, my chest growing tight with anticipation.

"He's dead, Liam. There were no survivors," she replied. I'd heard that revenge was hollow and unsatisfying, but this felt like something entirely different. We hadn't hunted down our adversary -although, if I'd had some idea how, I might have. There was no guilt, because MacAsgaill had decided on this path, not us. No, I mostly felt relieved. The man who had ordered my father killed was dead as well as the executioner who had performed the murder and the universe was a better place for it.

"Understood. Good. We haven't found Mussa or Tullas yet," I said.

Mussa, under MacAsgaill's orders, had actually launched the missiles at our peaceful co-op in the Descartes asteroid belt He wasn't any less guilty of murder than MacAsgaill and I wasn't sure what I'd do if we found him alive.

"We have another situation. I'll explain more when we get there, but the short of it is we have pregnant women aboard, giving birth."

"Say again," Mom requested. "You haven't been gone long enough."

I laughed, despite myself. "No one you know," I said. "We rescued a group of mostly women. It's a long story, but the short of it is that thirty-eight of them are pregnant."

"Thirty-seven," Marny corrected, pointing to a corner of the forward vid-screen where Ada was kneeling next to a woman who held a newborn baby to her chest. The Norigan, Jester Ripples, stood next to Ada, adjusting blankets.

"Oh, man," Understanding hit me quickly for once. I flicked the image over the comm to Mom.

"Liam, a warship is no place for pregnant women or babies," she reprimanded. "What am I looking at?"

"That's Jester Ripples," I said. "I really don't have time to explain, but we're headed your way in a few hours. Grab me on the comms if something urgent pops up."

"I can't believe you're going to leave me hanging like this, but I understand. I love you, Liam," Mom replied. "Petersburg Station out."

"Cap, we need to board *Justice Bringer*," Marny said. "The surviving crew has surrendered, but we haven't made contact with anyone of command rank."

"Jonathan, I trust you're comfortable in the seat," I asked. "Xie, you're with us."

"We are, Captain," he replied.

Without further conversation, the three of us exited the bridge and made our way to the armory. "Who has the gunnery nest?" I asked as we equipped what had become a fairly standard loadout: pistols, nano-blades, sensor pucks, flash-bang discs and grenade marbles.

"Sendrei, but only with Jonathan unlocking the guns. I'd like a little more time with him before I give him too much control," Marny replied, handing me a snap-on attachment for my blaster rifle. "Sticky rounds. Good for subduing without injury."

"You kids coming?" Tabby asked as I established our tactical channel.

"Just leaving the armory. See you in a minute," I answered.

"Grab that laser pistol I like. We don't have any on *Hotspur*," she requested.

We exited the armory, worked our way through the air-lock next to the cargo-hold and jetted over to *Hotspur*'s open door.

"Just hang in the hallway," Tabby announced as we landed. "Nick will ferry us over."

Justice Bringer's cargo-hold door was raised and eight suited figures knelt on the deck with hands over their heads, the postures of several indicating injury. Twelve figures lay prone, lined up in a row just aft of the crew.

"Xie, Tabby, verify the casualties," I requested as we came to rest just above the deck. Someone had rigged a gravity generator, but at .1g it did little more than hold down the surrendering crew.

"All deceased," Tabby announced.

"What are the scope of your injuries?" I asked.

"May I?" A man located in the middle of the group asked. I nodded and he flicked a synopsis of the crew's injuries. None were currently life threatening. We worked quickly to bind their hands behind their backs.

"Where's Tullas?" I asked.

"On the bridge," the same man replied. "They still have atmo and power." He sounded annoyed.

"Davey Jones' Brig?" Tabby asked, using a term she'd coined

when we set prisoners adrift in space without the benefit of AGBs.

"I don't think they're going anywhere," I said.

"We've got 'em," Nick said from *Hotspur* as he spun the top turret over to line up on the hold.

"Let's move," Marny said. "Tabby, you have point. Liam, number two. Xie, you've got our backs." We'd used the formation before and quickly moved through the already open airlock into the decompressed passageway on deck three. *Justice Bringer*'s layout was identical to *Intrepid* and we easily made our way to the bridge door after making a single circuit of the passageways on the second deck, dropping sensor pucks along the way.

"Tullas, are you in there?" I asked, after activating an acoustic coupler that would transmit conversation through the nano-steel door. We waited twenty seconds and I asked one final time.

"We'll have to breach," Marny instructed, pulling charges from a pack on her back and placing them strategically on the hatch.

Without atmo to transmit a pressure wave, the only danger with explosives was line of sight and ricochets. Even so, we positioned ourselves in the aft corridor, near the captain's quarters. A cloud of atmo escaping from the bridge was the only indication Marny had ignited the charges.

"Go, go, go," Marny said, spurring us inside.

"Clear," Tabby announced, sweeping to her right and forward.

"Clear," I called, sweeping aft. While true, our status reports didn't even begin to describe the scene. There were no targets; only bodies still at their posts, without vac-suit helmets.

"What in the frak?" Tabby asked as the four of us gathered in the center of the bridge. The four officers we'd found at their stations each had a single head wound.

"She murdered them and then suicided," Xie observed.

"That's barbaric," Tabby spat.

"She couldn't afford to be questioned," I answered glumly. "She was mad in her zeal."

Tullas sat in the captain's chair, arms open, pistol lying on the floor a meter from her body. The woman was smaller in death than I'd have thought possible.

***

"What do you mean, they want to start their own settlement?" Councilman Bedros asked, ignoring Flaer and Ganesh who had come with Sendrei to address the Yishuv Council. We'd just finished a meal provided by Yishuv and had transitioned to the purpose of our visit.

"You will address Ganesh on matters pertaining to Libertas," Sendrei replied, warning in his tone.

"I mean no disrespect." Bedros turned to Ganesh. "It is just that Yishuv is a thriving settlement and would welcome you with arms wide."

"What do a bunch of children know of hewing a settlement from the wilds of Ophir?" Peraf asked, clearly agitated. "We've barely survived after three centuries."

"And yet we did just that," Ganesh answered quietly. "Do you believe the Kroerak provided resources for our villages? They provided only access to water. It was up to us to establish shelter and defend ourselves from surrounding dangers."

"You've seen Jonathan's survey of the location," I said.

"You can't give them that spot," Peraf said. "We claimed it."

Ganesh looked at me, concerned.

"No we haven't." Bedros shook his head with a frown on his face. "We passed on the location and will certainly provide as much support as possible."

"What are you doing? You can't give away our planet," Peraf replied angrily. "They'll just keep bringing more people."

"Which will make us all stronger," Bedros replied. "Do you really believe we have the means or moral right to stand in the way of this?" When Peraf didn't respond, he continued. "The resources of Yishuv are at your disposal. Whatever we can do to help, we will do. Councilwoman Peraf no longer represents the majority opinion of the Council."

"Yishuv's knowledge of local agriculture would be much appreciated," Nick added.

"We'll arrange an expedition with farming equipment and seeds," Bedros replied. "It's late for planting most crops, but much work can be done to prepare fields for the next season. We should have livestock to trade within a stan or two."

"No!" Flaer answered vehemently, surprising Bedros.

Ganesh laid his hand on the healer's arm. "We'll appreciate your assistance with crops. We are uncomfortable keeping animals for consumption."

"Of course," Bedros answered, bowing his head graciously. "I meant no offense."

"If you are amenable, we'd like to give you a tour of Libertas," I said.

"You've already settled there? This is all just pretense?" Peraf asked.

"No pretense, Councilwoman Peraf," I answered. "We do not believe Yishuv is capable of controlling an entire planet and have made plans accordingly."

"Nor do we desire to," Bedros replied. "A trip to Libertas would be lovely."

As we stood and exited, I pulled Bedros aside. "Peraf seems ornerier than usual. What's up?"

"Lorraine Tullas promised Peraf she'd be rid of you all and be put back in charge. Suffice it to say, the councilwoman was disappointed by the recent turn of events," he said.

"Is that going to be a problem?"

"Not at all," Bedros replied. "Her approach has not won her any friends on the Council and I believe she'll be voted off in the next election cycle."

***

"Nice and easy, Tabbs," I called over the comms once we'd all loaded into *Hotspur*'s hold.

The trip took thirty minutes as we traveled the eight hundred kilometers to the location Jonathan had surveyed for the inhabitants of Yishuv many ten-day ago.

After setting down, we exited onto a green field. The sounds of rushing water from the nearby river and the backdrop of snow-covered mountains completed the idyllic scene. For not being human, Jonathan certainly knew how to pick a beautiful location.

As the growing settlement came into view, the smell of a campfire was evident and a thin column of smoke rose from above the cluster of temporary habitation domes. A construction bot was busy working on what looked like more permanent structures, pulling from a pile of sheet steel and armored-glass. Apparently, Merrie's glass manufacturing had already started production.

We were greeted by friendly waves as we passed residents who were busily moving between the habitation domes.

"We're building a central gathering hall, first," Ganesh explained. "Jonathan has been working with us to lay out our new city. His plans seem ambitious, but we have no real experience with materials such as steel."

"You've made quite a lot of progress already," I noted as we passed by one of four towers that had what I believed to be ship blaster turrets mounted on top. "I thought we felt the Ophies weren't a threat?"

"A necessary precaution," Jonathan answered, stepping up next to me. "There is some evidence of local predators."

"Are those turrets from *Justice Bringer*?" I asked.

"Yup," Nick answered.

I shrugged. "That's appropriate. Speaking of *Justice Bringer*. Any word on if we're going to be able to get her going again?"

"The frigates need repair, but they're both moving," he said. "I don't know what you're thinking next, but I'd say we should consider a trip back to Freedom Station."

Just then, a woman carrying a bundle in her arms approached our group. I recognized her as Isha, the first woman who'd given birth aboard *Intrepid*.

"Why don't you all go ahead," I said to the group. "Tabby and I will catch up."

"Liam Hoffen." She carefully pronounced my name, smiling.

"Hi, Isha. How are you feeling?" I asked, not really sure what to ask someone who'd recently given birth.

"I ask for your blessing," she said, handing me the bundle containing her infant. I looked at her, terrified. I had no idea how to hold a baby. She helped me by pulling my arm beneath its back and pressing it to my chest. Ada appeared and hustled up next to us. She, too, was smiling.

"I don't know what you're asking," I said.

"Just kiss her on the forehead," Ada said.

I looked to Isha and then to the baby, not sure which 'her' was being referred to.

"The baby, Liam."

"Oh ..."

I pulled the blanket away from the baby's face, leaned in and kissed her forehead, surprised at how sweet the child smelled as my nose brushed her skin.

"She's adorable," I said, enjoying the moment. My doubt as to the value of our mission disappeared in that single instant. Just this one life being saved from the Kroerak was worth all of the risk. I moved to hand the baby back to Isha, who accepted the bundle graciously.

"You're a natural," Tabby said, wrapping her arm around my waist. "Someday, we'll have our own."

"I sure hope so."

"Isha, is there something more you'd like to say?" Ada prompted the olive-skinned woman.

"Liam Hoffen Libertas," she said, shyly, almost embarrassed.

I pinched my eyebrows, not understanding.

Ada laid her hand on the woman's back, rubbing it reassuringly. "She named her after you, Liam."

I looked from Ada back to Isha who seemed to be cringing in anticipation of a rebuke. "That's perfect," I said wrapping my arms around the woman and her child. "You certainly have my blessing."

"Thank you," Isha kissed my cheek lightly and scurrying off.

"Hallo, Captain." Divelbiss said as we came into the center

court of the new settlement. The big man was smiling ear-to-ear as he carried a load of firewood.

"Divelbiss, I didn't expect to see you down here," I said.

"Master Chief gave me leave," he said, dropping his bundle onto a growing pile. A woman with long dark hair moved the logs into an organized stack. "But I've been looking to speak with you."

"Oh?"

"Arati, stop a minute," Divelbiss said. The woman who'd been stacking logs looked up to him and came over to his side. The difference in their sizes was almost comical as he towered over the much smaller woman, whose tummy bulged. "Cap, I know you've been more than fair to me and I committed to sailing with you, but I'm requesting to end my commission."

I looked from him to Arati and back. "Really?" I asked smiling. "How do you know so quickly?"

"It's not like that," he said, then looked at Arati with a horrified expression. "I guess maybe it could be … I don't know … I'm not great with words … I'd like a chance to find out, I guess."

"What does Ganesh have to say about this?" I asked.

"We live freely," Arati answered firmly, my AI's translation communicating her resolve as well as her words. "Ganesh will not object."

"Divelbiss, your sacrifice on the moon over Thren's Rest made all of this possible," I said. "If it is your desire to help build the village of Libertas, I will not stand in your way. You are relieved of duty." I snapped my hand up sharply into a salute, which caused the big man to tear up. "Know this, you're welcome on my ship anytime."

"Liam Hoffen," Jester Ripples hopped into view and upon reaching us, clambered into my arms. I'd finally become comfortable with the closeness required by the warm little creatures. "Isn't Libertas lovely?"

"Indeed it is. Have you explored much?" I asked.

"Indeed, yes," he said. "Blue Child and I very much approve of the location. The rivers are a wonderful treat."

"Have you decided if you'll make your home here or continue

with us?" I asked.

"Nicholas James says he expects to travel to my home-world. Is this true?"

"It is," I said. "It might take us a while, but we would very much like to be introduced to your family and see what sort of trading might be accomplished between friends."

"We have no capacity for creating nano-steel," Jester Ripples answered. "It would be highly sought after. But my family would simply enjoy welcoming such a wonderful species onto our pads - or homes, as you refer to them. I would accompany you on your journey, if welcomed. Blue Child has expressed a desire to stay in Libertas. He was taken at a much younger age than I and his heart is with his family here."

"It might be dangerous to travel with us," I said.

"Then you will certainly need my help."

HORSE TRADING

"This place looks great," I said as we finished a tour of Petersburg Station. All of the rooms previously closed by Belirand's attack in Descartes had been cleared, pressurized and reopened. Merrie and Amon had set up an efficient manufacturing space for pressing steel plate as well as firing armored glass.

"Wouldn't be possible without all the materials Ortel and the boys have been mining," Merrie said.

Priloe stopped in front of me. "You haven't seen the best spot."

"Really? I thought we'd just received the tour," I said.

"Not everything." He and Ortel grinned at each other.

"Seriously? Show me," I said. "Mom, do you mind?"

She nodded. "I wouldn't dream of standing in the way."

"We're just over half done," Ortel said as Tabby and I followed the two through a rough-hewn, poorly lit hallway.

"Merrie found replicator plans for the goals and ball returns." Priloe said excitedly. "She also created a bunch of really fun mods for changing up the terrain."

"Here we are," Ortel said as we popped through a steel entry door into a podball court that only a kid could love. Two goals had been hastily erected on opposite ends of a large, open space and gravity generators were haphazardly spread along the floor.

"Fire it up," Tabby said, pulling a ball out of the near goal.

"Try to score on me," Priloe taunted. "Bet you can't."

"Been training, have you?" she asked.

He turned the gravity down to 0.05g. "Sure have."

Tabby bounded through the space and allowed Priloe to block her out.

"Gotta be careful," she warned as she spun unexpectedly and fired the ball into the goal. "Sometimes people can be tricky."

"You're super-fast," Priloe said, awed by the woman who'd rescued him from the top of Léger Nuage so long ago.

"Bring it." Tabby challenged, floating back as Ortel picked up the podball. The two of them attempted to play keep away. I saw the error of their plan about the time Tabby easily intercepted the ball and rocketed back to the goal.

"What do you think?" Ortel asked, giving up.

"We'll let the construction bot have a run at it after you've cleared it all, but I love what you've completed," I said. "Maybe you and Priloe could run tournaments once it's up and running. You could even charge tourney fees. Who else plays?" I asked.

"Jenny Caton is good. Merrie, Amon and Zebulon aren't too bad," Ortel said. "You know - for grounders. I've heard there are a bunch of ex-Belirand from *Cape of Good Hope* who'd like to play."

"We'll need to work on getting a few more shuttles so you can ferry people from the surface," I said. "Tournaments would be good social interaction."

"As long as we can charge fees," Priloe said.

Ortel put his hands out. "With what currency?"

"Oh." Priloe looked dumbfounded.

"We'll get a currency figured out sooner or later," I said. "Jonathan and Nick are already working on proposals."

"You kids ready to eat?" Mom asked over the comms. "Amon made fresh bread."

"On our way." I wasn't overly hungry, but fresh bread sounded appealing.

"What, no beer?" I asked as we entered the room they'd converted into a combination mess and galley. Amon called it a kitchen, whatever that meant. The smell of bread had changed my mind on just how hungry I was.

"There's a mead to be had in Yishuv," Amon offered.

"Tastes like burned piss," Jenny Caton added, joining us. "I'd kill for a liter of real vodka."

"We'll make sure alcohol is on the trade list," I said. "When we were on Freedom Station, I got a ping from this guy, Jerry Sailer who runs the Contraband Distillery. I didn't think much of it then, but he was looking for grain. Seems like we could trade Yishuv grain for good liquor since we're headed that way."

Mom cocked her head. "Are you planning another trip to Freedom Station?"

"We are," I said. "*Intrepid* is down two engines and we've barely been able to get *Justice Bringer* moving again. Freedom Station is currently the only location we can safely get repairs. We also need food replicators for Libertas. Even with Yishuv helping, Libertas will never be independent if they have to rely on others for food."

"When will you leave?"

"As soon as we can load fresh supplies," I said. "We've no time to waste."

"I don't understand," Mom said. "We stopped Belirand, what's the rush?"

"The citizens of Libertas are just the lucky few we were able to save," I said. "We had to leave thousands behind."

"Even with two operational frigates, you could only carry a few hundred people. What else will a trip to Freedom Station do for you?" Mom asked.

I smiled and nodded. She was right, but I wasn't about to broadcast our plans to such a large group. "I guess we'll have to improvise."

***

"Mars Protectorate, this is *Hotspur*. Come in please," I said for the fifth time. Jonathan, Tabby and I had taken command of *Justice Bringer*, but I wasn't about to explain to Mars Protectorate why we were calling from the third Belirand ship we'd acquired. *Intrepid* and *Justice Bringer* had been underway for seventy hours and had an additional fifty hours of fold-space before arriving at Freedom Station. We were sailing light-handed again with just Tabby, Jonathan, Jester Ripples and me in Tullas's captured flagship.

"Do you think they've stopped monitoring the crystal?" Tabby asked.

As if in response, the communication device crackled to life. I relaxed when I heard Gregor Belcose's deep Russian voice. "Go ahead, *Hotspur*, you have Belcose."

"Gregor, so good to hear your voice," I said. "Liam Hoffen."

"Greetings, Captain Hoffen. It is indeed pleasant to hear your voice," he replied. I could imagine the heavily muscled man straightening his vac-suit as he spoke. "How may Mars Protectorate be of service to you today?"

"I need to speak with Commander Sterra," I said.

"I'm afraid her schedule is rather tight. Is there a message I could pass along?"

"Are you in a secure location, Gregor?" I asked.

"Relatively," he said.

"The information I have is dangerous," I said. "I'm hesitant to say anything."

There was a long pause. "One moment please." When he spoke again, his voice sounded different, like he was inside a shell. "Our conversation is secure, but you must know that I'm bound by duty to report what we discuss."

"Gregor, if Mars Protectorate is party to what we've run into, your life will be forfeit. Are you sure you want to continue?"

"I've sworn my life to the service of my home-world and its people. I am not fearful of reprisal," he said.

I blew out the breath I'd been holding. I'd never be able to un-ring the bell I was about to sound. "TransLoc gates are not necessary for faster-than-light travel," I said. "Belirand has been withholding technology."

"This is not news, Liam Hoffen. Even in the beginning, Belirand had the capability to travel without TransLoc gates," he replied. "That's how they discovered the initial systems."

"Three centuries ago, Belirand discovered a sentient species. They abandoned the mission on that planet, hoping the colonists would perish," I said. "They didn't. Two centuries ago, they ran into a particularly evil species called Kroerak. Gregor, they've been trading humans, who are being used as a food source, to gain favors with the Kroerak Empire."

"That's preposterous," Belcose snapped. "Belirand reports on their missions and they haven't found another inhabitable planet since Tipperary. They all but mothballed their fleet over a century ago due to their inability to achieve a reasonable return on their investment."

"Search for Sendrei Buhari of the North American Navy. He was killed in a training accident twelve years ago," I said. "Only he wasn't. Gregor, be careful with this information. Belirand will do anything to keep it quiet."

"What happened to Lieutenant Buhari?" Gregor asked. Apparently his AI had located Sendrei's record.

"Set up a meeting and you can ask him yourself," I said. "We rescued him from a planet controlled by the Kroerak."

"Stay by the comm-unit," Belcose replied. "I'll pass along your message. Captain Hoffen, I hope you aren't up to something here. The people who will become involved in this do not have a sense of humor."

"Copy that," I said and closed the comm.

"Like he does?" Tabby quipped nervously and we both laughed, to Jonathan's confusion.

"He sounded angry," Jester Ripples said, pulling himself onto my lap and wrapping a single, spindly arm around my shoulders to steady himself.

"It's not uncommon for people to sound angry when they are concerned," I explained. "The news I was giving him was upsetting."

"Thomas Phillipe Anino would not have taken the same risk you now take," Jonathan said. "He believed governments to be corrupt."

"Weigh the risks," I said. "We don't have the capacity to save the people on Cradle. If Mars Protectorate is in on this with Belirand, we're no worse off - unless they catch us."

"How difficult will it be for them to catch you?" Jonathan asked. "You've requested a meeting."

"A fine point, my friend," I said. "But you're not correctly weighing the risk. My experience with LaVonne Sterra and Gregor Belcose leads me to trust them. I weigh that and the lives of ten thousand people against the lives of my crew."

Two hours later, the quantum radio chirped, signaling an incoming message.

"Liam Hoffen, go ahead," I answered.

"Captain Hoffen, I've been given clearance to arrange a meeting. Would you be able to meet at Valhalla Platform in sixty-two hours?"

"We can make it, Gregor, but I need assurance from Commander Sterra that neither my crew, my passengers, nor my ship will be detained after our meeting is complete," I said.

"I'm afraid that's not possible, Captain Hoffen," Belcose replied. "Commander Sterra is not available."

"That's going to be a problem," I said. "We're taking quite a risk here."

"Ahh, bullcrap," a bombastic voice cut in. I wasn't completely sure, but I thought I recognized the speaker. "If we'd wanted to grab you, we would never have let you off the *Bukunawa*." The reference to the Red Houzi dreadnaught confirmed my suspicion.

"Admiral Alderson?" I asked, confused. "What's going on, Gregor? I thought you said you were with Commander Sterra."

"You'll need to forgive Gregor's deception, Hoffen. Lieutenant *Commander* Belcose was under orders to do whatever was necessary to maintain contact with you once it was made. He's moved up in rank and no longer serves with Sterra aboard *Kuznetsov*," Admiral 'Buckshot' Alderson answered. "You and your crew have been branded as terrorists by NaGEK vis-à-vis Belirand Corporation. Why do you think for one minute we'd believe your ridiculous story or give you any assurances? Seems to me, you need to be put down like a pack of wild dogs."

"Gregor, did you check Sendrei Buhari's story?" I asked.

"His presence wouldn't confirm your story," Belcose answered.

"What if I told you we had a Kroerak corpse aboard?" I asked.

"Son, if you can produce a real alien corpse, I'll personally give you that get-out-of-jail-free card," Alderson said.

"Are you giving me your word?" I asked. I'd learned that for all his bluster and political maneuvering, Buckshot Alderson both cared for the people of Mars and was a man of his word.

"If half of what you've said is true, we'll be so deep in the shite, you're the least of my concerns," he said. "You have my word that I'll release you if you produce a viable, sentient alien corpse. Honestly, I don't believe you're making as much trouble as Belirand would have me believe."

"In sixty-two hours, we'll arrive at the following coordinates," I said and rattled off the coordinates I'd worked out. "Please make sure that you don't have anyone sitting within a twenty kilometer radius. I'd hate to bump into them. Hoffen out."

"Where was that?" Tabby asked.

"Just outside Platform Valhalla's security perimeter. It's exactly where Commander Joe Alto picked us up and escorted us in from last time. I might like to make an entrance, but I'd prefer not spooking the types of folks they'll likely send to escort us," I said.

"Alto was a good man," Tabby said, causing me to wince. I'd forgotten that Alto and the *Walter Sydney Adams* had been in the response group that had been destroyed in the battle for Colony-40. It was the same battle where Tabby had nearly died.

"A real hero," I agreed.

The remainder of the trip to Freedom Station went without incident. That is, if you consider playing cards with an alien comprised of fourteen hundred thirty-eight sentients and a frog-like creature with genius-level spatial and mathematical skills without incident. Fortunately, Jester Ripples, while extraordinarily bright, was easy to bluff and Jonathan seemed more interested in our inter-personal interaction than actually winning.

"Here we go," Tabby announced from Tullas's chair. It was a seat I'd refused to occupy. "Transition in five … four … "

"Any contact?" I asked, when my vision finally cleared.

"Sensors are clear," Jonathan reported. "*Intrepid* is forty kilometers off our starboard bow at forty degrees and ten degrees of declination."

Open comm channel with Intrepid.

"Good morning, Liam." Ada sounded tired. I figured she'd

arranged shifts so that she was at the helm when we arrived in Sol.

"Good morning," I answered. "You all doing okay?"

"We had a few decompression events during our trip, but no casualties. That's one benefit of sailing light," she replied.

"Prisoners?" I asked, remembering the last decompression that killed three.

"All accounted for," she replied. "How was your trip?"

"Since most of the ship is closed off, it was pretty quiet," I said. "Looks like we're getting some sensor activity from the station, I'd better ring 'em up."

"Understood, we'll stand by."

Hail Freedom Station.

"Freedom Station, go ahead," a cheerful woman's voice answered.

"Captain Liam Hoffen requesting permission to approach the station," I replied.

"We're picking up two ships, Captain; one of Belirand registration. Please maintain standoff distance" the woman replied.

"Roger that, Freedom Station," I answered. "There's been a change of ownership, both ships are property of Loose Nuts corporation."

"Do you think that's going to be a problem?" Ada asked over the comm.

"I don't think so," I said. "I doubt they've forgotten the reception we received from Tullas last time."

"Agreed," Nick answered.

Several minutes later, the comm channel with Freedom Station reopened.

"Captain Hoffen, you old pirate." A familiar voice, with what I'd learned was a Latin accent, preceded the face of Admiral Jorge Penna showing up on the vid-screen. The camera was close in, although I could make out that he was sitting on the edge of a bed. "How in the Constellation of Antlia did you come into possession of *Justice Bringer*? And don't you ever sleep?"

"Sorry for the spacer hours, Admiral Penna. Let's just say that Admiral Tullas was overly persistent and we've resolved our differences," I said. "I was hoping you might have some interest in a lightly-used frigate."

"It wasn't two days ago I told Bard that we hadn't seen the last of you," he answered. "I'll send you back to Central Command and get you some docking instructions. Would you be open for breakfast at 0730?"

"It would be my pleasure, Admiral," I said and checked the clock. At 0430, it was indeed early.

"We'll send a breakfast service out to The Collet once you dock. I feel we owe your crew an apology for their treatment on your last visit. I'll also send Lieutenant Fuentes to escort you and your command crew so we might review your proposal," he said smoothly.

The comm abruptly switched from his bedroom back to Central Command where the uniformed woman who'd originally answered my hail picked back up. "Captain Hoffen. Admiral Penna has given permission for your entry to Freedom Station space. I'm transmitting a navigation path and docking instructions."

"Copy that, Freedom Station. Hoffen out," I closed comm.

"Ada, did you get all that?" I asked.

"We'll follow you in," she replied.

"Jester Ripples, you should move to *Hotspur*," I said. "I'm not sure that Freedom Station is quite ready to be introduced to Norigans."

"That is disappointing," he replied, using the common language of Earth and Mars. We'd all been surprised at how quickly he picked up our language. His voice sounded like a child's, but Jester Ripples was sixty standard years old, still relatively young for his species.

"I promise, on our next stop, you'll get to meet more humans. They're very interested in meeting with you," I said.

"I heard your conversation with Admiral Alderson and Gregor Belcose, Liam Hoffen. You were deceptive about my presence," he said. "I wonder why that might be, but I trust that you are my friend."

I scrubbed the warm, yellow fur above Jester Ripple's eyes, a gesture I'd learned he found soothing. "We are friends, Jester Ripples. Believe me when I say my only objective is to see that the people on Cradle are returned home. That includes Norigans as well as humans."

"That is something I've wanted to discuss with you, Liam Hoffen," he replied. I'd tried to get him to shorten my name. He seemed incapable of the change. "Blue Child and I may eventually visit our home, but we will not stay. The Kroerak made it clear they will raid our home world if Norigans attempt to rescue their families."

This took me aback. "Are you saying your family won't let you come home?"

"Oh yes. Of course they would. But I could not be so selfish to allow that. It would endanger them," he replied innocently.

"You always have a place with us, Jester Ripples," I said.

"Liam, we're here," Tabby interrupted. "Do you want to transfer Jester Ripples through the cargo bay airlock?"

"No. We'll walk him through the terminal," I said, changing my previous position. "If someone sees him and has questions, let them ask."

"Are you sure?"

"It's not my secret to hold," I said, parroting Ada.

As it turned out, all of my posturing was for naught. We left *Justice Bringer* and traipsed through the deserted jet-way of The Collet, at the dead center of the uniquely shaped Freedom Station. We passed Xie enroute as she transferred to join Jonathan in removing the fold-space generator from *Justice Bringer*.

"Welcome back, Cap," Marny greeted us as we entered the bridge.

"Any issues?" I asked.

"Negative. Freedom Station upped the security in the jet-way for the duration of our visit and will have a patrol boat swinging by every hour or so," she said. "Lieutenant Fuentes was quite apologetic for our experience here last time and mentioned a breakfast delivery coming in forty minutes. Do you know something about that?"

"Compliments of Admiral Penna." I heard the bridge open behind me and turned to see Nick enter.

"Good. You're here already," he said.

"What's up?" I asked as he passed and made his way to the conference room attached to the bridge. I decided I'd best follow him in.

"We'll need a firm idea on what we want for *Justice Bringer*," he said. "I wasn't expecting to have this conversation quite so quickly."

I smiled. For once Nick didn't have everything figured out.

"You mind if I clean up?" Tabby asked, leaning on the hatch. "I haven't had a good shower since we left Ophir."

"Sure, I'll catch up in a couple," I said. "Ada, can you find Jester Ripples accommodations?"

"I sure will," she answered.

"I think I've got a pretty good idea of what we need," I said, turning my attention to Nick. "There's no way I want to add another ship to our fleet and I'd be willing to bet Penna is drooling over the idea of sailing a first class frigate like *Justice Bringer*."

"I just don't see how you're going to realize the couple hundred million credits that ship is worth," he said.

"If we can get back to whole and I get the items I want, I'll be okay with it," I said. "Good will with Freedom Station can't be underestimated. The bottom line is we need our ship back just about as bad as we need solid trading partners."

Nick rolled his eyes upward and shook his head. "I hate going into these things blind."

I smiled. "I know. It's not something you can put a spreadsheet to. Trust me on this one?"

"I was afraid you were going to say that," he said. "Just like I'm sure I'm not going to like our conversation with Buckshot."

"Probably." I stood up from the table. "I'm going to get cleaned up for breakfast. Meet at the airlock at 0720?"

"Yup," he agreed.

By the time I made it back to my quarters, I found a well-scrubbed and naked Tabby lying under the sheets of our bed - asleep. It hadn't been that long, but we also hadn't gotten much sleep while sailing short-handed on *Justice Bringer*. Instead of taking advantage, I pulled a blanket over her and dimmed the lights. I didn't have time to sleep, but I could at least run my suit through the cleaner and hit the head.

After getting cleaned up, I considered the beautiful woman who lay in my bed. She might like to go to breakfast and meet the reclusive Bard Sanderson, but I couldn't bring myself to wake her. I quietly slipped out of the room and met up with Marny and Nick at the main airlock.

"Where's Tabby?" Marny asked.

"She ran too many shifts on *Justice Bringer*. I couldn't bring myself to wake her," I said.

Upon exiting onto the jet-way, we found Lieutenant Wilmarie Fuentes waiting for us, talking with two uniformed soldiers.

"Right on time," she said, extending her hand.

"Doesn't seem like the sort of thing we should be late to," I replied.

She smiled, but didn't answer other than to gesture down the jet-way, following us to the elevators in the center.

"We'll be taking the Dirt Side elevator," she explained as we approached the very center where another uniformed guard was holding an elevator open.

"Should we be concerned about the uniforms?" I asked.

We entered the elevator car and it began lowering. "I don't think so. The Admiral was embarrassed by your treatment on your last visit and has asked me to make sure we don't have a repeat. I'm just being careful."

"Much appreciated," Marny replied. "I'd like to trade notes with you after our breakfast. I have information you might find interesting."

As the doors opened, we found ourselves looking out over a green field of grass. In the center of the field sat a long table with a stark white table cloth. Two men were already seated at the table and were being attended by three others. A fourth man, in a formal looking vac-suit stood stiffly by the elevator door.

"Jasper, we have Ms. Marny Bertrand, Captain Liam Hoffen, and Mr. Nicholas James for breakfast," Fuentes announced formally, without responding to Marny's offer to share information.

"Very well, Lieutenant Fuentes," he replied. "If you'll follow me." He looped his arm through Marny's and led us across the surreal landscape. From the angle we found ourselves, the armored glass was nearly transparent and it very much looked like we were walking across a field hovering in the middle of space.

"Ah, Captain Hoffen, Mr. James. Welcome." Penna stood as we approached. "And this lovely woman must be the much talked about Marny Bertrand." His accent was, if anything, thicker as he welcomed us. "Please allow me to introduce you to the founder of our beautiful station, Mr. Bard Sanderson."

Sanderson wasn't a particularly large man and had straight black hair and a fair complexion. He wore an easy smile as he extended his hand to Marny, turning it over as she accepted and kissing the back with a mischievous grin.

"Oh," Marny giggled. "Very nice to meet you."

I looked at Nick. I'd never seen Marny flummoxed before and his wide eyes told me he hadn't either.

"Please, please, have a seat," Sanderson said after we'd shaken hands and completed introductions. "To be honest, I like to pull this little stunt when I want something. I find it puts my trading partners on tilt. Is it working?"

"The view is amazing," I said, looking out toward where I was sure Mars was.

"I'm from farm country on Earth, Mr. Hoffen, and I love the idea of living in the stars. This station was the best way to achieve both objectives. Would you care for a cup of coffee?" He nodded to the man who stood behind where we'd sat.

"I'd love one," I said, hoping the coffee was as good as the surroundings were unbelievable.

"How did our livestock travel? Did they make it okay?" Sanderson asked.

"They did and the people we delivered them to were appreciative," I said. "We even brought a few tonnes of milo back with us, hoping we might trade with one of your distilleries."

"Mr. Sailer will be pleased to hear that," he said as plates filled with eggs and sausage links were placed in front of us. A thick white sauce with black flecks covered two lumps on the plate, but I wasn't about to ask what I was looking at.

"You mentioned you might be interested in parting with *Justice Bringer*, Captain Hoffen," Penna said once we started eating.

The sauce covered a biscuit and I discovered the combination of the two items to be delicious. "That is true. We're not looking to expand our fleet and as you've probably been informed, *Intrepid* has taken quite a beating," I said.

"Are you just looking for repairs?" Penna asked hopefully, to which Nick coughed inadvertently, most likely gasping at the suggestion.

The table had become very quiet and I knew I had both men's full attention. "No. I don't think that would make us very good trading partners. Let me be clear; I'm not looking for full value of the ship but I'm also not about to give it away. My guess is that Freedom Station would have a very difficult time procuring a ship as well outfitted as *Justice Bringer*, what with all of the military grade systems."

"We're not without our resources," Sanderson replied, stiffening slightly.

"You mind if I just lay out what I'm thinking?" I asked. "Maybe skip all the normal posturing?"

Penna blinked twice, as if in astonishment. "That would be refreshing."

"Kind of takes the fun out of it though," Sanderson answered. "But I suppose there is something to be said for laying one's cards on the table."

"Especially if it benefits both parties," I said. "For *Justice Bringer*,

I'd like ten pallets of missiles, four General Astral Mark IV Defensive Cannons or their equivalent, two of *Justice Bringer*'s engines transferred to *Intrepid* - you'll find we've lost one engine and the other needs repairs that will take longer than we have patience for, a full set of repairs to *Intrepid*'s armor and one of Robert Beer's Chinese portable armor repair stations."

Sanderson picked up a white napkin, blotted his lips, and placed the napkin carefully on his plate. "Mr. Hoffen, I believe you over-estimate the value of your frigate. A Mark IV Cannon is worth nearly twenty million credits on the open market and a portable armor repair station is worth forty million. And that's not considering the missiles," he said. "If my math is right, you've valued your ship at one-hundred fifty million credits and that's with substantial repairs required and two broken engines."

"We also removed two of the smaller bow turrets," Nick added.

Sanderson smiled and shook his head. "You're off by twice."

"A frigate of this class is worth six-hundred million credits," I replied. "My offer is more than fair. The repairs required can't add up to more than sixty million credits, most of that being in the engine. Wouldn't you like to have one of the fastest warships produced? You've built an incredibly well defended installation, but with this ship, you'd be able to confidently strike out. What you can't swat down, you can outrun. It's the best of both worlds."

"Two cannons, the Chinese portable repair facility, armor repairs, engines moved and fifteen palettes of missiles," he answered.

"Make that three Mark IV Cannons and I'll throw in the milo grain," I said.

Sanderson laughed and held his hand out. "Three cannons and I'll even send you back with ten cases of Sailer's best stuff. Believe it or not, he calls it Contraband."

CARDS ON THE TABLE

"I can't help but feel you gave that ship to Sanderson," Nick said once we were back aboard *Intrepid*. "Conservatively, a damaged *Justice Bringer* is worth four-hundred million credits. Your trade is worth one-hundred-thirty million, max. You left two-hundred million on the table."

I smiled. "Listen to us. Arguing about a hundred million credit trade. You're right, of course. We got taken. It's also all he was going to offer. We showed up with a ship he hadn't asked for and traded for his critical supplies. Look at the bright side. We'll finally have a decent stock of missiles and the capability to do structural repairs on larger ships. That's freedom if you ask me. I'll pay a lot for that."

"I suppose if you look at it that way," Nick replied. He was grumpy, but he'd get over it.

"We need to take off in six hours," I said. "I'd like to bring the four of us, Jester Ripples, Jonathan and Sendrei."

"That would just leave Ada and crew," Marny said as we approached the station-side of the catwalk where Baker was armed with a blaster rifle and fully dressed in an armored vac-suit.

"Don't forget Xie," I said.

"Are you sure, Cap? I think you need to talk with her. I walked past her bunk this morning and it looked like she was packing," Marny replied.

Locate Xie Mie-su.

"*Xie Mie-su is currently in her assigned quarters,*" my AI replied.

"What are you going to do?" Nick asked.

"Talk to her, I guess," I said. "It's not like I'm going to require someone to stay on the ship as a prisoner. Well, that is with the exception of our actual prisoners."

"This is a mess," he said. In all of our time together, he had always been one step ahead and now twice in the same day he was struggling. It occurred to me that we might need to consider just how hard we were pushing the envelope.

I wrapped my arm around his shoulders. "I agree. We just need to keep our eye on the goal. We have ten thousand people whose only hope for survival rests in our hands. We need to block everything else as noise. So what if Xie talks about Kroerak or Norigans or even Ophir for that matter? People will believe what they want. We didn't create the secret and we have proof that the secret is hurting people."

He sighed. "I suppose. Do you want help talking with her?" We passed through the ship-side airlock and started aft, toward the bridge.

"Nah. I got this." I peeled off to the port where Xie's bunkroom was located.

When I knocked on the open hatch to her room, she looked up. "I was expecting you," Xie said. Her voice lacked the normal sultry lilt she used when in a larger group.

I looked at the single duffle on her bunk. "All packed up?"

"I'd like permission to disembark, Liam," she said.

"You're a valuable member of the crew, Xie. Are you sure?"

"The universe as we know it is about to change," she said. "Your crew is on the front line of a war I'm not sure we can win."

"Never known Xie Mie-su to run from a fight."

"But then, you've never really known me, Liam Hoffen," she purred, the silky quality returning to her voice.

"I think of you as a friend, Xie," I said. "I don't buy this image you portray to everyone around you."

She nodded. "You're a strange man. I've given you no reason to trust me, but you see good in me that even I'm not sure exists."

"Will you stay on Freedom Station?"

"For the time being." She took a deep breath as she stood. "There's work here with Beth Anne."

I pulled her into a hug. "I'll miss you, Xie. You need to believe in yourself."

"We would make a formidable team, Liam. Look me up," she said and brushed my cheek with her hand as she broke free and sauntered from the room. I walked out behind her and watched her disappear down the passageway.

"A jealous woman might make something of this." Tabby's voice caught me by surprise, causing me to startle.

"Shite, Tabby," I said. "I thought you were asleep."

"Let's just say I have a subroutine that tells me when you enter another woman's bunkroom." She suggestively slipped her hands around my waist.

I glanced sideways at her, wondering if she was telling the truth. "Seriously?"

"Don't worry, you're in the clear," she said, tapping my nose with her finger. "I think I might skip the trip to Valhalla Platform."

"Oh?"

"Too many memories. I just don't want to go back there," she said.

***

"Transitioning to normal-space in three … two …," I warned. I hoped Buckshot Alderson had taken me seriously and left open the coordinates I'd provided. In a close-in trans-location like we'd just done, our accuracy was within a kilometer. Longer transitions were less accurate, but we'd yet to miss by more than twenty kilometers, which is relatively pin-point when you consider the distances we were traveling. According to Jonathan, the accuracy issues were caused by our inability to measure time as accurately as required. He'd wanted to explain with more detail, but I'd suggested I was okay with some variance.

"We have multiple hostiles targeting the ship," Nick announced as my vision cleared.

"*Incoming hail, Battle Cruiser George Ellery Hale,*" my AI announced.

The forward holo-display showed three ships. The *George Ellery*

Hale was flanked by two destroyers that looked positively puny next to it.

"*Hotspur*, Captain Liam Hoffen, go ahead," I said.

"Captain Hoffen, I'm Captain Gregory Munay. I'll need you to accept our turret lockdown before we proceed." The man who appeared was everything I'd come to expect from a senior Naval officer; neatly dressed, polite and straight to the point. A blinking acknowledgement flashed, which I accepted.

"Thank you," he replied in response to my acceptance. "That was quite an entrance you made. You made my gunnery chief rather nervous. Mind explaining how you accomplished showing up in that manner?"

"That's much of the reason for our visit," I said. "Can I count on you to share your observations with Admiral Alderson?"

"Son, that's the reason I'm out here," he replied. "To that end, I'm sending navigation instructions for docking in fighter bay twelve. If it's all the same to you, I'd appreciate it if you'd proceed to the flight deck the good old-fashioned way, to avoid any misunderstandings."

"Copy that, Captain Munay. We understand the pecking order here and will comply," I said, to which he smiled and gave a curt nod of acknowledgement. "Hoffen, out."

As we sailed closer to the large ship, it just seemed to continue to grow. At two hundred and twenty meters in length and with a mass in excess of sixteen thousand tonnes, I couldn't imagine how anyone aboard would be made nervous by any action we took.

"Look at that," I said in wonder as we sat down in a bay that was empty except for two stubby Tison-4X Bumblebee fighters that had been pushed to one side. It was the same fighter Tabby had been training for. There was nothing extraneous or subtle about a Tison-4X. Large engines, externally mounted missiles and a single, forward, articulating turret were all built around a heavily armored cockpit that was filled with gel and surrounded by inertial systems. Perhaps most striking was the complete lack of anything resembling armor glass. The entire shell was armored with nary a peep hole. In all, it was ten meters of death for anything smaller than a frigate.

"I like the paint job," Nick said. The Bumblebee designation was lost on most spacers, but Tabby had shown me pictures of the rounded insects that were their namesake. The two ships were brightly painted with black and yellow stripes.

"Are you ready for this, Jester Ripples?" I asked as we descended to the bridge level. The Norigan had been playing a castle defense simulation game I'd shown him on the bridge's table next to the couch where he sat.

"I get to meet more humans?" he asked.

"Trust me, they'll be very interested in meeting you," I said as he scrambled up into my arms, wrapping his spindly legs around my waist. I stroked the back of the coarse, yellow stripe of fur that surrounded his bulbous eyes in greeting. His wide eyelids blinked in appreciation.

"The bay is pressurized and we've equalized, Cap," Marny announced as we approached the external hatch. "I'm going to stay behind with our guests, however." She was referring to the six crew we'd recovered from *Justice Bringer* as well as Moon Rastof, all of whom were in *Hotspur*'s hold with restraints that kept them from approaching the airlocks or control systems.

"Thanks, Marny," I said.

"Good luck." She popped the hatch after allowing the external stairs to descend to the deck.

A squad of Marines in armored vac-suits stood at attention in a line at the bottom of the stairs, perpendicular to *Hotspur*. A group of three officers stood at the end of the line, facing us. I immediately recognized Captain Munay standing forward in the middle.

"Welcome aboard, Captain Hoffen, Lieutenant Sendrei, Mr. James, and Jonathan," he said as we descended the stairs. He'd certainly been well-briefed. "May I introduce you to my senior officers, Lieutenant Commanders Carmine Jandry and Jensen Biggwort."

"I'd also like to introduce a recent addition to our crew," I said as I shook the proffered hands. "This is Jester Ripples. Say hello to

Captain Munay, Jester Ripples."

Jester Ripples squirmed on my hip and I released him to the ground. He quickly approached Munay and lifted his thick, three fingered hand. The Captain didn't miss a beat and extended his own. Unfortunately, Jester Ripples took this as an invitation for closeness and climbed the surprised man, spurring the Marines into action.

"Stop!" I exclaimed, jumping between Jester Ripples and the flood of Marines coming to their Captain's aid. I was knocked to the ground before Munay was able to intervene.

"Hold!" Munay recovered his composure. "Release Mr. Hoffen, please."

"What is wrong?" Jester Ripples asked in his child-like voice, clinging to the grey-templed captain, unwilling to believe that anyone would mean him harm. The Marine who dropped me helped me back to my feet, but didn't look the least bit apologetic.

"It's okay, Jester Ripples, people aren't used to Norigan closeness. The Marines thought you might be trying to hurt Captain Munay," I explained. Fortunately, my grav-suit had absorbed most of the blow that had knocked me down, although I'd be sore for a few days.

"I would never," he said.

"Would you care to explain?" Munay asked. "I thought you had simply brought an exotic pet along."

"Jester Ripples doesn't understand human issues with physical closeness. He is a Norigan, a sentient species. He's also a valuable member of my crew. Jester Ripples, perhaps its best if you came with me," I said.

"But you said I'd get to meet more people," he argued.

"True, but I think you're making Captain Munay uncomfortable," I said. "People take a little while to get used to Norigan closeness. Remember we talked about this?"

"Yes. I apologize. I got excited," he said glumly and released his hold on Munay, clambering back into my arms.

"Our flight deck is probably not the right place for this discussion," Munay said with a shake of his head. He continued to stare at Jester Ripples with wonder. "Would you follow me?"

Passing guards at each intersection, I wondered just how much of a threat Alderson really thought we were.

"Here we are," Munay announced as we arrived at a spacious conference room. Gregor Belcose was already in the room and talking in a low whisper with Admiral Alderson and Commander Sterra. I mentally kicked myself for not recognizing why the show of force, including a full battle cruiser. I'd assumed our meeting was on Valhalla Platform, but it looked as if we'd be meeting right here.

"Liam Hoffen," Commander Sterra said as we entered. She looked exactly as I remembered her, a petite ball of energy with a presence that demanded respect.

"Commander Sterra," I said, smiling and closing the distance between us as the three stood to greet us.

"Mr. Hoffen," Admiral Alderson's deep voice caused me to pause. I wasn't sure of the correct order of introductions. Sensing my hesitance, he gave me a break that I hadn't expected. "Don't be shy, Hoffen, we're not standing on formality today. But for the sake of expediency, assume we've been watching you since you entered our vicinity and know all your names and can skip all the pleasantries."

Sterra smiled, ignoring the Admiral for a moment and gave me a quick hug, eyeing Jester Ripples as she did. "Good to see you well, Liam. I've been worried," she said quietly, but not quite in a whisper.

"Tell me, Hoffen." Alderson held out his hand in greeting. "Is the little guy really sentient or are we looking at a monkey which resembles a frog?"

"Gregor, ask Jester Ripples a ridiculously hard physics, spatial, or mathematics question," I said.

Gregor raised his eyebrows and rattled off a navigational question related to the pull of Sol's sun on Earth's moon and how a ship could utilize the associated gravitational fields. Jester Ripples giggled his high-pitched trill and easily answered the question.

"This is fun, do another," he said, pushing off, suddenly more interested in Gregor.

Before I let him go, I warned Gregor, "He's going to want to hold on to you. Don't be alarmed; he's harmless."

"Very well. We saw this interaction on the flight deck," he said.

"You will find your ability to measure spatial and mathematical capability to be un-equal to Jester Ripple's understanding. Only your software systems have the level of understanding common to the Norigan race," Jonathan explained.

"You are an expert on this?" Alderson asked.

"We are," Jonathan replied.

"Are you carrying a frog in your pocket too, son? What's with the royal we?"

"Admiral, in the interest of expediency." I echoed his phrase. "Let's just think of Jonathan and Jester Ripples as very special guests. They aren't the primary point of our visit, but both have agreed to meet with you so that you would take seriously the information we're relaying," I said.

"Jonathan here is an alien too?" Alderson asked, edging toward belligerent.

"We are, Admiral Alderson," Jonathan replied. "We have assumed human form so that we might interact with humanity more efficiently."

"You'd have me believe that not one, but two alien species chose to interact with these yahoos instead of making contact with any of the myriad of representative governments in the system?" Alderson asked, looking first at Sterra and then Munay when he failed to receive any acknowledgement.

An awkward silence fell over the room as Munay closed the door after ushering out his two subordinates.

While I hadn't been expecting a warm welcome, Alderson's derisiveness was unexpected. I'd yet to feel settled around the man and his attitude pushed me back on my heels.

"It would seem that those representative governments have spent the better part of the last three centuries ignoring crimes against humanity," I said. It was risky to verbally dual with the

Admiral. He could easily have me locked up, but I refused to allow him to run roughshod over the conversation. "I can't fathom why any self-respecting alien would care to even bother contacting any of you. If the lives of thousands of people didn't rely on my ability to convince you of a moral obligation, I wouldn't be here either."

Alderson grunted out a chuckle. "You have some huevos on you, don't you, Hoffen? Tell me, what makes you think we have any idea about what you think you've seen?"

"I know for a fact you can track any ship in Mars territory," I said. "If you don't believe me, you can ask Mr. Belcose about how the *Kuznetsov* tracked four ships closing on Ceres from halfway across the solar system back when Red Houzi was trying to put us out of the game."

"Explain how that's relevant?" he asked.

"Belirand has been jumping ships in and out of Sol," I said. "There's no way that's escaped your notice. Commander Munay might have been startled by our appearance with *Hotspur*, but he certainly wasn't surprised. Let's not pretend here. You already know about fold-space generators and contact with aliens. We're just gambling that you're too decent to actually be complicit. There are too many lives at stake. And for the record, the reason Jester Ripples trusts us is because we risked our lives to save him."

Alderson sighed. "Show us what you have."

HARD BALL

"What do you think of all this, LaVonne?" Alderson turned to Commander Sterra who'd remained still throughout Nick's forty-minute presentation.

"We must tread carefully," she answered. "The implications of what we've learned today could very well send us to war with the North Americans. If not us, the Chinese have a valid complaint."

"Commander Munay?"

"Commander Sterra is right, of course, but I am more concerned about the enemy we don't know than the one we do," he answered. "Specifically these Kroerak and what they represent."

"And yet we saw but a single ship," Alderson replied.

"A battleship class ship guarding a farm," Munay said. "That's the equivalent of stationing this Battle Cruiser to watch over Jeratorn or Colony-40." He nodded in my direction.

"Mr. Belcose? Have you been able to get a read on the veracity of the data-streams?" Alderson asked.

"They've been cut down and put back together. Nothing that can't be explained by a desire to shorten the presentation," he said. "Mr. James has already provided access to the source data. It will take a few hours for full validation."

"Lieutenant Buhari." Alderson turned to Sendrei. "What's your part in this, beyond being rescued."

Sendrei cleared his throat. I'd seen the man strike down a charging Kroerak and yet I could read his nervousness from here. "I was a gunnery officer aboard the Destroyer *McCain*. This was twelve stans back, I'm sure you recall this was toward the end of the Amazonian War."

"I do," Alderson acknowledged. "Yet you were on a patrol in

space."

"You're aware of the involvement by the Chinese and their attacks on our mining colonies?" Buhari asked.

"I am," Alderson answered. "Please continue."

"We received a mayday from a Belirand vessel, eight days out. By the time we got there, the ship was dead, not a single crew left alive. The ship had been breached in multiple locations. I don't know if you're familiar with the Earth creature called a porcupine, but this ship looked like it had tangled with one and lost. There were hundreds of what looked like giant quills sticking into the ship and in some cases it looked like those quills had just gone completely through the ship's hull. At first, we thought it was some sort of new pirate weapon."

"Do you remember the designation of the Belirand ship?" Belcose asked.

"Hold on, Gregor," Sterra interrupted, "Mr. Buhari, what happened to the crew?"

"The ship's name was *Prosperity* and we didn't find out right away what happened to the crew," he said. "I have an advanced degree in engineering and so I was part of the crew sent over to try to get the ship's systems back online. To answer your question, Commander Sterra, the crew had been eaten. There were Kroerak onboard and they'd killed the crew while in fold-space."

"How'd you escape?" I asked, unable to hold back.

"I ran," he said, tears running down his face. "The Kroerak attacked my crewmates and I didn't do anything to help them. I ran away. I just let them die."

"How did you end up on the Kroerak world?" Munay asked after Sendrei recovered enough to speak.

"It was just me and another officer who survived," he said. "Once back on the *McCain*, we were taken into custody by my commanding officer and eventually handed over to Belirand, who in turn, transported us to Cradle and turned us over to the Kroerak." Sendrei took a deep breath, looked down and then back up. "Just so we're clear, Cradle is not their home-world. Every year or two, we'd get visitors who would come and look over the farms where we grew our crops and prepared for the upcoming harvest. They were more like the Overlord."

"Explain harvest," Alderson pushed.

"You need me to say it?" Sendrei asked. "Fine. The Kroerak harvested the people of our village. They were clear about the fact they were using us as food."

"How is that?" Munay asked. "And what do you mean by more like the Overlord?"

"Smaller and smart. The average Kroerak warrior doesn't have a lot going on upstairs, but these others, you can tell they're smart. They talked about bringing us home."

"In your language?" Alderson asked.

"Yes. They liked to taunt us, letting us know how inferior we were," he said.

"You served your time, son," Alderson said. "You need to let go of the guilt. I'm not saying what you did was right, running that is, but you weren't on a combat assignment and someone dropped the ball if you didn't have Marines on that ship."

"It was dead," Sendrei replied. "There were no signs of life, movement or anything."

"We found the same on the moon over Thren's Rest," I said. "The Kroerak appear to be able to evade our sensors, especially when they're at rest."

"Can you corroborate any of this beyond these data-streams?" Alderson asked.

"We captured crew from *Justice Bringer*," I said. "Thought you might like to interrogate them. To be honest, we don't have any capacity to hold prisoners and were hoping you'd take them off our hands."

"You don't say," Alderson said. "Commander Belcose, would you send a squad to gather the prisoners?"

"Aye, aye, Admiral," Belcose answered stiffly.

"We also have a Kroerak corpse," I said.

Alderson and Belcose exchanged a look. "Take it to Dr. Mensching's lab?" Belcose asked. Alderson just nodded his head affirmatively.

"So, what's your end-game here?" Alderson asked as Belcose walked to the end of the room and spoke quietly into his comm. "You've known about this for months. Why tell us all this now?"

I couldn't fathom a man with his military mind hadn't already figured out the obvious, but I indulged him just the same. "Look, I don't know if we can trust you. It's hard for us to believe you don't know what's going on here. I'd like to say we came to you out of a sense of duty, but that's not really true either."

"You understand it's within my purview to take your ship and dump you all in a big dark hole, never to be seen again," he said. "Your lives aren't worth diddly squat when compared to the people who are going to die because of this big pile of shite you just laid at my feet."

"It's not our pile of shite and it's too much for us," I said. "We're not in any position to make those decisions."

"Yet you have been," he said.

"You need me to admit we need help? No problem. We need your help. We can't possibly save all those people."

"What do you want us to do? It's not like we can jump to another system," he said.

"It's not a jump," Nick muttered between clenched teeth.

"I'm proposing a trade," I said.

"Ahh, here it is," Alderson said. "This ought to be good."

"It's not what you think."

"Yeah. I'll bet."

"How would you like to catch up on four hundred years of technology?" I asked.

"Be more specific." Alderson licked his lips in anticipation, a tell I'd never seen from him before.

"There are three components to fold-space travel." Unexpectedly, Jonathan had jumped in.

He was diverting from the plan. Something had changed.

Jonathan continued, "The first, the design for TransLoc engines, is widely shared and available to most ship manufacturers. In fact, the very ship on which we reside today is equipped with the modifications required to travel within a fold-space bubble."

"Tell me something I don't already know," Alderson said.

"The second component is the process and technology of generating a fold-space bubble. This information is a shared secret between the Anino Corporation and the Belirand Corporation. It's widely believed that this is only possible through the use of the Trans Location gates as are installed in each of the solar systems within humanity's known universe," he continued.

"Brilliant," Belcose muttered.

"Pardon?" Alderson asked, annoyed.

"It's brilliant. Anino Corporation maintained control over the process by keeping the key. What is the third component? A crystal? Some kind of fuel? It would have to be unique, unbreakable to have remained secret this long," Belcose asked.

"Thank you, Mr. Belcose, for that assessment," Jonathan replied. "And in fact, you're right, the third component, Aninonium, is the crucial ingredient for the fuel required to generate a fold-space bubble. The recipe is so closely guarded that it has remained unwritten and can only be produced by its inventor."

"Thomas Anino?" Alderson asked.

"But he's dead!" I exclaimed. What Alderson didn't know was that we were in possession of the only remaining Aninonium based fuel, as Anino's factory had been destroyed.

"What are you trying to pull here, Hoffen?" Alderson asked.

"I'm afraid that Captain Hoffen is quiet unaware of this particular wrinkle," Jonathan replied.

"Jonathan? What's going on?" I asked.

"A necessary ruse," he replied. I suddenly realized his speech pattern had changed.

"Would someone explain to me why we're talking about a man who's been dead for three hundred fifty stans?" Alderson demanded.

"I'm not dead, Buckshot," Jonathan replied.

"Phillipe?" I asked.

"Always the quickest in the group," Jonathan replied. "Yes."

"But" I felt myself trying not to stammer. "how?"

"He didn't die on *Mastodon*," Nick said. "That's why they built that ship with paper-thin armor. It didn't make sense until now. He figured out how to transfer his consciousness to Jonathan. What I don't understand is why he decided to let his body be destroyed."

"Tullas," Jonathan/Anino replied. "She'd infiltrated every level of my company and I'd been on the run for too long. I needed a way out."

"We were your way out?" I said. "You played us?"

"But that happened only a few months ago and it was Phillipe Anino who died." Belcose said with confusion.

"Phillipe was Thomas Anino. They are one and the same," explained Nick.

"How'd he stay alive that long?" Belcose asked.

"A simple medical process if you have sufficient funds," Jonathan/Anino replied. "It's illegal on Earth and Mars, but that certainly wouldn't stop someone of my means. Belirand introduced me to the possibility. They didn't like the idea of their supply of Aninonium running out, so I didn't even have to foot the bill."

"We know of the procedure," Alderson said. "So you pretended to be your own descendants to explain your regenerations. That doesn't explain how you're in another man's body."

"This body is a simulacrum," Jonathan/Anino replied. "A golem, if you will. I manufactured it to play host for the fourteen hundred thirty-nine sentients you refer to as Jonathan."

"That's not possible," Alderson answered. "The regeneration process doesn't put you in a new body."

"You know an awful lot about this process, have you been out shopping?" Jonathan/Anino quipped.

"You've always been an ass." Alderson's face was red, but he looked under control.

"I've missed you too," Anino replied.

I looked at Jonathan/Anino. "Are you changing the deal?"

"Not at all. The floor is yours," he replied. My mind reeled with the implications and I struggled to find a firm footing. I looked to

Nick, lost.

"Cradle, Liam. Nothing has changed," he said.

I blew out a hot breath, momentarily calming the fire in my belly, and tried to recall the details of what we'd discussed.

"We'll share the technology of TransLoc," I said. "Everything but the recipe for Aninonium."

"The technology is useless without fuel," Alderson shot back.

"It's a deal that's worked for Belirand for centuries," Jonathan/Anino replied. "It's also not negotiable. As long as I have the recipe, my friends and I are less likely to come to premature ends."

"The deal worked until it didn't," Alderson answered. "From where I'm sitting, it looks like Belirand wasn't interested anymore."

"I recently discovered Belirand had traded my technology to the Kroerak," he said.

"Without fuel, the Kroerak had nothing," Alderson said. "Just like what you're offering us."

"What you might not know is that the TransLoc gates operate with an extremely small amount of Aninonium. Once the fold-space lane is established, with sufficient power, the gates can remain active almost indefinitely."

"Even Belirand wouldn't be stupid enough to help the Kroerak come back to Sol," Alderson said.

"But there were Kroerak on *Prosperity* twelve years ago," Sterra said. "Could an invading force take control of the TransLoc gate in Sol and pair with it?"

"Yes," Anino answered. "This is the information Belirand didn't want anyone knowing and why they'd been willing to cut off their only supply of the fuel."

"You've leveled some serious accusations," Alderson said. "You'll understand if I don't just take this at face value."

"It changes nothing," I said. "We're here to talk about the rescue of ten thousand people on Cradle."

"It's like I'm talking to children, here," Alderson said. "First you tell me there's a possibility of a Kroerak invasion and then you tell me you want my help lifting ten thousand colonists from an alien planet."

"They're not colonists," Sendrei said, standing. "They're prisoners who've been sold out by the people entrusted to protect them."

I stood up in support of Sendrei and placed my hand on his shoulder. "The information we've provided is free, Admiral. It's information your intelligence service would have paid millions of credits for and would also have risked their lives to obtain. We brought it to you and I won't have you throwing in our faces.

I turned to the rest of the room. "Maybe this isn't as easy of a decision as I originally thought for you, but let me lay it out, just so we're clear. You will mount a mission to Cradle that includes the rescue of the human, Norigan and whatever non-indigenous species we run into who need rescuing. You will deliver these people to Ophir and provide sufficient support to house and feed them for at least a year as they become independent. You will also clear our names with the Nuage government in Tipperary. And finally, you will defend us legally from Belirand and ensure our safe travel within the Mars Protectorate."

"What do we get out of this?" he asked, shaking his head with his eyes closed.

"We'll equip whatever ships you specify for the mission and in the process, train your scientists and engineers on how to replicate the technology," I said.

"What about fuel?"

"I've already begun work on a new manufacturing plant," Jonathan/Anino replied. "I'll supply your first year free. After that, I'm sure we can come up with an arrangement that is mutually beneficial."

"You know I can't possibly make this deal," Alderson said. "At a minimum, I'd need to get buy-in from the executive branch."

"I'd recommend making that call, then," Jonathan/Anino replied, "because you're not getting the technology otherwise."

TIME TO GET ROWDY

"Cap, sorry to wake you." Marny's voice stirred me from sleep. It had been forty hours since our meeting with Alderson and I was sleeping fitfully in my quarters aboard *Hotspur*.

"I'm not really sleeping," I said groggily.

"There's a Marine at the airlock asking for us," she said.

"Copy that," I replied.

Ten minutes later, we all met in the galley.

"Ready for this?" I asked.

"What if they say no?" Sendrei asked.

"They can't," Jonathan replied. I wasn't sure if it was Anino or Jonathan talking and for a moment I felt like I'd lost a friend, knowing that the dominant personality of Thomas Phillipe Anino would likely take over speaking responsibilities.

When we arrived back in the *George Ellery Hale*'s conference room, we found a haggard looking team. Along one wall, vid screens displayed Cradle, its moon and the Kroerak battleship. On the table lay one of the spears the battleship had pinned to *Intrepid*. Another wall of screens displayed twenty different views of the two Kroerak species we'd run into. Bleary eyes regarded us as we took the seats left open.

"We're in, but you're not going to like it," Alderson started. "We need more data on that battleship of theirs and you're going to get it for us."

"What are you talking about? We get within thirty kilometers and they'll obliterate us," Marny said.

"True for *Intrepid*, but you're going to take a wing of Tison-4Xs with you," he said. "With luck, the fighters will be able to get close enough to gather the information we need."

"What kind of information?" I asked.

"We need to know if we can actually penetrate the hull of that battleship," he said. "The Tisons aren't much good against a ship of that size, but we don't need them to kill it. As nice as that'd be, we just need to see what we're up against."

"Sounds like a dangerous mission for that wing. We have no idea what kind of close-up defenses they might have," I said.

"Maybe you don't get it, Hoffen," Alderson responded. "That's what we do. We run toward danger so you don't have to."

"That's not fair," Sterra said, quietly. "Hoffen and his crew have consistently put their lives on the line for the good of others."

Alderson shook his head but didn't push it further. "Point is, we need data before we engage that ship with any sort of fleet."

"Give me a Tison," I said. "No, give me two Tisons. We'll get your data."

"That's crap. Naval Aviators train months to fly a Tison and it takes them stans to become proficient," Alderson shot back.

"What do you have in a Tison? Twenty, thirty million credits?" I asked. "That's nothing for you. Tabby is already trained on it and if you spent two weeks checking me out on one, I could get you your data. I'm guessing it will take you that long to put together a mission of this size anyway."

"Don't be stupid, Hoffen. You can't expect to outfly a Navy pilot."

"We're not going up against Navy pilots," I said. "We're going up against Kroerak."

"I'll put up the money for two Tisons," Jonathan said. "They're not that hard to come by on the black market if you're trying to keep your name clear."

"Commander Munay?"

"I'm not totally against the idea, Admiral," he said. "At a minimum, we'd learn about the Kroerak close-in defenses against small craft. Our fighter jocks would have a lot better idea what they were up against. If it's cost-neutral, I like it."

"We'll supply the Tisons, but I'll need payment in advance," Alderson said.

"Give me an account number," Jonathan said.

"What about the rest of the plan?" I asked.

"Once we take out that battleship, the rest of this is easy," Munay said. "You've already done the hard work on the ground by bringing back that corpse and modifying your firing package. Your makeshift 816s were moderately effective and from that we can make adjustments. We'll put a battalion of mechanized infantry on the ground and take the fight right to the enemy. They won't know what hit them. We should be able to complete the mission in forty-two hours."

"You plan to be on the ground for forty-two hours?" I asked.

"We do," he said. "Moving that many bodies takes time, especially if they aren't expecting us. The key to this mission is overwhelming firepower. We need to send a message to the Kroerak. Mess with us, we put you down."

"Oorah!" Marny said, bringing her fist down on the table, startling several of the bleary-eyed analysts who looked like they'd been awake for way too long.

"Damn straight, Marine," Munay said.

"What will you have us do?" I asked.

"Frankly son, I don't believe you'll be with us at that point," Munay said. "For the sake of argument, let's say you are. In that case, I'll have a special mission for you."

***

"You want *what* as your navigator?" The training officer looked at me like I'd grown a third ear. The name on his uniform read Lt. Commander Jacobs.

"His name is Jester Ripples. He's a Norigan and it's not up for discussion. We've talked about it and this is what he wants," I said.

"Your funeral, pal. My job is to get you ready and that's what I'm going to do," he said, running his hand back over his buzz-cut skull. "The first thing you and your monkey friend need to understand is that you're the most dangerous things in this cockpit."

We were standing next to a brightly painted simulator. The cockpit was designed for two and roomier than I'd expected. The two seats faced each other and had room enough to stretch out completely.

"He's not a monkey," I said. "And you're insulting the first alien Mars Protectorate has ever encountered. Is that really how you want to be remembered?"

"That a fact," the man replied, clearly not impressed. "The first thing most trainees notice is that the ship here is completely filled with nav-gel. The second is that there are no windows. If you're prone to claustrophobia, welcome to hell.

"Climb up in there," he continued. "Might as well get on with this. The AI is set up to orient you and start on basic training."

We did as he suggested. "This is very interesting, Liam Hoffen," Jester Ripples said, holding my hand as we climbed into the heavily armored cockpit. "It appears your species places quite an emphasis on survival. I appreciate that."

"Lifespan of an active fighter pilot is precisely twenty-two point two stans," Jacobs explained as he made sure we were tucked in correctly. "That's seventeen stans for primary and secondary education, three stans for the academy, and two point two stans to turn into a ball of flaming glory."

I had to smile at the man's patter. I wondered how many recruits he'd laid this spiel on.

I'd be a liar if I said that I didn't panic when the nav-gel filled the cockpit after we'd been closed in. The viscous fluid made all movements within the cockpit slow and exaggerated. It was almost the exact opposite of experiencing zero-g.

"This nav-gel is quite remarkable," Jester Ripples cackled in his high voice. "It's such a wonderful idea. I'd wondered how they could allow us to face each other, but this gel is brilliant."

"Quiet in there," Jacobs demanded from outside. "The AI will run you through a number of self-paced simulations. It's not too late to punch out if you're getting squeamish."

I looked at the display that had popped up in front of me. A reticle tracked my eye movement and an AI's voice instructed me to lightly flick my finger to select the currently focused option. There were two options; start the training or exit the cockpit. I focused on the training menu option and flicked my finger. A display popped up showing an oversized picture of my finger movement and prompted me to repeat the gesture, but with less movement. I complied and the option was selected.

For the next five hours, the AI continued to walk both Jester Ripples and me through a series of exercises. By the end of it, I was both tired and exhilarated. Flying a Tison was all about micro-gestures, something I was already attuned to with my AGBs. About ten minutes into the training, the ship's AI recognized that I already had an understanding of these micro-gestures and we set about mapping them to ship commands.

"Give up?" Jacobs asked as we both exited.

I smiled. "Do you fly?"

He nodded affirmatively.

"I bet you know the answer to that, then," I said.

"Well then, all right," he answered. "Maybe there's hope for you yet. I want you to get grub and be back here in thirty minutes."

"Let's do it now," Jester Ripples said. "I'm having so much fun!"

I pulled two meal-bars from a pack and handed one to Jester Ripples. "Give us five and we'll be ready to go."

"You have ten," the man said.

***

About halfway through our fourteen days of training, the newly repaired *Intrepid* arrived at our staging location and Tabby and Nick joined in with the training. Tabby refreshed her skills in the bumblebee while Nick served as navigator. Much of the thrill of piloting the Tison had worn off - or rather had been ground off by the grueling pace. Days melded from one into the other and by the end of it, I had difficulty imaging I hadn't always flown a bumblebee. The Tison-4X designation had been lost so many days before.

"Here's to you not pasting yourself the first time you come in contact with the enemy." Lieutenant Gentry Jacobs toasted us on the flight deck. He opened a bottle of sparkling wine, filled disposable cups, and handed them out. "Remember. The most common way for a jock to die is ... "

"...to turn into a fine red paste due to excessive g-forces." Tabby, Nick and I finished for him. He'd drilled the idea into our heads over and over again.

"Don't be a statistic," he said. "It reflects badly on me."

"It's been an honor." I saluted him back. Jacobs had been a jerk for the better part of the two weeks and when we'd actually started flying the fighters for real, it had become entirely obvious that he'd earned that right. The man could literally fly circles around us and frequently had. His ability to push his craft to the edge was well beyond our own capacity and my respect for professional pilots had grown by an order of magnitude. It hadn't been completely one-sided, though. Both Tabby and I had moments of brilliance and while those moments were far exceeded by our blunders and near catastrophes, I felt like given time, I'd have been able to give him a run for his money.

"I guess we better get these birds back to their new home," I said. At the moment, I would have preferred to simply lie down on the deck and go to sleep, but the entire fleet was scheduled for departure in less than an hour.

Naval engineers had modified the hitch used to lock in *Hotspur* so that it was compatible with the two, much smaller craft. In addition, they'd also installed a retractable cowl that hid the existence of the fighters as well as plumbing for the nav-gel reservoirs. We could now load into the fighters without being exposed directly to space.

"Hold on there, kids," Jacobs said, smiling. "You've missed the best part of our little ceremony."

"Really?" Tabby asked, eyebrows raised high in surprise. "But we didn't finish all of the training."

"Absolutely. You're headed into combat; you've earned it," he explained. "Unlike our North American counterparts, Mars Protectorate provides call-signs for the birds their pilots fly. As the pilot moves, so moves that call-sign. Captain Liam Hoffen, I understand you do a little boxing. Your bird's call-sign will be Sugar, after one of the greatest boxers from an era long ago. Tabitha Masters, I stuck with the theme and your bird's call-sign will be Rowdy after the martial artist from the same time period named Rousey. Now, you go fly these birds like their namesakes and report back to me when you make it out on the other side."

And that was that. Without any further conversation, Jacobs walked over to the two Tisons which Anino had purchased and pulled a sheet of sticky paper from the hull, exposing the painted names he'd assigned. He then left the flight deck without so much as looking over his shoulder.

"Load 'em up," I said with more enthusiasm than I felt and palmed the security panel on the side of low-slung fighter. The cockpit hinged open, exposing a clean interior. Jester Ripples and I had re-configured the seating so that he sat in front of me and down, with both of us oriented forward. We'd learned that I had a predilection for forward flight and there was a slight advantage in absorbing g-forces in the forward facing seat. The nav-gel almost made it a wash, but not completely. Jacobs had talked with me about working to overcome my forward bias. His argument was that if I were to dog-fight with any decent pilot, they'd pick me apart once the bias was recognized. The second advantage to our orientation was that I could see Jester Ripple's displays almost as well as I could see my own.

"The wet interior makes me wish for home," Jester Ripples offered as the interior filled with gel.

Hail George Ellery Hale, Jester Ripples requested. "*George Ellery Hale,* this is Loose Nuts fighter wing one. We're requesting an all-clear for the attached local-space maneuver." I'd been impressed how quickly Jester Ripples had adopted the protocol required by Mars Protectorate.

"Loose Nuts, you're cleared for close-in operation."

"Tell me about home, Jester Ripples," I said as I lifted the fighter from the deck and backed out. In that there were no windows in the craft, backing out was easy as I was able to rotate my view so that it felt like I was flying forward.

"Rowdy, we're all clear," he continued before answering me. It was a pattern Jester Ripples and I had adopted, official communication interrupting conversations as if they weren't even happening. "Jonathan and I feel the best translation for our home planet is Norige."

"We read you, *Sugar*," Tabby replied with a mischievous lilt to her voice. "We're on your wing."

"Try to keep up." I juiced the fighter out between the *George Ellery Hale* and her twin battle cruiser, *Messier*. In all, the battle group consisted of the two cruisers, five destroyers and two personnel carriers, each carrier as large as a battle cruiser. For the most part, we'd been kept out of the battle plans, aside from our part in it, which was simply to gather intelligence in advance of the invasion.

"*Intrepid*, we're requesting permission for mating," Jester Ripples said in his sing-song voice.

"Pardon me?" Ada asked, chuckling. "You're clear for docking."

"I made a funny," Jester Ripples squeaked. "My apologies, Ada Chen."

The flight of a Tison-4X bore virtually no similarity to that of a normal ship. I'd learned the engines produced as much power as *Sterra's Gift*, yet we were one-twentieth the mass. At short distances, it felt more like you squirted from one location to the other, instead of accelerating, gliding and decelerating. Travel was possible in virtually any direction, which was why Jacobs was so concerned with my predilection for forward flight.

As we approached the belly of *Intrepid*, Jester Ripples changed the cockpit view to give me a panoramic view. It was as if I was able to see completely through the gel and the ship's hull as we approached, giving me one hundred percent confidence of our attitude in relationship to docking. At ten meters, Jester Ripples provided a popup window showing the vector of travel between the fighter's docking rails and *Intrepid*'s extended docking clamps. I confidently dropped into place, toggled the virtual switch to lock us in and drained the cockpit. If there was a downside to the fighters, it was the time it took to recover the nav-gel. For the same reason the gel was valuable as a conductor for the inertial system, – basically, it helped the system manipulate forces – it was easy to coax off vac-suits and every surface within the cockpit.

We were first to the airlock and waited inside for Nick and Tabby, who were only a few moments behind us. "Do you need me for anything?" Tabby asked as atmo filled the chamber.

"Nope, we're outta here in forty-five minutes or so, but Ada has that under control," I said. "What's up?"

"I haven't had a decent workout in forever," she said.

"I'm just going to check the watch schedule, but I don't have a workout in me," I said. "I need sleep."

"I'll find you," she said.

"Captain on the bridge," Marny announced smartly as Nick and I entered.

"Liam, Nick. Good," she said. "All systems are reporting green."

"Copy that," I said. "Let's get this show on the road."

"We've been given instructions not to leave until the top of the hour," Ada said.

"In that case, it's a good thing we're not Navy," I said. *All ship announcement. Play AC-DC, Back in Black.*

"Seriously?" Ada asked.

"Let's hit it," I said as the music started.

Back in black, I hit the sack
I've been too long I'm glad to be back

FIRE IN THE HOLE

"Liam, we're two minutes to transition to local-space," Ada said.

After twenty-two days in fold-space, we were preparing to drop into Cradle's solar system. I was tense with excitement. For all the talk of accomplishment in getting Mars Protectorate to mount an emergency mission in record time, none of it meant anything if we failed on this portion of the plan.

We'd loaded into the Tisons and I breathed deeply, trying to calm myself. The plan was to separate immediately from *Intrepid* upon arrival. Everything after that point depended on the Kroerak. When we dropped in, *Intrepid* would require two hours on hard burn to reach Cradle. *Sugar* and *Rowdy* would cover that same distance in seven minutes, five if we pushed hard.

The wave of transition hit me hard and I felt the familiar tug on the ring I wore on my left hand. Tabby knew I still struggled through transition and let me know she was thinking of me.

"*Rowdy* is off," Jester Ripples announced. My vision had just started to clear as I released the clamps holding us to *Intrepid*.

"We're reading six bogeys," Ada's voice announced over our tactical channel.

"We're tucked in, let's hit it," Tabby urged, orienting *Rowdy* on my starboard wing.

Jester Ripples zoomed in on the enemy ships. The worry I'd been nursing in the pit of my stomach for the last eighteen days in fold-space bloomed into a fresh rush of adrenaline. The battleship-sized potato we'd so easily evaded on our last trip had been joined by five frigate-sized, but no less potato-shaped, ships. They were spread out over several hundred thousand kilometers.

Floating tactical labels appeared next to the ships. Marny's doing, no doubt. *Alpha-prime* for the battleship and *Beta-one*

293

through *Beta-five* for the smaller ships.

"Nothing changes," I said. "We hit *Alpha-prime*." I pushed forward and we hurtled toward the giant ship.

"We've been made," Ada said. "I'm taking a defensive vector." Our original plan had been to have *Intrepid* make a close pass on Cradle, keeping the battleship at a distance.

"Don't get trapped," I said. "We don't know the speed of those beta ships."

"Copy that." Her reply was a good indication of the stress she felt, as she rarely utilized military speak.

"They've seen us," Nick announced at the same time I saw a stream of smaller ships detach from the battleship. It was as if small portions of the *Alpha-prime* simply flaked off. Up to that point we had no idea the fighter-sized ships even existed; their hulls blended in with *Alpha-prime's* perfectly.

"Frak." I accelerated hard to port and with a declination of twenty degrees, wanting to move away from *Intrepid's* flight path. The wave of Kroerak fighters mirrored our actions, albeit with no discernable formation. If anything, the fighters flew like a school of fish, maintaining positioning between themselves but easily trading places, no particular individual in the lead.

The good news was they weren't headed for *Intrepid*. We still had no idea how our weaponry would affect their armored hulls. The bad news was their acceleration was significant. My AI currently estimated the Tisons at a twenty percent advantage. In combat, speed and agility were king. If I could count on twenty percent, we'd be in good shape.

"We're going to punch up through them," I said to Tabby. The flock of fighters were curving down onto us, reversing their acceleration in an attempt to keep us from passing them at high speed and rounding their flank.

"They're firing," Jester Ripples said, highlighting a cloud of unidentified, incoming small projectiles.

"Evasive," I grunted and pushed downward and back.

Tabby spun off upward. We'd agreed beforehand on how we'd separate so as to avoid a collision. As with the battleship, the cloud of projectiles was fast, but had no tracking. My AI projected a curve of acceleration around the cloud and I adjusted accordingly. Then I saw my opening. The tail of the enemy flock would pass close enough for me to orient and take a swipe.

I was equipped with two heavy rockets and three missiles. The primary difference between the two was that the rockets were slow and had a sizeable payload, while the missiles were fast and had a smaller punch. I dialed in a single missile, locked the target and fired, then followed up with my articulating turret which had been converted to a hybrid: one barrel tossing slugs, the other a modified particle blaster. I'd been instructed to follow the fire as closely as possible so that *Sugar's* sensors would record the damage meted out. It was a feat easier said than done. Upon firing, the entire flock of fighters oriented on me. Suffice it to say, I bugged out, angling hard; away from the angry aliens.

"Sensors were obscured," Jester Ripples reported. "Low data quality."

We were now literally running for our lives. The Kroerak fighters fanned out as I pushed *Sugar's* acceleration hard. It was as if they'd constructed a wall behind me. A warning of excessive g-forces first showed on my display, followed by a narrowing of vision and browning out. The Kroerak fighters were fast. Whatever advantage I had in acceleration wouldn't get us away quickly enough.

"Shite, this isn't going to work," I uttered through clenched teeth and reversed the acceleration, flying directly at my opponents. I felt like my face slammed into a steel bulkhead as I abruptly turned into my attackers.

"They're firing," Jester Ripples said. "We can't escape."

Indeed, a cloud of projectiles had been launched. At least they were consistent in their thinking.

"Don't need to," I said and launched a heavy rocket at nothing in particular. I followed the path of the rocket which barely out-accelerated us and lay into my turret. As the rocket met the cloud, it exploded violently. Too far away to damage either my ship or the Kroerak, it had punched a nice clean hole for me to pass through.

I used to watch nature vids and remembered one in particular about a school of fish and how they reacted to a predator being dropped into their midst. It was chaos. Such was the Kroerak's reaction to my about-face and subsequent rocket attack. I picked out my prey and lay fire into it with both barrels, following with a missile. For a moment, the ship attempted to flee and I watched with disappointment as the damage from my turret seemed inconsequential. The missile, however, was another matter. A bright explosion on the enemy fighter's starboard wing - if you could call the irregular flat shape a wing - sent it spinning into a second ship. I continued to accelerate out the back side of the wall of fighters, when I saw a familiar object swoop down from the starboard side. Tabby, hot on our trail, had taken advantage of the chaos I'd created by laying into the injured ships, ripping the wounded pair apart with her fire. There would be no recovery for them, although we were still outnumbered thirty-eight to two.

"Point Masters!" she exclaimed.

"Bug out!" I replied. She'd picked up a tail and I turned to it, blasting away with my turret and loosing my final missile. "Head for *Alpha-prime*."

I didn't need to tell her twice. We'd gained necessary positioning on the fighters and it would be a foot race to the capital ship.

"Uploading combat data to *Intrepid*," Jester Ripples informed me.

As we raced ahead, the resemblance between our current fight and a podball game flitted through my head. Having jumped ahead of the defenders, we had a clear shot at the goal and the point was ours to lose. Of course, where this broke down was the fact that the goal would be shooting back at us. We also had an angry horde on our trail that wouldn't give up once we reached goal.

"We're receiving a hail from the planet," Ada informed me over the tactical comm.

"Ignore it." We were seconds from *Alpha-prime's* weapon's

range and I didn't need the distraction.

"Follow me in, Tabbs," I said and squirted toward the already launched flight of spear-shaped missiles. We'd calculated the ship's reload time and would have to hit and run at top speed to have any chance at survival. Our mission had come down to this moment. Jacobs and the other tacticians had worked out a complex maneuver where the lead ship would attempt to lock in on one of the projectiles and deflect, protecting the trailing ship. It was generally understood, but unspoken, that the lead ship would be committing suicide in order to allow the second ship through.

"I don't buy this plan. We need to work around it," she said.

"Trust me. I've got this." I shot forward even faster, my vision once again narrowing into a tunnel from the G forces. That was fine. We needed speed and if it didn't work out ... well, that wasn't an option.

I launched my final heavy rock, as Jacobs referred to it. This time, I targeted the back of the rocket and fired upon it just as the wave of missiles overtook our position. I blacked out as the blast wave rocked *Sugar* to the side.

"Liam!" I finally heard over the comm as I came to. It was Tabby. She'd stayed on mission and had cleared the blast in my wake.

"I'm up. Go!" I said and diverted, raking across the front of the huge ship and reversing acceleration in a complex maneuver that I'd dreamed of, but hadn't been willing to discuss with anyone. I slowed ridiculously hard and was thrown into the nav-gel, my face once again feeling like it had come into contact with steel.

Jester Ripples and I landed in the wash of the massive engines behind the Kroerak battleship. I was out of rockets and missiles, but spun around violently to open up with my turret. The impacts chipped away at the outer edge of the peculiar engine housing. I wasn't having a lot of effect, but then what should I expect from a lone fighter plugging away at the massive, armored beast?

I jumped out from my position and watched for a signal from Tabby. Our next move had been Tabby's idea and we'd briefed Nick and Jester Ripples as we loaded up. Predictably, another salvo of weapons fire from the behemoth sought to take us out. As planned, Tabby and I both veered back toward the ship. A clunk of metal on metal sounded through my nav-gel. We'd impacted something and nav-gel started draining from the hull.

"We're holed," I said and Jester Ripples sprang into action, applying an emergency patch. We'd lost nearly a third of our gel by the time he got the breach covered.

"Tabby, we can't make it back to *Intrepid*, we're losing gel" I said. "Those fighters will run us down."

"Plan B," she said.

"Frak!" We peeled off toward the planet. My ability to accelerate was severely limited. Without a full load of gel, the material would become a deadly wave each time we changed direction.

"Jester Ripples, send the data-stream now!" I said as we came in contact with the atmosphere of the planet and his patch was sucked through the large hole.

I dialed up the controls and vented the remaining nav-gel from the cockpit, as it was now more of a liability than anything else.

None of the Kroerak fighters had followed us in toward the battleship as they'd been avoiding the ring of death caused by the ship's kinetic weapons. I now waited and watched our sensors, hoping against hope that they didn't possess the same capacity for atmospheric flight as did we.

"Let's just see how well defended this cow-town is anyway," I said and laid in a course, transmitting it to Nick.

"Cow town?" Nick asked.

"Livestock ... I don't know," I said. "It was the first thing that came to mind."

With no evidence of pursuit, we rocketed across the sky at seven thousand meters above the surface toward our secondary objective.

"I see it," Tabby said as Nick lit up our destination and sensors started resolving visual images. We'd tracked the location from where the Kroerak Overlord had transmitted its previous messages. "I've got a rock left."

"Drop it." We streaked toward the alien looking city of rounded rock spires and hills that teemed with Kroerak warriors and vehicles. It looked like a child's clay art project. What I assumed were buildings looked more like lumps of mud, lacking any discernable features. More significant was the total paucity of the ordinary tell-tales of electromagnetic radiation.

"There could be people down there," Nick said.

"Too late," Tabby responded. We both peeled off, not wanting to get caught in the explosion that would level forty square kilometers.

"I'm not buying it," I said. "No way they'd have anyone but Belirand down there. And that was our secondary target from Munay. He gave it to me before we left, just in case we survived our primary mission."

"Frak, frak, frak," Tabby said. "All I saw were bugs."

"Knock it off, Tabbs, it was our mission. These shites came after us, we had to hit back hard," I said. "Munay's team thought that location was probably command and control. From what it looked like to me, that was a reasonable assessment."

"Liam. We're picking up an explosion on the planet's surface," Ada said over the comm a few seconds later. The delay period on her comm the result of her distance from the planet.

"Copy that, Ada. That was us following up on a secondary objective," I said.

"Munay arrived ten minutes ago," she replied. "The whole battle group jumped right on top of that butt-ugly potato. It was over before it started. One minute we were being chased by those frigates, the next Munay showed up and the gates of hell opened up. The Navy launched two wings of fighters and they're working on the remnant frigates. It's a complete rout." She'd loosed a fusillade of words, betraying her excitement.

"Where are you?" I asked.

"We're sailing in to join the battle group," Ada said. "We're still two hours out. Frak, there goes one of the Kroerak frigates now!"

"We're being hailed, Liam Hoffen," Jester Ripples said. "It is Lieutenant Sendrei Buhari."

"Ada, I'm going to take this."

"Understood, Chen out."

"Sendrei. I'd have thought you were tucked deep in a drop ship," I said. The plan had been that Sendrei would accompany the Marines and attempt to interface with the villagers. He couldn't be at every location but his local knowledge was critical.

"Aye, Captain. Can't give up operational details, but let's just say this is terrifying," he shouted. "The Major would like to extend his invitation for you and *Rowdy* to join the planet-side squadron."

"Roger that," I said. "We're all in." I accepted the tactical channel invitation that accompanied his message and shared it with Tabby.

"See you on the ground. Buhari out."

Instead of crossing the globe by flying through the atmosphere, I led us up and out. The cockpit was still open to vacuum, but as long as I kept the sudden navigational adjustments down, we'd be fine, not to mention we'd be able to meet up with the Marines more quickly.

Upon approach, our tactical channel lit up with targeting. I felt fortunate that Marny had already familiarized us with targeting priority principles. Wing on wing, Tabby and I sailed over the top of several mechanized squads engaged in ground combat with a veritable horde of Kroerak. Unlike our experience, the mechanized Marines were making good progress, although not quite the rout Munay had experienced above the planet.

We picked priority targets from the local Marine platoon leader and lay fire into the swarm. Best I could tell; the Marines were constructing a beach head right on top of one of the five main Kroerak defense installations. The planet-side Kroerak airships proved to be no match for *Sugar* and *Rowdy's* turrets. Not only were the alien ships dependent on airfoils to keep their ships aloft, but their weaponry was forward facing. They'd certainly caused our mechanized infantry problems by dropping explosives, but once we arrived we ripped through them.

After an hour of heavy fighting, the Kroerak's defense of their installation started to wane as fewer and fewer Kroerak poured from the ravaged buildings. Finally, the Major ordered his Marines to switch to explosive rounds and raze the defensive installation. As was obvious from the influx of warriors, a massive network of tunnels existed beneath the Kroerak's rounded stone structures.

"Sappers," Major Wiggsly called over the tactical channel as our fight turned from battle to cleanup. A squad of Marines jumped to the forefront, standing on the rubble of the ruined buildings. Their suits were emblazoned with a sledge hammer driving a lightning bolt into the ground and the digits four and nine. From special weaponry, they started lobbing what I suspected were explosive charges into the tunnels and then covering them with foam.

"FIRE IN THE HOLE!"

"Shite!" I wasn't sure how big of a blast they were expecting, but every Marine below was running pell-mell from the site. I banked away and dropped lower to the ground.

"What does 'fire in the hole' mean?" Jester Ripples asked.

"Incoming explosion," I explained just as the ground buckled beneath us and collapsed in a spider web of veins leading out from the original detonation site.

"You are such a mix of the literal and the figurative," he mused.

"We're Oscar-Mike," Wiggsly announced. "Appreciate the assistance *Sugar, Rowdy*." And with that he jumped over the pit and charged forward.

With two hundred mechanized infantry on the ground, I couldn't imagine that anything we'd seen would stand in their way. From my viewpoint, they could have achieved the same objective with a quarter of the force they'd brought. When pressed, Alderson had scoffed at the notion. Overwhelming firepower, he'd said, was what he wanted to bring. He had a point, I'd seen the flip-side in the battle for Colony-40, where the Red Houzi dreadnaught *Bakunawa* had done much the same to a substantial Mars Protectorate fleet. I wondered how much of this battle had been shaped by that drubbing.

The fight continued well into the night, pockets of Kroerak showing up from who knows where, some obviously having run from a great distance. By the time Cradle's star was cresting over the horizon, however, the mission turned from combat duty to sentry duty. I'd just taken my second hit of Navy provided stimulants when I received a message from Commander Munay. He was requesting our presence on *George Ellery Hale.*

We signed out with the Ground Forces HQ and made way for space. I smiled as we set down on *Hale's* flight deck next to *Hotspur.* She'd been left out of the action for once and looked great, not a fresh crease anywhere. A wave of nostalgia rolled over me. It felt like the end of something, seeing *Hotspur* sitting out the battle.

A Marine Lieutenant greeted the four of us as we exited the fighters. "Greetings, Captain Hoffen. James Pugno." The young lieutenant offered his hand. "I've been asked to accompany you."

I smiled, it was a much warmer reception than we'd first received aboard the *Hale.* "Nice to meet you Lieutenant Pugno. Lead the way."

He handed each of us a med patch and then explained. "We're reading combat stims in your bios. Be best for everyone if you weren't amped up when talking with the commander, if you don't mind." He had a good point, I was feeling pretty frakking edgy.

We walked deeper into the ship than we'd ever been and I wouldn't have thought we could have gone any lower when Pugno finally stopped and gestured to a hatch. "Far as I go," he said and palmed the door.

The room we found ourselves in was a plainly decorated meeting room, with steel chairs and a utilitarian table. The room looked onto another, separated by armored glass. Inside of that room were four of the smaller, more colorful Kroerak. I recognized the Overlord of the North as one of them.

"They can't hear us," Munay said, standing up from his chair. "But they can sense us, even with a hermetically sealed room. That's not even armor glass, but a vid-screen. Going to drive the lab-coats nuts."

The Cradle's Overlord looked directly at me as I crossed the room. "Yeah. That's officially creepy," I said as I paced backward just to make sure it was actually tracking me, which it was.

"I see you, Liam Hoffen," the Overlord said, its horizontally opposed jaw not moving in any way I associated with making sound.

"The audio sensor is not currently turned on," Munay said. "Like I said, lab-coats are already going nuts."

"How can we help?" I asked.

"You can't," he said. "I just wanted you to see that we caught these guys - help put a bow on it for you. Admiral Alderson sends his regards and thanks you for your service."

"Really?" I asked. "I'm pretty sure he thinks I'm a clown."

"You're misreading him," Munay said. "Everything that man says is calculated to elicit a reaction. What'll drive you nuts is when you realize that and then try to figure out how many people he's targeting or what he's trying to accomplish. One of the smartest men alive."

"You're frakking with me," I said.

"He's the top-ranked admiral in Mars Protectorate," he answered. "Just led the biggest mission in its history, rescued ten thousand orphans and defeated and captured a powerful alien race no one knew existed. Play it anyway you want, he got what he was after."

"But ..." I started, only to be interrupted.

"We are not defeated, Liam Hoffen," the Overlord said. I looked around and tried to discern where its voice was coming from. "I may have underestimated your resolve in the matter of our livestock, but there are tens of trillions of us and your scent has been communicated. Humanity thinks too much of itself, winning such an unimportant battle and for what? Food? You are all weak. Go home. Celebrate. For we are coming soon and there will be no joy when that day arrives."

"You underestimated us," I said, looking straight back at the Kroerak Overlord and its companions. "The message you should be sending to your empire is to flee. But I suspect that's just not in your DNA. What you don't understand is that by attacking us, you've done something no person has ever managed. You'll unite all of humanity against your precious bug empire. And if you do come for us, God help you, because nothing else will."

EPILOGUE

To say Mom was shocked when we showed up in local-space next to Petersburg Station with the *George Ellery Hale* and personnel transports, was something of an understatement. Munay had sent *Messier* and the destroyers back to Sol, but had been given instructions to personally check out Ophir.

"Lieutenant Hoffen," Munay smiled as he shook hands with Mom. "I'm surprised your boy didn't rope you into this last mission. I believe it was right up your alley.

"My days of dropping boys and girls out of perfectly good transports are long gone. I much prefer the anxiety of carving a space station out of an asteroid and convincing small minded people to share with their neighbors because it's the right thing to do."

He smiled. "Apple doesn't fall far from the tree, I see."

"Coffee?" Mom asked as she led Munay, Nick, Tabby and me into the galley Merrie insisted on calling a kitchen. Katherine LeGrande was already seated, talking with Jonathan, but stood to greet us. I crossed the room and hugged her in greeting.

"I have a proposition to discuss with you all," Munay said.

"How can we help?" Mom asked.

"Mars Protectorate would like to formally colonize Ophir," he said, looking at me and then to Mom. "We wanted your feedback on the idea."

"Not really much for small-talk, are you?" Mom asked.

"Strategically, Ophir is perfectly aligned for travel to the Dwingeloo galaxy. More importantly, Mars population is bursting at the seams. We need a colony."

"It doesn't seem like we could stop you," I said.

"True. However, if the human settlements of Ophir endorsed

the colonization, it would eliminate future legal challenges," he said.

"I think you just said you're coming either way," Mom replied handing him a cup of coffee with a smile I recognized as anything but friendly.

"With our recently gained knowledge, we believe we could establish a TransLoc gate system between Mars and Ophir."

"Would Ophir be given a seat in the Senate?" Jonathan asked.

"That's something that would have to be discussed," Munay replied. "If not, there are protections for colonies. I believe you're already familiar with the political structure of Colony-40."

"Yeah. M-Cor charged so much in delivery that miners barely survived," Mom said. "All legal within Mars Protectorate. Pick a better example, Mr. Munay."

"Those rates were negotiated with the colony," Munay said. "You'd have the capacity to shape that policy, Mrs. Hoffen. I'm authorized to put that in writing."

"A TransLoc gate would bring a lot of change to Ophir," Jonathan said. "What about protecting the indigenous species?"

"It is a primary concern," he agreed. "Look, I'm not asking you to sign something right now, but rather to start a conversation. Surely, you understand that if it's not Mars Protectorate, it will be the North Americans or the Chinese."

"We do understand that," Nick answered. "We also know we have no expertise in negotiating this type of deal."

"To me, it's fairly straightforward," I said. "For the same reasons we needed help rescuing the people of Cradle from the Kroerak, we need help integrating Ophir with the rest of humanity. I have one question, though, is this the reason M-Pro was so quick to authorize the Cradle mission?"

"You're asking for a simple answer to a complex question. It certainly weighed heavily," he agreed. "Can I report back to Alderson that there is enough agreement to move forward on negotiations?"

I looked around the large table and caught the eye of each member of my family and crew. To a person they agreed.

"We're in, Commander. I appreciate that you're not just rolling over the top of us like you did the Kroerak. Which, by the way, I'd like to understand better. I thought the idea was for you to drop in at some distance and engage more slowly, not jump on top of them," I said.

"The first rule of battle is to know that no plan survives first contact with the enemy," Munay said. "When we received the data you and Ms. Masters gathered, our engineers quickly recognized a flaw in the Kroerak armor. A flaw we were prepared to capitalize on. By jumping in close, we were able to engage before the Kroerak battleship recognized our plan. It was a measured risk, but there is another axiom you should not forget - *Audentes Fortuna Juvat.*"

"Fortune favors the bold," Marny translated for us.

"Quite," Munay replied. "There was some chance the Kroerak would adjust to their discovered weakness. By jumping on them, we eliminated that possibility."

"I sure wish I could have seen that," I said.

"Will you join us for the celebration in Libertas tonight, Commander?" Mom asked. "I understand substantial progress on habitats has been made."

"Last report I received was temporary housing would be complete within the next month," Munay said. "What we really need is a steady supply of ore. You wouldn't happen to know any miners who are looking to set up operation on the third moon, would you?"

"I suspect we could find interested parties," I said.

"Mars Mineral exchange rates?" Nick asked.

"Whoa, getting a bit ahead of things aren't you?" I asked.

Nick raised an eyebrow which I knew meant I should shut up.

"We'll accept the mineral exchange rates," Munay held his hand out to Nick. "How quickly can you ramp up production?"

"We might need some help from an industrialist who has access to ready capital," Nick said, turning to Jonathan. "Do you have any interest in investing in a startup?"

"If you give me a ride back to Tipperary so I can transfer to a body of my own, I'll fund your project, but I'll expect a significant ownership stake," he said.

I gave Nick a pinched - things are moving too fast – look.

"We'll set up a new company," Nick said. "I'll send you a proposal, but we need fifty-one percent control."

"We can work that out," Jonathan/Anino agreed. "And we were wondering … any word on that missing fold-space generator?"

"What?" I asked.

"Happened while we were training on the Tisons," Nick said. "The fold-space generator from *Justice Bringer* went missing while we were on Freedom Station. Everything was happening so fast that we couldn't run it down. M-Pro knows about it and they're looking into it."

"Xie Mie-su," Tabby said. "I *told* you she couldn't be trusted."

"We'll find it," Munay replied, with ice in his voice.

"Good luck with that," I said. "If it was Xie Mie-su, you never will."

Munay smiled but didn't take the bait.

"So, tell me, Captain Hoffen. What's next for you? How do you top this adventure?" he finally asked.

"Well, we've only scratched the surface of Belirand's abandoned missions. I've got an entire trunk of comm crystals I promised to run down," I said. "There's one that's transmitting what sounds like bubbles …"

But that's another story entirely.

ABOUT THE AUTHOR

Jamie McFarlane is happily married, the father of three and lives in Lincoln, Nebraska. He spends his days engaged in a hi-tech career and his nights and weekends writing works of fiction. He's also the author of:

Privateer Tales
1. Rookie Privateer
2. Fool Me Once
3. Parley
4. Big Pete
5. Smuggler's Dilemma
6. Cutpurse
7. Out of the Tank
8. Buccaneers
9. A Matter of Honor
10. Give No Quarter
11. Blockade Runner (Coming end of 2016)

Guardians of Gaeland
1. Lesser Prince

Witchy World
1. Wizard in a Witchy World
2. Dark Folk (Coming Fall 2016)

Word-of-mouth is crucial for any author to succeed. If you enjoyed this book, please consider leaving a review at Amazon, even if it's only a line or two; it would make all the difference and would be very much appreciated.

If you want to get an automatic email when Jamie's next book is available, sign up on his website at fickledragon.com. Your email address will never be shared and you can unsubscribe at any time.

CONTACT JAMIE

Blog and Website: fickledragon.com
Facebook: facebook.com/jamiemcfarlaneauthor
Twitter: twitter.com/mcfarlaneauthor

Made in the USA
San Bernardino, CA
29 December 2017